THE GOD GENE

F. PAUL WILSON

FORGE®

A TOM DOHERTY ASSOCIATES BOOK
NEW YORK

THE GOD GENE

Copyright © 2017 by F. Paul Wilson

A Forge Book
Published by Tom Doherty Associates
175 Fifth Avenue
New York, NY 10010

www.tor-forge.com

Forge® is a registered trademark of Macmillan Publishing Group, LLC.

The Library of Congress Cataloging-in-Publication Data is available upon request.

ISBN 978-0-7653-8519-2 (hardcover)
ISBN 978-0-7653-8560-4 (ebook)

Our books may be purchased in bulk for promotional, educational, or business use. Please contact your local bookseller or the Macmillan Corporate and Premium Sales Department at 1-800-221-7945, extension 5442, or by email at MacmillanSpecialMarkets@macmillan.com.

First Edition: January 2018

Printed in the United States of America

0 9 8 7 6 5 4 3 2 1

ALSO BY F. PAUL WILSON

Repairman Jack* *The Tomb / Legacies / Conspiracies / All the Rage / Hosts /
The Haunted Air / Gateways / Crisscross / Infernal / Harbingers /
Bloodline / By the Sword / Ground Zero / Fatal Error /
The Dark at the End / Nightworld*

The Teen Trilogy* *Jack: Secret Histories / Jack: Secret Circles / Jack: Secret Vengeance*

The Early Years Trilogy* *Cold City / Dark City / Fear City*

The Adversary Cycle* *The Keep / The Tomb / The Touch / Reborn / Reprisal / Nightworld*

Omnibus Editions *The Complete LaNague / Calling Dr. Death* (3 medical thrillers)

The LaNague Federation *Healer / Wheels Within Wheels / An Enemy of the State /
Dydeetown World / The Tery*

Other Novels *Black Wind* / Sibs* / The Select / Virgin / Implant /
Deep as the Marrow / Mirage* (with Matthew J. Costello) / *Nightkill*
(with Steven Spruill) / *Masque* (with Matthew J. Costello) / *Sims / The
Fifth Harmonic* / Midnight Mass / The Proteus Cure* (with Tracy L.
Carbone) / *A Necessary End* (with Sarah Pinborough) / *Panacea* /
The God Gene*

The Nocturnia Chronicles *Definitely Not Kansas / Family Secrets / The Silent Ones*
(with Thomas F. Monteleone)

Short Fiction *Soft & Others / The Barrens and Others / The Christmas Thingy /
Aftershock and Others / The Peabody-Ozymandias Traveling Circus
& Oddity Emporium* / Quick Fixes—Tales of Repairman Jack* /
Sex Slaves of the Dragon Tong / Ephemerata*

Editor *Freak Show / Diagnosis: Terminal / The Hogben Chronicles* (with
Pierce Watters)

* See "The Secret History of the World" (page 365).

ACKNOWLEDGMENTS

The usual suspects: my wife, Mary; Jennifer Gunnels and Becky Maines at the publisher; Steven Spruill, Elizabeth Monteleone, Dannielle Romeo, Ann Voss Peterson, and my agent, Albert Zuckerman. Thanks for your efforts.

Conspicuous by his absence:
David G. Hartwell
RIP

THEN

Sunday, May 8

MAPUTO, MOZAMBIQUE

Amaury Laffite stared at the photo for a moment, then shifted his gaze to the man on the other side of the counter, the thin, thickly bearded Afrikaner who had handed it to him. He wore a slouch hat and a safari vest. Trying to look like Indiana Jones, perhaps? Or perhaps not. Under the hat his scalp was bare. And the outfit was practical in East Africa.

Amaury rubbed his prickly jaw. He used a stubble trimmer daily, set at the Jason Statham length of 0.4 millimeters. Women liked that. He kept his dark brown hair tied back in a short ponytail. Women liked that too, as long as it wasn't too long. He didn't let it reach past the base of his neck. His mother had been a not-too-dark Algerian from Oran, his father a somewhat-white Marseillais, leaving Amaury's skin just light enough and his hair just straight enough to make both affectations work.

This odd South African gave him a frisson. He'd heard talk of him, wandering both shores of the Mozambique Channel, from South Africa all the way up to Zanzibar and Tanzania on this side, and all along the west coast of Madagascar. And everywhere he went he'd show his picture of a strange little primate to anyone who would look. Amaury had never doubted that he eventually would show up here. In all the man's travels he would inevitably run across someone who would say, *You're looking for an exotic animal? Go see Amaury Laffite.*

Easier said than done, however. Amaury did not make himself too easy to find. He'd grown up on the docks of Marseilles, and had entered the smuggling trade at an early age. He knew how to keep his head down and stay off the police radar. Eventually he'd drifted to his mother's homeland in North Africa, and finally landed here on the east coast of the Dark Continent, where rules were less stringent and the police even more corrupt than in Marseilles.

Even so, the endangered species he dealt in carried certain risks, such as fines and jail time. The former were tolerable, the latter unthinkable. He never housed the animals where he did business. He moved his signless storefront from time to time and stocked his shop with photos only.

And now, in his hand, lay another photo.

He looked at it again, studying it more closely this time. The creature in question crouched on a man's shoulder; the man himself had been cropped out, leaving only the monkey or prosimian—he couldn't be sure—staring at the camera. It had eyes like a lemur, only bigger. And bright blue—clear winter-sky blue. Some lemur species had blue eyes, but this wasn't like any he'd ever seen.

Lemurs, especially the ring-tailed variety, had been a gold mine for a while, demand sparked by that first *Madagascar* cartoon back in 2005. No matter that they were among the most endangered vertebrates on the planet, no matter that they made lousy pets, people wanted them. After a while, business fell off as dealers in places like Texas and Florida started breeding them, but it had been great while it lasted.

This wasn't a lemur, though. It lacked the bushy tail. More like a monkey.

"I cannot tell the size from this," Amaury said, angling the photo this way and that.

He spoke English. He and this stranger had established in their first few sentences that this was their lingua franca. Marten Jeukens spoke no French, negligible Portuguese, but excellent English. In addition to French and English, Amaury spoke Portuguese—an absolute necessity for doing business in Mozambique—but no Afrikaans.

"It weighs about eight hundred grams," Jeukens said.

Convenient weight. Nothing threatening about a monkey weighing less than a kilo. He looked again at those big blue eyes and that sad expression. He could sell a ton of these, five grand retail, three grand wholesale. Yes, he could move every one he laid his hands on.

"You wouldn't happen to have one for sale?" the Afrikaner said.

"I *wish* I had one for sale. But I've never seen anything like it, and I've seen just about every monkey and prosimian in this part of the world."

He snatched the photo from Amaury's fingers. "Then you are no use to me."

Another frisson. Not the words so much as the tone. It seemed to imply, *You might as well be dead for all I care.*

Under normal circumstances Amaury would be glad to see him go. But the creature's eyes . . .

"Wait! What is it?"

"New species."

"'New'?"

"New to me. New to almost everyone I've asked."

"'Almost'?"

"Two people say they have seen what they claim is the exact same animal, only dead. One was washed up on shore near Toliara, and another washed up right here."

Amaury considered that: one in Madagascar, on the far side of the channel, and one here in Mozambique. He knew it hadn't originated on this side, and he'd mined the exotic species of Madagascar to the fullest extent without ever seeing a trace of this blue-eyed monk—an occasional blue-eyed lemur, yes, but not this monk.

"Both drowned? Odd, don't you think?"

The Afrikaner stared at him with his cold eyes. "Not if they're confined to an island."

Amaury frowned. "Island? Where?"

"Where else? The Mozambique Channel."

"There are islands in the channel, *monsieur*, some so inconsequential that they disappear at high tide. But they're all well explored." He pointed to the photo. "None contain an exotic species such as the one you have pictured here."

The slam of Jeukens's fist on the countertop startled Amaury.

"Do *not* tell me that! It *is* there! It *must* be!"

"I speak the truth when I tell you there is no undiscovered island in the channel, *monsieur.*"

Jeukens calmed as suddenly as he'd flared. His eyes narrowed and his tone turned mocking. "You're sure? Absolutely sure? It is said that to be absolutely certain about something, one must know everything or nothing about it."

"Well, no one can be absolutely sure about anything, can one? No one can know everything about the sea, but—"

"The Mozambique Channel covers one and a third *million* square kilometers—half a million square miles of open water. Do not presume to tell me there couldn't be a small undiscovered island in all that expanse."

"Well, it is possible, of course, but—"

"Millions of years ago, lemurs floated on debris from Africa to Madagascar. Eventually they became extinct on the continent but they thrived on Madagascar." He waved the photo. "Who's to say these creatures didn't do the same, but wound up on a tiny island instead?"

"Anything is possible, I suppose."

"By my calculation, the island lies north of here."

Amaury nodded. "Obviously."

The Mozambique Channel flowed north to south. The drowned monks would have entered the water upstream.

Jeukens slipped the photo into a breast pocket of his vest. "I am going to find that island."

"Where was this monk found?" Amaury said. "The one you have there?"

Jeukens tapped the pocket. "Floating in the channel, near the Madagascar coast. A sailor fished it out, thinking it was dead. But it sputtered to life once it was onboard. He sold it to a street vendor in an outdoor market near Quelimane town center."

Amaury nodded. Quelimane . . . about halfway up the Mozambique coast from here. "Have you checked with that vendor?"

"Of course. You think I'm an idiot? But he says he'd never seen one before and hasn't since."

Amaury smiled. "It appears you will be renting a boat soon."

"'I must down to the seas again, to the lonely sea and sky.'"

"That sounds like a poem."

"Masefield. But first I must learn to navigate."

"I suggest you search satellite maps before you start searching the horizon."

"I've already done that."

"And?"

"No unnamed islands."

Amaury was about to say *I told you so*, but thought better of it.

"However," Jeukens went on, "I have noticed areas where clouds always seem to cluster. An island could be hiding beneath them."

"True," Amaury said. But not likely. "Are you in a hurry to find this little creature?"

"I am on a mission."

A wild light grew in the Afrikaner's eyes. He seemed filled with an almost religious zeal. Amaury was going to ask, *For God?* but thought better of that too. "For yourself or someone else?"

"For civilization. To save the Giordano Brunos of the world."

Without another word, Jeukens turned and strode from the tiny storefront.

His departure left Amaury nonplussed. An idea had come to him and he had been searching for the best way to present it. A fortune awaited in the sale of those monkeys. An exclusive deal could keep the gravy train running for years. Jeukens didn't know navigation but Amaury was a veteran of the seas. Theirs could be a match made in heaven.

He ran out into the street. Downtown Maputo at midday . . . crowds of pedestrians and bicyclists winding past and through street vendors and smoky buses and taxis. But nowhere was Marten Jeukens. He seemed to have vanished into thin air.

NOW

Tuesday, May 17

1

EAST MEADOW, NEW YORK

What do you say to a man you crippled for life?

Hi, Mister Fife. Remember me? I'm Laura Fanning—the girl who caused you irreparable brain damage twenty years ago.

Laura stood at the Advocate's reception desk and watched the man in the electric wheelchair roll toward her from far down the hallway. He worked the controller with his right hand while his left—splinted to the forearm—lay useless in his lap. As he neared, she saw how the left corner of his mouth sagged. Persistent left hemiplegia. Just the way she'd left him two decades ago.

James Fife . . . a fresh stab of guilt knifed through her. She'd hoped to find that he'd regained some function over the years.

His paralysis seemed to be the only thing that hadn't changed, however. He looked older—obviously—and grayer and heavier than she remembered.

Her gut squeezed at the prospect of facing him again, but she had to do this. She'd somehow forgotten about him, and she couldn't allow that. Ever.

And maybe . . . just maybe the damage didn't have to be permanent. Maybe she could change that.

"So it's you," he said with a slight slur as he rolled to a stop before her. "I didn't see how it could be anyone else, but I still couldn't believe it."

"Not be anyone else?" Laura said, startled. "How could—?"

He nodded to the receptionist who'd called the dining room to tell him he had a visitor. "Ceil here. When I asked what you looked like she said 'dark-skinned and-blue eyed.' I've only met one person who fit that description."

Yeah, well, Laura herself had never met anyone who looked like her either. Her Caucasian father had been blue-eyed, and her Mayan mother must have had a blue-eye recessive hiding in her genome. The result was a striking combination that turned heads.

"I didn't mean to interrupt your lunch."

He shrugged one shoulder. "I was finished anyway."

"How . . . how are you?" She hated how lame she sounded but was unable to come up with anything better. The sight of him had gummed up her brain.

"Still half paralyzed," he said, but she could detect no malice in his tone. "Have you come to tell me of the death of my nephew?"

So . . . he knew.

She shook her head. "No, I came to see you. I heard you were on Long Island and—"

"Did Nelson tell you that?"

What to say? During the few remaining minutes of his life Nelson Fife had said that his uncle was "stuck in an East Meadow nursing home." It had taken a while but she'd managed to track him here to this facility run by the Catholic Church.

"Yes. He said you were 'suffering every day.' I'm so sorry."

James Fife offered half a smile. "Nelson was like a son to me, but he had a tendency toward the dramatic. Let's go someplace we can talk."

"Someplace" turned out to be his apartment. She followed him back down the hallway to a studio with a full bath, a tiny kitchen equipped with a microwave and half fridge, an electric bed tucked into the rear section, and a small sitting area at the front. A crucifix and a Sacred Heart of Jesus print adorned the walls.

Leaving the door open, he gestured to one of the two easy chairs flanking an oval throw rug. "Please."

Since he was already seated, she complied.

"And for the record," he added, "I'm not suffering. I've accepted, I've adapted, and I bear you no ill will."

Laura felt her throat thicken. "I was so irresponsible."

"You were seventeen."

Yeah . . . seventeen and using the rearview mirror to apply mascara as she blew through a Salt Lake City stop sign and hit an unsuspecting pedestrian.

He added, "Even though I wasn't fully aware during the days that followed in the hospital, I know you came to visit me every day."

"I felt so helpless. I ruined your life."

Another lopsided smile. "No, you merely *changed* my life. You set it on another course."

But not one of your choosing, she thought.

"Your nephew wasn't quite so forgiving."

She didn't mention that Nelson had meant to kill her.

"I know. We discussed you shortly before his death."

"You did?"

It shouldn't have surprised her, but it did, and not in a pleasant way.

"Yes. I know you're a county coroner, and I'm glad you've put your life to good use. I assured Nelson that the accident wasn't your fault, that you were simply an instrument of God's will, part of the Divine Plan."

Uh-oh. Like nephew, like uncle? Nelson had been a total fanatic.

"It doesn't feel that way," she said.

"It rarely does. Since there wasn't enough of Nelson left to bury, I can assume you weren't with him when he died."

"No . . . not with him. But I wasn't far away."

"You were on the island?" Fife leaned forward in his wheelchair. "Can you tell me what happened? I was told an explosion of some sort."

"Yes. A big one. I'd just left the island and was in a boat. I was told . . ." She had to say it. "I was told that he fell victim to the fate he had planned for me."

Fife winced and squeezed his eyes shut. When he looked at her again, he said, "Saint Augustine told us to love the sinner but hate the sin. It took this"—he gestured to the inert left side of his body—"and the changes it caused in my life to make me appreciate that. But Nelson couldn't separate the two. Do you know any more about it?"

"Apparently something didn't go as planned, but I don't know the details."

She did know them, but this man probably wouldn't believe her if she told him.

He gave her a hard look. "You're not one of *those*, are you?"

" 'Those'?"

He leaned back with a frustrated expression. "All right, I'm going to say a word that I hope means nothing to you: *panacean*."

Panacean . . . brewer of the mythical panacea . . . which had turned out to be not so mythical after all.

"No, not one of them. In fact, I became aware of their existence less than two months ago when I was hired to bring back a dose of the tea they brew."

"And did you?"

None of his business.

"I'm not at liberty to say."

He jabbed his right index finger toward her. "Is that why you're here? Is that why you've shown up after all these years? To assuage your guilt by slipping me a dose of that diabolical potion?"

His vehemence startled her. "Not at all. I—"

"I forbid it! Pour it down a drain! What happened to me is God's will and you shall not undo it! Is that clear?"

She managed a shrug. "It's a moot point. I don't have any. I just came by to see if you needed anything, if I could do anything for you."

That seemed to mollify him, but only a little. His eyes remained narrowed with suspicion.

"I hope that's true. And if it is, I appreciate it. But I need nothing. I'm comfortable here. I have friends, I pray, I meditate, I feel closer to God than ever. Don't ruin that."

Laura couldn't imagine not wanting to regain the use of half of your body. She almost envied the peace that came with imagining yourself part of a divine plan . . . a peace she'd never know.

"As I said: I don't possess the means to do that." She gave him a long look. "Do I have anything to fear from you, Mister Fife?"

He shook his head. "In case you haven't noticed, I'm confined to a wheelchair."

"That's not an answer."

"You mean, am I a member of the Brotherhood?"

"Yes. If I lift your right sleeve will I see a *536* tattoo?"

He raised his chin. "You would. I've been their abbot for many a year. But . . ." He sighed.

"But?"

"With Nelson's death I relinquished the title. And that was all it was: a title. I took no part in the Brotherhood's activities, and now I'm officially retired."

So . . . 536 was still out there. Not what she'd wanted to hear.

"How many are you?"

"Not your concern. But I will tell you this: They don't know about you, and I won't tell them. If what you say is true and you aren't brewing the panacea, you have nothing to fear. But if you are . . ."

Laura had no plans to make any, but if Clotilde held to her promise, she'd be dispensing a dose now and again.

"If I am, they'll what? Burn me at the stake?"

"They'll track you down and deal with you, and I won't be able to help you."

"You?" That last surprised her. "Why would you want to?"

His look softened. "Because you're not an evil person. Nor are the panaceans. Just terribly misguided."

Laura disagreed with that, but saw no point in challenging him.

He yawned. "Sorry. I usually nap after lunch."

"One more thing, then I'll be out of your life." This had been bothering her ever since she'd returned to the States. "Have you ever wondered how the woman your nephew chased all over Europe turned out to be the same person who hit you with her car all those years ago?"

That half smile again. "You're calling it a coincidence, I suppose."

"Well, yeah. An amazing coincidence, don't you think?"

He shook his head. "There are no coincidences, young lady. What you call 'coincidence' is the hand of a provident God, writing the story of your life."

"If you say so."

"You're not a believer, I take it."

She shook her head. "I can't believe. I've never been able to believe."

She'd been raised a Mormon but had merely gone through the motions as a child. None of it had made any sense to her. No religion did.

"Then you will not be saved," he told her.

A thought occurred to her. "Some people are born unable to believe. If you believe in a provident God, that means he created them that way. How can God expect them to believe when he made them incapable of belief?"

Fife blinked, then said, "Even Saint Thomas the Doubter came to believe in the Resurrection."

"But only after sticking his fingers in the wounds."

"For some, faith takes effort. For me it is like breathing." He extended his hand. "Go with God."

Laura shook it, but Fife didn't let go. He was frowning.

"Something wrong?"

"Redemption," he said, staring at her. "Redemption in your future."

What now? A vision?

She broke contact. "Well, that's good, I guess."

"Oh, it is. And remember: There are no coincidences."

She smiled, waved, and headed for the parking lot.

No coincidences . . . James Fife might find that comforting. Laura found it deeply disturbing.

When she'd made the decision to visit Fife, she'd planned on making him the beneficiary should she ever come into possession of another dose of the panacea. But he'd just made it quite clear that he wouldn't consider it a benefit.

Fortunately she had another candidate.

2

SHIRLEY, NEW YORK

Laura pulled into her driveway but didn't bother opening the garage door. She'd never been good about disposing of belongings and the car had been crowded out long ago. She stared through the windshield without focusing on anything as she thought about her strange encounter with Fife. She hadn't known quite what to expect, but she hadn't expected *that*.

So accepting of his nephew's death, of his own awful fate. *Let go, let God* . . . she wished she could.

Sighing, she picked up her phone from its usual spot in the center-console cup holder and checked her email for any new messages since leaving East Meadow. She nodded with satisfaction as she saw confirmation that the Stritch School of Medicine had sent her transcript to the residency-match folks. She could cross that off the checklist of items she needed in order to apply for the neurology residency she wanted. So different from when she'd registered for pathology over a decade ago. Now everything was online or through email.

After her daughter Marissa's ordeal and miraculous cure last month, she'd decided she'd spent enough time with the dead and was ready to deal with the living. She'd handed in her notice to the Suffolk County Medical Examiner's Office; they needed time to find a replacement, so she'd stayed on, limiting herself to half days. Good thing, those half days. She still enjoyed the challenges of being an assistant medical examiner—sussing out causes of death and all that—but more important, the job gave structure to her life. All this free time . . . she couldn't remember when she'd had so much of it and had yet to figure out how to fill all the open hours.

She pocketed her phone and grabbed the Barnes & Noble shopping bag from the passenger side. She'd done some book browsing on her way home. Marissa's science class was covering evolution and Laura had thought it couldn't hurt to have a couple of relevant coffee-table books lying around the family room.

She stopped halfway along the walk when she spotted a cardboard cube, barely big enough to hold a softball, sitting on her colonial's front stoop. She approached and squatted next to it for a closer look. *L. Fanning* was block printed on the label with no return address. Her mouth went dry when she saw the Crymych, Wales, postmark. Only one possible sender: Clotilde.

And Laura knew what it contained.

Ikhar.

The panacea. *The* panacea. The universal cure-all. The real deal.

The irony . . . While she'd been assuring James Fife that she possessed no sample of the "diabolical potion," it had been sitting on her doorstep.

Clotilde had promised her a dose every few months. She'd kept that promise. Here was the first. And now the promise felt like a threat.

As she carried the package inside, the empty house greeted her with silence. Until two weeks ago, when Marissa had gone back to school, someone had always been home. Marissa for sure—her human contacts had been strictly limited after her stem-cell transplant and so she never left the property—and usually Natasha, her homebound instructor.

Marissa's leukemia, her failed trials of chemotherapy, followed by her successful stem-cell transplant had dominated the past two years of Laura's life. And then last month she'd almost lost her to a CMV infection.

But now she was cured. She'd gone from knocking on heaven's door to completely cured overnight—literally overnight. Not one of all the specialists and subspecialists who'd attended her in the Stony Brook PICU could explain the miracle then. To this day they remained baffled.

But Laura knew: Half an ounce of a foul fluid had saved her.

Ikhar.

Now Marissa was back in William Floyd Grammar School. She'd returned too late for softball tryouts, but the coach was letting her practice with the team.

Laura placed the box from Wales on the counter and stared at it.

Well, it's not going to open itself.

She continued to stare.

It's still not going to open itself.

Finally she took a breath and slid out the shit drawer—her private name for it, not used in front of Marissa—and extricated the box cutter from the Gordian knot of charger wires and key rings and such. She popped out the blade and slit the tough fiber packing tape along the seams.

Inside, swaddled in bubble wrap, a small, crimson ceramic jar embossed with a Chinese character.

A Chinese snuff bottle? It felt cool as it settled in her palm. She shook it. Liquid inside. A handwritten sticky note clung to the back.

Let the All-Mother guide you.
C

C for Clotilde . . .

The promised *ikhar*.

Or as Rick called it, "worm juice."

She'd felt torn since Clotilde had made her promise. Would the old woman follow through? Laura couldn't be sure, but had been setting the stage for its advent, if it ever happened. Today's visit to James Fife had been part of that.

Now it had arrived, but the responsibility it carried tied her in knots. A dose could cure one person—just one—of any illness, but that meant denying it to everyone else who so desperately needed a cure.

Choosing life for one and leaving thousands of others to their fate, which too often meant death. How could she—?

A knock on the front door.

Who on Earth . . . ?

Quickly she closed the box and placed it on a high shelf among the decorative bowls she rarely used. She hurried to the door. A peek through the sidelight revealed a familiar face.

Rick.

"You're early," she said, feeling a tingle of delight as she pulled the door open. She'd invited him over for dinner.

Tall, with lean muscles and a wedge-shaped upper body that owed more to genetics than weight training, he looked fit and trim in a dark blue polo shirt and tan slacks. A brown paper bag dangled from his hand. With his thick brown hair, dark gray eyes, and a perpetually sardonic twist to his lips, he looked the proverbial hunk. At least on the outside. Inside she knew he was something quite other.

"I know. If that's a problem . . ."

"No problem at all."

True. Not only was she glad to see him—she'd been looking forward to his arrival all day—but she needed a distraction from the *ikhar*.

After a fleetingly awkward pause, he wrapped his arms around her and gave her a quick kiss on the top of her head—he was that much taller—and then broke away. The hug felt good and Laura wished it had lasted longer, but even after all they'd been through, he still acted so hesitant around her.

She wondered about that. He seemed supremely confident in all other areas of life, but she hadn't seen him around other women. Was he skittish with all women, or just her? She hoped it was just her.

She pointed to the bag in his hand. Obviously a bottle. "Bubbles?"

"Veuve Clicquot."

"Ah. The good stuff."

According to Rick, he'd been mostly a beer drinker until their trip through France where he discovered how much he liked Champagne.

"What are we celebrating?"

"How about . . . it's Tuesday?"

"Good enough for me." She took it from him. "I'll stick it in the fridge till dinner."

After a rocky start, she'd come to like having him around. Parts of him scared her. He'd done terrible things in his life, but only to terrible people—or so he said. And in Israel she'd witnessed firsthand his ruthless efficiency in dispatching a deadly threat. But she harbored not the slightest doubt about his unswerving loyalty to her.

And Marissa adored him—always a good sign.

In the weeks since their return to the States, he'd become a frequent visitor. After her divorce she hadn't wanted a relationship, but then Rick had been forced upon her, and she found it good to have a man in her life again, even if this one confined himself to the periphery.

Was this a relationship? She wasn't sure what to call it. They'd teetered on the edge of intimacy in that hotel in the Orkneys—the end of their mission, too much to drink—and might have taken the leap had they not been interrupted. Rick had never followed up on that, never once made a pass at her. She wasn't yet sure how she'd respond if he did, but she would at least like the opportunity to find out.

She kept remembering what he'd said outside that dead kibbutz in Israel: *Relationships are overrated.* Did he mean that, or had he said it to blow her off because he felt her questions were getting too personal? And was he wrong?

He was so hard to read. Sometimes he seemed almost afraid of her, or rather afraid she'd shatter at the slightest touch. She wasn't a china doll. She'd done bioprospecting in jungles, been married, had a child, gone through a divorce, shepherded her child through leukemia. And just last month—as Rick knew all too well—she'd been chased across various continents by assorted psychos who wanted her dead, and had somehow managed to survive.

Not that she was craving male companionship. She and Rick had their own spaces and lives, but they remained intersected to a certain degree. The scientist part of her brain couldn't help visualizing a Venn diagram with their lives as circles, hers red, his blue. The overlap was a small area of purple. Sometimes she wished for more purple, but saw no need to rush it. What would happen would happen. In the meantime, she had her own agenda, so much of which did not involve Rick.

And yet, for someone not craving male companionship, she found her thoughts straying often to this man.

He followed her into the kitchen. "How's the residency hunt?"

"Still tracking down and collecting data for the application."

Her decision to change the focus of her medical career had come too late for this year's residency match, so she was laying the groundwork to put her name in the neurology pool for next year.

"And then what?"

"And then next spring I hope they match me with a convenient hospital."

He smiled. "Oh. Sort of like a Sorting Hat."

"Never thought of it like that, but you're not far off."

The National Resident Matching Program wasn't exactly a lottery, but close. All medical school seniors—and occasionally a doctor already in practice, like her—looking for postgraduate residencies in specialty training had to join the match program. She wouldn't be able to officially register for a neurology residency until September; then she'd apply for interviews with area medical centers like Columbia, Mount Sinai, Stony Brook, and NYU–North Shore. She'd take any of them, but really wanted one of the latter two because they were practically in her backyard.

She stowed the bottle in the fridge and turned to him. Should she tell him about the *ikhar*? He knew about Clotilde's promise, but seemed to have forgotten about it. Telling him the *ikhar* had arrived would ignite a discussion about who she'd dose with it and she didn't feel like getting into that. At least not at the moment.

So she kept the chatter neutral. "What brings you over so early?"

"Stahlman's idea."

"Oh? He's scheduling your social life now?"

"Why not? He's already scheduling the rest of my life. Keeps me jumping on multiple projects. He's got so many irons in so many fires . . . ever since we cured him he's been a dynamo."

Clayton Stahlman had financed their trip last month. He was stupid rich and had been terminal with pulmonary fibrosis when he'd sent her out to find a cure. Rick at the time was already managing his security and backgrounding key employees, so Stahlman had sent him along.

"You mean ever since *you* cured him," she said.

"We found the panacea together."

This was one of the things she liked about Rick. He never hesitated to share credit.

"But you're the one who delivered his dose."

Insisted on seeing that his boss received a dose, even when neither of them was sure it would work.

The result had been another miraculous cure and, as Stahlman had promised, a multimillion-dollar windfall for Laura. Most of it was tagged for Marissa's future, and Laura had hired money managers to figure out the best way to preserve it for her until she reached adulthood.

"Anyway," he said, "told him I wouldn't be available tonight because you'd asked me over for dinner. And he said something like, 'Perfect! I want you to ask her something.'"

"I'm afraid to hear."

"He's picked up rumors of some miraculous cures right here on Long Island and wanted to know if that was you."

Laura tensed. "And you said . . . ?"

"Said no way. You used up all you had."

"You didn't tell him about—?"

"Clotilde sending you more?" He made a face. "Seriously?"

"Sorry. I just want to keep all that under wraps."

No worry where Rick was concerned. His time in the CIA had left him silent as a clam. He never volunteered information.

"Makes two of us. Anyway, people are saying there's some doc somewhere on the North Shore with a healing touch. Stahlman wants us to track him down."

"Why does he think he needs me for that? Because I'm a doctor too? No thanks. Besides, whoever he is, he's either a charlatan or a kook."

"And if he's not?"

"It's a super–long shot that he's the real deal." A month ago she would have said "impossible," but impossible had become an opinion. "But if he is, we should leave him alone."

"Amen to that."

She noticed a spoon in the sink. She rarely left utensils about, but she'd been distracted this morning by the prospect of meeting James Fife. She pulled open the dishwasher to put it away.

"Whoa!" Rick said as she slid out the Miele's utensil tray. "Serial-killer dishwasher!"

"What?"

"Take a look," he said, pointing. "You've got all the long forks lined up next to each other, and all the short forks together, same with all the teaspoons and tablespoons."

"So?"

"Serial killer," he said with a sage nod. "No question. I know these things. Only serial killers go to that sort of trouble."

"You know nothing of the sort. And it's no trouble at all."

Was he serious? Sometimes she couldn't tell.

Okay, sure, she had a little OCD going for her. But so what? It made her a better ME. When posting a corpse, it paid to do everything the same way in the same order every time. That way she didn't miss anything.

Playing along, she held up the tablespoon. "Look. I've got to put this someplace, right? So I put it next to another tablespoon." She did just that. "See? Simple. Same with a dessert fork: next to another dessert fork. And so on and so on. Why? Because it makes unloading a breeze. Just grab all the dinner forks at once and drop them into the dinner-fork slot in the utensil drawer. Bam. Done in one shot. Nothing to it."

He was still nodding. "Uh-huh. Where are the bodies buried? Under the rhodos?"

She put on a shocked expression. "Don't be ridiculous! Their roots are too thick."

"And what if I took this," he said, reaching for a steak knife, "and put it with the forks?"

"Well, then I'd have to kill you—with the steak knife, of course." She grinned as she closed the dishwasher. "When did you become funny?"

"'Funny' as in 'strange'? Always been strange."

"You hid it when we met—under a thick layer of crankiness, as I recall." She remembered not liking him much at first.

"Because I didn't know if I could trust you. I'd experienced the inexplicable and you hadn't. Now you have."

"The *ikhar*."

"The *ikhar*. Its existence is proof that there's more to life on Earth than what we see. You've accepted that all is not as it seems, so now we are simpatico."

"I wasn't given much choice, was I. Dragged kicking and screaming to acceptance, but yes, I have to admit that all is not as it seems." To change the subject, she pointed to the B & N bag. "Before we wade too far into the Sea of Paranoia, would you mind putting those out in the family room?"

"More neurology books?"

She explained Marissa's current class work.

He shook his head. "It's baseball season."

"You mean spitting season?"

He grinned. "That bothers the hell out of you, doesn't it."

"It's disgusting."

No lie. Baseball players couldn't seem to go ten seconds without spitting something. And not one of them seemed capable of chewing with his mouth closed. Yuck.

"Well, spitting season's fully up and running. Got a feeling her discretionary reading is going to be limited to *Sports Illustrated* and the back pages of the *Daily News*."

Marissa loved all baseball but loved the "Metropolitans"—as she insisted on calling the Mets—most of all. And miracle of miracles, the Metropolitans were doing well again this year.

Laura tapped her temple. "There's method to this madness. I picked out a couple of big books, heavy on illustrations. We both know she'll balk at the idea of 'learning' during one of her precious games, but if someone, let's just say her mother, or perhaps a guy she thinks is really cool and pretends to like baseball as much as she does—"

"Hangin' in there. Hope I can last. MLB season goes on like a Castro speech."

"'Oh what a tangled web we weave . . .'"

"Tell me about it."

Another likable trait. To get on Marissa's good side, Rick had pretended to love baseball when he hated it. Neither he nor Laura had anticipated him being a semi-regular visitor then, but Rick hadn't let Marissa down. He'd studied up on the sport and could now trade stats with the best of them.

"So," she said, "what if, during a commercial break, you casually picked up one of the books and found a cool picture and said, 'Hey, look at this!' Who knows? She might do some page flipping during subsequent breaks, or even when nothing is happening on the field. Which is often."

"Except for spitting."

"Spitting excepted, of course."

"Your optimism is inspiring. Naïve, but inspiring nonetheless."

"I'm counting on your help, Rick."

"I'm on it."

She handed him the B & N bag. "Kindly find strategic places for these in the family room."

"Any suggestions?"

"Well, they're called coffee-table books. Why not start there?"

"You have a coffee table?"

"It's that low flat thing in front of the couch."

"Oh, the footrest."

She laughed. "Yes, that too."

"Got it."

A few seconds after he left the kitchen she heard him say, "I'll be damned! That's my brother!"

She hurried into the family room, expecting to see him staring at the TV. Instead his gaze was fixed on the book in his hands.

"Brother? You have a brother?"

"Yeah, well, I'm not in touch with my family much." He held up one of the books she'd bought: *The Ties That Bind* by Keith Somers, Ph.D. "But that's him. That's my bro."

Keith Somers . . . okay, right. Rick's real name was Garrick Somers, not Rick Hayden ("like the planetarium, not Panettiere," as he was wont to say). He'd arrived at his Rick Hayden identity via a long, arduous, devious, and deadly path.

With all that had happened, with all their time together in Europe, why hadn't he ever mentioned a brother? He'd been there for her when Marissa was near death. Didn't he know she was here for him?

"You never told me you had a brother."

"You never told me you had a coffee table."

"I'm serious. Aren't you worried about him?"

He frowned. "Worried? What's to worry about? The cover says it's an international bestseller."

He looked puzzled. Which meant he didn't know. How could he not?

"He's missing."

His expression went slack. "What?"

"He disappeared."

"When?"

"Weeks ago—probably over a month, month and a half now. It's been all over the news. How could you not—?"

"Whatever news I get comes over my phone—headlines, mostly—and Stahlman's kept me so busy I must have missed it."

"Didn't anyone in your family call?"

"My family? Not likely."

"But—?"

"It's complicated. Just let me say the radio silence is no surprise. And let me tell you: Keith's a little weird."

"What's that got—?"

"Not as weird as my sister, of course."

"Sister? You have a *sister*?"

He sighed. "Yeah, two sibs, one of each sex."

"And a mother and father too, I assume."

"Dad died. Cancer."

"Oh. Sorry."

"Years ago. When we moved back from Switzerland, he quit the phar-maceutical biz and cofounded a clothing company. Not sure how he did it, but it got huge. Let himself be bought out after he heard the terminal diagnosis. Left my mother a very wealthy widow. I mean, *very* wealthy. Who knew there was that kind of money in retail clothing?"

"You don't have that scion vibe."

"Cylon? You mean like in *Battlestar Galactica*?"

She found it hard at times to tell when he was putting her on, so she said, "*Sci*-on—son of a rich family, a trust-fund kid."

"Well, first you need a trust fund for that, right?"

"You mean your father—?"

"Like I said, he left it all to my mother, and she's not my biggest fan."

Laura narrowed her eyes. "All right, what did you do?"

He shrugged. "The ultimate filial betrayal: joined the CIA."

"And that's a problem?"

"With my mother it is."

"But you're still her son."

"Welllllll . . ." He drew out the word to its tensile limit.

Laura got it. "You're adopted."

"All three of us. I'm the middle child. Keith's the elder Cylon."

"Scion."

"No, if you knew Keith you'd know Cylon is closer to the truth."

"Whatever. So he's not really your brother."

Rick rubbed his jaw. "Not biologically, I guess, but the way I look at it, if you're both adopted by the same people, if you shared the same last name and were raised in the same house, you're brothers."

"I can't believe you've never mentioned them. Especially after you know all about *my* family."

"Well, it's never come up. And your having a Mayan mother was kind of germane to our mission, wasn't it?"

Point taken. "Still . . ."

"You know that old cliché about knowledge that can drive you mad? That describes my family."

"Aren't we exaggerating just a little?"

"Not really. If you ever see where I come from, I'll never hear from you again."

Well, nice to know she mattered that much to him. Still . . .

"You ought to know by now I'm not easily put off."

"You've never met my mother. We're talking about a migraine in loung-ing pajamas."

"Nobody wears lounging pajamas anymore."

"You have no idea."

No question: Rick seemed to find his family truly embarrassing.

"But your brother . . . he's missing." She took his arm and pulled him toward her home office. "Come on. We can Google the news and catch you up. The munchkin's got softball this afternoon so we've got plenty of time to get you up to speed on your brother. And you need to know."

"Can we debate that?"

"No."

She led him into her office off the family room where she settled before her aging Dell. She hopped into Google news and immediately found a raft of articles on Keith Somers, Ph.D., a zoologist specializing in evolu-tionary biology and the application of genetics to taxonomy, assistant pro-fessor in NYU's Department of Biology, author of the hugely successful bestselling pop-science book *The Ties That Bind*.

As she opened successive links, Rick leaned forward, resting one hand on the edge of the desk and the other on her shoulder. So intent was he on the screen he seemed unaware he was touching her. But Laura was aware. A vague electric tingle trickled from the gentle pressure of his palm. She liked it.

She focused on the screen where scant details about Dr. Somers disap-pearing between his home and office six weeks ago were recounted. Police statements from that time provided no useful information.

The news pieces tapered off quickly after the disappearance as more sensational stories captured the fickle attention of the news cycle, and there'd been no mention of Dr. Somers for weeks.

"Well," Rick said, his hand sliding off her shoulder as he straightened, "that was a waste of time."

Laura felt his frustration. She cleared her throat. "It's as if they've for-gotten about him."

"Either that or my mother's negotiating a ransom."

"The quotes from the police said they didn't suspect foul play."

He shrugged. "Keeping police away may be part of the ransom demand. Look at what we know: This rich guy leaves work and never arrives home . . . that means he's either been snatched or he's running from something. Keith is a biology nerd. Spends his life deciding how various living things should be classified. Not the type to get into anything shady. That leaves a kidnapping."

Why wasn't Rick more disturbed? Maybe he just didn't show it. They'd gone through a few hairy moments in their quest for the *ikhar* and he'd never once lost his cool.

"For all we know, he could be back by now." He sighed. "As much as I know I'm gonna regret it, I don't see any choice but to go straight to the source. And that means doing something I haven't done in years . . . something I dread more than anything else in the universe."

Laura couldn't imagine. "What?"

"Gonna have to call my mother."

3

Laura had left him in her office and returned to the kitchen to work on dinner—*so ET can phone home alone,* as she'd put it.

Rick still remembered the home phone number, at least what the number used to be. How many years since he'd called home? He didn't remember. Wasn't even sure his mother still lived in the same house. But then, she'd need an awful good reason to leave a waterfront property on Long Island Sound. She sure as hell didn't need the money from the sale, so odds were high she'd stayed there.

He held off punching in the number and looked around. He'd never been in here before. He moved to the nearest wall and browsed the photo gallery. Sprinkled among the many pics of Marissa were a sampling from Laura's youth. Her Mormon father had met her Mayan mother while doing a missionary work in Quintana Roo.

Laura had grown up in Salt Lake City and did she ever stand out in her school photos. This beautiful dark-skinned, dark-haired, blue-eyed girl surrounded by all her lily-white Mormon classmates.

Rick wondered how that must have felt growing up. He'd been born with a face and a name that would be welcome in any country club in the world, while Laura had grown up a swan among ducklings.

Ah, but what a swan she'd turned out to be. He'd hesitated to rest his hand on her shoulder but the urge had been overwhelming. He'd settled for simply touching her when what he'd really wanted to do was knead her shoulders until she was good and relaxed and then slide his hands down her front to her—

Whoa. Stop. Not the time or place for fantasies. Like thinking about the night in Kirkwall when, after a *lot* of wine, they'd started kissing. What might have happened if Clotilde had waited an extra hour before interrupting them?

He shook it off, pulled away from the photos, and punched in the old phone number.

A woman answered in accented English. *"Allo?"*

Obviously not his mother.

"Is this the Somers's residence?"

"Yes. Who is it calling?"

"Rick—Garrick Somers." He'd almost said Rick Hayden. "May I speak to Mrs. Somers?"

Some muffled conversation as the receiver's mouthpiece was covered, then a familiar voice came on.

"Garrick? Is this really you?"

Paulette Garrick Somers had given him her maiden name as his first and had never once called him "Rick."

"The one and only, Paulette."

And he'd stopped calling her "Mom" sometime during college.

"Where have you been? I've been trying to contact you."

"You have?"

"Well, not me, personally. Lena tried, but your number has been given to someone else."

He'd had easily a dozen or more phone numbers since they'd last spoken.

"Who's Lena?"

"My assistant. She even called that gang of thugs you joined but they said they'd never heard of you."

No surprise there. Part of his deal upon leaving the CIA was that all records of his connection with the Company would be buried.

"Not with them anymore."

"Now that's the first good news I've had in weeks."

"Look, I'm calling about Keith."

"Well, it's about time."

"Only heard about it twenty minutes ago."

"How is that possible? He's your brother."

"If it's not front-page news, I usually miss it. And frankly, what I looked up just before I called doesn't tell me much. Was he kidnapped? Have you had a ransom demand?"

"No, nothing like that. I haven't heard from anybody, especially Keith."

"What about the police?"

"Worse than worthless, as expected when it comes to anything other than abusing minorities! They think he pulled a disappearing act on his own. Patently ridiculous! Something happened to him and it's all because of that damned monkey."

"Monkey? What—?"

"It's too involved to go into."

"Isn't *anybody* looking for him?"

"I am looking for him. But I'm the only one. First you left to join those thugs, then Cheryl left and won't tell me where she is, and now Keith." Her voice broke on the name. Keith had always been her favorite. *"I'm all alone in this."*

Was she looking for his help? Paulette would never come straight out and ask—especially not someone even remotely connected to the CIA.

"What can I do?"

"Nothing. I've got everything under control."

Sure as hell didn't sound like it.

"Look, I'm not far away—just down in Shirley. I'm coming over."

"Don't put yourself out."

"See you soon."

He hung up and walked back to the kitchen where Laura was chopping romaine. He stood and watched her for a moment. She had such a unique look—slim, sturdy frame, inky hair, olive skin, but those eyes . . . those startling pale-blue eyes were the cherry on the whipped cream.

But her looks were just the wrapper. Inside she had smarts, she had guts, she had character. She was funny, she was true-blue, all the corny stuff that goes into being a *hausfrau* and mother. And still something oh-so-sexy about her.

Not to mention her aura. Not the new-agey nonsense, her *presence*. It suffused her home. The world outside was ugly and petty and populated by trolls and leeches. But here in this place, this home, he sensed serenity. All because of Laura.

He wanted her. God, how he wanted her.

Here was the woman who could save him. But what would save Laura from him? That mission in Düsseldorf . . . he'd discovered a darkness within him. He'd made the world a better place, but at such a cost.

The Company had assigned him to infiltrate a group of violent young Germans. Despite being into anarchy and nihilism, they seemed more into talk than action until a mysterious stranger gave them an old book by a long-dead Düsseldorf native. They took to it and it led them into an unspeakable vileness that defied categorization, performing ceremonies that involved mutilating children in the hope of summoning something they called the Dark Man.

Rick had trapped them in their farmhouse and ignited the explosives and incendiaries they'd stockpiled there. They'd booby-trapped the barn where they kept the children—couldn't allow anyone to see what they'd done—and when the farmhouse went up, so did the barn.

Eleven adults gone—good riddance—along with fifteen irreparably damaged children.

And as they'd burned, Rick had seen something in the flames . . . something dark . . .

The shrinks who'd debriefed him afterward had tagged him with PTSD, and maybe they were right. He'd faked getting over it but he hadn't. Not really. Because he couldn't be sure it wasn't all going down again. Right now. Had the man with the book given another copy to another gang of psychos and were they now doing the unspeakable to other children?

Yeah . . . PTSD all right.

But he hadn't been prone to fits of violence, he hadn't been suicidal. He'd have to *feel* something for any of that, and he'd felt *nothing*.

Which didn't mean that he couldn't project feelings. He learned to fake them really well, enough to fool the shrinks, enough to fool the various women who'd passed through his life since Düsseldorf. He conned them all, ushering them past the Potemkin village of his emotions.

But Laura had awakened something he'd thought dead forever. He cared about someone again. And that felt so damn good. He'd discover her traipsing across his field of thought at the oddest times.

He'd told her about Düsseldorf, but not the whole story. Three quarters of it, but not the worst part, not the part that made him a monster.

The truth will set you free? Yeah. Set him free from Laura, set her running from him. She could never know. Because if she ever did . . .

She deserved better. He believed that—no, he *knew* that.

And yet he couldn't stay away.

He stepped through the doorway. "Looks like I'll be making a quick trip home."

She put down her knife, wiped her hands, and trained those eyes on him. "And where might that be?"

"The Incorporated Village of Monroe."

"Really? That's North Shore."

"*Preferred* North Shore, don't you know. Do you mind?"

"You're going to make it back for dinner, right?"

"Better believe it. Keep the bubbly cold."

He'd need it after visiting with his mother. Might even have to pick up a second bottle on the way back.

And what the hell had she meant by "that damned monkey"?

4

NORTH SHORE, LONG ISLAND, NEW YORK

Rick was cruising Cedar Swamp Road, about five miles out from Monroe, when his phone rang. He didn't recognize the number—wait, yes he did. His mother. He hit the accept button on his steering wheel and Bluetooth did the rest.

"Thought you didn't have my number."

"*Caller ID tell me,*" said Lena.

The wonders of modern technology.

"What can I do for you, Lena?"

"*Mother say you pick up accountant at Boulevard Motors in Glen Cove.*"

"What?"

"This is what she say."

Boulevard Motors had been fixing local cars for generations. What was an accountant doing at Boulevard Motors? And why an accountant?

"I don't understand."

"Mother say all explained when get here. But you pick up Harry Tate at Boulevard Motors. Very important."

How long had it been now? Five . . . seven years without a face-to-face and already she was sending him on errands.

Plus ça change . . .

"All right. Be there soon."

He piloted the Ford pickup—part of Stahlman's fleet, but he'd used it earlier today so he'd kept it—up to Sea Cliff Avenue, then headed for Boulevard Motors.

Stepping into the repair bay, he flagged down a guy in appropriately greasy overalls.

"Looking for a Mister Tate."

"Tate?" He shrugged and pointed. "Got me. Check the waiting area."

Rick followed the point to a tiny room with battered furniture, an old tube TV, and a Keurig machine. The only occupant was a squat Indian woman in a yellow-and-orange sari shuffling through a pile of papers on her lap. She had a gentle round face framed by short dark hair that made her look like a contented housecat ready to purr.

"You work here?" she said as he stepped in.

"No, I—"

Apparently she wasn't listening because she glared at him and pointed across the room. "What's the idea of having a Keurig machine and no K-cups? Not a single goddamn K-cup in the whole place. That's like torture to someone who needs coffee."

Okay, make that a hungry feral cat.

"Just looking for a Mister Tate," he said. "Any idea—?"

"I'm Tate and I ain't no mister."

"Really? Harry Tate?"

"That's H-a-r-i Tate."

Her garb might have been Mumbai but her accent was pure Mineola.

"Sorry."

"Happens all the time." She shoved the papers into a briefcase that had been hiding beside her chair. "So you're Garrick?"

"Rick, please."

"I didn't even know you existed."

"Really?"

"She never mentions you. Only Keith-Keith-Keith."

"Yeah, well, I'm sort of the Jan Brady of the family."

"When your mother told me her son was going to pick me up, I was shocked. Thinking she meant Keith, I said, 'He's back?' and then she explained." Hari snapped her briefcase shut. "Where the hell have you been and what do you do?"

Not exactly a shrinking violet.

"Investigations and security work out of Westchester."

"How many employees?"

"Three: me, myself, and I."

Straightening her sari as she rose, Hari said, "My Mercedes won't be ready for at least another hour. Let's get outta this dump."

As they headed for the exit, she said, "How's sole proprietorship working out for you?"

"Great. Nobody argues with my decisions."

"I'll bet the company picnics are lame, though."

"Yeah. Me and a six-pack. At least I always win the horseshoe tournament."

"Busy?"

"Very."

"Need an accountant?" After a beat, she added, "I'm asking for a friend."

"Not yet, but I hope to someday. Right now I've got only one client, so keeping the books is a breeze."

True. Almost everything he did was for Stahlman.

"The accepted wisdom of small-business management recommends spreading yourself around."

"So I've heard."

Yeah, if Stahlman took a turn on him, things could get tight pretty fast. But then again, Stahlman owed his current good health and therefore his life to Rick.

He led her into the parking area. She stopped dead when she saw he was headed for the F-150.

"Wait. We're riding in a pickup?"

"Something wrong with that?"

"Nothing, I guess. I'm just used to foreign cars—more reliable."

"Oh, like the one that's on the lift back here?"

She made a face. "No wonder your mother never mentions you."

Rick held the passenger door open and noticed her having a little trouble hoisting herself onto the running board. He was tempted to help her but decided better not to. Human bites were dangerous.

"We need to stop at a Seven-Eleven or something," she said as she snapped her seat belt closed. "The Keurig at the garage was useless and I need coffee. Boy, do I need coffee."

Rick got rolling. "So, you're an accountant? Where's your office?"

"Flatiron District. And I'm a *forensic* accountant."

"Which means . . . ?"

"I usually work on criminal cases involving fraud and money laundering."

Rick didn't like the sound of that, but couldn't make a connection.

"Has this got anything to do with Keith?"

"One month before he disappeared, your brother started liquidating all his assets, converting them to cash. For the police, that signaled a plan to disappear."

"Sounds like it."

"Your mother contends there was no reason for him to run, and I have to agree. Everything was going his way. He was moving up in the NYU biology department, his book was a bestseller, and his publisher was offering him big bucks for a follow-up. And one more thing: All his belongings, including his passport, are still at his apartment. He didn't even take a toothbrush."

Not proof positive, but pretty damn convincing. It seemed like Keith had the perfect life. With his trust fund and bestseller royalties, he couldn't have been running from debt. But what had Paulette said?

"My mother mentioned something about a monkey . . ."

Hari laughed. "Oh, she's fixated as all hell on that monkey. I never saw it myself, so I'll let her tell you about it, but she thinks the monkey is at the root of everything."

"A monkey?"

"Nutshell version: She's convinced someone was extorting money from Keith—either through blackmail or threats—and that the monkey was somehow at the heart of it. Find the money and we'll find the bad guy. So she hired me to do what I do best: Follow the money." She pointed through the windshield. "Hey, there's a place. Pull in."

Rick followed her point to a storefront called Fly-By and pulled into the lot. A quick look-around showed three high-schoolers drinking the place's Slurpee equivalent by the ice freezer over on the left, while to the right two roofers leaned against a van, smoking and drinking coffee.

"If this is a chain, I've never heard of it," he said.

"Who cares? As long as they have coffee."

A landscaping van pulled in just as she was sliding from the passenger seat.

"Get moving!" she said.

"Why?"

"Quetzalcoatl clown car!"

"What?"

"Just get inside so we can grab our coffees before them."

Once inside the front doors, she pointed through the window at Mexican laborers piling out of the van one after another. It went on and on until they formed a cluster of a dozen.

"What I tell you?"

"You afraid of them?"

"I'm afraid of being behind them in line. Come on. Fix your coffee."

Fly-By was more of a convenience store than a coffee shop: no cappuccinos, no baristas, just half a dozen urns of varying flavors and octanes. The Mexicans filed in as Rick fixed himself a dark roast with sugar and light cream. He didn't see what Hari made but he'd barely snapped on a lid when she pulled him over to a spot six feet back from the cash registers. An older white couple ahead of them at the counter were mulling over the array of donuts.

He leaned close to her. "I still don't get your problem with these Mexicans."

"Being Mexican has nothing to do with it—it's everybody. People take for*ever*. They stand in line and yak-yak-yak."

"Isn't that what we're doing?"

"Not quite. We've fixed our coffees and we're gonna be ready—money in hand—when it's time to pay. You *do* have your money ready, don't you?"

Rick showed her the fiver in his hand.

"Excellent. But people these days don't give a damn about anybody else. They'll wait till they reach the counter, *then* they start studying the sandwich warmer—'Do I want it with cheese or not?' You know, like they'd never consider using the time they've been standing on line to devote a single thought to it. Finally they make their momentous decision, and then, when everything's tallied and the cashier tells them the amount, they're suddenly like, 'Oh, hey, I gotta pay!' Like there was a possibility it was gonna be free? 'Oh, here, let me wiggle my wallet from my pocket or bag and paw through all the compartments for some cash.' And you think the next guy in line is gonna get a clue from watching this? No way. Same nonsense with every one of them. I don't have time for that."

Rick fixed his gaze straight ahead. "Wow."

"Hey, don't go hanging some kinda racist sign on me. I'm a minority too. And female to boot. That makes me a two-fer. Lack of anticipation has become the way of the world. The gene pool lifeguard went out for lunch and never came back, so these escapees from the skimmer are everywhere. No race has a lock on them. They come in every shape, size, and color—*especially* white. Take those two honkies at the counter now. No anticipation. Not a bit. The ones from the van just happen to come from south of the border, that's all."

"What side of the bed did you get up on?"

"Just low on caffeine is all. My ex-husband kept saying I need an anger management course, but that's bullshit."

"Really."

"Yeah, 'really.' I just need a world with fewer people who piss me off." She pointed to a clear plastic container in a nearby display case. "Hey, will you look at this? Cannoli filling with a side of crackers—let's sell a lump of fat-and-sugar paste as a cracker dip. Are they kidding? I mean, who eats this crap?"

"Ever consider drinking your coffee while standing in line? It's allowed, you know."

"Yeah, maybe you're right." She took a deep gulp. "My filter tends to slip a little when my caffeine level drops."

"Yeah?" He left it at that.

Rick paid for her coffee so she could continue drinking. The obligatory Pakistani counterman was making change, saying, "Would you like to buy a lottery ticket?"

"No," Hari snapped.

"Would you like donuts to go with your coffees?"

"No."

"Would you like a bag?"

Hari leaned over the counter. "What we'd like is to pay up and get the hell out of your store."

Rick managed to get her back to the pickup without her mauling anyone along the way. When they were rolling again, he turned the conversation back to Keith.

"So what have you forensicked so far?"

She tapped the briefcase on her saried lap. "That either your brother knew a lot about moving money around the world or someone else was involved."

Keith was smart. He could have learned, but . . .

He said, "Not the sort of thing you pick up on your way to a Ph.D. in zoology."

"My thought too. As he liquidated his assets—not all of them, but very nearly—he deposited the proceeds in various accounts around the world."

" 'Very nearly'?"

"Well, not his apartment. Worth a lot but hardly liquid."

"This means you've identified the accounts."

Rick was far from an expert in offshore banking, but he'd run across international money laundering during his time with the Company and had been staggered by the almost unimaginable sums secreted in offshore accounts.

Hari nodded. "All over. We're talking Caymans, Belize, Luxembourg, Bermuda, etcetera. But they're mostly empty now. The funds were deposited, then transferred to other accounts, and from them to still others. I haven't ferreted out where the money's landed yet. But I will. And if that final account is owned by your brother, well, that means he's on the run. If not . . ."

"Could still be him under a different identity."

"Correct. But if not, then we will have found the one who coerced him into doing this."

"Keith is such a nerd. Can't imagine anyone could have something to hold over him to that degree."

"How about threatening to kidnap his mother for a horrible death if he didn't comply?"

Rick smiled and shook his head.

"What?" she said. "That's funny?"

"I'm seeing a *Ruthless People* scenario—you know, that flick with Bette Midler and Danny DeVito?"

"You mean, where no one wants her back?"

Exactly.

"Forget I mentioned it," he said. "I can see threats working on Keith. But where does this monkey come in?"

She shook her head. "Your mother's theory, not mine. I'll leave that for her to explain. Weird stuff going on inside that head."

Rick deadpanned, "Well, you've got to understand, she's never been the same since Dorothy threw that water on her."

A heartbeat of silence followed, then Hari guffawed. "I think I like you."

"That's a pretty exclusive club."

"And your mother's not a member, I take it?"

"Correctomundo."

"Well, she's definitely a fan of your brother. The only time she's not wailing about her missing Keith is when she's ranting about *My Fair Lady*."

"The play?"

Hari nodded. "They're reviving it again on Broadway."

Rick knew he'd regret asking: "And what's her beef?"

"She wants them to change some of the songs."

"What? They're classics."

"Whatever. I don't know the play, but apparently she thinks some of the songs are too misogynistic. In case you never noticed, your mother is a granola-chewing, chai-sipping, PETA-donating crackpot. And I mean that in the most respectful way."

Rick smiled. "Taken in the most respectful way."

Hari, he thought, you've only scratched the surface. You've no idea.

5

SHIRLEY, NEW YORK

Laura couldn't resist any longer. She had the chopped romaine in the colander and some finely sliced Parmesan ready for the Caesar salad; she'd debated making the dressing from scratch but opted for bottled when she found some in the pantry. She had a couple of New York strips marinating. She'd dragoon Rick into grilling those. Which left her with not much else to do.

And idle hands . . .

She pulled the box from the top shelf, parted the bubble wrap, and removed the crimson snuff bottle. She wondered what the symbol meant, if anything. She'd seen snuff bottles in Chinatown, but they were usually much more ornate. This one seemed merely functional, and didn't contain snuff.

The *ikhar* sloshed within as she reread Clotilde's note.

Let the All-Mother guide you.

The All-Mother . . . Clotilde's Gaia-type goddess. Her pagan cult had been brewing the *ikhar* since the sixth century and doling out the curative tea to the lucky few designated by their deity. Curative was an understatement—the tea was the legendary panacea, able to cure *every* ill. But they kept its existence on the down-low because their goddess wished to be niggardly with it, dosing only those she deemed worthy of healing.

Clotilde had never explained just how the *sylyk*, as they called their healers, recognized the chosen recipients. Laura suspected each *sylyk* made his or her own choice and attributed it to the All-Mother. Whatever. She could see how leaving it to the goddess lightened the hellacious burden of deciding who got well and who stayed sick.

When she had asked why Clotilde was designating her a *sylyk*, she'd said Laura had "the soul of a healer" and that the All-Mother "smiles on you." Again, whatever. She didn't believe in the All-Mother any more than she believed in hobbits and elves.

However, she had no choice but to believe in the *ikhar*.

Educated in the scientific method, Laura had vigorously resisted the possibility of a cure-all. But finally she'd come to accept its existence. What other option did she have? She'd seen it bring her own daughter back from the brink of death. Stahlman's pulmonary fibrosis—a terminal diagnosis—had cleared overnight. The scientist part of her demanded to know its method of action, but the *ikhar* had resisted all analysis. Finally she'd raised a white flag of intellectual surrender and simply gone with it.

As for choosing who would get this dose, Laura wasn't about to wait for the All-Mother. The *ikhar* was a miracle waiting to happen, so she'd decided to choose her recipients carefully. After weeks of careful consideration, she'd settled on James Fife. She'd harbored a deep, personal reason for gravitating toward Fife, but he hadn't worked out. She had other possibilities, though. Hopeless cases, nearing the end of their ordeals. But they had to be *worthy*.

A couple of weeks ago she'd found the perfect candidate at the VA Medical Center in Northport: Emilie Lantz met the criteria of hopelessness and worthiness—in spades.

She squeezed the snuff bottle. Less than an hour's ride to the medical center. If she left right now . . .

No, if she hit traffic in either direction she wouldn't be here when Marissa came home, and that wouldn't do at all. Besides, tomorrow was her usual volunteer day. They'd notice her, ask why she'd shown up on a Tuesday instead of her customary Wednesday. And then if Emilie woke up tomorrow fully cured, they'd remember.

If . . . Listen to me. *If Emilie woke up tomorrow fully cured* . . .

Despite the testament of her own experience, part of her—a big part of her—still resisted the *ikhar,* still refused to believe any such thing could exist.

But if Emilie woke up cured, someone might well say, *Hey, that Laura Fanning volunteer showed up unexpectedly yesterday. Didn't her daughter have a miracle-cure too? What's up with that?*

She had to be careful, so very, very careful. People had died horribly for dispensing the *ikhar*. Rick and Stahlman already knew about it, of course—they were in on the discovery—but she'd told no one else.

She'd wait until tomorrow. That meant another day of misery for Emilie. She felt bad about that, but it couldn't be helped.

Laura replaced the snuff bottle in the box and returned it to the upper shelf.

6

THE VILLAGE OF MONROE, NEW YORK

Rick found Monroe pretty much as he'd left it: a charming little village stuck between Glen Cove and Lattingtown on Long Island's preferred North Shore. Years ago the city fathers had overhauled the downtown area into a faux whaling village design, and that hadn't changed—still as faux as ever. He was glad to see Memison's still in business. Back in the day it had gained a rep as the best restaurant in town, renowned for its fish dinners.

Hari yakked on and on as he piloted the pickup along Main Street, past the Monroe Yacht and Racquet Club; rows of garden apartments followed, segueing into postwar tract homes, and then finally into the chi-chi environs. He turned onto Shore Drive where the waterfront homes were mansion class.

"I'll never get why some people name their homes," Hari said as they cruised along. "Here's one: Toad Hall. Really? You've got a waterfront mansion and you name it Toad Hall? I don't get it."

Rick glanced at the willow-lined yard. "Never read *The Wind in the Willows* with Mister Toad?"

"I went on Mister Toad's Wild Ride at Disney World when I was a kid. I hear they've closed it down. Is that the same?"

"The same."

She shook her head. "Now I get it even less."

Finally he came to a white-columned mansion and turned onto the long driveway.

"Home sweet home," she said. "You miss the big old place?"

"Nope."

He stepped out and paused to look. It had a majestic front with a high, rounded portico and stately columns. But this place had never been home. He'd grown up in Switzerland. When they all eventually returned to America, Long Island real estate had been in a down cycle and Dad got a good deal on the place.

Rick's two-bedroom apartment in White Plains was perfectly fine with him.

They passed between the columns to the front door where a dark-skinned woman who appeared half African, half Asian answered his ring.

"You must be Lena," Rick said, extending his hand. "I'm Garrick."

She gave his hand a quick shake. "Yes-yes. Please to meet you. And I already know Ms. Tate. Come in."

They entered the foyer just as his mother was making her entrance, breezing down one side of the curved double staircase. Really, who needed two staircases in a foyer, no matter how big?

"Well, well," she said in a tone even more imperious than he remembered, "the Prodigal Son returns."

She wore a floor-length gown of some sort of shimmery blue material. She'd stayed slim but had let her hair go silver and cut it short and close to her scalp. Going for a Judi Dench look?

"Hello, Paulette."

She drifted past him without stopping or even slowing. "Come into the sitting room and we'll discuss your brother."

He shook his head and had to smile as he followed. After years away, that was his welcome home. He hadn't expected a big hug and a kiss—she probably thought she'd be contaminated with CIA cooties—but she didn't even offer to shake his hand.

Rick realized he was fine with it. Home was where the heart was. And his heart had left this place a long time ago.

He had no desire to tour the place for old times' sake. He'd been in touch with his sister Cheryl for a while after he'd left. She'd said Paulette had remade his old bedroom into a guest room and had completely gutted and refurbished Dad's study, erasing all trace of him.

Hari started setting up in the sitting room but it quickly became apparent that it offered insufficient tabletop space, so they moved to the dining room, where she could spread out her voluminous paperwork.

Rick had to admit she knew her stuff. She'd tracked the sales from Keith's brokerage account and the withdrawals from his IRA through various banks around the world. She even had a graph showing the progress of the funds from bank to bank, country to country, until they all wound up in a single Grand Cayman account.

"The money was transferred from that account just forty-eight hours before he disappeared," she said as the three of them stood around the long, littered mahogany table.

"Where to?" Rick said.

"That's the big question. The account was in the Bodden Bank of the Caymans, privately held with its only office in George Town, and fiercely secretive."

"What are our options?" Paulette said.

Hari said, "I propose to open an account there simply to initiate contact. Once I have people to talk to, I'll press for information. Money may have to change hands."

"You mean a bribe," Paulette said.

Hari snapped her fingers. "*That's* the word I was looking for."

Paulette—immune to sarcasm—groaned. "How many more banks before we reach the final destination?"

"I think the next bank will be the caboose to this train. Someone did a very good job of diffusing the funds to blur the trail. But they all wound up in the Caymans. I'm reasonably sure the next stop will be the last one."

"Whatever it takes, then," Paulette said. "I want an answer. Find who wound up with the money and we'll find whoever took Keith."

Rick waved his hand over the papers before them. "This is all very elaborate, but ultimately cut and dried. A paper trail." He looked at his mother. "How's it connected to the monkey you mentioned?"

Paulette rolled her eyes. "That Mozambique monkey! That little blue-eyed devil! Keith was entranced with it."

"A pet monkey? Keith?"

Paulette shook her head. "I know. So unlike him."

"And since you've seen it, I assume he brought it here."

Paulette made a face. "Unfortunately, yes. The thing was his constant companion. He called it 'Mozi.'"

"Mozi from Mozambique . . . how original."

"Don't be snide about your brother. He missed you."

No way was Rick buying that. "You're kidding, right? I doubt he even knew I was gone."

Paulette shook her head. "On the contrary. He asked quite frequently if I'd heard anything from you."

"Bull."

"It is true," Lena said. "Many time he ask for you."

Rick stared at her, shocked. He could write off Paulette's claims as fabrications or, at best, wishful thinking. But here was a stranger backing her up.

Keith . . . wondering about him . . . asking about him? Totally out of character.

Paulette said, "I know Keith could be aloof, and he didn't pay much attention to you or Cheryl when you were here, but he definitely seemed to miss you when you weren't. And as for that monkey, he might not have given it the most original name, but he certainly doted on it."

She sounded almost jealous.

"Keith? Affectionate?"

Had he stepped into the Bizarro World? Or had he been misreading his brother all along?

"I know. It shocked me too. The disgusting little thing seemed quite attached to him as well—figuratively and literally. The only time it left his shoulder was to pee or poop in one of my plants."

Keith with a monkey on his shoulder . . . Rick just couldn't see it.

"How big was it?"

She shrugged. "Hard to say. Lots of tail, I'll tell you that. But I'd be surprised if that oversized, tree-dwelling rat weighed even two pounds."

Rick smiled. "I'm getting a feeling you weren't a fan."

"I'm sure Keith was taken in by its cute face and big blue eyes. But not me."

Definitely jealous.

"So anyway, what could this monkey have to do with his disappearance?"

"He said it was very important. An ancient undiscovered species. He was working on where it fit in the evolution tree and said he might even get it named after him. He liked to joke that this way the Somers name would live on after all." She gave a dramatic sniff. "That's something, at least, since I don't expect any help in that quarter from my children."

A thought struck Rick. "Wait. Did he disappear with the monkey?"

"Mozi died," Paulette said. "Keith appeared here one day with the monkey's ashes. He wouldn't say what happened, just that it had died and he'd had it cremated."

"He cremated his monkey?"

"Yes. He was very upset." She pointed toward the Long Island Sound. "He went down to the dock and scattered the ashes on the water."

"Ashes," Rick said, thinking. "So no one actually saw a dead monkey."

"Thank heavens, no," Paulette said.

His years with the Company had taught him the hard way never to believe someone was dead unless you saw their corpse. And even then . . .

But this was a monkey, not a person.

Rick shook his head. "Bizarre."

"Quite. But not as bizarre as what he said to me before he left. I remember the words exactly, because they were so disturbing: 'I'm being backed into something I would have considered inconceivable just weeks ago.'"

"He didn't elaborate?"

She shook her head. "Wouldn't say another word about it. And that was the last time I saw him. The following day was the last time *anyone* ever saw him. He walked out of his office and disappeared."

Hari said, "I'm not a family member, so I hope I'm not out of line . . ."

"Go ahead," Rick said.

"Could it be connected to his book? Once Paulette hired me, I sat down and read *The Ties That Bind*. Have you read it?"

Rick shook his head. "Didn't even know it existed until this afternoon."

Paulette shook her head. "Garrick, Garrick, Garrick."

Rick could only shrug.

"Well, it's *very* Darwinian," Hari said, "showing the interrelations between the human genome and other animals, even plants, past and present. My point is: Could he have ticked off some crazy creationist?"

"It's possible, of course," Paulette said. "Keith is a staunch evolutionist. Mere mention of creationism or intelligent design sets him off on long rants. This book was an in-your-face evolutionist manifesto."

"Well, then," Rick said, "seems Hari might have a good point."

"Except . . ." Paulette raised a finger. "Keith has a chapter about certain unique features in the human genome, exclusive to humans among the primates. Oddly enough, religious factions across the globe leaped on that. They called it the God Gene, and pointed to it as proof that God started evolution and let it run its course until a certain point when he intervened and infused mankind with a soul."

Hari shrugged. "Hasn't the Catholic Church been saying that for a long time?"

"I wouldn't know about the Catholic Church," Paulette said. "Believers all over the world took this as vindication. Keith was incensed at first but stopped protesting when he learned how sales to Christians and even Muslims were going through the roof. Everyone, believers and skeptics alike, seems to love the book. So I don't think it was the book." She turned to Hari. "Do you have anything more for us?"

The accountant shook her head. "Not till I work through the Bodden Bank."

"Good. Thank you for coming."

On impulse, Rick said, "I'll bring Keith back."

He wasn't sure why he said that, but he meant it.

"But we don't know where he is."

"Hari's homing in. When she finds him, I'll go get him and bring him back, no matter where he is." He looked at Hari. "You'll keep me informed?"

She glanced at Paulette who gave a curt nod. "Sure. No problem."

He found his mother staring at him. "You've changed, Garrick. You're different. What did they do to you?"

"'They'?"

"Those thugs in the CIA. What did they make you do?"

"Nothing too terrible. Toppled a few legitimate governments and replaced them with puppet regimes, sold drugs to schoolkids so we could supply guns to psycho insurgents, and generally crushed the hopes of freedom-loving people everywhere. You know . . . the usual."

She sniffed. "I can see I'm not going to get a straight answer out of you."

Lady, he thought, a straight answer would stop your heart cold.

Hari was checking her phone. "Sorry to interrupt this warm family moment, but I'll need a ride back to the garage. They just texted me that my car is ready."

Rick said, "I'll drive you. Give you my contact info on the way."

"Great." As Hari started gathering her papers, she said, "Oh, by the way, Paulette. How's the *My Fair Lady* thing coming?"

Paulette put on a pained expression. "Excruciatingly slow. Like banging my head against a brick wall."

Rick did *not* want to get into this, but had to ask. "Just what is it you're trying to do?"

"The right thing, of course. I decided that someone must speak up about this latest revival. I'm organizing a petition and a protest."

"Against what?"

"Two of Professor Higgins's songs are paeans to misogyny."

Rick bit back a laugh. "Well, yeah. Because he's a misogynist! That's the whole point of the play. Contact with Eliza changes him. If he starts out as some kind of feminist, where is there for him to go?"

"You're missing the point. 'I'm an Ordinary Man' and 'A Hymn to Him' denigrate women. Lyrics like, 'Why can't a woman be more like a man?' Can you believe it? I want them deleted. Any right-thinking person would agree."

Hari snapped her briefcase closed. "I'm with your mother here. I think it would be wonderful if they dumped those songs and substituted something like John Lennon's 'Imagine.'"

Paulette puffed herself up and pointed to her. "There! See? That's the kind of out-of-the-box thinking we need around here. I knew I liked you from the very beginning, Hari."

Rick found himself incapable of a coherent response.

Hari smiled sweetly and winked at him. "Shall we be off?"

Rick mumbled a good-bye to his mother and led Hari back to the pickup.

"Are you kidding me?" he said when they reached the truck. "On the way out here you called her a 'crackpot.'"

"A granola-chewing, chai-sipping, PETA-donating crackpot, I believe."

"And then you come up with substituting 'Imagine'?"

She grinned. "That was brilliant, wasn't it? I mean, even if I do say so myself."

"Not even close."

"Look, I don't know the first thing about *My Fair Lady*, but I figured it was what she wanted to hear."

"Is that so? Because in the brief time I've known you, I haven't quite gathered the impression that you say what people want to hear."

"I do when they're writing the checks. She seems like the type who'd get all swoony over utopianist garbage like 'Imagine,' so I laid it on her."

"'Garbage'? I'd hardly call it garbage."

Rick kind of liked "Imagine."

"Hey, I like a lot of Lennon's stuff, but everybody sharing all the world? Get real, Johnny Boy. Not on this planet."

"That's why he says 'Imagine.'"

But Rick had to agree with her. He could imagine peanut-butter swirl ice cream flowing over Niagara Falls and knew he'd have a better chance of seeing that.

Hari was tapping her watch. "Can we get moving?"

7

SHIRLEY, NEW YORK

Marissa came home and headed immediately to the fridge for a snack. The eight-year-old's skin was lighter than her mother's and darker than her father's, but her eyes matched the blues of both her parents. She had Steven's strong chin and Laura's straight jet hair, most of which she'd lost during chemotherapy, but it was growing back with a vengeance since her cure.

"I want you to get an early start on your homework," Laura said. "Rick's coming for dinner."

"Yay!"

"And we're having steak."

"Double yay!"

After sending her off to hit the books, Laura settled herself in the family room and opened *The Ties That Bind*, the coffee-table book by Rick's brother. She found it fascinating and easy to read, but her thoughts kept wandering away to Emilie Lantz and how Laura could get that dose of *ikhar* into her without anyone knowing—especially Emilie.

By the time Rick returned, she'd made it halfway through the book—his brother Keith had crammed it with photos. Marissa, still dressed in her softball shorts and jersey, ran to the door to let him in. She heard their voices approaching from the front hall.

"Did you see the game?" Marissa said. "Did you see?"

"Only parts of it. Had some work to do."

Laura smiled. That meant Rick had watched highlights on *Sports-Center*.

"The Metropolitans were *awesome!*"

Laura had gathered from Marissa's cries of *"Yes! Yes!"* last night that the Mets had won their game.

"Had some hot bats, that's for sure. Let's just hope they stay hot."

"They will," Marissa said. "This is *our* year."

The eternal optimist, she thought.

"Sure is, kiddo." Rick deepened his voice into announcer mode. "The Year of the Metropolitans!"

"Yeah!"

"Hey, how'd softball go?"

"Super. Ms. Hernandez says I've got a great arm."

"Well, you practice enough."

"Rick's here," Marissa announced as the pair entered the family room.

Laura closed the book. "Well, that's a relief. I was wondering who that strange man's voice belonged to."

Rick looked offended. "Who's strange? I'm not strange." He looked at Marissa and scrunched up his face. "Do I look strange to you?"

Marissa thought this was hilarious, as only an eight-year-old could.

"Finish your homework before dinner so you can just hang out the rest of the night."

As Marissa took off down the hall, Laura held up the oversize book.

"Your brother did a good job with this."

Rick shrugged. "Knew he was smart, but never read anything he wrote."

"He's a good explainer. He makes a convincing case that every living thing on the planet is genetically connected. I don't see how anyone could read this and deny evolution."

"Unless you're someone like Bishop Ussher."

Laura couldn't resist. "When did he become a bishop? I thought he was still rapping."

Rick didn't miss a beat. "Between concerts and recording sessions he calculated that the world is only six thousand years old."

"Doesn't leave much time for dinosaurs."

"Everyone knows dinosaurs are a hoax."

"Oh, right. Forgot." She replaced the book on the table. Time to get serious. "So what's the story with your brother?"

Rick paced back and forth while he told her about Keith liquidating his assets, about the forensic accountant and the trail of money to Grand Cayman, about the apartment he abandoned, passport and all.

"So," she said when he was through, "the consensus is foul play?"

Rick nodded. "Had everything going for him, and nothing to run from. Can't see it being much else. Paulette's sure it had something to do with this monkey he brought back from Mozambique."

"Based on what?"

"Her intuition."

"Well, never underestimate a mother's intuition where her child is concerned."

"Except he's not her natural child."

"Speaking of which, did you ever hunt down your natural folks?"

Rick shrugged. "Every orphan's quest, right?"

"Not all."

"Well, if they're not looking, I guarantee you they've thought about it. Anyway, I wasn't a true orphan at first. My mother gave me up. But she'd been dead for years by the time I tracked her down. Overdose."

Laura laid a hand on his forearm. "How awful."

"Giving me up was probably the best thing she could do for me."

"And your father?"

"Unknown. Not listed on the birth certificate." He sighed. "So . . . I told Paulette—who's not my natural mother—that I'd help find Keith— who's not my natural brother."

She was catching a strange vibe from Rick. "You're not sure how to react about Keith, are you."

"If Hari locates him, I said I'd go bring him back."

"I get the feeling you didn't like him too much."

Rick shrugged, looking uncomfortable. "I worshipped him as a kid—absolutely worshipped him. To my mind at the time, my older brother knew *everything*. I'd follow him around the yard and into the woods we had in Switzerland and he'd name everything we passed—animal, vegetable, mineral, didn't matter, he knew the common name and the scientific name."

Laura grinned. "Impressive. Maybe he was making them up, trying to impress his kid brother."

"But he wasn't trying to impress anyone. He was testing his knowledge. And if he'd come across something he couldn't identify, he'd pull out his little notebook and jot down a description."

"So you were close?"

"Not a bit. I was closer to my sister Cheryl."

Laura shook her head. Baffled. "I don't get it. You worshipped him but—"

"Oh, I wanted to be close to him but it never worked out."

"Was he your mother's fave? Got a Tommy Smothers thing going here?"

He laughed. "You mean, 'Mom always liked you best'? No. Even though she did, that wasn't the problem. The problem was that Keith was so self-contained. Didn't need anybody else. And something like that—not being allowed past the gate—only makes you want to get inside more."

"Did you ever get past?"

He shook his head. "No. And eventually I realized there was nothing for me on the other side. What's the expression? 'There's no there there.' That fits Keith. Had his own world and wouldn't let anyone in it."

She recalled his brief Wikipedia biography. "Yet he managed to get a doctorate and a position at NYU, and then write a bestseller."

"I know. Amazing. That's why his getting attached to this mystery monkey was so out of character. Maybe it broke through his shell."

Laura was developing a mental picture of Keith. She had some half-formed ideas but didn't want to say anything yet.

"So let me get this straight. He's not your real brother and he never let you in, but you're going to find him and bring him back."

He shrugged. "Well, yeah. Still remember the good times. Fond memories of those walks in the woods and how I looked up to him. Sure, I was frustrated that he was so unreachable, maybe even a little hurt."

Oh, I'm betting a lot hurt, Laura thought.

"But he's my brother. And when someone abducts your brother, you do something about it."

And there it was. This was the Rick she'd come to know. In so many ways an independent spirit and free thinker—some of his ideas were *way* out of the box—but when duty called, Rick answered.

8

After Champagne and steaks and wine, Laura walked Rick out to his car—or truck, rather. He stopped on the walk and looked up.

"Clear night."

He pulled out his phone and took a picture of the sky. She'd seen him do that before—in Quintana Roo, in the Negev, in Orkney—and had never given it much thought. Foreign skies, she'd thought. But here? On Long Island?

"Going for a Junior Astronomer badge?"

"I've been putting together a collection."

"Of sky pics? Why?"

He looked at her. "Do you really want to know?"

"Is it involved?"

"Yeah, pretty much."

"Then I'll take a rain check. Back here on Earth, when do we start poking into Keith's disappearance?"

"'We'?"

"I'm helping, of course."

"Not necessary. You have that whole residency-matching thing—"

"—totally under control. I want to do this. I *need* to do this."

She didn't say it, but she owed Rick for Marissa's life. If he hadn't sneaked those samples of the *ikhar* back from Scotland, well . . . her mind refused to go there.

"All right, if you insist. But not much to do until the accountant finds the end of the money trail."

Laura shook her head. "I disagree. It doesn't sound like the cops did much. You were with one of the world's biggest intelligence services, and you and I have already proven we're a pretty good team when it comes to tracking down something no one else could find. I think we should do our own investigation."

"Okaaay," he said, drawing it out. "You really been giving this some thought, haven't you?"

"If it's important to you, it's important to me."

"I appreciate that. But you think we'll find something the cops missed?"

"It doesn't sound like they even looked."

"Good point. So where do we start?"

"Your brother's apartment, of course."

"Of course."

THEN

Tuesday, May 10

MAPUTO, MOZAMBIQUE

After two days of searching, Amaury Laffite had found not a trace of the Afrikaner. He'd checked along the docks where he moored his own boat, and no one had heard of Jeukens. Which was good news. It meant he hadn't chartered a craft.

Finally he resigned himself to the probability that Marten Jeukens had moved on, either up or down the coast, in his continuing search for the blue-eyed monkey.

He found him quite by accident in a bar on Ponto Do Ouro. Amaury stepped in for a drink and maybe some female companionship. Bruce Springsteen's "Hungry Heart" was playing softly in the background. He'd always identified with the song, and liked to change the words to his own situation: *Got a wife and kid in Oran, Jack.* And like the guy in the song, he'd gone out for a ride and never looked back.

Except he did look back. Not often, but now and then he'd think about his daughter. A dozen years since he'd walked out. She'd be sixteen now. He wondered if she remembered him at all. He wondered if his wife had remarried. Was another man raising his child? Casting secret lustful glances her way? In those moments a pang of guilt would overcome him and he'd send some money—no return address, of course.

He'd been going through a hard time when he left. Things were better now but he had no desire to go back. He liked the unattached life. Many women in his bed since then, but he limited himself to flings. No strings on Amaury Laffite. Never again.

He looked around, checking out the women, and there sat Jeukens, a very white man alone at the bar surrounded by very dark locals, a nearly empty bottle of Pinotage before him.

Typical, he thought. As soon as you stop looking for something, you find it.

The Afrikaner had set his hat on the bar and presented an odd sight without it: His face was tan below a line that ran an inch above his eyebrows, but above that his denuded scalp was white as a cherub's behind. The overhead lights gleamed off its glossy expanse.

Amaury sidled over to the bar.

"Did you find your monkeys yet?" he said in English as he took the seat next to him.

Jeukens started in surprise, then gave him a confused, heavy-lidded stare. The blankness lasted a few seconds, then his eyes lit with recognition.

"Laffite?"

"That is correct."

"I wasn't sure it was you, what with the hat."

"Women like it."

He adjusted the compact straw fedora, neglecting to mention that it covered where his hair had begun to recede on the sides.

"Do they like that ponytail too?"

"Love it."

The women love Laffite and Laffite loves the women.

The bartender came by and Amaury ordered a Laurentina Preta. He offered to buy something for Jeukens but the Afrikaner shook his head.

"I've still got some of this left," he said, pointing to the bottle.

Pinotage . . . how did anyone drink that swill?

Small talk first . . .

"If I remember correctly, the other day you said you were on a mission."

Jeukens nodded. "That is correct."

"To save the Giordano Brunos of the world, I believe?"

"Correct again."

"I had never heard of him, so I looked him up. *Mon ami*, how do you save a man who died in the year sixteen hundred?"

The Afrikaner's face twisted. "He didn't just '*die*.' He was martyred for science. He was a friar who subscribed to the Copernican theory that the Earth revolved around the sun. For that, the Inquisition burned him at the stake!"

Amaury wanted to probe further but he was thinking this man might be a little crazy. Really, how do you get upset about something that happened centuries ago? He backed off.

"That is a terrible thing. I am glad we don't do that anymore."

"Don't be so sure."

"Well, anyway, I am glad you are still in town. You are a hard man to find."

"From that I gather you've been looking for me?"

"Yes. All over."

"You found me just in time. I won't be here for long."

"Oh? Should I assume that means you have found your monkey?"

Jeukens shook his head. "No. But I will. They're out there somewhere. Sooner or later I'll find them."

"Which is why I have been looking for you."

Amaury's beer arrived with a glass that he pushed back. As he sipped from the bottle he caught a woman looking at him. She had dark mocha skin and bleached kinky hair piled atop her head. She'd squeezed her curvy body into a tight red dress. She smiled, he smiled back. He'd come here with the intent of meeting someone just like her.

But first . . . Jeukens.

"I have a proposition," he said.

Jeukens emptied the last of the bottle into his wineglass and swirled the deep red liquid. Keeping his gaze fixed on the mirror behind the bar, he drank deeply, then wiped his beard. Amaury winced. He supposed you had to be born in South Africa to stomach Pinotage. He, however, had been raised in France . . .

"I'm listening."

Amaury had rehearsed his spiel as he'd searched through Maputo, so he was prepared.

"Business has been slow of late in the exotics trade. I have a boat—"

"Do you, now?"

"Yes. It is old but solid."

"How old?"

"Its keel was laid in 1988—a forty-eight-foot Krogen."

"That's pretty old."

Spoken like a typical landlubber. Lots of aged ships still toiled the seas. They built them better in the old days. Amaury had sailed the *Sorcière des Mers* back and forth to Madagascar countless times, returning with the belowdeck brimming with exotics—mostly lemurs, but with a sampling of sifakas, tenrecs, mongooses, and even flying foxes.

"Not if you take care of it. She's a sturdy ship. If your island is findable, we will find it."

Jeukens's eyebrows lifted. "At what cost?"

Just then the bar band started playing, blasting something with a frenetic *marrabenta* beat. The woman in red began gyrating. Amaury smiled at her again and held up a finger—wait one minute. Then he picked up his beer and leaned toward the Afrikaner's ear.

"Let us go outside where we can hear each other," he said, gesturing toward the door.

Jeukens nodded and drained his wineglass. He wiped his beard on his sleeve, replaced his hat, and followed Amaury out.

On the bustling sidewalk, they took up a position beside the entrance and leaned against the stucco wall. Amaury watched the constant flow of club people in various stages of inebriation and levels of high. Maputo had the best nightlife in all of Africa. Better than the Muslim countries, of course; better even than Cape Town and Johannesburg.

"How much?" Jeukens said.

Amaury had already decided on the price he wanted but he started higher.

"Four thousand a week."

Jeukens laughed. "You're crazy! I could rent ten boats for that."

"Ah, but not for the distance we must travel. And you would not have Amaury Laffite guiding you."

"Lafitte . . . like the pirate?"

"Two f's and one t—the way he spelled it, the proper French way to spell it. The Americans changed it."

"Any relation?"

Amaury nodded. "Distant but direct."

A complete lie, but one he wished were true. In many ways he was like his namesake, who made his living as a smuggler before becoming a privateer. Amaury smuggled too, but his contraband was alive.

"Anyway, I know the Mozambique Channel. We do not know where your island is, but I know where it is not. That will save us much time."

Jeukens considered this, then said, "I'll go two thousand and that's it."

Just what Amaury had been hoping for. He'd have settled for less. If those monkeys were out there, he wanted to know where. They'd be worth a fortune on the exotics market—especially if they all had blue eyes. But still, it couldn't hurt to push now for just a little more.

"This is a low price for traveling much distance. The only way I can make that work is if you pay for the food and fuel."

Diesel was on the rise again. The *Sorcière* had a thousand-gallon tank, but the area of search with the best chance of success was six hundred nautical miles away. The *Sorcière* burned half a gallon per mile at her top speed of nine to ten knots. The fuel bill would run no small sum.

Sensing his hesitation, Amaury gave him a gentle slap on the shoulder. "It is only money."

"And you think I am rich?"

"Richer than I, I am sure, *monsieur*."

Jeukens shrugged. "'Who is rich? He that is content. Who is that? Nobody.'"

"Wise words, *monsieur*."

"They belong to an American named Ben Franklin."

He certainly liked his quotes. How many had he memorized?

"Food and fuel . . ." Jeukens chewed his upper lip. "I can see you've inherited some of your namesake's piratical genes."

If only that were true, Amaury thought.

Jeukens added: "You need to find a higher purpose."

"A higher purpose? What does that mean? Working for God?"

"God?" The Afrikaner's eyes almost glowed in the night. "Hardly! I serve mankind. And I am simply saying one needs to live for more than profit and pleasure."

Amaury shrugged. "I am a simple man and, if truth be told, rather fond of profit and pleasure."

But he understood. Like his namesake, he felt he was destined for greater things. Maybe not a place in the history books, but greater than an animal merchant. But he'd done nothing about it, and time was passing him by—already half a century gone. He'd better get to seeking that higher purpose soon. He doubted it would come looking for him.

"Perhaps I can guide you to that next level." Abruptly Jeukens stuck out his hand. "Two thousand a week plus food and fuel."

Amaury grasped it and gave a firm shake. "We have a deal then?"

"We do." The Afrikaner's eyes narrowed as he released Amaury's hand and grabbed the front of his shirt. He jerked him close until they were nose to nose. "But if you try to cheat me, I will gut you like a fish and watch you flop around until you're dead. Clear?"

Amaury's gut knotted. Where had that come from? And he'd said it so calmly, so matter-of-factly.

"Amaury Laffite cheats no one! I am a man of my word!"

Jeukens released his shirt and smiled as if he'd simply mentioned a possible change in the weather. "Then we shall get along splendidly. When do we leave?"

Amaury wondered if he was making a mistake, allying himself with this man. He shook it off.

"I-I will need tomorrow and Thursday to fuel up and have her seaworthy. We can leave at dawn on Friday."

"I'll be there."

"I will need an advance for the fuel."

"I'll drop it off at your shop tomorrow."

Amaury forced a smile. "Excellent, *mon ami*! We shall hunt down this island and make it our own!"

He watched Jeukens stroll away. A strange, strange man. A little voice from the back of his brain cried out to stay away from this man. He shut it down.

Those monkeys . . . a fortune beckoned from their blue eyes.

But first . . . the woman in the red dress was waiting for him . . .

NOW

Wednesday, May 18

1

MANHATTAN, NEW YORK

"I'm surprised he didn't choose a place with a doorman," Laura said as they waited outside Keith's Upper West Side apartment building.

She'd spent much of her morning on paperwork in Hauppauge at the coroner's office while one of her fellow assistant MEs did the post-mortem exams. As she'd trained into Manhattan to meet Rick, the small container of *ikhar* nestling in her shoulder bag seemed almost alive, awaiting its moment. Today was Emilie's day . . .

She banished the poor woman to the back of her mind as she waited with Rick. Keith lived in an ornate corner building with a Beaux Arts feel—not as cake-decorated as the Ansonia, but in the running. She counted eight stories. Street level was all retail, and the rest apartments. The rounded corner edge with the bay windows on the upper units added to the vintage look.

"Doorman?" Rick shook his head. "Keith wouldn't want to deal with a doorman every day. Or tip him at Christmas. Too much hassle. He's the type who likes to come and go without having to talk to anyone. Not into human interaction."

Rick seemed different out here in the world. At her place last night he'd been relaxed and warm, bantering with Marissa. Today his gray eyes had regained that hard, flat look, like smooth, dark stones—the look they'd had when she first met him. Back then she'd thought he looked like a man prepared for the worst and expecting it. Now she knew that he'd already seen the worst.

He'd told her about what he'd witnessed and what he'd done in Düsseldorf. He'd come back scarred and damaged. But had he told her all of it?

So she stood with him here in the middle of a Columbus Avenue sidewalk. Tourists would do that: block the pedestrian flow to gape at a sign or an iconic building. Annoyed Manhattanites on their way to work would often purposely bump obstructing gapers. No one bumped Rick. They flowed around him. He had that look.

She liked the other Rick better.

"By the way," he said. "How does it feel?"

"How does what feel?"

He smiled and it changed his whole face. "You and me, back on the road together."

"Well, it's not quite the globe-trotting we did last month, but it feels . . . good."

And it did. In fact it felt great being out here with Rick.

"Yeah. It does."

A voice behind them said, "Are you Mister Somers?"

Laura turned to see a slim young woman with platinum hair in bangs who couldn't be more than twenty-five. She wore a blue skirt and jacket. Next to her stood a young man, equally blond, equally banged, dressed in a blue pinstriped suit.

Somers? she thought. Oh, right. Only natural to assume Keith's brother would use the same surname.

Rick nodded. "That's me. And you must be Hari's assistant."

"Casey," she said, extending her hand. "And this is my brother, Peter."

Laura had to ask. "You wouldn't happen to be twins, would you?"

Peter smiled. "How'd you guess?"

"Identical?" Rick said.

Laura nudged him. Seriously?

The twins glanced at each other, looking a little uncomfortable.

Casey said, "Well, no. You see, to be identical we'd have to—"

"—be the same sex," Rick said, waving off the explanation. "Just kidding. You both work with Hari?"

Casey's blond bangs fluttered as she nodded. "I'm the firm's IT nerd; Peter's—"

"I specialize in corporate tax," Peter said. "We share an apartment and we were both heading out at the same time, so . . ."

"I see," Rick said. "By the way, how are things in Midwich?"

They looked confused. Laura felt the same. *Midwich?*

"Is that in Connecticut?" Peter said.

"Not quite. Got something for me?"

Casey handed him a manila envelope with *7D* scrawled on the front in Magic Marker. "The keys are in there. Please drop them back at the office when you're through. Hari's card is inside with the address on it. Oh, and I need to warn you about the computers."

"What about them?" Rick said.

"Well, I borrowed the laptop and removed the desktop's hard drive."

How strange.

"Why would you do that?"

"Hari needed them for her investigation, and I'm sort of the in-house hacker. She wanted me to check the drives for any bank records or financial transactions, and a hard drive is much more portable than lugging a whole desktop downtown."

"Find anything?" Rick said.

The young woman shook her head. "Someone used a shredder on the drives. I'm pretty good at data recovery but couldn't pull out anything."

Rick frowned. "Hillary-ed it?"

"Yeah. But more thorough. Whoever did this knew what he was doing. Way too overwritten to dig up anything."

Laura was confused. "The drives were shredded?"

"I'll explain," Rick said. He nodded to Casey and Peter. "Thanks, guys."

"What's a shredder?" Laura said as he unlocked the building's front door.

"Software. When you delete something on your computer, it's not really gone."

"Well, right. It's in the trash bin. It's not gone until you empty the trash."

"Well, even then it's not really gone. All you've done is remove the codes that allow your computer to find that data. The data remains on the drive until it's overwritten. And even after it's overwritten it's often still recoverable. A shredder program overwrites multiple times with random data. DoD recommends seven overwrites."

"DoD?"

"Department of Defense. Most people say four overwrites are enough."

Laura was going to ask him how he knew what the DoD recommended, then realized she'd be surprised if he didn't.

Rick led her through the foyer to where the elevator stood open. They entered and he jabbed the 7 button.

"Why would your brother do that?"

"Normal reasons are because you're either selling the computer or giving it away. If you've been doing, say, your banking online, you don't want someone else seeing all your transactions."

"Likewise," she said, "if you were planning on disappearing, you'd want to shred all evidence of where you might be headed."

Rick looked at her as the doors opened on the seventh floor. "Thinking he ran off?"

"Shredding his drives seems like premeditation, don't you think?"

"Not necessarily. If he was being pressured about something he knew, makes sense to want to erase all trace of it."

Laura hadn't looked at it that way.

"Or," he added, "maybe whoever grabbed him snuck in and shredded the drives."

"Maybe that's the way we should approach this," she said. "I'll spin everything we see toward running away and you spin it toward abduction, and we'll see who makes the best case."

"Deal." He unlocked the door to 7D.

Early afternoon sunlight glaring through the southern windows brightened the room. She'd anticipated the musty-dusty odor—inevitable after six weeks with no open windows or air-conditioning—but she was taken aback by the blaze of colors on the walls.

"Wow," Rick said, closing the door behind them. "Didn't know he was so into photography."

"In his book he's credited on a good number of the photos."

The photos were all colors and varying sizes. He'd used glossy, heavy-duty photo paper but hadn't bothered with frames. It looked like he'd simply printed them out and either tacked or stapled them to the walls. And not haphazardly. Despite the different sizes, he'd fitted each snugly against its neighbors. Some appeared to have been trimmed to fit, but the effect was a huge, room-size mosaic that spread from wall to wall to wall. Virtually nothing of the original surface remained visible.

"Oh, man," Rick said, turning in a slow circle. "Must have taken a lot of work—a *huge* amount of work."

They did a quick tour and found every room, even the small but functional kitchen, bedizened with photos of every imaginable variety of plant and creature—mammals, reptiles, birds, fish, insects. She recognized some from *The Ties That Bind*. Only the bathroom had bare walls.

"A photo-free zone," Rick said.

"Probably because the moisture from showering would ruin them."

"All these photos," Rick said, shaking his head as they returned to the front room, "and not a single human being in any of them."

Laura realized with a start that he was right.

"But . . . but there's got to be one picture of his family here—his parents at least. Doesn't there?"

"You find one, give a holler," he said. "Meantime, keep an eye peeled for any photo of a blue-eyed monkey."

"You think that's key?"

"Don't know. Paulette thinks so. We might as well know what it looks like."

They divided up the rooms: Rick took on the major task of combing the large front room while Laura started on the bedroom. She figured her best chance of finding a photo of something supposedly as near and dear to Keith's heart as that monkey would be where he slept.

The bed was made, the closets and bureau drawers full of clothes. He didn't appear to have taken anything with him. She gave each photo a brief glance and then moved to the next. Many were labeled with "MZ" or "TZ" or "EAR."

Nothing. Maybe the office . . .

As she was leaving the bedroom she glanced up at the high ceiling and froze. Keith had arranged dozens, maybe a hundred or more, photos up there in a giant pinwheel mosaic. Or maybe whirlpool was more like it. Did he lie in bed and stare up at it?

She spent a while checking out each photo, but no blue-eyed monkey.

She moved on to the spacious office in the bay-windowed corner. Lots of natural light here, with a great view of Columbus Avenue. Neat and tidy, the office boasted a large oak desk against the wall, a Dell computer on the floor next to it with its housing removed, exposing its guts. An oversize Canon printer sat on its own table on the other side of the desk. As for the photos, same story here, although she did find a cluster of blank spaces on the wall above the desk. She could tell from the tack holes in the wallpaper that something—a number of somethings, from the look of it—had been pinned there. With all the walls obsessively covered, the effect of empty space was jarring. Why had he chosen to remove these particular photos?

She opened the wide center drawer over the kneehole and spied a U.S. passport. She flipped through it. The country stamps inside—Mozambique, Tanzania, Kenya, Zambia, Madagascar—confirmed what all the photos suggested: Keith had spent an awful lot of time in East Africa.

She looked at his ID picture: brown eyes, full lips, a bored expression, thick, bushy brown hair.

Rick stepped into the room, saying, "I get 'MZ' and 'TZ,' but what's this 'EAR' he keeps writing on photos?"

"He discussed it in his book: the East African Rift. It's a huge valley that runs from Kenya down to Mozambique. Scads of early hominid bones have been found there. Some people call it the cradle of humanity."

"Guess I need to read his book."

Laura pointed to the empty spot on the wall. "Something's missing."

Rick leaned closer. "Yeah. First blank spot I've seen. No sign of anything behind the desk?"

"Already checked. Not on the desk either, although I did find this."

She showed him Keith's passport.

"That's pretty much the way I remember him," Rick said, glancing at the photo. He returned his attention to the big blank spot. "What do you think he posted there?"

"I'm going to bet on the monkey. Because I'm going to bet you didn't find a single photo of it."

"You'd win."

"And so now I'm becoming convinced your mother is right."

"That the monkey's involved?"

Laura nodded. "From what she told you, it was his constant companion—

even brought it to her house. He had it cremated and discarded the ashes off the shore of his family home. That *screams* attachment. Add that to his taxonomy work—"

"What's that mean?"

"She told you he was trying to find its place in evolution and maybe get it named after him, right?"

"Right."

"That's called taxonomy. He was looking to classify it. That involves comparing characteristics with others of its type. So if he was doing that, wouldn't he have photos of it all over the place?"

Rick looked around. "Sure as hell would. Or at least on his computer."

"Which he shredded." This wasn't piecing together right. "It's almost as if he was trying to wipe out any trace of the monkey's existence."

"Makes no sense. Paulette said he mentioned getting the species named after him. Why erase your chance for academic immortality?"

"I can't see it either." An idea was taking shape. "Unless . . ."

Rick beat her to it. "Unless he was being coerced. Paulette quoted him as saying, 'I'm being backed into something I would have considered inconceivable just weeks ago.'"

"Could that 'something' be liquidating his assets and depositing them around the globe?"

Rick smiled. "Aren't you supposed to be countering that theory?"

"Oops."

She stared at the open case of Keith's desktop computer. If only his hard drive were readable. She shifted her attention to the big Canon printer. She checked the output tray but, as expected, found it empty.

"Heavy-duty photo printer," Rick said. "Looks like a professional model."

Right. That would account for the high quality of the prints. And then Laura remembered something . . .

"We had this coroner's case where a murder victim's computer was stolen, but the forensics folks were able to get evidence off the printer in his office."

Rick snapped his fingers. "Right. High-end printers have their own hard drive. And I saw a toolbox of sorts in the front closet."

Handing her the passport, he took off, leaving Laura alone in the office. She seated herself in the desk's swivel chair and started going through the drawers. Rick returned holding a couple of screwdrivers.

"Find anything?" he said.

"Lots of pens and paper clips. Flashlight . . . scissors . . . calculator."

"In other words, no help."

"Right."

She continued pawing through the drawers while he unplugged the Canon and tackled the access panel with a Phillips-head. She finished her fruitless search and moved to the bookcase. There she found half a dozen copies of his own book and a slew of textbooks, mostly old and worn.

"No novels," she muttered. "A whole bookcase and no fiction. You'd think he'd have at least—wait a sec."

"What?" Rick said from over by the printer.

She lifted a pile of half a dozen DVDs off a shelf. "Looks like he's got movies here."

"Monkey porn?"

They were hand-labeled with a green Sharpie. "They look homemade."

"No *King Dong*?"

She looked at him. "Seriously?"

"Hey, you never know."

"The first one says 'Conan.'"

"You're kidding. The Schwarzenegger movie?"

"No, wait. The second says 'Fallon.' Must be TV shows." And then she knew. "He had a big bestseller. I'll bet his publisher booked him onto these shows. I'm going to take these."

"Why?"

"I want to see him live, so to speak. You grew up with him but all I've seen is a passport photo. I want to get a feel for him."

"Good luck. Like I said: There's no there there."

She wandered over toward Rick where he had the printer's back open and was fiddling inside.

"You know, I'm leaning more and more toward the foul-play scenario," she said.

"Why's that?"

"Because it's getting harder and harder to counter it. He doesn't appear to have taken anything with him but the clothes on his back."

"And maybe a handful of photos."

Laura shook her head. "If the missing photos are of his monkey—and I think they are—I don't see him taking them with him. If he shredded his drives, he shredded the photos too."

"None of this makes one goddamn bit of sense," Rick said as he detached the hard drive. He held it up. "But maybe this has answers. Let's see if Hari's gal can find anything on it."

2

Rick drove down Broadway thinking about his brother. Yeah, his disappearance was looking more and more like an abduction. But why, damn it? What possible reason could anyone have to snatch Keith?

He found a garage on Twenty-first near the Flatiron Building and parked. As they came up the ramp, he did a quick look-around as they hit the sidewalk. Skateboarder, long hair, skinny tattooed arms poking from the sleeves of his T, rolling their way. Gonna pass close, maybe close enough to grab Laura's shoulder bag.

Rick stepped out and eyed him, making him swerve curbward, out of reach.

"Hey, watch where I'm goin', asshole!" the kid shouted, flipping the bird as he rolled away.

"That was close," Laura said.

"But at least I made a new friend."

"Really? How can you tell?"

"He thinks I'm number one."

"Is *that* what that means?" she said, grinning, then glanced around. "Which way to this Hari's office?"

He looked at Hari's card and pointed uptown. "Right around the corner on Twenty-second."

A few minutes later they entered the offices of Hari's firm. Rick had called ahead and Casey was waiting for them.

"Gift for you," he said, handing her the apartment keys and the hard drive.

She gave him a puzzled look. "Your brother had another computer?"

"From his printer."

Her eyes lit. "Ah! Why didn't I think of that? I'll get right on it."

"Hari around?"

"Yeah. She wanted to talk to you." She pointed to a door. "Go right in."

Hari had a fair-size office overlooking Twenty-second Street. She was dressed in a dark green pantsuit. Rick introduced Laura.

"No sari?" he said.

"Hardly ever. Only for certain clients."

"Like my mother?"

A nod. "It fits her narrative."

As Laura and Hari engaged in some get-acquainted chitchat, Rick stepped over to a large, well-lit fish tank filled with crystalline water. A number of rugged lava rocks nestled on a thick layer of white sand, but that was it. Not a single fish or plant in sight.

He turned to Hari. "Did Doctor Serizawa stop by recently, by any chance?"

"Who?"

He could see the reference had zipped right past her.

"Not a *Godzilla* fan, I take it?"

"What? That old movie with a guy in a rubber suit stomping on Tokyo? Not likely." She stared at him. "*Ruthless People* and *The Wizard of Oz* yesterday, *Godzilla* today. You some kind of movie nut?"

"Me? Nah. Just seen a bunch."

After Düsseldorf, during the endless debriefing and psychiatric sessions, he'd found himself alone. A lot. So he'd watched movies. A lot.

He pointed to the aquarium. "Why an empty tank?"

"It's not empty."

"Coulda fooled me. Oh, wait—you're gonna tell me it's not empty because it has water in it."

"Not at all. Hang on a sec."

She opened a door in a wall cabinet, revealing a tiny refrigerator. She pulled out a resealable pouch of tuna and removed a few small chunks.

"Watch."

She dropped them into the water. As the pieces began to sink, a six-inch blue crab popped out of the sand.

Laura gave a little jump. "Didn't expect *that*."

"Meet Pokey," Hari said.

The crab darted through the water and snagged the biggest chunk with a claw. Then it settled to the bottom and began feeding bits into its busy little mouth.

"A lot of tank for one crab," Rick said.

"Y'think? Let me tell you, it didn't start out this way. I had a whole tankful of fish and plants—not the junk kind, I'm talking high-end tropicals. Everybody getting along and thriving. Then I'm at the beach with my nephew last summer and he shows me this cute little two-inch crab he's caught. For laughs I bring her home, name her Pokey, and drop her in the tank. You know, just to see how she'd get along."

Rick could see what was coming. "And she's all that's left?"

"You got it. I was feeding her chunks of sushi-grade tuna and she started molting, getting bigger and bigger each time. Then I made the mistake of going away on vacation. I had my usual someone come in to feed the fish while I'm away but she neglected the tuna for Pokey."

"Uh-oh."

"Damn right, 'uh-oh.' She ate every living thing in sight. Gobbled up a couple thou worth of tropical fish. Since then she's uprooted all the plants because she likes to dig. She even rearranges the goddamn rocks."

Rick couldn't help giving Laura a knowing look.

"So, you had a tropical paradise going and you introduced a foreign element to shake things up."

Hari said, "I wasn't looking to shake things up, just figured they'd all adapt."

"But the result was *Paradise Lost*."

Laura rolled her eyes and Hari caught it.

"Am I missing something?"

"Just a weirdo theory Rick has," Laura said.

Rick said, "But we don't need to get into that here."

Hari looked from one to the other, then shrugged. "Whatev." She jabbed her index finger at the tank. "Anyway, she cost me a fortune."

"Then why do you keep her?"

"Because she's got a few more molts to go. And pretty soon, right after

one of those molts, she's going to wind up the world's most expensive sau-
téed softshell crab sandwich."

She glared at the oblivious Pokey for a few heartbeats, then headed
back to her desk, saying, "You learn anything new at the apartment?"

Rick shrugged and told her about giving Casey the printer's hard drive
and their growing conviction that the monkey was an important piece of
the puzzle.

He finished with, "Any progress on the money trail?"

"I've started the rigmarole of opening my Cayman account."

Frustration gnawed at Rick. "So there's not much for me to do but wait
and see how that pans out?"

"If you think the monkey is a player, then you might want to drop in on
Keith's NYU colleagues. I didn't bother because I saw no way it would help
with the money trail, but they're all biologists and could maybe shed some
light on the mystery monkey."

Rick liked the idea. "You wouldn't happen to have any contact numbers, would you?"

"As a matter of fact, I do."

As Hari checked her computer, Casey arrived, grinning and waving a
sheet of paper. "Did someone say 'monkey'?"

She handed Rick a low-res photo on ordinary printer paper.

"He looks a little chunkier than he did in his passport photo," Laura
said, leaning in for a look, "but that's your brother, right?"

"Right. And chunky was his default mode. Keith liked his carbs."

Damn, why was he using past tense?

"Don't we all?" Laura said.

"Yeah, but Keith never met a dessert he didn't like—twice." Rick's attention was drawn inexorably to the little blue-eyed monkey perched on
Keith's shoulder. It sported dark brown fur all over except on its throat and
belly, where it was almost white.

"And that must be Mozi," Laura said.

The big blue eyes gazed out from the photo, directly into the camera,
deep into Rick. He wasn't a zoologist, and he hadn't had any more expo-
sure to simians than the average American, but he'd never seen an animal
like this one.

He had a sudden strange feeling about this monkey.

"Oh, he's so cute!" Hari said, peeking at the photo. "I want one."

"Me too," said Casey.

"I'm told that what you're calling a 'he' is a she." He looked at Casey. "This the only photo on the drive?"

"I found a good sampling of others, but if you checked out his walls, you've already seen them. This was the only one that was new to me."

"I'll bet this was in that empty spot over the desk," Laura said.

Rick nodded. "Good bet. Mozi looks pretty healthy there. Wonder what she died of."

He turned his attention to Keith. The guy in the photo looked happy, actually smiling. Rick could count on one hand the times he'd seen his brother smile. The monkey was balanced on his left shoulder while his right arm was extended forward, mostly out of frame. Obviously a selfie.

Keith had found a friend. No surprise to Rick that it wasn't human.

"Can I keep this?"

Casey said, "Sure. I'll pick up some photo paper and run off a hi-res glossy for you."

Hari gave him the numbers for the NYU Department of Biology. Since he and Laura were already in the city, and NYU was only a dozen blocks or so downtown from here, he figured right now would be as good a time as any to check out Keith's office and his associates. But when he called he was told that everyone in the department had either gone home for the day or had meetings scheduled. So he wrangled an appointment to meet tomorrow with a Dr. Willard Salas, the head of the department; at first he was turned down, but when he said he was Keith's brother, a late-morning time slot magically opened.

"Our work here is done, I guess," he said. "But before we go . . ." He turned to Hari. "When did Keith start liquidating?"

"March second," she said without hesitation. "Sold his first block of stock then, and kept on selling. Ran through his bonds, his retirement fund, his trust fund, everything except the apartment. By the eighteenth he'd turned it all into cash in various accounts. Then he started moving it around. By the twenty-third the whole caboodle landed in the Caymans."

He patted his pockets. Damn. Hadn't brought a pen. "The second to the twenty-third. Could you write that down for me?"

She jotted on a small square pad of yellow sticky notes and handed the whole thing to him. "Here. Keep it."

"Thanks. And the date he disappeared?"

"Last seen April first—a Friday, so it was days before he was missed."

April Fool's Day—easy enough to remember. And how appropriate.

He looked at Laura. "What say we find us a bar and then head back?"

"Why don't we head back and *then* find a bar."

He had to admit that was probably a better idea. "Okay. Let's do that."

She looked at him. "But can we make one teensy little stop along the way?"

3

NORTHPORT, NEW YORK

Laura guided Rick to the VA Medical Center in Northport. Under different circumstances she would have enjoyed the alone time together, but the closer they got, the more tense she became.

"What's here?" he said as he pulled into a parking space.

"I need to check on somebody."

"Relative?"

She shook her head. "A new friend."

Should she tell him? She decided to hold off . . . wait until this was all a *fait accompli*. After all, he had strange ideas about the origins of the *ikhar* . . .

He said, "I'll wait here. Not a fan of hospitals."

"You've got plenty of company there. I won't be too long."

Inside, the receptionist returned her wave as she entered the lobby and made a right turn for the elevators.

"Happy Tuesday, Sarge," Laura said after knocking on the doorframe to Emilie Lantz's private room.

Emilie smiled and mouthed *hello*. A nice smile. Her teeth were big and white, her skin a lighter brown than Laura's—a Beyoncé shade—her hair done in neat cornrows. They took good care of her here.

Laura wasn't here as a doctor, simply a volunteer. She'd started using a few hours of one of her afternoons off to help out. Since she was heading for a neurology residency, she gravitated toward those patients with neurological disorders.

Emilie had been a military intelligence staff sergeant in Marine Air Control Group 1 during the first Gulf War. She'd accompanied her unit into Iraq itself. Her multiple sclerosis was diagnosed in 1991, shortly after the combat phase ended. In the decades since, her condition had gradually deteriorated to the point where she could no longer walk, no longer raise her arms, and barely speak.

She was perfect.

A woman who had feared nothing in her prime had been reduced to complete helplessness and chronic pain by an autoimmune disease that gnawed the insulation off her nervous system.

The MS itself wouldn't kill her. She'd die of a complication of some sort: pneumonia or a pulmonary embolism. To Laura's mind, she deserved a whole lot better. Laura wasn't a fan of her country acting as the world's policeman; in fact, she flat-out hated the idea of spilling American blood on foreign soil. But none of that mattered where Emilie was concerned. She'd enlisted, and when called on to go fight, she'd gone. 'Nuff said.

A special woman laid low.

Well, Laura could fix that. Or rather, the *ikhar* could.

Laura simply had to administer it without Emilie knowing she was being dosed. And she thought she'd found a way.

"Thirsty?" Laura said.

Emilie gave a tiny nod.

Slipping the half ounce or so of the not-so-great-tasting liquid into a few ounces of juice had done the job before. She figured the trick was to choose just the right amount of juice—too much, she might not finish, too little and she'd taste the *ikhar*.

By the next morning all signs of her illness would be gone, vanished as if they'd never been.

Or so Laura hoped.

"How about some apple juice?"

Another tiny nod.

"I brought you the healthy kind," she said, pulling a sixteen-ounce bottle from her shoulder bag and holding it up. "It's unfiltered. Supposed to be better for you."

The cloudy *ikhar* would change the clear look of the filtered and pasteurized juice they served here at the VA. The unfiltered kind was already cloudy.

She stepped out of Emilie's line of sight and found a six-ounce plastic cup. She pulled the snuff bottle from her pocket, removed the stopper, and emptied the *ikhar* into the bottom of the cup. She swirled it as she half-filled the cup with juice, then held it up. Perfect. She grabbed a straw and approached the bed.

"Here you go." Laura fitted the straw between Emilie's lips. "Okay. Drink."

Poor woman . . . couldn't even hold a cup. This *had* to work.

Emilie quickly sucked up the three or four ounces. She released the straw and made a sour face.

"What? You don't like it?"

A *meh* expression.

Laura got a fresh cup, poured in a few ounces of juice, and quaffed them.

"Tastes okay to me. Maybe you were expecting something different. Try a bit more."

She poured a couple more ounces of juice into Emilie's cup. She wanted her to get every drop of the *ikhar*. This time when Emilie finished it she gave a little nod of approval.

"Good job."

Laura slipped Emilie's cup into her bag. She'd leave the bottle of leftover juice behind.

"All right. Reading time."

Emilie couldn't hold a book, couldn't even touch the screen of a Kindle. So Laura read to her. She knew Rick was waiting but she had to make this look like a routine visit.

"What'll it be? More Hammer's Slammers?"

Now a smile with the nod.

Laura had learned that Emilie liked science fiction, specifically military

SF. Since Laura didn't come by often enough for them to get into a novel, she'd looked for a collection of short stories. She'd Googled around and found *The Complete Hammer's Slammers Volume One* by someone named David Drake—twenty stories about a future tank war. Perfect.

She pulled out a pair of reading glasses and turned to the table of contents. She could read without them, but had picked up a +1.5 diopter pair at a dollar store. She'd leave them behind when she finished here. All part of her plan.

"Okay, 'Hangman' looks good. Let's do that." She thought of Rick outside. "Trouble is, I've got an appointment so I don't think we can finish today."

Emilie said. "'S'okay. Bushed."

With a bittersweet pang Laura realized this would be her last reading session with Emilie. By tomorrow she'd be cured and would be able to hold a book on her own.

If it worked.

4

She found Rick dozing behind the wheel when she returned. She watched him a moment. He seemed able to sleep anywhere. His face had lost all its tension. He looked almost . . . innocent. He didn't jump when she rapped on the driver's window, simply opened his eyes and gave her a little wave.

"Napping?" she said as the glass rolled down.

"Never pass up a chance to grab forty. Everything good in there?"

Tell him or not? She felt guilty for holding back. But they'd be returning to the city tomorrow to visit NYU. She could tell him then.

"As good as can be expected in a VA hospital."

"I hear you. Where to next? We were heading for a drink, as I recall."

She felt the need for a drink—a stiff one—but she wanted to make one more stop before that.

Keeping her tone as offhanded and casual as she could, she said, "I was thinking of retracing our steps a ways."

He frowned. "Toward the city?"

"Only about twenty miles or so back along Northern Boulevard."

"But that would put us—" His eyes widened. "Ohhhh, no. Don't even consider it."

"Why not? If I'm going to be any help in finding your brother, I need to know where he came from, I need some insight on his decision making. And for that I need to meet your mother."

Probably true, but Laura was really looking for insight on Rick. And she was pretty sure his mother wasn't anywhere near as bad as he made her out to be. A man's relationship with his mother can reveal a lot about him, and Laura wanted a firsthand look.

"First off," Rick said, "as I told you, he's not my true brother and not her true son—no shared blood between the three of us. So, on the nature-versus-nurture front, there's no nature and minimal nurture."

"Didn't you tell me he was her favorite?"

"Yeah, but—"

"Then I need to meet her. She must have had *some* influence on him. I'm serious, Rick." She sensed him wavering so she moved in for the kill. "Marissa's going over to a friend's house after softball, so we have time for a visit before I have to be back. A quick fly-by. What can it hurt?"

He stared skyward. "If you only knew."

"Rick . . ."

"Okay, okay. But promise me one thing."

"What?"

"You'll still be talking to me afterward."

He had to be overstating this. Didn't he?

5

THE VILLAGE OF MONROE, NEW YORK

"So," Laura said, staring at the house as they pulled up before it, "you never told me you grew up in Tara."

The front of Rick's family home had a high, rounded portico supported by cylindrical columns. He remembered Tara as being far more angular, but he guessed every big house with tall white columns was a Tara of sorts.

"Yep. Butterfly McQueen will be opening that front door any second now."

Instead, Lena let them in. He'd phoned ahead so Paulette knew they were coming. She appeared from the left as they stepped into the foyer. She was dressed in royal blue silk lounging pajamas—the things Laura had told him no one wore anymore. Add opera gloves, a long cigarette holder, and she could be a gray-haired Auntie Mame.

Immediately upon her entrance—before she could speak—he jumped into an introduction.

"Paulette, this is Doctor Laura Fanning."

Her eyebrows rose as she extended her hand. "How do you do, dear?"

Laura gave her hand a single shake. "A pleasure to meet you, Mrs. Somers."

"'Doctor,' is it? MD?"

"Yes."

"What would you be doing with my—?"

"We work together," Rick blurted. "On occasion, that is." Why am I sweating? "She's going to help us find Keith."

"Really." She elongated the word. "And just what kind of doctor are you?"

"I'm with the county medical examiner's office."

Paulette gasped and her hand flew to her chest. "You don't mean—?"

"Oh, no-no-no!" Laura said.

Rick wondered how to salvage this . . .

"No, it's oaky," he said. "We haven't heard anything about Keith. It's just that Laura is very good with forensics—a different kind of forensics than Hari. You know, evidence and such."

"Oh, dear. You gave me such a fright."

"Sorry," Laura said. "I realize how that must have sounded."

She gave Laura a thorough up and down. "You're quite striking. How did you become paired with Garrick?"

Rick said, "We're not 'paired.' We—"

Paulette shot him a look. "Your friend appears capable of coherent speech. Why don't we let her answer?" To Laura: "Is he always like this with you?"

She smiled. "Not at all. We were hired separately and sent out as a team by a man who wanted us to track down a medication."

Paulette frowned. "Why would someone send a coroner in search of a medication?"

"It's complicated," Laura said.

"As are most things. Were you successful?"

"Yes."

"And so now, because of that, you two are going to play detective?"

Laura didn't miss a beat. "I prefer 'sleuth.'"

Rick resisted a fist pump. Yes! Right back in her face.

A smile twisted Paulette's lips. "Sleuths . . . hmmm."

"What?" Rick said.

"It just occurred to me that 'Rick and Laura' rhymes with 'Nick and Nora.'"

Fearing Laura would miss the reference, Rick said, "*The Thin Man* couple?"

"Yes. That means you must have become adept at making martinis."

"Never had one," he said. "Don't think I'd like them."

"They're an acquired taste . . . for the more sophisticated palate. Lena makes a good one. I'll have her make us some. You really should try them if you're going to be a detective couple."

"We're not a couple," Laura said, looking Paulette in the eye and not backing down an inch. "But I'd love a martini."

What was she doing? Going toe-to-toe with Paulette? He'd never seen Laura drink anything stronger than wine.

You're gonna hate it, he thought.

Paulette was looking at him. "And you, Garrick?"

"Beer?" he said with faint hope.

A bad-taste purse of the lips. "What would make you think I'd have beer?"

What indeed?

"Champagne then."

6

Laura looked longingly at Rick's Champagne flute. The first sip of her martini had almost gagged her. Like straight gin. Awful. She'd never had one before and never would again. How did they ever become popular?

But she'd be damned if she'd let Paulette know.

Sophisticated palate, my gold-plated patootie.

She choked down another sip and said, "So tell me about Keith."

Paulette sighed. "My dear, beautiful, brilliant boy. A mother's dream. Never an ounce of trouble." She cocked her head at Rick. "Unlike this one, who was nothing *but* trouble." She leaned forward and lowered her voice. "Tell the truth: In your search for this medication, did he make any indecent proposals?"

Was she really asking this? Right in front of Rick? She wanted to say, *I wish,* but she'd only just met the woman.

"Never. He has always been a perfect gentleman."

Unfazed, Rick waved his empty Champagne flute. "The CIA had mandatory etiquette classes. I got all A's."

Paulette kept her gaze trained on Laura as Lena appeared and refilled his glass from a bottle painted with flowers.

"The reason I ask is because before he left to join that gang of thugs, he ran through a slew of girlfriends. Their fathers hated him. No respect for their rules. He'd keep them out till all hours and bring them home any damn time he pleased. The complaints I heard!"

Laura wanted to drive her point home. "Perfect. Gentleman. At least in my experience. In fact, he even saved my life at one point."

Paulette straightened in her chair. "Really? How—?"

Rick jumped in. "I believe the subject is Keith?"

Laura knew he hated to be the topic of conversation. Not one of those people who went on about themselves. Apparently he liked it even less when someone else was talking about him.

"Yes, yes, of course," said Paulette. "My dear Keith. Did you discover anything at his apartment?"

Rick pulled the folded photo from his jacket pocket. "We found this on his printer's hard drive. That's Mozi, I suppose?"

Paulette took a quick glance, then handed it back. "Yes, that's the horrid little creature."

Laura asked, "Did he ever say how it died?"

She shook her head. "No. He seemed barely capable of speech when he arrived with its ashes."

"Laura also found some DVDs," Rick said. "Recordings of TV shows."

Paulette was nodding. "His publisher arranged a lot of interviews when the book was released. I caught most of them. Did you happen to notice one from *The Anthony Akins Show*?"

Laura pictured the array of disks . . . "I believe I did."

"I missed that one. Would you mind terribly if we played it?"

"Of course not." Laura was planning to watch them anyway. Why not start here? "They're in Rick's truck . . ."

"I'll get it," he said, hopping out of his seat.

When he was gone, Laura found herself again under the scrutiny of Paulette's hazel gaze.

"You appear to be an intelligent, accomplished woman. How you must have struggled to get where you are."

She shrugged. "I've always had good study habits."

"I meant all the gender prejudice."

"You mean glass ceilings and all that?"

"Yes. No matter what they say and what laws they pass, it's still a man's world."

No argument there, but . . . "Well, my boss, Doctor Henniger, the chief medical examiner, is a woman."

And can be a real bitch at times. The sociologists didn't realize that certain women could be worse than men in keeping their own gender down. Once someone like Susan Henniger reached the upper echelons, she didn't want competition from *anyone*.

"But you must have encountered . . . prejudice."

She means because of my Hispanic coloring and features?

"Nothing overt. I mean, half my fellow students at Stritch were female, with a lot of minorities. But what gets to you are the *unconscious* attitudes—like being constantly underestimated."

Being *underestimated* . . . that was the most insidious. During her training she tolerated the older docs calling her "dear" and "honey," but being underestimated was the hardest to fight.

"Well, be that as it may, why on Earth is someone like you involved with Garrick?"

"We're not 'involved.' We're . . . we're coworkers who've become friends."

"That's all? I sense a bond between you."

A bond? Laura thought. Yes, she supposed there was.

"Well, we shared some stressful experiences."

"Stressful" barely touched it. They'd walked through fire together and made it to the other side. Two people couldn't do that without forging some kind of bond.

"You're sure there's nothing more?"

Well, there was that time in the Orkney Islands when we were on the verge of tumbling into bed.

"Absolutely."

Though sometimes I wish . . .

"Well, there will be."

Laura shook her head, baffled. "Why are you so insistent—?"

"I see the way he looks at you. I don't recall ever seeing him look at a woman that way before."

Did this woman ever hold anything back?

Rick returned then, holding up a disk. "Got it."

But Paulette's words stuck with her: *I don't recall ever seeing him look at a woman that way before* . . . Laura wasn't sure what that meant, but she liked the sound of it.

"Before we watch," Paulette said, "I've had Lena set out a selection of cheeses along with some Château d'Yquem."

"Oh, you shouldn't have," Laura said, and meant it.

"It's for my benefit as well. I rarely eat full meals these days. I prefer to graze. And besides, I have a charity function I must attend later."

"What's the cause?" Laura said, just to be polite.

Paulette waved her hand. "Some -itis or dystrophy. I've forgotten."

"Probably 'Save the Beluga Caviar Sturgeon,'" Rick muttered as he surveyed the table.

Laura realized she was hungry and was impressed with the variety: Brie, Camembert, Gouda, Dorblu, Edam, Gruyère, Roquefort.

But apparently Rick couldn't resist a dig.

"What? No pâté?"

Paulette gave him an icy look. "You know very well the barbaric torture ducks and geese must suffer to make their livers suitable for pâté."

"You used to serve it all the time when we were kids. That's how I acquired a taste for it."

She looked embarrassed. "I've evolved."

"Guess you have." He made a show of inspecting the table. "So, no veal then?"

She walked away, saying, "You are insufferable."

Laura gave him a reproving look. "Maybe you should lighten up. Just a little?"

He sighed. "You're right. It's just that her outrage buttons are so big and fat and tempting."

"Which means she's too easy. You need a worthier opponent."

"You're on her side?"

"I always tend to side with the underdog, and you definitely outgun her."

"Oh, I don't know about—"

She leaned closer. "Look, what can she say that'll penetrate your defenses? Nothing. While she's basically a collection of trendy outrages waiting to be triggered."

His expression said he knew she was right.

She nudged him. "Let's grab some cheese and go watch your brother."

7

"Isn't he wonderful?" Paulette said as the recording ended.

Rick shook himself back to the here and now. He'd been only half watching, thinking about Laura's admonition to back off. She was right of course. Back in the day, Paulette had subjected him to a relentless onslaught of criticism from the moment he announced he was joining the CIA until the day he walked out. It had mattered back then. He'd been a lot younger and she was his mother, after all. Years of complete radio silence had followed, which, though a relief at first, had hurt in its own way. He'd gotten over it. Larger traumas later on had put all that in perspective.

"He's such a natural for TV," she added.

Rick noted the use of present tense, and that was good. But her remark proved that a mother's assessment of her child's performance in any field should always be suspect.

Keith gave bad interview—mumbling, rambling, looking everywhere but at the camera and the interviewer.

That's the Keith I know.

Laura cleared her throat. "Did Keith have any repeat interviews?"

Paulette frowned. "I'm not sure what you mean."

"I mean, did anyone ever ask him back?"

Rick repressed a nod. Yep. Laura had the same opinion: a stinkaroo guest.

"Not that I know of. The publishers arranged the original publicity, and once the book was out, that was it. Why do you ask?"

Rick could almost see Laura's mind racing for an inoffensive answer. "Oh, just wondering if, when the God Gene publicity hit the media, they wanted to question him about it."

Paulette shrugged. "If they did, he never told me."

Laura rose from her seat. "Well, I have a daughter to collect. It was very nice meeting you."

Blah-blah-blah . . . The conversational trivialities of parting passed through Rick's head like ghosts as he guided Laura through the door and out to the driveway.

"Well," she said as Rick started the pickup, "that was . . . interesting."

"You're still speaking to me?"

She smiled. "You can't choose your parents."

What a relief.

"Just keep in mind that I'm adopted," he added.

"Well, you do have that to thank her for."

"I think I have my father to thank more. I gathered growing up that he was the one who wanted kids around the house and Paulette agreed because she'd have a nice family photo for the Christmas cards—sorry, *holiday* cards."

She stared at him. "Boy, that's toxic. She's an absolute horror. Might be the most toxic woman I've ever met. I bet she'd feel right at home running a Nazi death camp. Or maybe—"

Rick raised his hands. This wasn't like Laura. "Hey-hey. She's not *that* bad."

Laura smiled and laid a hand on his arm. "Just seeing if I could get you to defend her. And you did. So I guess it's okay for *you* to come down on her, but let someone else try . . ."

"Well, when someone rags on your mother, even if she's not your biological mother—"

"—you've got to stick up for her, right?" She laughed. "That is so you."

He sighed. Yeah, he guessed it was. Didn't like being so predictable, but very much liked the feel of Laura's hand on his arm.

"Well, you did warn me about her," she went on, "but you never mentioned that your brother was on the spectrum."

"What spectrum?"

"The autism spectrum."

That shocked him. "Hey, Keith's weird but he's hardly autistic."

"Well, the spectrum contains all degrees of developmental disorders. I think he'd be considered a sort of Asperger's if they were still using the term. I'm hardly an expert—I mean, my patients don't exhibit *any* sort of behavior—but he showed a lot of the signs in that interview."

"You mean the lack of eye contact?"

"That and his flat affect and atonal speech. You said he never had any friends."

"His chatter could drive you crazy at times. He didn't seem to need friends. He built a computer and he'd spend all his time making lists on it."

"Of what?"

"Who knows? He wouldn't let anybody see."

"Did he have any obsessive interests as a kid?"

"Oh, hell, did he ever. A mania for classifying things. Our sister didn't have a pet cat, she had a . . ." Rick sifted his memory for the terms. "She had a *Felis catus*. And he'd recite the subfamily and family and order and class. Somebody wouldn't be walking a dog, they'd be walking a *Canis lupus familiaris* and so on."

"You have a good memory."

Rick shook his head. "I can't *not* remember. He grew out of it after a while, but as a kid, every time he saw Cheryl's cat or a dog, or even a freaking rose in the garden, he'd go through its classifications."

"Back when you worshipped him?"

Rick sighed. "Yeah. I thought he was so smart, thought he was so cool for trying to teach me. But he wasn't. He was just reciting what he knew. He'd have done the same if I were miles away."

"That jibes with his biographical sketch in his book: expert in evolutionary taxonomy. Which means he put his obsession to work for him."

Keith . . . on the autism spectrum . . . Asperger's syndrome . . .

Rick thought about that as he drove. He didn't know much about—what had Laura called it?—developmental disorders, but it explained a lot. He'd gone from admiring Keith to almost hating him when he'd concluded his older brother was rejecting him because Rick wasn't smart enough to keep up with him. But the truth was more like Keith had been incapable of including him in his life.

That changed everything, didn't it. Keith hadn't rejected him . . . Keith had barely known he was there.

A little knife of guilt twisted its blade inside him. All those years of bad feelings about a guy who couldn't help it.

Ah, well. The past is past and what's done is done. None of that offered answers as to where Keith was now.

"All this has got me rethinking my original position even more," Laura said.

Rick snapped back to the here and now. "What position?"

"That your brother ran off. Everything pointed to a man who was planning to change his life—liquidating assets, moving the money around, shredding his computer files. It all seemed so premeditated and purposeful. But after seeing that interview . . ."

"How's that change things?"

"People on the autism spectrum, especially the high-functioning ones, tend to like their daily routines and familiar surroundings."

"But then how come every time you turn around you seem to hear about an autistic kid wandering off?"

"The 'elopers' tend to be low-functioning. They get it into their head that they want a donut or a swim or whatever and, because they're nonverbal, they simply head out the door looking for a bakery or a swimming pool. They fully intend to return, but they get lost so easily."

Rick found himself nodding. "Yeah, from the look of things, Keith's apartment was definitely a comfort zone."

"Right. You saw how he'd arranged his photos. Your brother is very high-functioning and that apartment means something to him. I can see him leaving it for research trips, knowing he'd return, but I can't see him voluntarily giving it up altogether."

Rick couldn't see it either. "But there's the matter of shredding his drives."

"As you said, if he was being 'backed into something' or pressured about it, he might want to erase all trace of it."

"Or maybe someone else wanted all trace of his involvement with Keith erased and did it after he disappeared. Either way, I've got a feeling that little monkey's right in the middle of it all."

Laura's expression went into mock shock. "What? You agree with your mother?"

"Even a stopped watch is right twice a day. And I never underestimate a woman's intuition."

Laura leaned back and stared out at the road. "If only we could learn how it died, I think we'd be a lot closer to finding out what happened to your brother."

"Maybe the people he worked with will know."

Laura nodded. "Maybe. Let's just hope Keith didn't suffer the same fate."

Rick shook his head. "Hey, you're supposed to be the optimistic half."

"Which means?"

"Which means you believe we live in the best possible world."

"And you . . . ?"

Rick said, "As the pessimist half, I'm afraid you're right."

But he knew what she meant. After this long without a peep from Keith, the likelihood of a happy ending had become vanishingly small.

THEN

Monday, May 16

THE MOZAMBIQUE CHANNEL

From his position behind the wheel, Amaury Laffite watched his passenger as the *Sorcière des Mers* chugged along at a steady six knots through the western expanse of the channel, approximately six hundred miles from their starting point in Maputo and one hundred miles west of Belo Tsiribihina on the Madagascar coast. Straight ahead in the prow, Marten Jeukens stood in his customary stance: leaning against the rail with binoculars glued to his eyes as he scanned from port to starboard and back again, over and over.

Amaury had told him it wasn't necessary—he had his radar dome directly overhead on the wheelhouse roof, doing the same thing, only better. He'd told him his radar would detect an island before his eyes could, but the stubborn Afrikaner could not be dissuaded.

The first day out had been uncharacteristically rough and Jeukens had spent much of it hanging over the stern puking his breakfast into the channel. But he never complained and by nightfall his stomach had calmed enough to allow him a light dinner.

Amaury piloted the *Sorcière* the first hundred miles or so to move them out of the busiest shipping lanes, then let Jeukens take a turn at the helm while he napped. For sixty hours they ran night and day at eight knots on a northeastward course through mostly empty water, crossing the Tropic of Capricorn along the way. The Afrikaner soon gained his sea legs and seemed comfortable above and belowdecks.

He did not prove a very communicative travel companion, except to complain about the heat. Though he revealed little about himself, Amaury managed to learn that he hailed from the temperate climes of Cape Town, which would explain his intolerance of the tropical heat here. Standoffish as he was, Jeukens somehow managed to draw out Amaury's life story—the various enterprises, legal and not-so-legal, he'd engaged in during his checkered life, even the wife and daughter he'd left in Oran.

"Oran?" Jeukens had said. "Albert Camus, the famous French writer, set *La Peste,* perhaps his greatest novel, in Oran."

"Never heard of him," Amaury said.

He had dropped out of school early—life on the Marseilles docks was so much more interesting—and did not care much for books.

"He espoused absurdism which, I am sure, is something else you've never heard of—or would have any interest in."

He thinks I am a dullard, Amaury thought. Just because I do not read books does not mean I am stupid.

"One never knows, *monsieur.* Try me. We have plenty of time."

Jeukens shrugged. "There's not much to it, really. Camus thought it's natural for humans to look for meaning in life; the absurdity comes when we realize there *is* no meaning in life."

"You sound as if you disagree."

"Oh, I agree wholeheartedly with the absurdity. There is a group in the United States called 'Black Lives Matter.' The harsh reality is that *no* lives matter."

Amaury's feeling that he was destined for something greater . . . was that just a delusion?

"This does not seem to me a philosophy that fills one with hope and joy, *monsieur.*"

"Well, hope and joy are illusions. Camus's mistake was in thinking that humans actually bother to look for meaning in life. The vast majority of them do not. They simply exist moment to moment—like you. After all, didn't you tell me you lived for profit and pleasure?"

"I enjoy them," Amaury said, offended. "But I do not live solely for them." Or did he?

"I diverge from Camus in that I believe we can and must *create* a purpose in life. Our lives do not matter to the universe, but we can make them matter to *ourselves.*"

"The 'higher purpose' you mentioned in the bar."

"Yes! I have found mine—a way to make my life matter."

"Your mission for civilization . . . to save the Giordano Brunos of the world."

"Exactly!"

"But how *exactly* will you do this?"

"That is my secret. Find your own mission."

Well, the crazy Afrikaner may have found his higher purpose, but together they had not found the island. Perhaps today, their fourth day out, would prove lucky. Amaury couldn't complain about the weather. The morning had broken clear and calm, with only a hint of haze on the limitless horizon.

On the bow, Jeukens lowered the glasses. They swung from the cord around his neck as he turned and made his way aft. Amaury thought he might be headed to the galley for a bite of lunch, but instead of going below, he climbed to the wheelhouse.

Now what?

"We've worked this area to death," he said, scratching his beard. "I want to try north."

Amaury repressed a sigh. They hadn't worked it to death, not nearly. This was not the first time they'd had this conversation. Very well, once again . . .

He set the autopilot for due south and motioned Jeukens to the map table. He tapped a spot to the east of Belo Tsiribihina where the Madagascar coast curved inward.

"The Mozambique Channel is well traveled, especially the shipping lanes northward from Durban to India and the Arab countries. Those lanes run along the western side—which is why so many fall victim to the Somali pirates. Here on the Madagascar side, the area we have been exploring, is the least traveled."

"So you've said. But we've been exploring it up and down with no results. We haven't seen a thing since those barren atolls we passed on the way in."

He was referring to Île Europa and Bassas da India, two of the Scattered Islands well known to anyone who sailed the southern reaches of the channel. The latter was dangerous because with every high tide it disappeared below the surface.

"We've barely scratched the surface." He moved his finger north on the map. "If we go north . . . up here . . . see how the Madagascar and Mozambique coastlines both belly into the channel. It's narrowest there, and the shipping lanes all crowd together. Any islands up that way, no matter how small, have been spotted and charted."

Jeukens's expression was grim as he tugged off his slouch hat and rubbed a hand over his pale bald pate. "As one of your countrymen said, 'One doesn't discover new lands without consenting to lose sight of the shore for a very long time.'"

Yet another quote!

"Which countryman would that be?"

"André Gide."

"But of course," Amaury said, though he had no idea who that was.

The Afrikaner's eyes narrowed. "Are you leading me on a fool's errand?"

"Not at all," Amaury said quickly. He'd seen this look before. "It is too early to quit this area. We have ten thousand square miles where a tiny island might hide." He pointed out the salt-streaked port window. "Look out there. We are a hundred miles from the coast but the horizon is only a few miles away. There is so much yet to see."

If the island existed, Amaury wanted to find it as much as Jeukens—perhaps even more. A steady supply of those blue-eyed monkeys would put him on Easy Street. If he started breeding them, perhaps he could even retire.

After squinting through the glass, Jeukens abruptly yanked open the door and hurried down to the main deck where he raised his binoculars toward the east.

"What is it?" Amaury called. "Do you see something?"

Jeukens lowered the glasses with a slow, disappointed shake of his head.

"No . . . just a little cloud on the horizon."

Amaury stepped outside and looked up at the pristine blue of the sky, then toward the horizon. He could see nothing. Jeukens had been hogging the *Sorcière*'s field glasses, so he stepped back inside and opened the cabinet where he kept his rifle—a .30-30 Marlin. He unzipped the padded cloth case and removed the Nikon 2-7×32mm scope from the rail atop the receiver housing. He stepped outside and focused on the horizon.

He could just make out a puff of white along the line where the darker blue below met the lighter blue above.

Amaury felt a tingle of excitement.

"You know, *mon ami* . . . we are going to investigate that."

"A cloud?"

"Warm moist air rises from an island as the day heats up, and condenses in the cooler air above it. Could be nothing, but we are not going to ignore it."

He returned to the wheelhouse and immediately checked his radar. No signal, but that meant nothing, even though he had the gain already set to max. His radar was old and wide-beamed, and not very sensitive. He had little need for a more sensitive unit—or a fly bridge or a radar arch, which would have increased its range—because he used it only at night or in fog or rain, to let him know if a freighter or other large craft was near. But even if a land mass was causing that cloud, no radar, no matter how narrow the beam, would pick it up if it lay below the horizon.

He began turning the *Sorcière* to port. By the time they were pointed east, Jeukens was back on the prow with his glasses. Amaury opened the throttle and the cruiser's speed rose to nine knots. He'd been running at lower speeds to conserve fuel, but this was excuse enough to waste a little.

The tingle in his gut increased as a green glow began to grow at the top of the black radar screen. Possibly a container ship but he couldn't imagine what one would be doing this far east in the channel. Besides, this appeared stationary. Container ships could run a quarter mile in length these days, but they wouldn't have their own pet cloud.

Had to be an island. Eventually his passenger's binoculars saw it too. Without turning, Jeukens raised his fist with a thumb up.

I'm way ahead of you.

An island, a tiny one not on his maps. But was it the one they were looking for? Did the object of their search even exist?

Jeukens joined him in the wheelhouse. "It looks volcanic, don't you think?"

"I do not have the advantage of your binoculars, but I believe that a safe assumption. You saw Bassas da India—that atoll is volcanic, not coral. Its base is thousands of feet below the surface. I would not be surprised if what we see ahead of us is similar."

Less than half an hour later Amaury was able to throttle back and coast toward a steep, sheer, dark wall studded with ferns and vines and other greenery clinging to its surface. It rose to a uniform height, perhaps twenty feet above the waves. A narrow beach, little more than a strip of sand, supported an array of palms. Gulls and terns wheeled above.

"Most definitely volcanic," he said.

Jeukens seemed almost frantic. "How do we get to the top? Climb?"

"I doubt that will be necessary. I am sure we will find a break in the wall. Let's take a tour, shall we?"

He turned on his depth sounder—he didn't want to run aground on some sneaky underwater reef jutting from the island—and throttled up, spinning the wheel to port and taking them northward at four knots. The face there was just as sheer but had less vegetation, clearly revealing a volcanic origin. The island proved slightly oval. He guessed its diameter at roughly half a mile.

But nowhere did they find a break in the wall.

"Most unfortunate," Amaury said as they returned to their starting place.

He idled the engine and the *Sorcière* immediately began drifting south in the current. It seemed especially strong here.

"Pull in and we'll go ashore," Jeukens said.

"'Pull in'?" Amaury had to laugh. "This is not a car. You cannot just 'pull in' to the curb."

"Well, then, drop anchor or whatever you do. I want to see if we can climb that wall."

"You expect to see a horde of your little monkeys?"

"I have no idea what to expect up top. It could be a barren plateau. Or the wall could be the rim of a caldera filled with life. If it's the first, we keep on searching. If it's the second . . ."

"Then we look around to see if we can spot one of your little friends."

Please, God, Amaury thought. Let there be a caldera and let it be crowded with them.

"At least get closer."

Keeping an eye on the depth sounder, Amaury put the engine in forward. The *Sorcière* slowly reversed her drift and began to chug east. The gauge was giving him no readings, which meant the seabed was far down, beyond its range.

As the boat inched toward the island, Jeukens stepped out onto the deck and lifted his glasses to scan the bushes and small trees clinging to the rock. Suddenly he stiffened and leaned over the railing.

"What is it?"

"See that queen palm?" Jeukens started kicking off his shoes. "I saw something move in it."

"What are you doing?"

The Afrikaner said nothing as he stripped down to boxer shorts.

"Let me get closer!" Amaury shouted. "The current—!"

Without a word Jeukens leaped in. Not a natural swimmer—about as graceful as his clumsy leap—but his skinny arms stroked him to the beach about thirty feet downstream from the tree he had indicated.

Pulling himself up on the ribbon of shore, he shook himself off and made his way toward the palm. He stepped gingerly with his bare feet on the rough surface. About ten feet from the tree he stopped. His bald head gleamed in the sunlight as he crouched and peered into the palm's gently waving fronds, leaning this way and that for a better view.

Suddenly something small and furry with a long tail leaped from the tree and grabbed hold of the wall. Amaury watched it scurry up the rocky surface and disappear over the top. He couldn't tell if it was one of the creatures they had come looking for, but when he saw Jeukens shaking triumphant fists in the air, he knew.

Excellente!

The Afrikaner dove back into the water and started stroking toward the *Sorcière*. Amaury lowered a rope ladder over the side and was waiting with a towel when Jeukens climbed aboard.

"Strong current," he panted.

"I warned you. We've found them?"

Obviously they had, but he wanted to hear it from the lips of the man who had been closest.

Jeukens nodded as he dried himself. "That was one of them. No question. Its blue eyes looked directly at me before it ran off."

Amaury hid his elation. He'd begun the voyage with little hope of success. Chances had been low that the island even existed, and even lower that they could find it. But his strategy of concentrating the search where other ships did not go had paid off.

Now he had to get back to Maputo, gather up a couple of the experienced men he used on poaching trips, load the *Sorcière* with traps and cages, and return to this nameless hunk of rock as soon as humanly possible.

But he wasn't sure about his passenger. Jeukens might have different ideas.

"Congratulations," Amaury said. "What next?"

Jeukens stared at the island. "I got a close look at that wall. I don't think it's climbable."

Good. Just what Amaury wanted to hear. He'd feared that Jeukens would want to spend days trying to conquer that wall.

"But it is not insurmountable, *mon ami*. Only twenty feet or so high. With a little help we can conquer it. All we need do is return with the right ladder and—"

Jeukens turned to him. "You want to trap them and sell them, don't you."

What was this? A challenge? He couldn't tell. He had to tread carefully with this man.

"Exotics are my business, after all. And these are as exotic as they come. Do you find that a problem?"

"Not a bit. Take as many as you can carry. It's of no concern to me."

Well, that was a relief. Amaury wasn't in the mood for a rant on animal rights and ecology and the rest of that nonsense.

"So, what is *your* plan?"

"I wish to study them in their natural habitat."

Amaury laughed and clapped him on the shoulder. "Then we are in accord! I will leave you plenty to study. I am no fool. I will treat this as a preserve where these creatures can be fruitful and multiply. I will take the older ones and leave the younger to breed, creating an endless supply that you can study to your heart's content."

"Obviously you are coming back soon."

"As soon as I can gather a crew and load my equipment."

"Good. I will return with you."

Amaury hadn't planned on that.

"Five people, cages, traps . . . it will be crowded."

"That is of no concern. Do not play games with me. You wouldn't know about this island if I had not chartered you to find it. You'll become a rich man because of me."

Amaury couldn't argue with that, so he did not try. "No games, *monsieur*. We head to Toliara immediately. The sooner—"

Jeukens frowned. "Toliara? That's—"

"Madagascar, yes. We don't have enough fuel to make it back to Maputo. We burned up too much running our search grid. It will add a day but cannot be helped. We will be back in Maputo early Friday."

Jeukens looked back at the island. "I can put the extra day to good use. I have preparations to . . ." His voice trailed off as his expression went slack.

Amaury followed his gaze.

Arrayed along the fern-fringed rim, hundreds of blue eyes stared down at them. Amaury stared back until the Afrikaner spoke behind him.

"Is this thing loaded?"

Amaury repressed a gasp when he saw Jeukens holding the Marlin.

"Yes." Five rounds in the tube. Keeping one stored in the chamber would allow six shots, but Amaury had never been comfortable with that, so he always left the chamber empty. After all, it took but a second to work the lever and make her ready to fire. "What are you doing with that?"

"I want to see how they react when I kill one of them."

"I do not think that is a good idea, *monsieur*." He wanted these things alive—all of them.

"I'll decide that. Is it ready to fire?"

"No, you must work the lever,"

Jeukens did just that, then raised the rifle to his shoulder and fired. Above, the monkeys merely looked curious. He worked the lever, ejected a shell, and fired again. And again. And again. Fortunately he was a terrible shot, missing every time. Amaury did not mention the scope resting in his pocket.

"Damn!" Jeukens said, wheeling so the rifle pointed at Amaury—whether accidentally or on purpose wasn't clear. "How many shots left?"

"Please, *monsieur*, point that in a safe direction."

Jeukens didn't move it. "You didn't answer my question."

Amaury's mouth went dry. "One . . . one more."

Jeukens worked the lever. Glittering brass tumbled through the air. He turned and fired once more at the island, with as much effect as before. Then, with a smirk, he handed the Marlin to Amaury and headed below.

That night, as the *Sorcière* sped southward with the current along the moon-lit channel, Amaury put aside his deep misgivings about his passenger and broke out the bottle he kept tucked away in one of the galley cabinets. The radar showed clear water ahead, so he poured glasses of the amber fluid for Jeukens and himself. He noticed the Afrikaner wince at the burn accompanying his first swallow.

"Cognac?"

"Armagnac, far superior."

Not like your awful Pinotage, eh? he thought.

Earlier, just after they'd got under way, the Afrikaner had made a couple of manic calls on his sat phone—at least they seemed manic—but he was more relaxed now. Not that he ever seemed truly relaxed.

Amaury had had time to think since they'd left the island. At first the future had looked clear and sunny—so many sets of blue eyes staring at them from the rim. But a cloud had appeared on the figurative horizon. He turned to the source of that cloud.

"So," he said to Jeukens, "are you planning on publishing papers about our island?"

He was careful not to say *my* island, which was how he was already thinking of it.

Jeukens shook his head. "Not immediately. I want to keep it and its inhabitants secret for a while—as long as possible, actually—so I can study them without interference." He tossed back his Armagnac with another grimace and poured himself a healthy second helping without asking. "So I hope you will keep the island's existence to yourself as well."

Amaury was so relieved he almost burst out laughing. "Keep it to *my-self*! Of course I will! I do not want anyone poaching that island. I was worried about *you*."

"Don't worry about me. Worry about the crew you will be bringing back."

He finished his second glass and poured a third. Amaury hadn't finished his first yet.

"Pace yourself. That is strong stuff. And as for my crew, they are mostly muscle." He tapped the side of his head. "Not much up here."

"But I can hear one of them now, in his cups at a bar, talking about traveling to an uncharted island populated by those strange, blue-eyed monkeys Laffite sells at such a profit."

Amaury had already considered this.

"But he won't be able to tell anyone more than that, because he will not know the coordinates."

"Do you?"

"Of course. I took a GPS reading before we left." He'd noticed the Afrikaner doing the same. "My men won't know where they're headed until they get there."

"Good. I don't want interference until I'm through." He took another gulp. Already his eyes were looking glassy. "If the wrong people get a look at those creatures they'll start 'missing link' talk."

"'Missing link'? Is that what it is?"

Jeukens shook his head. "No. It's more. Much, much more."

Now *this* was interesting. Would it increase the monkeys' price tag?

"Explain, please."

The Afrikaner waved him off and set down his glass. "I'm more used to wine. And I've said too much already."

"What? About a missing link?"

The Afrikaner's face contorted. "Do not mention that again!"

Why so upset? The man looked ready to fight. Amaury didn't think he had much to fear from those skinny arms, but a fight would be bad. This odd man might prove useful in the future.

He raised his hands, palms out. "After tonight I say nothing. But for now, just one more question. Please?"

Jeukens spoke through his teeth. "What?"

"Your little primates—they're so tiny. How can they be the missing link? Missing link to what?"

"To madness. To more Friar Brunos."

"The one who was burned at the stake?"

"Yes. For merely recognizing that Earth was not the center of the universe. You've heard of Galileo?"

"Of course."

"The Inquisition bearded him for the same thinking, threatening torture and death if he didn't recant. Knowing what happened to Bruno, he complied."

This made no sense. Was he already so drunk?

"What does Galileo have to do with these missing links? Seriously. You must have a better answer than that."

"Not for you. I doubt we'll ever learn what they link to. I, for one, am not sure I want to know."

Jeukens turned away and staggered toward the bunks below.

NOW

Thursday, May 19

1

GREENWICH VILLAGE, NEW YORK

With only one postmortem scheduled for her at the morgue, Laura had been able to leave a little early and train into the city. During the trip her head had been filled with thoughts of Emilie and the potion she'd sneaked into her. Was it doing any good? Or more important, was it doing any harm?

All it would take to find out was a simple call. But she'd never called before, and that was just asking for people to connect her to whatever happened overnight. Besides, calling wasn't enough. She wanted—*needed*—to see for herself. Assuming the *ikhar* had worked, of course.

As they'd arranged, Rick met her at the arch in Washington Square and the two of them walked east on Waverly Place. Keith's office was in a six-story building near Mercer Street. The glossy black steel and glass of the modernized entrance jarred with the old red stone of the upper stories.

"The Center for Genomics and Systems Biology," Rick said, reading the etching on the glass door. "Impressive."

The same title was displayed in huge letters along the rear wall of the long foyer that stretched to the right.

Just so no one forgets, Laura guessed as they stepped inside.

A low reception desk sat directly opposite the entrance

"We have an appointment with Doctor Salas," Rick said when they reached it.

The young man behind the desk seemed prepared for them. "Oh, yes, I'm sorry. You wanted to talk to him about Doctor Somers, right?"

Laura had a sudden feeling their meeting wasn't going to happen.

"Right."

"Well, he was called away unexpectedly and we didn't have your phone number. But he left word with Doctor Somers's assistant who'll be glad to talk to you if you wish."

"I guess so," Rick said. He glanced at Laura. "Okay?"

"Fine," she said, thinking this might work out better.

The receptionist made a quick call and turned to them. "He'll be right down."

Minutes later a twenty-something guy appeared at the far end of the foyer: short reddish beard, glasses with thick black rims, a muddy gray-brown plaid shirt, dark green bow tie, skinny jeans, dirty white bucks, and . . .

"Is that a man bun?" Rick muttered as he approached.

Laura nodded. "A top knot. Total L train."

"Top knots should be limited to people with a katana and a first name like Toshiro."

They saw the young man stutter-step when he saw them, then continue approaching. Some people reacted to Rick that way.

"This must be him," Laura said. "Put on your nice face."

"This *is* my nice face."

"Grady Fehr," the fellow said, extending his hand. "I'm Doctor Somers's grad student."

Rick introduced himself and Laura, then followed him back to an elevator.

"How long have you been with Doctor Somers?" Laura said.

"Just going on two years. Have you heard anything from him?"

"No. That's why we're here. We're hoping someone in the department can shed some light on where he might be."

"I can tell you straight up front that no one here's got a clue. His disappearance was all we talked about for a while, but no one could come up with anything. We were all like, 'What's happening?' First Kahlil, then Keith.'"

"Who's Kahlil?" Rick said.

"One of the genetics profs. Iranian, worked right here in the center. When he returned to Teheran to visit his mother last fall, he was arrested. The Supreme Leader had issued a fatwa against him for blasphemy."

"Blasphemy?" Laura said. "What did he say?"

Grady shrugged. "Published papers on the genetic basis for male homo-sexuality. He's been in jail ever since. Your brother was really upset."

"Were they close?"

"No. Just the fact that it could happen in this day and age is enough, don't you think? Truth is, he wasn't really close to anyone."

"Yeah," Rick said through a sigh. "Not exactly a warm fuzzy guy."

"Don't get me wrong," Grady said. "No one disliked him, it's just that he kept to himself. He was hard to know. I've worked with him steadily for two years and I don't feel I know Doctor Somers at all."

Laura remembered Rick's assessment of his brother: *There's no there there.* She said, "Was he always 'Doctor Somers'?"

Grady nodded. "Well, not behind his back. Then he was 'Keith.' But face-to-face he insisted on 'Doctor Somers.'"

A distancing thing . . . Laura wasn't surprised.

"Well, Grady," Rick said, "we're interested in anything you can tell us, but we're particularly interested in the monkey."

"Mozi? Well, technically speaking she wasn't a monkey. I mean, at first we all thought she was a new species of monkey when he brought her back, but evolution-wise she predates monkeys."

"It's that easy to bring an unknown species into the country?" Laura said, frowning. "What about diseases and such?"

"It's not easy at all. Easy to get them out—the Mozambicans have all sorts of laws against exporting animals but a little cash passed here and there opens pretty much any door. Not so easy after that. The U.S. has lots of hoops to jump through before letting them in. But we have ways. He housed her at a pharmaceutical company's primatarium on Long Island for the first week or so."

Primatarium . . . Laura hadn't heard the term before but the meaning was obvious.

"Which company?"

"Schelling, I believe."

Rick nodded as if this made some sort of sense. "Okay."

"Anyway, he never even mentioned he'd brought a primate back from Africa. He was home about a week or so when out of the blue he shows up with her. Said she didn't like the accommodations at the primatarium."

Rick shook his head. "Heard of 'Take Your Daughter to Work,' but 'Take Your Monkey'?" Grady opened his mouth to speak, but Rick cut him off. "I know, not a monkey. But in the photo I saw she looked like a monkey to me so . . ."

Grady smiled. "Gotcha. Anyway, he brought her every day. She became a fixture around here."

"How'd that go over?" Laura asked.

"Not so great at first, but Mozi was well behaved, stayed in Keith's office, and won over everybody in no time. It was those eyes, man. People started asking where they could get one like her. And of course, Keith doted on her."

Rick was shaking his head. "My brother with a pet . . . who'da thunk?"

"Yeah. He'd talk to her like he never talked to people. I mean, you'd go to drop off some papers or something and you'd hear him in conversation on the other side of the door. But when you went in, it was just him and Mozi."

Rick said, "Next you're gonna tell me the monkey answered him."

Grady grinned. "Now *that* would have sent me running. Anyway, we kept trying to classify her but she kept defying expectations. Pretty soon we began to suspect that she might be some sort of an adapiform that had somehow survived—a living transitional fossil—the bridge between the Haplorhini and Strepsirhini."

"The what?"

"Sorry. Evolution-speak. Somewhere around sixty million years ago the primates experienced an evolutionary split into the Haplorhini—who evolved into the higher primates such as monkeys, apes, and humans—and the Strepsirhini who became our modern-day lemurs and lorises and such. Mozi had both lemur and monkey characteristics, but more monkey, including grasping hands with opposable thumbs and nails instead of claws; she had a dry nose but she could still make vitamin C."

"Vitamin C?" How odd, Laura thought. "How does that matter?"

"Yeah," Rick added, "and what's a dry nose got to do with anything?"

"When the primate split occurred, the Haplorhine branch—the one that evolved into us—had dry noses as opposed to the wet noses of the Strepsirhini, and they lost the ability to synthesize ascorbate. Monkeys and humans can't make vitamin C; lemurs and lorises—who are in the

Strepsirhine line—can. The combination of features put Mozi in both camps."

"The missing link?" Rick said.

"We don't use that term—we prefer 'transitional species.' But even if we did use it, there's no such thing as *the* missing link. There's a ton of them along the branches of the various evolutionary trees. But yeah, she could have been one of many missing transitional species in the primate-to-hominid chain." He sighed. "But she's gone now and I don't know if we'll ever find another."

Rick shook his head. "Really? There have to be others. I mean, Mozi had to have had a mother and a father, right?"

"Of course, but by all rights Mozi should be extinct. Her species should have died out with the adapiforms and other contemporary primates in the Miocene."

Laura had never been able to keep the various -cenes straight. "How long ago are we talking?"

"Five–six million years."

"But she somehow survived," Rick said. "If Keith found her, why can't someone else?"

"I'm not saying it'll never happen, but Keith's circumstances were a total fluke. He found her in an outdoor market near the town center in Quelimane—that's on the central Mozambique coast. She caught his eye as he was walking by."

"Those big blue eyes, I'll bet," Laura said.

Grady nodded. "Yeah. They're startling. You can find blue-eyed lemurs and cats and malamutes, but Mozi had the biggest blue eyes I've ever seen—proportionally, that is. Keith told me he knew right away something was different about her, beyond her eyes. At first he thought a new kind of lemur—after all, Madagascar is just across the channel—but on closer inspection he discarded that: no grooming claw and no toothcomb."

"You realize that means nothing to us," Rick said.

"Yeah, sorry. It means she was def some type of primate but a very unusual one. He asked the vendor where he found her and he said he'd bought her from a fisherman who'd found her floating off the Madagascar coast. Said he sells lots of animals but had never seen one like Mozi."

"Could she have been trying to swim from Madagascar?"

Grady shook his head. "First off, you're talking hundreds of miles even at its narrowest point. But even if just half a mile, I doubt she's from Madagascar. That place is a biodiversity jewel—ninety percent of its species exist nowhere else in the world. Zoologists have been fine-combing its biosphere for, like, forever. If Mozi's kind had a colony there, they'd have been found by now."

"Well, she had to come from somewhere," Laura said, realizing too late how obvious that sounded. "She didn't just pop into existence."

Rick wiggled his eyebrows. "Or did she?"

"Oh, no," she said. "We're not going there."

"Why not? A species that should be extinct shows up out of nowhere?"

Laura held up a hand. "Stop right there."

Grady looked puzzled. "Am I missing something?"

"Nothing. Trust me." She tried to jump to the heart of the matter. "Did Mozi carry that so-called God Gene?"

Grady's laugh was brief and almost bitter. "We may never know. But oh, man, the ribbing Keith took around here for that. Even though he'd never written or uttered those words, they stuck to him like a graft. All because he'd mentioned miR-941 a couple of times in his book."

Laura remembered that. "Right. I just read a passage about it."

"It's nothing terribly new . . . discovered years ago. But when he described how it seemed to appear *de novo* out of non-coding DNA—"

"Non-coding?" Rick said.

"The layman's term is 'junk DNA.'"

"Okay, that I've heard of."

"The term's passé. It's not junk at all. It accounts for something like ninety-eight percent of human DNA. It doesn't encode proteins but it does produce RNA that has functions. So maybe 'non-coding' may wind up in the dustbin as well. Anyway, the miR-941 gene pops up a few million years ago and plays a pivotal role in human brain development—neurotransmitter signaling, specifically. People read that and blew it all out of proportion, saying it didn't just 'pop up'—*God* put it there. Divine intervention and all that."

"Thus, 'the God Gene,'" Laura said with a glance at Rick. "It's not found in any other primates, right?"

Grady nodded. "Right. But I can think of about twenty other genes that appeared since we split from the chimps. And if you want to go into greater detail, I can get into human copy number variations."

Laura could feel her eyes preparing to glaze over, but said, "Try me."

"Okay. We used to think it highly unlikely that evolutionary processes could produce a functional protein-coding gene from inactive DNA. New genes could only evolve from duplicated or rearranged versions of preexisting genes—what we call copy variations and transposable elements or jumping genes. Then a couple of researchers in Dublin found a number of human-specific genes that arose from non-coding DNA after the split from the chimps. Best of all, they learned that these were more likely to be expressed in recently expanded human brain structures, like the neocortex and prefrontal cortex. Get it? Newer genes connected to the newer parts of the brain."

"So in a sense," Laura said, "they're what make us human."

"Part of it."

"More than one God Gene, it seems," Rick said. "I'm told my brother wasn't happy about that whole God Gene thing."

Another laugh. "That's the understatement of the year. Drove him crazy. But it started him digging deep into the human genome, looking for more genes unique to *Homo saps*. He discovered one similar to miR-941. He designated it hsa-mir-3998."

"Meaning what?" Laura said.

He shook his head and raised his hand into the oath-taking position. "I can't say. He swore me to secrecy—no formal NDA or anything like that, but I intend to honor it. We put in a lot of hours on it. He wanted to nail down its role in the evolutionary process before he went public with it."

Laura had a feeling this was important. "What *can* you tell us about it?"

"It plays a major role in human creativity."

Laura blinked as an epiphany hit her. "Creativity . . . that's huge."

He was nodding, grinning. "Tell me about it. Civilization can't exist without creativity."

Rick said, "That's all you can tell us?"

"'Fraid so. But I can *show* you something."

He led them to his cramped office, where Laura noticed a porkpie hat sitting on his crowded desk. He stepped to a pair of rickety bookshelves leaning against each other and began pawing through a stack of papers that functioned as a bookend.

"It's here . . . I know I put it here. Ah!"

He yanked on a sheet, and as it came free the whole bookcase began to tilt away from the wall. Rick's quick reflexes prevented a bibliolanche. He pushed it back but it wouldn't stay.

"Hold that," he told Grady.

While Grady steadied the bookcase, Laura watched Rick pull a zip tie from a pocket and use it to lash the wobbly case to the sturdier one.

"Thanks," Grady said. "That's been threatening to happen for ages. You always carry zip ties?"

"Thousand and one uses," Laura said, beating Rick to it.

"So what's on that sheet?" Rick said.

Grady showed them a diagram, half printed, half scribbled.

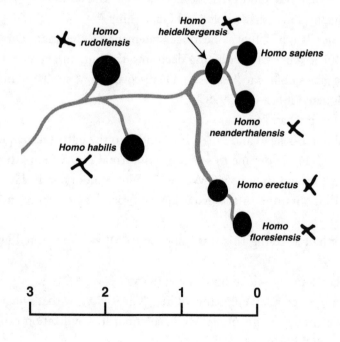

"Are those Keith's X's?"

"Yes. I found this behind his desk. He and I have spent the last year tracing 3998 back through the hominid tree, but I never saw this."

"How far back did you go?"

"We stopped at *rudolfensis*. If we hadn't found 3998 by then, there seemed no point in going further back. We found it only in *Homo sapiens*. Emerged sometime after *heidelbergensis*—post the Neanderthal split, 'cause we didn't find it in *neanderthalensis*."

"Isn't that odd?"

"Yes, and no. Under environmental stress, formally coding genes can stop coding and formerly non-coding genes can start—the now-famous miR-941 is a good example of that. Hsa-mir-3998 is apparently the same. Can't be a hundred percent sure, but we're working on that."

"Under different circumstances I'm sure this would all be fascinating," Rick said, "but it doesn't help us locate him. Is there any way we can check his office computer?"

She knew what Rick was thinking. Maybe Keith had left an email or some record of whoever had forced him into liquidating his assets.

"He kept all his files encrypted—but even if someone knew the key, it wouldn't help."

Laura thought that an odd comment, and then realized why the encryption didn't matter.

Rick was nodding. Obviously he got it too. "Because someone shredded his hard drive."

Grady's eyes widened. "How did you know?"

"His home computer was found in the same state."

Grady looked crestfallen. "I was hoping he'd backed up all our data there. We had everything organized but Keith wanted to go off and think it all through for a while before we started writing. He said he was going to visit the Rift Valley for inspiration. When he returned we would prepare everything for publication. I was going to be the first author."

"I take it the paper was never published?" Laura said.

Grady shook his head. "When he returned he had Mozi with him and she became the focus of his attention. And now the data's gone."

"Gotta be a backup somewhere," Rick said.

"He would never back up to the cloud or to the university servers. Didn't trust them. Worried about an EMP wiping them all out. He'd only back up to optical media."

"DVDs?" Laura said. "Well, where are they?"

Grady looked glum. "I wish I knew. His home maybe?"

Laura shook her head. "We searched it. The only ones we found were video."

"But his computer's not all that's erased," Grady said.

"Oh?"

"No. He wiped all of Mozi's genetic data from the sequencer."

Laura stiffened. Now there was a shocker.

"That doesn't make sense."

"Tell me about it."

Rick said, "Are you sure he ran Mozi's DNA?"

"Absolutely." Grady looked hurt. "But he must have run it when I wasn't around and never told me."

Laura wondered about that. "If it was erased, how do you know he even ran it?"

"After Keith disappeared and we found his hard drive wiped, I searched his office and stumbled on that chart there. When I saw 'Mozi' with a question mark I suspected he might have started sequencing her. I checked the log book and Keith's last run on the sequencer was labeled 'unknown primate.' But the results were gone."

"Don't you back up?" Laura's boss was fanatical about that at the ME's office.

"Of course—to the cloud—but Keith had it erased from the cloud as well, so there's no record."

"What the hell?"

"Exactly what I thought. And I'll tell you something else: He didn't erase it just once, he erased it *three times*."

"You mean he was trying to overwrite it?"

"Sorry, I guess I didn't say that right. The sequencing folks told me that, after the first run, he came back to them all upset, saying they'd botched it. He gave them a second sample from the same primate and made them run it again—but a larger sequence. After he had that one, he returned yet again, even more upset, and insisted they run a *third*, even larger sequence."

"Three? But why?"

"It seemed he didn't believe what he was seeing. And then he came back one last time and stood over the techs until they'd erased the results of all three runs, backups and all."

"That's allowed?"

"They said he was scary . . . looked crazy. And he's one of the bosses, so they did what they were told. When I saw the date of the sequencing I realized that was when he changed."

"Changed? Changed how?"

"He became, I don't know . . . distracted."

Rick shrugged. "Wasn't he always distracted?"

"In social situations, or a conversation like this, sure. I mean, he was a terrible conversationalist. But when he had a problem to solve, well, I've seen him put in fifteen-hour days, sometimes even more. His focus was incredible. But all of a sudden he couldn't focus at all."

Laura was baffled. "Why do you think he was upset with Mozi's genome?"

"Who knows?" Grady said with a shrug. "I've been through his desk and there's nothing there. And if he left any notes on his hard drive, they're shredded. I'd love to ask him."

Rick said, "Do you think he was expecting this 3999 thing to be there and got all bent out of shape because it wasn't?"

"It's 3998, and it would have been super if it had been there, but that's highly unlikely. Besides, I doubt 3998 was even on his mind. He seemed to have forgotten about it since his return with Mozi. Most likely he was running her genome so he'd know where to place her on the evolutionary tree. Taxonomy was his specialty, after all. I can't even guess what the problem was, but the sequencing crew said he looked positively spooked."

"Spooked?" Laura tried to imagine that . . . and failed. "What could spook you about a genome?"

Rick was giving her that look. "How about something that wasn't supposed to be there."

Laura was *not* going there. "It was just DNA. Nothing spooky about combinations of base pairs."

"Still," Grady said, "that was the word they used: 'spooked.'" He looked at his watch—an old Mickey Mouse model, Laura noted. "Hey, I've got a meeting." He grabbed the porkpie from his desk and plopped it over his topknot. "I'll show you out."

"Before we go, do you remember the date he got 'spooked'?" Rick said.

"No. But I can find out in a sec." He leaned over his desk, barraged his keyboard with a series of lightning strokes, then squinted at the screen. "February twenty-fourth. Why?"

Rick pulled out a pen and a pad of yellow sticky notes and scribbled something. "Just keeping track."

Grady led them down to the first floor and onto Waverly Place.

"If I can help in any way," he said when they reached the sidewalk, "just call me here."

And then he was off, skinny jeans and all. They stood and watched him go.

"I'd have liked to have spent some time searching through Keith's office," she said.

"Sounds like his colleagues have picked it over pretty well."

"Yeah, I suppose. Still . . ."

He was staring at his notepad.

"What?"

"Keith runs Mozi's DNA on February twenty-fourth. Six days later, on March second, he starts liquidating his assets. By the twenty-third all his dough ends up in the Caymans. April first—just nine days after that— is the last time anyone ever sees him. So in the course of one month he goes from a rich and famous—and 'spooked'—zoologist to a missing person."

Laura shook her head. "Well, that's spooky right there. But what does it mean?"

"It says to me that Mozi and his disappearance are linked."

"But how?"

"Don't know. But I do know I need lunch." He pointed to a sandwich shop on the corner. "Let's give that a try."

Laura shrugged. She could do with a bite.

Inside, the food prep area was exposed to view. Laura took one look and pulled Rick back outside.

"Something wrong?" he said.

She didn't say that it looked like the kind of place petri dishes went to feel clean. "I'd like someplace quieter." She spotted a bar across the street with a sign advertising *Food and Fine Ales*. "How about there?"

"Sold."

Inside, the White Oak Tavern was all dark wood walls and floors and tables arranged around a big horseshoe bar. It felt new but the sconces and the wrought-iron chandeliers with their frosted globes looked like holdovers from the gaslight era. A young woman in a black apron led them to a window table with a view of Waverly Place, directly across from something called the Torch Club. A blonde dressed exactly the same dropped off menus and took drink orders—an iced tea for Laura and a Pabst for Rick.

"Pabst?" she said. "I didn't know they still made that."

He grinned. "Never stopped. Did your father drink PBR?"

"He was a Mormon, remember? But I remember the kids at college guzzling lots."

"The right price for college kids. Grady made me yearn for one. You know: When in Rome . . ."

"Well, where are we—really?" she said. "How do you feel about all this?"

"'Feel'?" he said, picking up the menu. "Rather think than feel. And now I think more than ever that Keith's little monkey is at the heart of this whole deal."

"No question. Especially after that story about erasing Mozi's genome from the sequencer. How bizarre is that?"

"Very. But Keith's mind never worked like other people's."

She glanced at the menu—soups, salads, sandwiches, and entrées. "That's to be expected with someone on the spectrum, but Grady said 'spooked.' Said it twice. Spectrum or not, what could spook a grown man, a scientist, no less, about that little monkey's DNA?"

"Not a monkey, remember?"

"Oh, I remember, all right. I'll rephrase: What could spook your brother, a guy who was sequencing DNA up and down the line, what could spook him about that particular little primate's genome?"

Rick banged his fist on the table, earning a few stares. "Damn, I wish I knew genetics!"

Laura understood his frustration. "Don't feel bad. I studied it in medical school and everything they taught me is obsolete. We've learned so much in the past decade, and the pace of discovery keeps accelerating. Unless you work with it every day and keep up with the journals, you're left in the dust."

"So you're saying neither of us knows enough to figure out what spooked him?"

She nodded. "Exactly. If he'd left a copy of Mozi's genome on his computer and you showed me a printout, I'd be at a loss to tell you what was wrong with it. But I know people who could."

"'Wrong with it' . . ." Rick shook his head. "How could a primate's DNA be 'wrong'? And wrong enough to spook you?"

Laura had been thinking about that. "What if it showed some sort of defect in Mozi's genome, something that would doom her to a premature death?"

Rick gave his head another shake. "If you had some emotional attachment to the monkey, sure you'd be upset. But that wouldn't make you erase all the data. Pretty obvious Keith didn't want anyone else to see what he'd seen. But why not?"

The waitress returned with the drinks and Laura asked for the crispy brussels sprouts while Rick ordered the pulled pork sandwich.

As the waitress left, Laura had an awful thought. "What if Keith killed Mozi to keep her genome a secret?"

Rick's lips twisted. "Thought of that. But not likely with the way everybody says he doted on her." He went silent for a few heartbeats, then shook his head again. "Doesn't jibe. He wouldn't have to kill Mozi to keep her genome secret—just keep anyone else from sequencing her DNA. Which would be easy enough to do."

"Then why is she dead?"

"The zillion-dollar question."

They lapsed into silence. Rick broke it with: "Grady said Mozi had been kept at a lab for a while."

"A primatarium."

"Why don't we make that the next stop?"

Laura couldn't see it. "What for?"

"It may be a wild goose chase, but I'm figuring one of the vets there must have examined her. Maybe he can tell us something."

"Or *she*," Laura said.

"Or she."

Their food arrived.

Rick looked askance at her plate. "Brussels sprouts? Really? My mother used to make us eat those when I was a kid. Hated them."

"So you said the first day we met."

"I did?"

"Uh-huh. You told me you didn't like dogs, cats, children, spectator sports, or brussels sprouts."

He looked embarrassed. "Well, I make an exception for Marissa in the children category, but I stand firm on the sprouts."

"Your mother probably boiled them. These are roasted with olive oil and asiago. Try one."

"No, thanks. I'll pass."

She pointed her fork at him. "Try. One. Now."

Making a face, he speared one of the halved sprouts and popped it into his mouth. A chew. Another chew. And then his face lit.

"Hey, these *are* good."

"See?"

He quickly speared and devoured two more, then came back for thirds.

"Hey," she said, pulling her plate away. "Leave some for me. You've got your pulled pork."

"Which *you're* gonna try."

"Nope. I don't think I could eat anything that was 'pulled.'"

He sipped his beer. "You need to loosen up. You don't like baseball because the players spit, you don't like—"

"Can we not talk about spitting while I eat?"

"Sorry. Yeah, let's get to it. Grady mentioned Schelling Pharma. Our dad used to work for them, so no surprise at the choice. But they're global. All over the place. Where did Keith house Mozi? I should have asked."

Laura realized she couldn't put off seeing Emilie any longer.

"Well, our hipster pal is off to a meeting," she said as Rick raised his sandwich, "so we'll save that for tomorrow?"

He looked at her over his *bitus interruptus*. "You've got someplace you need to be?"

"Yeah."

2

NORTHPORT, NEW YORK

Laura managed to put off telling Rick about the *ikhar* until they reached the VA hospital, but couldn't hold out any longer. If she couldn't trust him about this, she couldn't trust anyone.

"You know the friend I visited here yesterday?" she said as he pulled into a parking spot.

Her voice sounded as shaky as her insides. She clasped her hands to stifle the tremor that had started. It had to have worked—*had* to.

"Something wrong?"

"I sneaked her a dose of the *ikhar* during my visit."

He jerked upright in his seat. "What? How—?"

"It came Tuesday."

"Why didn't you say something?"

"I'm saying it now."

He unlatched his door. "Let's go. I'll walk you inside."

"I thought you didn't—"

"This is different—way different."

She sat there. She'd been dying to know all day, had wanted a firsthand look, and now the moment had arrived. So why was it so hard to get out of the car?

Rick opened her door, took her hand, and helped her out.

"You still don't believe, do you."

"It's hard."

"I know," he said softly. "I know."

He took her arm as they crossed the parking lot and held the front door for her.

"Just follow my lead," she whispered as she slipped past him into the lobby.

She didn't recognize the receptionist at the desk—maybe twenty, short-short black hair, tiny stud above her left nostril—but noted the odd spelling on her nameplate: *Gale.*

"Hi. I'm Laura Fanning. I was volunteering here yesterday and forgot my reading glasses."

Out of the corner of her eye she caught Rick's raised eyebrow but didn't acknowledge it.

Gale smiled and said, "I'll check the lost-and-found box."

"If I left them anywhere, it would be in Emilie Lantz's room."

The receptionist froze. "You visited Emilie yesterday?"

"Yes. I read to her once or twice a week."

Gale looked agitated. "How—how was she when you left?"

"Same as always." Laura put on a puzzled look to hide her growing excitement. No doubt about it: *Something* had happened. "Is anything wrong?"

"No . . . yes . . . no. I mean, she's cured!" Her words came in a rush. "Okay, I shouldn't say she's cured because nobody's said she's cured yet but what else can you call it? They found her walking up and down the hall outside her room this morning screaming for everyone to come see!"

Laura had to lean against the counter for support. *Yes!*

"Standing? She couldn't even hold up a paperback when I left her."

"I know, right? Yet she woke up completely cured. It's a miracle!"

Miracle . . . how many times had she heard that word in the past couple of months?

"Can I see her?"

Gale checked her computer screen. "She's on her way to radiology. They're running *scads* of tests on her. You know—MRIs, labs, the works."

I'll bet, Laura thought.

Disappointment dampened her elation. Though it should have been enough to know that Emilie had been cured, a part of her needed to *see* her on her feet. But she hid it.

"Okay, I'll come back later."

"Don't you want me to check for your glasses?"

"They can wait."

Laura suddenly wanted out of here. But as she turned toward the door, an unfamiliar voice rang through the lobby.

"Laura! *Laura!*"

She turned to find a grinning Emilie being pushed down the hall in a wheelchair by an aide. She motioned to the aide to stop. And then she levered herself to her feet.

"Can you believe it?" she cried, grinning as she stood with spread arms. "Can you *fucking* believe it?"

"Oh, god!" was all Laura could manage before her throat locked.

And then she found herself hurrying down the hall as Emilie stumbled toward her. They wrapped their arms around each other and both began to sob.

Finally Laura broke the clinch and wiped her eyes. Had to appear clueless . . .

"Emilie . . . what . . . how?"

"I don't know! Nobody knows! And you know what? I don't care!" She laughed. "Maybe it was that apple juice you gave me yesterday!"

No, no, no! Laura didn't want her even joking about that. Be cool. Go with it . . .

"Well, I . . . I left the bottle for you. If that's it, maybe you can spread it around to the other patients."

Another laugh. "Maybe I will!"

"Excuse me, ma'am," said the aide. "I'm supposed to have you in radiology."

"Okay, okay." Emilie squeezed Laura's hands. "We'll have to get together after I get out of here."

"Yes, def," Laura said, knowing she couldn't let that happen. She might let something slip.

They exchanged waves as Emilie was wheeled away; then, all wobble-kneed, she returned to the lobby. Without waiting for Rick, she hurried out the door and across the parking lot. She was aware of him close behind her but more aware of the pressure building in her chest. The door locks popped as she approached the pickup, but before she could climb inside, she burst into tears.

"You okay?" Rick said as he came up beside her.

She nodded and waved a hand for him to give her a moment, then leaned against him and sobbed. His arms went around her and she clung to him. And kept clinging after she'd regained control. It reminded her of that night in Kirkwall when they'd both had too much to drink. Where would they be now, relationship-wise, if they hadn't been interrupted? As much as she liked the clinch, she finally pushed away.

"Sorry."

"No apology necessary."

"I'm not usually this emotional. It's just . . ." Her throat tightened again. "It's just so wonderful to see her on her feet . . . cured."

Rick stared at her. "After all you've seen, you're still surprised?"

Good question. She'd witnessed two impossible cures back to back in the Stony Brook PICU, so why had Emilie's hit her like a runaway train?

"Well, the *ikhar* could've spoiled in transit."

A dubious look. "That really it?"

"I mean, the possibility was in the back of my mind." Way back. "Okay, I admit it: I can't help it. There's no question that it works and yet I can't wrap my mind around the reality of it. All science and reason says it can't work, and yet it does."

A wry smile. "Well, if it's gonna cause you such torment, maybe you should just flush the next dose down the toilet."

"You know damn well that's not going to happen."

"I do. But more importantly, how are you going to keep it secret?"

"By changing the places where I volunteer. I've got months to find my next 'patient.'"

"Just be careful," he said, his tone now grave. "Someone connects the dots, life as you know it is over. If people think you have a supply of the real panacea—and once that thought gets in their heads, convincing them otherwise will be damn near impossible—they'll hound you to the ends of the earth."

The truth of that made her stomach crawl. Because Marissa would be involved as well. But she couldn't discard a panacea. Too many desperate people out there . . .

"I'll be careful."

"Great. And meanwhile . . ." He tilted his head back and thumbed his nose at the sky.

She had to smile. "That's for the vast, cool, unsympathetic intellects out there?"

"You got it."

Early on she'd dismissed Rick's wild theory that sapience was so rare in the universe that it attracted attention—the wrong kind. As a result, humans had become the playthings of "intellects vast, cool, and unsympathetic"—a phrase he'd snagged from H. G. Wells. He claimed the panacea—the *ikhar*—had been created by these intellects to throw a monkey wrench into all of humankind's concepts of a knowable universe by breaking all the rules.

Ridiculous, right?

But that blithe certainty had been turned on its pointy little head. After seeing the *ikhar* cure a raging viral meningitis, a cardiomyopathy, and now end-stage MS, she had to wonder if maybe it had truly originated, as Rick put it, *outside*.

Like a little blue crab dropped into a tropical fish tank.

Laura had yet to buy totally into Rick's scenario, but just for fun she mimicked his gesture.

Rick gave her shoulder a friendly squeeze. "Way to go. But 'intellects, vast, cool, and unsympathetic' is kind of unwieldy, don't you think? They need a handy acronym, so I've settled on 'ICE.'"

"ICE . . . meaning?"

"Intrusive Cosmic Entities. They even have a theme song." He hummed a stuttering bass line.

"That's not . . . ?"

"Uh-huh," he said, nodding. "'Ice Ice Baby.'"

Laura couldn't help laughing. She never knew what to expect from Rick.

"Feeling better?" he said.

"I wasn't feeling bad. Not really. Just a lot of pent-up emotion. When Clotilde said she'd be sending me an occasional dose, I never realized the burden it would carry. It means every so often I can dramatically change the course of a life for the better, provide a future where there wasn't one. The responsibility is . . . daunting."

"Yeah, but Clotilde knew what she was doing. She chose a healer."

"Some healer. One who works with dead people."

"One who's been hiding behind dead people. Time to enter the land of the living."

Which was just what she intended to do.

FRIDAY

May 20

1

MAPUTO, MOZAMBIQUE

"It's settled, then?" Amaury said after they'd tied up the *Sorcière*. "You will be here on this very dock first thing Sunday morning."

Marten Jeukens nodded as he hefted his duffel bag's strap onto his shoulder. "I have business later today and tomorrow, but if all goes well, I'll be here bright and early on Sunday."

Business . . . Amaury wondered just what that might be. Nothing connected with their island, he hoped. All along the 1,100-kilometer route from Toliara the Afrikaner had seemed to spend more time on his satellite phone than off it, always near the bow or the stern, out of earshot. Whatever he was cooking up, he didn't want Amaury to know about it.

But Amaury had been doing a little cooking of his own. He'd come up with a scheme that would allow him to corner the market on these little monkeys. All commerce was ruled by supply and demand. Low supply and high demand pushed up the price. So the key was to control the supply. This would be easy when he first brought the creatures to market, but after a while, exclusive access to the island wouldn't matter. Inevitably other dealers in exotics would buy a male and a female from him and start breeding their own. As the supply rose, competition would put downward pressure on prices.

So Amaury had come up with the idea of selling only males at first. This would not hurt the population on the island because a single male could impregnate many females. Later, as the profits started rolling in, he would import females and sell them only after he'd had them spayed.

But while selling the first primates, and establishing a market for them, he would start a breeding program. He knew from experience how labor intensive that could be with simians, but he couldn't predict how long he'd have access to the island. He might have years, or maybe only a few months. It all depended on how fast the UN acted once it got wind of a new species that might be endangered. Usually it reacted slowly, but one never knew. He must be prepared in the event his source was shut down.

At times Amaury couldn't help being amazed by his own brilliance.

But what was Jeukens up to?

Amaury took solace in the fact that the Afrikaner had seemed sincere when he'd said he didn't care if the monkeys were put on the market.

"I will tell you honestly, *monsieur*: If you are not here on the dock Sunday morning, I must leave without you. I will regret doing so, but you must understand that I cannot let too much time pass. Who knows if someone else might stumble across the island?"

This did not seem to faze Jeukens in the least. In fact, he seemed somewhat distracted, as if this "business" he was off to was suddenly more important than the island he had been so intent on finding.

"'Don't think twice, it's all right.'"

Amaury had to smile. "Even I know that one! But—"

"Truly, do not give it a second thought. If I'm not here, by all means, sail without me. I will catch up with you."

With that he stepped onto the dock and walked away without a backward glance.

I will catch up with you . . . ? How did he intend to do that? Hire a speedboat?

A secretive, sinister fellow, this Jeukens. Amaury would give much to know what was going on inside that bald head.

2

"You're late," Laura said as Rick unfolded himself from the driver's seat of his SUV. She'd been feeling a little anxious waiting for him. Rick was never late.

"Got lost."

"Ever hear of Waze?"

"Waze is for wimps."

Rick had offered to pick her up but she'd thought that a ridiculous waste of time. He lived to the northwest, in Westchester, over an hour's ride to Melville, while she lived another thirty miles farther east. They'd decided to meet in the Schelling parking lot.

"I got delayed at home as well," he said. "Thought the fact that my father had been a Schelling executive back in the day would open doors, but seems nobody here's ever heard of him. He worked at the corporate headquarters in Switzerland so I guess I shouldn't be surprised."

"But you did get us in, right?"

He nodded. "Yup. Managed to talk my way through to their vivarium and the gal there remembers my brother and Mozi. She's heard about Keith's disappearance and seems eager to help."

The Schelling Pharma research facility was one of many nondescript functional buildings occupying a huge industrial park just off the LIE. The Schelling structure was a three-story layer cake of alternating bands of red brick and mirrored glass.

The receptionist found Rick's name on her list and called the vivarium. A few minutes later a chunky young Asian woman in a lab coat exited an elevator. She had a blinding smile and wore her black hair in a short bob with razor-sharp bangs.

"Hi, I'm Mitoki Toda," she said, extending her hand toward Rick. Her English was accent free. "You're Doctor Somers's brother?"

"That's right. And this is Doctor Laura Fanning."

She gave Laura's hand a quick shake, saying, "DVM?"

"No. MD. Call me Laura. You're a vet?"

She nodded. "Call me Mito." She turned to Rick. "You don't look at all like your brother."

"I take after my father," he said, as if that should mean something.

Mito led them to the elevator and pressed the down button.

"As I said on the phone, I don't know what I can tell you about Doctor Somers. I only met him maybe half a dozen times, and then only briefly. He was hard to get to know. Kind of shy, y'know?"

"We know," Rick said. "But we're now more interested in his monkey."

"Well, you really can't call it a mon—"

"Sorry . . . primate."

"Did he ever classify it?" Mito said as the elevator stopped. "When he first arrived with Mozi he wasn't sure if she was a simian or prosimian. I mean, she had features of both."

"We don't know," Laura told her. "His records . . . aren't available to us."

Mito led them down a tiled, fluorescent-lit hallway. "I'd sure like to know. I combed through my entire NHP database while Mozi was here and—"

"NHP?"

"Non-human primates. We never see exotics in our primatarium."

"So Mozi was . . . refreshing?"

Mito nodded. "We've got some squirrel monkeys and spider monkeys, but almost ninety percent of our primates are macaques. So yeah, Mozi was refreshing. And so *cuuuute*. Those big blue eye didn't miss a trick. I was sure I could nail her species, but she didn't fit anywhere. Something would always be off."

"You keep the animals in the basement?" Rick said as they walked along.

"Uh-huh. Best place. No windows. If one gets loose, there's no way to get out except the elevator and stairs, which are always closed off."

She pushed open an unmarked door and ushered them into a small spare room with an oblong table and a half dozen chairs. A sink, a microwave, a Keurig, and a small fridge completed the furnishings.

"My office is too small to seat three, so we'll use the break room." She indicated the chairs. "Have a seat. I can offer water, coffee . . ."

Laura and Rick both declined.

"I've got to say I'm confused," Mito said. "I mean, you said you're more interested in Mozi than your brother."

Rick grimaced. "I guess I didn't phrase that right. We're looking for Keith but have almost nothing to go on. But we think the monk—Mozi might be somehow connected to his disappearance."

She looked surprised. "How can that be? I mean, you do know she's dead, right?"

"We do," Laura said. "But we don't know why or how. Are you aware that he had it cremated?"

"Well, yeah, seeing as I did it for him."

Laura sensed Rick stiffen. "*You* cremated Mozi? You have a crematorium here?"

"Of course. We go through a lot of animals in our research."

Laura felt a tingle of excitement. "So you saw her corpse. You wouldn't happen to know how she died, would you?"

"Doctor Somers wouldn't give me any details, but I could tell from the way her head dangled that her neck was broken."

Now they were getting somewhere. Or were they?

"Any idea how that happened?"

"Doctor Somers was too upset to talk about it."

"You think he might have been responsible?"

Mito shrugged. "I can't possibly say, but I seriously doubt it. He loved that little thing. And if he somehow was responsible, he sure regretted it. He was on the verge of tears the whole time."

Rick was staring at her. "Keith . . . on the verge of tears . . ."

"No question. I tried to talk him out of the cremation, you know. I mean, Mozi being a unique species and all that, but he wasn't buying. He kept saying, 'I must. I must.'" She shook her head. "Such a shame. I really would have liked a look at her brain."

Laura hadn't expected that. "Her brain? Why?"

"Smart as could be. In fact . . ." She popped from her chair and headed for the break room door. "Looks like we're gonna wind up in my office anyway. It's the only place I can show you."

"Show us what?" Rick said as he grabbed the door and held it for Laura.

"Mozi in action."

They made a right turn into another hallway where she led them to a door labeled *M. Toda, DVM.*

She wasn't kidding about the size, Laura thought as they followed

Mito into her cramped office: a littered desk against a wall, teetering bookshelves, and one extra chair, its seat piled with journals.

"Excuse the mess," Mito said. "You can see why I brought you to the break room."

She seated herself before the widescreen monitor that dominated her desktop, brought it to life, and began typing.

"I call this *Mozi's Greatest Hits*," she said.

As Laura squeezed behind Mito's chair, the screen lit with a grainy black-and-white view of a small, spare, dimly lit room with barred cages arranged on a shelf that ran along the three visible walls—one cage per wall. She froze the frame and rotated her chair to face them.

"Let me set it up for you. Down the hall we have a quarantine room where we separate sick animals from the general population. We test them and treat them if we can, and either return them to their fellows if they get better or sacrifice them if they don't."

"Sacrifice . . ." Rick said, his expression grim.

"A common euphemism. Sounds better than 'kill.'"

Rick nodded. "Akin to 'terminate' or 'sanction.'"

"I guess. You watch a lot of spy movies?"

A wry smile. "Yeah, sorta."

Laura said, "Does it ever bother you? The animals, I mean?"

Laura couldn't help remembering the dog she'd operated on in med school and finally had to sacrifice. Even though it was unconscious under heavy anesthesia, it damn near ripped her heart out when she'd tied off its main coronary artery.

Mito shrugged. "It did at first. But my job is to see that they stay healthy and are treated humanely. You can't romanticize them, or anthropomorphize them."

"Hard not to when we share common ancestors."

"Look, they play an indispensable part in saving hundreds, thousands, sometimes millions of human lives."

Laura raised a hand: peace. "Don't misunderstand. I'm not challenging the value of your work. Just having an emotional reaction."

"No problem. I understand perfectly. But back to Mozi. Doctor Somers somehow got her out of Africa and dropped her here for quarantine."

"Is that standard procedure?" Rick said.

"We have an arrangement with NYU. There are various ways to bring an animal in under the radar. I don't know what route Doctor Somers took, but he did the responsible thing by quarantining her."

"How long?"

"A week. We did blood tests, checked her stools for parasites, the usual. All negative. But on the second day of her stay, a tech came in and found that a granola bar she'd left on the counter had been opened. The wrapper had been chewed and torn, and the bar partially eaten. The door had been locked as always and Mozi was the only occupant. Her cage, however, was latched just as it should be."

"A locked-door mystery," Rick said. "I can already see where this is going."

"You have no idea." Mito turned and clicked on the screen. "Schelling keeps the whole building under surveillance, especially the vivarium areas. Animal rights activists are a constant threat. So I accessed the CCTV recording of the quarantine room. First check out this tech fixing Mozi a meal."

A young bearded man in a white coat slices fruit on a counter to the right. He scoops the slices into a tray and slips it through a slot into one of the cages on the left. Then he rinses the knife and puts it in the drawer below the counter.

"That's Mozi's cage on the left. Now we cut to hours later."

The image shimmers and it's the same scene, except a bar of some sort lies on the counter. A few seconds of no motion, then a tiny black hand snakes through the bars of the cage door and fiddles with the latch. Seconds later the door swings open and a tiny monkeylike figure with a long bushy tail hops to the floor.

Laura said, "I assume that's not so unusual for a primate like that. Their hands are very human."

"It's rare. But we're not through here. In fact we've only just begun. Watch."

Mozi scampers across the floor and lithely hops up on the opposite counter where she grabs what looks like a candy bar and begins biting the wrapper. She tears it open and takes a nibble off the bar, puts it down, then begins exploring the room. After returning to the bar for a few more bites, she scampers back to her cage.

Mozi hops back into her cage and closes the door after her. Then a little hand appears through the bars and resets the latch.

"See that?" Mito said, her voice rising with enthusiasm as she froze the recording. "A certain percentage of primates who manage to get loose will return to their cages, others won't. No big deal. But I've never seen or heard of one spontaneously closing and relatching the door from inside."

"Almost as if she was hiding her trail," Laura said.

"Exactly, although I find it hard to credit her with that level of cognition. My best guess is that she was simply returning her environment to its previous state. But she seemed so at ease with working the latch that I decided to try an experiment. Before we locked up the room for the night, I wired the latch shut and left another granola bar on the opposite counter. This is what happened . . ."

The same room with no sense that time has passed. Again, a little black hand slips through the bars; it fiddles much longer with the latch this time but eventually the door swings open and Mozi emerges. Jump cut to Mozi returning to the cage, relatching the door and fiddling with the wire.

"I cut out the middle with her eating and wandering around," Mito said, freezing the screen and rotating again. "But did you see what she did?"

Rick said, "It looked like she was trying to rewrap the wire around the latch?"

"Exactly. She did a poor job, but the point is she *tried*. I was stoked now. So I added a combination lock to the cage—nothing fancy, just a simple three-number model like you'd use on a school locker. I made sure we opened it and relocked it half a dozen times each day so she could see how it worked."

"Was she watching?" Laura said.

"Ohhh, yeah. She'd press her little face against the bars and watch with those big blue eyes, studying every move."

"I'm guessing she learned to open it."

"Not right away. That night the video showed two little hands poking through the bars working furiously at the dial but to no avail. But the second night . . ." She hit a few keys and the video began to race. "I'm fast forwarding through the first night and taking you to the second."

Two little black hands grip the combo lock and twist the dial this way and that until the latch pops open. The lock is pulled loose and drops to the floor.

"Incredible," Rick said softly. "She memorized the numbers."

"I don't think she has any concept of numbers. Probably more like pattern recognition. But she remembered the patterns in the proper sequence, and that's saying plenty about her intelligence. But wait, as the commercials say, there's more."

Mozi tears open the granola bar, takes a nibble, then leans over and pulls out the drawer beneath the counter.

"Now watch this," Mito said. "Here's where it becomes even more interesting."

Mozi extracts the same knife the tech used and, after a little trial and error, slices a couple of pieces off the granola bar. She returns the knife to the drawer, eats the pieces, then hops back to her cage.

"She learned how to use a knife?" Laura said.

Mito nodded. "Just by watching the tech every day."

"That's a little scary."

"Depends on how you look at it. I told Doctor Somers about it when he came to visit her and he was fascinated. He said he'd kept a padlock on her cage from the start so her getting out had never been an issue."

"So a padlock is the answer?" Laura said.

Mito nodded. "But that didn't stop her from trying to stick a piece of straw in the keyhole. Show me a chimp or gorilla doing what she did and I wouldn't be terribly surprised. But this is a tiny prosimian. She weighed in at less than two pounds. Relatively speaking, she had such a tiny brain. That's why I wish I could have had a look at it."

"What do you think you'd find?"

Mito shrugged. "Who knows? At the very least I could have compared it to other simians or prosimians of equal size. You know, encephalization quotient and such, see if certain areas of Mozi's brain were more developed than in comparable primates."

"Well, maybe another Mozi will pop up."

"I hope so. And I hope it's Doctor Somers who brings her in."

"Amen to that," Laura said. She was finding herself less interested in Mozi's brain and more interested in the effort Dr. Toda had put into her video. "Did he see *Mozi's Greatest Hits?*"

"Well, no. Not in this form. I showed him some raw footage on his visits."

"It must have taken you a while to assemble everything."

"Yeah, kind of." Was that a blush creeping into Mito's cheeks? "After editing it down I copied it to a disk for him and was going to send it to him, but then he showed up with her dead. He seemed so upset. I was heartbroken too. I mean, I'd only spent a week with her but I got to know her and we kind of bonded. Anyway, I . . . I didn't think it was the right time to give him the disk, and then he disappeared."

"Wait," Rick said. "You've mentioned how he'd visit Mozi?"

"Yes. She was really attached to him, and vice versa. He doted on her, bringing her treats and playing with her. Whenever he'd leave she'd sulk in the corner of her cage for hours." She looked from Rick, to Laura, and back. "Nobody has any idea where he is?"

"We have people following some leads," he said, "but nothing yet."

She bit her upper lip. "You think there might have been, you know, foul play?"

"We hope not." Rick pulled Hari's yellow pad from his pocket. "Say, do you remember the day you cremated Mozi?"

"Not off the top of my head, but I keep a log." She banged at her keyboard and a grid appeared. After a few seconds of studying it she said, "March thirtieth. Why?"

He made a note. "Making a timeline."

"Look, if there's any way I can help," Mito said, "any way at all, just let me know."

Sensing her sincere concern, Laura gave her a gentle pat on the shoulder. "We will. And thank you for your time. *Mozi's Greatest Hits* was fascinating."

Mito guided them back to the elevator. As soon as the doors pincered closed, Laura said, "I think your brother has a secret admirer."

Rick's eyebrows lifted as he flipped through the sticky pad. "Mito? Yeah, maybe," he said with a distracted tone.

"What've you got?"

"Well, today's takeaway is that at least now we know Mozi's really dead."

That surprised Laura. "You had your doubts?"

He shrugged. "Never take anything at face value. I confess it crossed my mind that Keith may have wanted everyone—including whoever might have been coercing him—to *believe* she was dead. His making such a public show of disposing of her ashes had me a little suspicious."

"But now . . . ?"

The doors opened and they stepped into the ground-floor lobby.

"Now we have an eyewitness account—the word of someone who knew Mozi from before, and who did the actual cremation. So she's truly gone, probably from a broken neck."

The broken neck had been bothering Laura since Mito had mentioned it. It didn't sit right, but she couldn't say why.

"Okay. We learned that Mozi was a very clever little primate and that she's dead."

"'Not only merely dead, she's really most sincerely dead.'"

Was the Munchkin coroner reference for her benefit? She let it pass. "What's our next move?"

Rick shook his head, his expression baffled. "I'm tapped out of ideas. Guess we'll have to wait until Hari finds the end of the money trail."

"And then what?"

"And then I go find the money. If Keith's got it and wants to stay off the grid, fine. That's the way it'll be."

"And if he's . . . ?"

"Dead? I'm counting on him being alive."

"But if he's not?"

"I'll bring back what's left of him, then go after whoever killed him."

"And then?"

"Depends."

"On what?"

"On a lot of things. I'm playing this by ear, one step at a time. Don't want to get too far ahead of myself or get locked into anything. Let's just say all options are open." He looked at his watch. "Gotta run."

"Stahlman?"

"Yeah. Wants to hire some new security guys. Needs me to background them."

Laura had been hoping to grab some lunch with him again.

"Something wrong with his old security guys?"

"Nah. Since his cure he's putting new irons in the fire one after another. He—"

His phone rang. As he listened, his usually controlled expression ran through a variety of emotions. The only real words he uttered were, "South Africa? No kidding." Then, "Okay. We'll be there. You call Paulette."

He hung up and turned to Laura.

"Hari's gal Casey has tracked down the transfer from the Cayman account. It went to a bank in Johannesburg."

"South Africa?" Laura said, realizing Rick had just said the exact same thing.

He nodded. "She wants us all to meet in her office tomorrow. Casey should have lots more info by then."

3

MAXIXE, MOZAMBIQUE

A dangerous fellow, this buyer-man.

Mahdi Mahdi knew little about him beyond his first name—Marten—and a guess that he was South African. But Mahdi had sensed the danger the instant he laid eyes on him. Dangerous . . . not desperate-dangerous like the *badaadinta badah* he worked with far up the coast in Somalia. This bearded bald man was crazy-dangerous.

But then again, he shouldn't be surprised. Who but a crazy and dangerous man would want to buy what Mahdi was selling?

Mahdi's father had started out a poor fisherman on the Galmudug coast who came to earn a much better living after he joined the local band of *badaadinta badah*. Mahdi grew up among the pirates, but his father made him go to school and would beat him if he neglected his lessons. So Mahdi learned many things. One was a smattering of English. Which was why he had wound up here with this crazy-dangerous Afrikaner.

Mahdi was not a violent man but he had come prepared with a five-shot .32-caliber revolver—not a terribly deadly weapon, but effective at close range. He'd never had a chance to reach for it, however. As soon as he'd entered this cinder-block box of a house on the western edge of Maxixe, the crazy-dangerous Afrikaner drew a much bigger pistol and shoved it in his face.

"Empty your pockets onto the table," he'd said in a voice Mahdi recognized from their numerous phone conversations over the past few days.

With shaking hands he complied, producing his revolver and knife along with his phone, money clip, and the keys to his rented truck.

"You weren't planning on using that, were you?" the buyer-man said, gesturing to the revolver.

He spoke too rapidly for Mahdi. "From our phone calls you know my English is poor. Please say again."

The buyer-man repeated, slowly this time.

Mahdi shook his head. "Only defense. I did not sail all this way to shoot you."

"Sail?"

"In my dhow."

"Why didn't you drive?"

"Too many borders."

"Ah, yes. Of course. Considering your cargo, that was a wise choice." He pushed the keys back, adding, "You'll get the rest on your way out."

The Afrikaner shoved his own pistol into his belt and stared at Mahdi.

"What?" Mahdi said, feeling uncomfortable.

"I believed I was dealing with Somali pirates. You don't look like a pirate to me."

"We are not pirates. We are coast guard. *Badaadinta badah* means 'savior of the seas.'"

"Spare me your euphemisms."

Mahdi did not know this word but let it go. The Afrikaner's dismissive tone exposed his contempt. A white man who thought he was better than the black man. He'd encountered such before.

But he was right in a way. Mahdi was not a true *badaadinta badah*. He belonged to the local group but had never boarded a freighter. He left that to the whooping warrior types with their Kalashnikovs and their speedy little skiffs. His work began when they returned with their loot and their ransom money. He sold or traded off the former and hid the latter.

Some of that loot sat in the truck outside. He'd never thought he'd be able to dispose of it, but then weeks ago whispers began filtering up the coast of a man who might want to buy "pesticides" in bulk. Normally Mahdi would have ignored them, but the whispers mentioned a preference for a product of "Syrian origin."

Mahdi knew exactly what the man was looking for, and could supply it.

During the revolt, under pressure from the UN, the Assad government started reducing its stockpile of chemical weapons. They kept their stock of chlorine, not banned in itself except when used as a weapon, but shipped off their organophosphates for storage in ally states.

Some of Assad's supply had wound up as loot in the hands of Mahdi's band of *badaadinta badah*. It seemed a good idea at first, but everyone became afraid of it. And if the Al-Shabaab madmen roaming the Somali countryside ever got their hands on that poison, only Allah knew what horrors might follow.

Mahdi and his fellows had buried the canisters and tried to forget about them.

But Mahdi remembered where and made contact with this stranger. They'd settled on a price—a remarkable five thousand U.S. each for two canisters. The buyer would call back with a delivery date. All good. Not only would the canisters go far away from Somalia and Al-Shabaab, but Mahdi would make a handsome profit along the way.

Then, four days ago, a call from the buyer with a time and place for delivery. Mahdi had set sail immediately. And here they were . . .

"Well, let's see what you brought me," the Afrikaner said.

He led the way outside to where Mahdi had parked his rented 1994 Toyota pickup next to the buyer-man's newer but equally dirty SUV. The squat house stood on an overgrown wooded lot surrounded by stinkwood and bushy ironwood trees. A hundred feet away, a dirt road ran by the far end of the unkempt driveway.

Mahdi untied and lifted the blue tarp that covered the bed, revealing two aluminum canisters painted dark green. Each had two sealed ports on the top end.

"They look like beer kegs," the buyer-man said. "How do I know they're not filled with Heineken?"

Mahdi had never seen a beer keg. He was a Muslim, yes, though not devout. Still he did not drink alcohol.

"They are not beer. They each contain one hundred liters of very strong VX."

"So you say. But you're charging me ten thousand dollars U.S. for fifty-some gallons of liquid, and I have only your word that it's VX." He gestured to the canisters. "Where are the biohazard symbols?"

"I painted over them—in case I was stopped."

The buyer-man nodded as if this made sense.

Mahdi was looking at the canisters as he spoke and noticed that some of the paint had scraped off right over a yellow biohazard icon. He pointed to the scratch.

"Look. You can see there. Just a bit of the symbol."

"Maybe so. But it still doesn't mean there's VX inside. I'm going to need proof."

Mahdi's gut clenched. Proof? He didn't like the sound of that.

"How do I prove it?"

The buyer-man's smile held no humor. "You do not prove anything. I prove it to myself. Oh, and by the way—where is the rest of my purchase?"

Mahdi pointed to the Toyota's cab. "Hidden under the front seat."

"Good. We'll get to that later. Wait here."

He stepped back through his front door. Mahdi guessed it was a rental house—perhaps rented just for this meeting. Even the poorest hut in his home village showed more personalization than this place. The buyer-man reappeared clutching a flimsy plastic shopping bag. He walked around to the side of the house and returned almost immediately with a cage. A large brown rat circled within.

"Maputo is a wonderful city," he said. "You can buy almost anything in its back-alley bazaars." He gestured to one of the canisters. "Open it."

Mahdi backed away. "No! I will die!"

"All right then, just loosen it. I'll do the rest."

"No . . . I . . ."

The big gun reappeared in the Afrikaner's hand. "If you don't open it, I can't test it. And if I can't test it, I'll have to assume it's not VX, which means you're trying to cheat me. No one gets too curious about a gunshot in this neighborhood."

Not seeing any alternative, Mahdi broke out in a sweat as he stepped toward the truck. He reached over the tailgate and placed both hands around one of the large, boltlike plugs screwed into the top of the nearest canister. His moist palms slipped a few times before they finally caught and he felt the bolt give a little turn. He turned it again, then backed away.

"It is loose."

Wearing bright yellow dishwashing gloves which he must have pulled on while Mahdi was working the bolt, the Afrikaner unscrewed it the rest of the way and dropped it on top of the canister. Then he pulled an odd plastic tube from the shopping bag.

"Never seen one of these before, I bet," he said, holding it up.

A rubber bulb was attached to one end of a ten-inch plastic tube that tapered almost to a point at the other.

"No, I—"

"It's a turkey baster. Do you have turkeys in Somalia?"

Mahdi didn't know this word "turkey" so he shook his head.

The Afrikaner dipped the end of the turkey baster into the canister and suctioned up enough VX to fill half the tube. It looked like water. Mahdi prayed it was the real thing, that he hadn't been duped.

The buyer-man pulled a clear plastic bottle from the bag. He transferred the VX to the bottle then firmly fastened a spray attachment to the top. He tossed the baster aside and adjusted the nozzle to a thin stream.

"There," he said, holding up the bottle. "A history lesson for you: Organophosphates were originally developed as pesticides, but reclassified as weapons of mass destruction once they proved as deadly to mammals as insects. The most toxic nerve agent ever synthesized, and it's odorless, colorless, tasteless." He smiled. "Do you know what 'LD-fifty' means?"

Mahdi shook his head, his mouth so dry he could not speak. Finally, he managed a "no."

"It's a scientific term. 'LD' stands for 'lethal dose.' A chemical's LD-fifty is the dose at which fifty percent of the test subjects die. Can you guess the LD-fifty of VX for human beings?"

Mahdi shook his head.

"Don't even want to try?"

He shook his head again.

"Ten milligrams." He hefted the spray bottle. "Spray just ten milligrams of this innocent looking stuff on a hundred humans and fifty of them will die."

Without warning, he directed a stream through the wire mesh at the rat, pumping the handle three times, soaking the fur on its left flank.

"There. That was more than enough to kill a human. The rat doesn't have a chance . . . *if* this is VX." With his free hand he pulled out his pistol again and stepped back. "So . . . either the rat dies or you do."

Knowing his lifespan depended on what happened next, Mahdi trembled as he watched the rat in horrid fascination.

"H-how long will the VX take?"

"Not long. It's quickly absorbed through the skin. But I hate to call it VX." He turned to the cage. "Dear rat, you've just been sprayed with O-ethyl S-two-diisopropylaminoethyl methylphosphonothioate. Isn't that a beautiful name? Why settle for a colorless abbreviation like VX when the full name has so much more character?"

Mahdi had no watch and wished he could check his phone to keep track of the passing time, but it sat on the table inside. He would leave it if he could and buy a new one in town. He wanted very much to be far, far away from this man.

The rat began to twitch.

"See? The acetylcholinesterase blockade is spreading, causing uncontrolled muscle contractions. After a series of normal contractions, the supercontractions start, effectively paralyzing the victim."

The rat's breathing became rapid. Soon it was trembling all over.

"Eventually the supercontractions hit the diaphragm, and when the diaphragm stops working . . ."

Suddenly the rat went into a prolonged fit—Mahdi had seen an epileptic seizure once and this was much like that, only worse. It ended in the stillness of death.

Mahdi let out a long, slow breath. The VX had worked . . . horribly. What an awful way to die, even for garbage-eating vermin.

"Seems like you brought me the real deal," the buyer-man said. "Lucky for you."

Mahdi asked the question he hadn't dared ask himself. "What do you plan to do with two hundred liters of this?"

"Do?" The Afrikaner gave him that long stare again. "I'm going to save the human race . . . save it from itself."

Mahdi had been right about crazy-dangerous. The words of a madman.

"I do not understand."

"You wouldn't. It's complicated. As is our present situation."

Mahdi didn't like the look in his eyes. "W-what do you mean?"

"I mean, you know I have this weapon of mass destruction. At least that's what the UN calls it. If you rat me out"—he nodded toward the still form in the cage—"and I use the term advisedly, I'll spend the rest of my life rotting in a Mozambique prison."

Mahdi backed away. "I would not do this! I brought it here! I will rot right beside you!"

"Good point. Still . . ." He raised the spray bottle.

"No! Please!" His bladder threatened to empty. "My people! They know I am here! They will come for you!"

Not true. His local *badaadinta badah* had no idea where he was, or why. They had abandoned the VX, so Mahdi had considered it his for the taking. This was a private side deal. But the threat seemed to make the Afrikaner think.

"Maybe you're right," he said. "You're just as guilty as I. And I don't want to have to go about my business constantly looking over my shoulder for pirates."

Mahdi's knees bent but didn't buckle. His bladder unclenched.

"You are a cruel man."

The Afrikaner shrugged. "Not really. Just cautious. And to that end, I'm going to need a little insurance . . ." He pulled out his phone and motioned Mahdi over to the truck. "Lower the tailgate and stand there."

The Afrikaner stepped back and took his picture with the VX.

"Good. Now load it into the back of my car."

The canisters were heavy but Mahdi managed to place both of them in the back of the SUV.

"Give me my money," he said, his voice shaking as he slammed the gate shut. "I want to leave."

"Our transaction isn't quite complete. Bring the rest inside and we'll settle up."

Mahdi grabbed the package from under the Toyota's front seat and followed the Afrikaner into the house. The crazy man pulled a manila envelope from a drawer in the table.

"It's all here, but feel free to count it."

Mahdi wanted to do just that, but the urge to be away from this man was stronger. He pointed to the table.

"Give me my things."

The Afrikaner took the small revolver, emptied the shells from the cylinder, then pushed it and the rest across the table.

He smiled and said, "A pleasure doing business with you."

Mahdi hurried out and gunned the pickup down the driveway at reckless speed. He wanted to be far, far from this man as quickly as possible. Ten thousand U.S. for something he'd wanted to be rid of anyway had seemed like such a wonderfully profitable opportunity. Now he wished he'd never heard those "pesticide" whispers.

The two hundred liters of VX were bad enough, but Mahdi had also sold him two bricks of C-4 and four detonator caps.

What was this madman planning?

SATURDAY

May 21

1

THE MOZAMBIQUE CHANNEL

Abilio Batalheiro steered his Hummingbird north along the Madagascar side of the channel. The twenty-year-old copter was cruising five hundred feet above the waves at a comfortable one hundred miles an hour. No need to climb higher over open water like this.

Toliara lay behind to the south. And ahead . . . who knew?

Abilio had learned to fly in Mozambique's Air Defense Force, and after an honorable discharge in 2011, he had invested all his savings plus some borrowed cash in this used Hummingbird. Now he eked out a living making express deliveries and ferrying passengers—mostly government officials—up and down the central coast.

Over the years he'd flown some strange charters, but this might be the strangest: the three passenger seats full—one with a human, the other two with heavy aluminum canisters—all headed nowhere.

Well, not exactly nowhere. The passenger had given him GPS coordinates, saying they would find an island. But Abilio knew the names and locations of all the islands of the Mozambique Channel, and knew they'd find nothing there. Granted, he'd never flown this area of the channel, but why would he? Why would anyone? The Madagascar coast held little of interest along these latitudes. No one came here because it offered nothing but open water.

His fare, a thin, gruff, bearded Afrikaner named Jeukens, had shown up late yesterday afternoon at Inhambane Airport looking to hire a helicopter he'd heard was available for charter. He'd arrived by taxi after ferrying across the *baia* from Maxixe in a single-sail dhow. With three kilometers or so by boat versus a roundabout sixty-kilometer car trip, most chose the water route. He wanted to be flown to an island at a specific set of coordinates. Abilio had assured him there was no island there but the man had insisted.

No point in arguing. The man was paying cash, and an all-day charter like this was rare, so Abilio shrugged and took his money. You wish to charter a flight to nowhere? *Bom.* Abilio will take you.

Jeukens had arrived on time at first light this morning, but not in a taxi. He'd driven the long way around with the two canisters in the back of his SUV. Abilio had asked him what was in them but he'd brushed him off, saying they were part of a scientific experiment that he wouldn't understand. No matter. Cash was cash.

Abilio helped him load them aboard and strap them into the rear seats. The Afrikaner sat in the front passenger seat with his backpack on his lap, his skinny arms tight around it as if loaded with gold.

They'd taken to the air and flown directly into the sunrise, straight across the channel to Toliara on Madagascar's west coast.

Officially Abilio's Vertical Hummingbird 260L had a range of 375 miles; by moderating his speed he could squeeze 400 out of the tank if need be. Toliara was a solid 500 miles from Inhambane Airport, however. No way could he make that with the Hummingbird's standard equipment.

But years ago he'd fitted his bird with a twenty-gallon auxiliary tank that extended his range an extra 130 or so miles. So, after topping off both tanks in Toliara, he and the Afrikaner had headed north.

His passenger's voice crackled in the little speakers of Abilio's headset. *"There it is. What did I tell you?"*

The unmuffled roar of the Hummingbird's six-cylinder engine along with the chop of its whirling blades made normal speech impossible. Even shouting was only sporadically effective. Headsets connected through the dashboard were the only way to go.

Directly ahead of them an island that should not exist had appeared on the horizon. Well, live and learn, they say.

"My apologies, *senhor.* I have learned something today. We are over a neglected corner of the channel. I had no idea this place existed."

"And now that you've seen it, find us a place to land."

"I do not see a place on this side. We'll fly around the island and see if we can find a beach that—"

"I've been all around it and there is no beach worth mentioning! We have to find a place to set down inside."

Abilio wasn't sure that would be possible. The closer they got, the more greenery he was spying beyond the upper edge of the wall.

He pointed to the blades rotating above. "Those span thirty-three feet. I have put this craft down in a fifty-foot courtyard, but that was under still conditions, and was not easy even then. We do not know what sort of updrafts and downdrafts and crosswinds we'll encounter inside."

" 'The world little knows or cares the storms through which you have had to pass. It asks only if you brought the ship safely to port.' "

"Pardon?"

"A quote from Joseph Conrad. Now . . . get me on the ground."

Abilio descended toward the island. The closer they approached, the greater his dismay. Yes, a volcanic island, but its caldera appeared choked with greenery—not brush but trees. That was bad enough, but then he recognized the unique configuration of the branches.

"Oh, no," he groaned. "Baobabs."

Jeukens jerked forward and stared through the windscreen. *"What? Are you sure?"*

"I believe so."

As they flew closer, all doubt disappeared.

"You're right," Jeukens said. *"And not just any baobabs*—Adansonia grandidieri. *Imagine that. They're endangered on Madagascar, and yet here . . ."*

"Yes, your island is full of them—*packed* with them."

Jeukens glanced at him. *"My island . . . if only it were so."*

Abilio knew then that his craft would not be landing on that island.

This baobab—this *Adams grandi* or whatever the Afrikaner called it—was like no other tree in the world. Its big smooth trunks, thick as the concrete columns supporting a highway overpass, grew to a height of eighty or ninety feet, with all their branches splayed at the top. Looking down now, Abilio could see nothing but broad, flat leaves forming a thick canopy over the entire caldera, obscuring everything beneath.

Jeukens pointed. *"There! An opening!"*

Abilio saw it. A hole in the center of the canopy. He approached, slowed, and hovered over it. And then he saw the reason: a lake.

It made sense. The low point of the caldera was near its center, and all the rain eventually collected there. And of course, since the baobabs couldn't grow in water . . . an opening. But with no pontoons, not useful to him.

Abilio moved on, and in no time the Hummingbird had traversed the small island. He banked around for another pass, slower this time. But no help. No place to land.

"No," Jeukens said, his voice hushed but audible through Abilio's headset. *"This can't be. It can't. There has to be—"* He twisted in his seat. *"You have a winch. We can use that."*

"That is for rescues."

As one of the few private helicopters in all of Inhambane Province, his Hummingbird was often called on to aid in sea rescues when Mozambique's Naval Command was delayed or simply not available. He'd often used the winch to haul up shipwrecked fishermen.

"Excellent. It's going to rescue this trip. How do I get into the harness?"

"Senhor, you cannot do this."

"I certainly can. You'll lower me to that wide section of the rim, and I'll climb down to the base of the caldera. Then you'll lower a canister through the branches to me at the point where you last saw me. I'll release it from the harness and we'll repeat the process. Simple."

"Simple" was not the word for it. Simple*minded,* maybe. *Insane* was much more accurate.

Despite Abilio's protests, Jeukens started to unfold the harness.

"It will be easier without your backpack," Abilio said.

"Oh, no," the Afrikaner said with a quick shake of his head. *"This stays with me."*

Abilio glanced at the fuel gauge. The main tank registered half full.

"Listen to me, *senhor.* We can spare maybe thirty minutes here, but absolutely no more before we have to head back."

"Thirty minutes should be fine."

"It will have to be. I know of no place to refuel between here and Toliara. So set your watch. I will sound my air horn when it is time. If you are not on the rim when I blow my horn, ready to be hauled up, I will leave without you."

Jeukens blinked. *"You'll abandon me?"*

"I will have no choice. We cannot escape the fact, *senhor*, that if my chopper ditches because it has run out of fuel, we both will die."

Jeukens looked at his watch and nodded. *"No escaping the cold equations, I guess. All right. Let's get to it then."*

He removed his headset and hat, then slipped into the harness. Sliding back the door on the passenger side, he clutched his backpack and eased out of his seat until he was standing on the landing runner. With his bare scalp gleaming in the sun, he glanced down at the narrow rim of the caldera. A sick-scared look slackened his features and Abilio felt a surge of hope that he'd lost his nerve and changed his mind. Abilio couldn't blame him. The top of the ledge was uneven and only three meters across at its widest.

But by the time he raised his head, his expression had hardened.

His lips moved as he pointed down. Abilio couldn't hear him, but the meaning was clear. He started the winch. Jeukens spun slowly on the way down. When the winch line played out—it didn't take long since it ran only fifty feet—Abilio had to lower his craft. Finally Jeukens's feet touched down on the rim. He released the catches on the harness and gave a thumbs-up.

Abilio hit the up button on the winch and watched Jeukens start to pick his way down the inside of the island wall. When the harness retuned to door level, he pulled it inside.

A gentle breeze was flowing out of the southeast, and the updraft from the island wall was minimal—helpful, really. Abilio steadied the chopper with his knees while he wrapped the harness around one of the canisters. He wondered what it contained. Some sort of liquid, certainly, but what?

No matter. A scientific experiment, Jeukens had said. Abilio wasn't into science—beyond aeronautics, of course.

He pushed the harnessed canister out the door. He had an instant of panic when it made a crazy tilt and he feared it might slip free. But no, it held.

He began lowering it over the spot where he'd last seen Jeukens. When it made contact with the top of the rim, he eased the chopper forward and let the canister descend through the baobab leaves. When the winch cable reached its end, he descended until his skids were just above the leaves.

The downdraft from the whirling blades set them into furious motion, clearing a view to the ground below.

Abilio was shocked to see that the caldera was much deeper than he'd expected. The outer wall was maybe twenty feet from sea to rim, but inside was easily three times that. The canister dangled close to a smooth, thick baobab trunk, but a good thirty feet off the ground. Abilio could descend no farther, and the trunk offered no branches for Jeukens to climb.

And where was Jeukens, by the way?

He waited. And waited.

What could he be doing? The fuel level was reaching the critical stage.

Movement to the right caught his eye. Jeukens was standing on the rim, waving for Abilio's attention. He looked furious. He kept making angry downward motions which Abilio took to mean *Lower it closer to the ground.* Abilio responded with gestures of helplessness and then slapping his hand against the winch cable.

Finally Jeukens seemed to grasp that the cable had played out to its end. His shoulders slumped in defeat for a few seconds, then he motioned Abilio to come closer. Abilio took this to mean *Bring the canister to me.*

Leaving the winch cable fully out, Abilio ascended slowly. The last thing he wanted was for the canister and its harness to become snagged on a branch. Once it cleared the leafy mantle, he eased it toward Jeukens, who was able to grab it and free it from the harness.

With the canister sitting on the rim, the Afrikaner began making wind-up and wind-down gestures while pointing to the copter. Abilio finally got the message: *Lower the other canister.*

No problem. Let's get this done and head back to Toliara.

As the cable wound up, Abilio wrestled with second canister. Damn, but it was heavy. When he started fastening the harness, he came face-to-face with an area where the paint had been scraped away, revealing . . .

His mouth went dry as he squeezed his eyes shut for a moment, then looked again. No doubt about it . . . the biohazard symbol.

What had he got himself into?

He scraped away a little more paint and saw a chemical formula he didn't understand. But he did understand the two letters printed beneath it: *VX*.

He almost dropped the canister. He'd heard of VX. Back in 2010, the U.S. Army had come in for joint military training operations and he'd spent half a day listening to lectures on chemical weapons. Among those mentioned was a deadly neurotoxin known as VX. The name had stuck with him because of its simplicity.

With sweaty, shaking fingers he tightened the last strap and pushed the canister out the door. Immediately he jabbed his thumb against the down button and watched with relief as it descended toward the waiting Jeukens.

What could the Afrikaner want with such a huge amount of neurotoxin? What was he planning? Certainly not mass murder—not out here on a deserted tropical island.

He held his breath as Jeukens grabbed the canister, eased it to the ground, and freed it from the harness.

What now? Was he going to try to carry them down to the bottom of the caldera?

Apparently, yes. Jeukens moved one of the canisters to the edge by rocking it back and forth on its rim. He lowered himself over the edge, then tried to hoist the canister onto his shoulder—and almost fell backward in the process.

The man was mad even to consider carrying that deadly poison down the cliffside or anywhere else on his back. Jeukens appeared to come to the same conclusion. He scrambled back up to the rim.

A glance at the fuel gauge showed the tank reaching the point of no return.

Abilio grabbed the air horn, held it out the window vent, and pressed the button. Its deafening blare could be heard even over the roar of the rotors.

The Afrikaner's head snapped up. He waved Abilio off—he needed more time.

Impossible!

Abilio sounded the horn again, longer this time.

Below, Jeukens went into a rage, stomping about in fury, waving his arms at the trees in the caldera and shaking his fists at the hovering helicopter.

Suddenly, to Abilio's shock, he kicked the nearer canister, sending it toppling into the caldera. Then he turned the second onto its side and rolled it over the edge where it disappeared into the leaves.

For a moment he stood on the edge, hands on hips, panting. Then he grabbed the harness and started slipping into it.

Abilio felt sick and sweaty. He'd had no idea he'd been transporting liquid death. If one of them had leaked, even a little . . .

He was tempted to jerk the Hummingbird upward, spilling Jeukens from the harness and leaving him here. But he couldn't bring himself to do that. So he held steady until the Afrikaner gave the thumbs-up signal for ascent.

As he awaited Jeukens's arrival, he gazed out over the island's leafy canopy and was shocked to see it alive with life. Little monkeys clung to the branches, hundreds of them, maybe a thousand or more, all staring his way with big blue eyes.

He was aware of the Afrikaner's arrival, mouthing incoherent curses as he clambered aboard, but Abilio paid no attention. The combined gaze of all those eyes transfixed him.

"*Damn you,*" Jeukens said after he'd strapped himself into the seat and replaced his headset.

Abilio pointed ahead. "Look. Do you see?"

The Afrikaner's angry expression slackened when he saw the monkeys. "*Yes, I see.*"

"Did you know they were here?"

He nodded. "*I knew. But I never realized how many.*"

"They're watching us."

"*They're always watching. Let's go.*"

"And why should I be damned?"

"*Because your winch has half the cable I needed.*"

"It is a rescue winch. I have no need of a longer cable. And you never told me you needed to use the winch."

"*I didn't know about the trees. If only I'd known about the trees . . .*"

As Abilio ascended and turned the copter south, he noticed something. "Where's your backpack?"

"*I left it.*"

"I thought you said it 'stays' with you."

"*That's all right. We're coming back.*"

Not *we*, Abilio thought. Not in my bird. Abilio wanted nothing more to do with this madman.

"No. I have no wish to come back here. It is too dangerous."

The Afrikaner gave him a curious look. "*You mean those little primates? No, they're not dangerous.*"

Should I say it? Abilio thought.

Yes, he had to bring it up. No civilian should possess VX—not even governments were allowed. He watched the Afrikaner's expression closely as he spoke.

"I mean the toxin—the VX. You pushed those canisters over the edge. One or both of them could have burst open. Any living thing that comes in contact will die."

He saw Jeukens stiffen, then relax. Another look, longer, less curious.

"*Whatever gave you the idea that was VX?*"

"I saw the biohazard symbol."

Jeukens shocked him by bursting out laughing. "*Oh, that!*"

"It is not funny, *senhor.*"

"*Well, yes, I'd quite agree if the canisters really contained VX. But they don't.*"

"How is that possible?"

"*The VX belonged to Syria and its disposal was overseen by the UN. But no one wants to waste excellent aluminum canisters like those, so they were cleaned and sterilized and put to better use.*"

Abilio didn't know if he could believe him. He knew he *wanted* to believe he spoke the truth—the thought of being so close to death was unnerving— but wanting had never made anything so, at least not in his life.

"*Be sensible,*" Jeukens added. "*I know what VX is. I would not be so reckless and downright foolish as to strap that sort of poison into a helicopter seat directly behind me. I value my life more than that.*"

Be sensible . . . What the Afrikaner said sounded logical. But still . . .

"You had me very frightened."

Jeukens laughed and clapped him on the shoulder. "*I'm sure I did.*"

"But you pushed them over the edge."

He sighed. *"What else could I do? They're nontoxic and I couldn't leave them on the rim. A storm could knock them into the channel and carry them away."*

Abilio remembered something Jeukens had said a few moments ago. "You say you are coming back?"

"Yes. Very soon. If you won't bring me, I have an offer by boat. I wasn't going to take it, but now I see I have no choice."

"This 'research' you are doing . . . does it have something to do with those monkeys?"

"Yes. That is why I would appreciate it if you did not mention the island to anyone just yet. Once I've finished my work, you may tell everyone."

Abilio didn't know anyone who'd care, except maybe as a curiosity. "Your work . . . it is important?"

"Extremely important. It will preserve the course of human history."

Preserve . . . an odd word to use. Most people would say their important work would *change* the course of human history.

Ah, well, what was important was that the Afrikaner was returning to the island. That was extra proof that the canisters held nothing toxic. No one would willingly return to the vicinity of a possible VX spill.

Well, nobody sane.

2

MAXIXE, MOZAMBIQUE

Abilio's phone read 11:48 as he stepped off the dhow that had ferried him across the *baia* from Inhambane. The tide was out and he had to climb a few extra steps on the ladder up to the top of the quay.

A long, strange day. After the initial torrent of words from the Afrikaner, the rest of the trip had passed in silence. What a relief to set the Hummingbird down at Inhambane Airport. Once the rotors had stopped, Jeukens had simply got out, paid the rest of the charter fee in cash as agreed, and walked to his SUV. No handshake, no thank-you for the safe trip.

Abilio had watched the taillights speed south and disappear into the darkness, then he'd set about cleaning out his copter and bedding her down for the night. He would give her a thorough inspection before taking her up again—she needed an oil change among other things—but that could wait until tomorrow. He was tired and she wasn't going anywhere tonight.

It had taken time for a taxi to answer his call, and more time to track down one of the ferrymen to take him back across once he reached the long Inhambane quay.

The ferry trip had given him time to think about the Afrikaner, his cargo, and the new island. Abilio had promised to say nothing about its location, and he would honor that. But what about those canisters? He wasn't sure he believed Jeukens about their not containing VX. It seemed logical they wouldn't—why would he bring a deadly toxin to a place where he wanted to study the wildlife?

Still, maybe he should make discreet inquiries among his old superiors in the FADM to see if any whispers about VX were in the wind.

The concrete quay was dark and deserted as he strolled toward the whitewashed Terminal de Passageiros da Maxixe on the shore. He lived in a rented apartment only a half dozen blocks away. The streets were empty, with only an occasional car or motorbike passing. Even on Saturday night most people here did not stay out late.

He had just passed the post office when he heard the scrape of a shoe on the sidewalk behind him. He turned and saw a silhouetted figure pointing something at him. He started to cry out as a tepid stream splashed over his face and neck, some getting in his mouth. No taste but it felt oily on his tongue and his skin. He spat and wiped it away.

"That's right," the figure spoke in English. "Smear it around, and get it on your hands as well. The more surface contact, the better."

Abilio recognized the voice. "Jeukens?"

"Keep rubbing, Abilio. It will work quicker that way."

Quicker? What would work quicker?

And then Abilio knew.

"*Ah, não! Não VX!*"

"Afraid so. You were right. And you've just been sprayed with it."

Abilio cried out but his tongue wouldn't respond, and his throat seemed locked. His cheeks were bathed in sweat as the muscles of his face began to twitch.

"I didn't want to do this," Jeukens said. "Truly, I didn't. But you left me no choice."

Abilio retched, then vomited the water he'd drunk on the dhow ride over. His legs would no longer support him and he crumbled to the ground.

Air! He couldn't breathe, couldn't draw air!

"Your diaphragm is seizing up now, Abilio. It won't be long. I didn't want to hurt you. You seem like a good man. We could have gone our separate ways, but it's just terribly bad luck that you recognized that canister. You must understand that I can't risk you talking about it. Not when my work is so important."

Abilio's vision was fading as Jeukens leaned over him.

"Do you have any children? We never did get around to discussing family. Well, if you do, your children and your children's children would understand. If they knew the holocaust I'll be preventing, they might even thank me for silencing you."

The Afrikaner's face faded as darkness roared in.

SUNDAY

May 22

1

MAPUTO, MOZAMBIQUE

There he is, Amaury thought as he watched the bearded figure stride down the wharf. Still the Indiana Jones hat and his skinny arms sticking out of his sleeveless safari jacket. The black duffel on his shoulder looked new.

"*Bonjour,*" Amaury said as Jeukens reached the *Sorcière*'s dock. "Right on time."

Jeukens seemed tense. He'd already glanced over his shoulder twice since he'd appeared.

"Is something wrong, *mon ami*?"

"What? No, nothing."

And now a third look back.

"I was wondering whether you'd show."

Jeukens stared out over the channel where the as yet unseen sun was starting to ignite the horizon. "You said to be here at first light Sunday morning. Sunrise is six thirty, so here I am."

"*Bon,* let us get you aboard and settled."

Jeukens handed his duffel across, then stepped onto the deck.

Amaury hefted the bag, surprised at the weight. "What do you have in here?"

"A tent and food."

"We have tents and food."

"I didn't know if you had a tent for me, and"—he winked—"I already know what your food is like."

Amaury laughed. "The more food, the better! As a matter of fact, my two helpers, Bakari and Razi, are in town stocking up. You will meet them soon."

Jeukens gestured to the two holding cages that crowded most of the aft deck space. "It appears you're planning on bringing back a lot of the little creatures."

"Depends on how plentiful they are. I want to be prepared if we find a large colony."

"I'm willing to bet you'll find more than you ever imagined. But where are the traps?"

Amaury pointed toward the foredeck. "Up there, under that tarp. Live traps, of course. They fold flat for transport."

"Spring doors?"

"Exactly. Designed to catch raccoon-size animals so they should have no problem holding our little primates."

"If I were you I'd worry less about their fitting inside and more about their staying in the trap until you can get them to your transport containers."

This bothered Amaury. "What do you mean?"

"They're smart and adaptable. They learn very quickly."

"Ah, but the cages are strong and the wire mesh is tight."

Jeukens was smiling. "We'll see. You're going to export all males at first, I assume?"

A smart one, this Afrikaner.

"Yes. Mostly. That leaves the females to continue breeding."

"And keeps your competitors from establishing their own breeding pairs, right?"

"Exactly. Do you have a problem with that?"

"Not at all." Another wink. "And I don't think the males you leave behind will have a problem with it either."

They both laughed at that, but the Afrikaner's bonhomie was out of character. His smile seemed forced and faded quickly. Another glance back toward the city.

"How much longer before we leave?"

"As soon as my men get back. Not long. Is everything all right, *mon ami*?"

"What? Yes, fine. I simply wish to be off. It's been my dream to see those primates in their natural habitat, and we're wasting time."

What was wrong with Jeukens? He looked as if the hounds of hell might be sniffing after him. What had happened since he left here Friday? Amaury had no idea, but he was sure it couldn't have been good.

2

MANHATTAN, NEW YORK

Laura glanced at her watch. The things were becoming obsolete, what with people using a phone as their primary timepiece, but she'd yet to join the iCult. She kept her phone in a pocket or her purse rather than adoringly clutched in her hand like a holy relic. Her watch read 2:11. Hari had set the meeting for two sharp.

"Your mother's late."

"Surprised?" Rick said, staring out Hari's window at Twenty-second Street below.

"She could be stuck in traffic."

"Yeah, probably it." He turned and stepped toward her, a sardonic twist to his lips. "Sunday traffic is such a bitch in the city."

She understood what he was saying: Laura had breezed in from Long Island via the Queens-Midtown Tunnel, and Manhattan's infamous crosstown traffic had been virtually nonexistent. She imagined Rick had had it just as easy from Westchester.

"My, my, aren't we crabby this morning."

"Speaking of crabs," he said, "let's check out Pokey."

Together they strolled toward the huge, virtually empty aquarium. Casey stood there with her back to them, feeding the crab.

As they approached, Laura said softly, "When you mentioned 'crab' I expected another crack about your mother."

He grunted. "Guess I didn't think of it. But this is just like Paulette. She's the client so she knows Hari won't start without her. The rest of us can just cool our jets and like it."

Laura shook her head. Rick had such a sore spot where Paulette was concerned. His moments with her were not his finest.

"You know," she said, "this meeting is all about her missing son."

"Exactly. So wouldn't you think she'd be on time?"

"Maybe she's worried, maybe she's afraid she's going to hear something she'd rather not know."

Rick stared at her. Obviously he hadn't thought of that. He nodded once and said, "Point taken."

They reached the tank with its sand, stones, and crystal clear water. Casey was feeding its single occupant, Pokey the blue crab, from the heel of a sub roll.

"No tuna today?" Rick said.

"Pokey eats pretty much anything," Casey said, turning. "Especially loves carbs. Hey, you hear about Staten Island last night?"

"How could I not?" Laura said. "It's all over the news." Fifty bodies shot, stabbed, and/or mutilated in some abandoned building in the kills. "The world's gone mad."

"And then that toxin downtown?" she said, turning. "What's going *on*?"

Her straight blond hair and bangs were as platinum as ever. She was dressed in skinny jeans and a *Midwich* sweatshirt.

"Wait a minute," Rick said, pointing. "You're kidding."

She grinned. "After you asked me if I was from Midwich I googled it and almost screamed when I saw the movie stills. Those village kids could have been Peter and me as children! Well, except for the glowing eyes. So I had to have a shirt made. Got one for Peter too. We wore them to a bar Thursday night and you wouldn't believe how many people got it. And I'm thinking, why didn't *I* get it when you said it?"

Laura was about to ask what on Earth she was talking about when Paulette entered.

"Sorry I'm late," she said as she strode in. "The car service couldn't find the house."

"Hail, hail, the gang's all here," Hari said, rising behind her desk. Her sari today was bright green. "Everybody take a seat and I'll let Casey fill us in on what she's discovered."

Paulette stopped in the middle of the room. "Nothing too bad, I hope."

Hari said, "Nothing directly about Keith, if that's what you mean. This is only about the man who's got his money."

Paulette looked relieved and Laura realized she'd been right about her being worried about her son.

She sat on the loveseat and Rick and Laura each took a chair. Casey picked up a yellow legal pad from Hari's desk and leaned against it as she began to speak.

"I was finally able to track down the transfer from the Cayman account. It went to the Market Street branch of the First National Bank in Johannesburg. The account holder is named Marten Jeukens." She looked around the room. "Anyone ever hear of him?"

With a baffled expression, Paulette gave her head a vigorous shake. "Never. And I'm sure I'd remember a name like 'Jeukens.' Who is he? And how does someone from South Africa force my son to give him all his money? And what did he do to Keith?"

"'Who is he?' is the most important," Rick said. "Answer that one and we may not have to answer the rest."

"I don't understand."

"Keith may have wanted to disappear and created a new identity named Marten . . ." He glanced at Hari. "What was that name?"

"Jeukens. Think of 'jukebox.'"

"Right. Jeukens."

"I think I can help there," Casey said. "Marten Jeukens is a real person."

"Oh, dear," Paulette said, her lower lip trembling. "I was so hoping it would be Keith."

Laura's heart went out to the older woman. The trail appeared to be coming to an end.

Rick's eyes were growing stony. "Details."

Casey said, "Well, I was able to cull a lot of information from the target account in First National. Once I snagged his tax number—the South Africa equivalent of a Social Security number—I was able to track him down." She checked her yellow pad. "He's forty-four years old, lives in a wealthy Cape Town suburb with his wife of seventeen years and two daughters."

Cape Town . . . Laura remembered watching footage of great whites chasing seals down there during *Shark Week*. But . . . "If I remember, Johannesburg is a long way from Cape Town."

"I was just about to bring that up," Casey said. "And you're right. Something like nine hundred miles. But we're talking a lot of money."

"Got anything else?" Rick said.

Casey consulted her pad again. "Well, he's got no criminal record and he's well off: owns a company called Jeukens Plastic Extrusion Molding. It makes what are described as 'plastic tube enclosures.'"

"Meaning?"

Casey was smiling when she looked up. "He makes those little caps for toothpaste and other tubes. And he sells a ton of them."

"Bullshit!" Rick said.

"I'm not kidding. Hey, somebody's got to make them."

"Not that." Rick shot to his feet. "The idea that this is a guy who could reach damn near halfway around the world to force Keith to liquidate his assets and send the cash to him." He shook his head. "Uh-uh. Doesn't wash."

The same thought had been running through Laura's head. "I agree. He sounds like a stable, upstanding member of the middle class. What possible connection to Keith?"

"He's sure as heck not hiding," Casey said. "I found an entry for him on LinkedIn." She turned to Hari. "You should still have the link on your screen."

"Yep . . . *za.linkedin.com*—got it." She clicked her mouse, then turned her monitor around. "There he is: Marten Jeukens."

Laura saw a completely bald man with a full beard and intense eyes.

"He doesn't look very dangerous."

"But he's got Keith's money," Paulette said, "and so he must know where he is."

"Oh, yeah," Casey said slowly. "About the money . . ."

Uh-oh, Laura thought. Now what?

"Yes," Hari said, taking the lead. "There's only fifty thousand left in the account. More than ten times that amount was transferred in seven weeks ago."

"Where did it go?" Paulette's tone was alarmed.

"We don't know yet," Casey said. "I was only able to access the daily totals in the account, not where the money went, but the total diminished by varying amounts every business day until it hit fifty *k,* then it stabilized."

"How?" Rick said. "In-person withdrawals, wire transfers, checks?"

"I can't say yet. There's a credit card attached to the account but I haven't been able to access it."

Paulette rose and began to wander the office. "This is so *frustrating!*"

"I know," Hari said, her tone soothing, "but we know so much more now than we did yesterday. We have a name, a place, a *face.*"

Paulette stopped her pacing and faced the room. "But we don't have Keith."

"And we still don't know *why,*" Rick added, pulling his notepad from a pocket. "Made a timeline that might help. According to his assistant, Keith ran Mozi's genome on February twenty-fourth. According to Hari—correct me if I'm wrong—he started liquidating on March second, right?"

Hari was nodding. "Right. That was the start."

"So, less than a week after being spooked by Mozi's genome, he starts his sell-off."

"And three weeks later," Hari said, "on March twenty-third to be exact, he finished. All his liquid assets had been converted to cash."

Rick said, "Okay, on March thirtieth, a week after everything's in cash, he shows up at the Schelling primatarium with Mozi, dead of a broken neck. March thirty-first he makes a trip home and dumps her ashes into the sound. April first he and his money are gone. So, Mozi dies and forty-eight hours later he walks out of his office and is never seen again."

"That monkey and Keith's disappearance," Paulette said. "I've always said there's a connection."

Rick nodded. "And I'm sure you'll say it again soon. But consider the timing: If we assume someone was pressuring him for a payoff—forcing him to liquidate all those assets for whatever reason—maybe that someone killed Mozi as a convincer, a preemptive strike to show Keith how serious he was."

Hari said, "You think it shook Keith up so much he ran?"

"Or maybe it ticked him off to the point where he told whoever to shove it and they, um, dealt with him."

Laura noticed Paulette's stricken expression and said, "Maybe we should ratchet down the speculation."

After a few heartbeats of silence, Rick looked Paulette's way. "You told me his strange parting remarks when you last saw him. Tell me again, with his exact wording."

"I'll never forget them. He said, 'I'm being backed into something I would have considered inconceivable just weeks ago.'"

Hari said, "Well, if that doesn't sound like coercion, I don't know what does."

Rick said, "Do we know where this Jeukens lives?"

"The only address the bank has is a Cape Town post office box," Casey said.

"What about his toothpaste cap factory?"

"That we have—it's in the LinkedIn entry."

"Write that down for me, will you? Looks like I'll be headed to Cape Town." His expression turned grim. "Got a few questions for Mister Marten Jeukens."

That sounded like trouble to Laura . . . trouble for Rick as well as the mysterious Jeukens.

"Do you think that's such a good idea?" she said.

He shrugged. "Got a better one?"

She didn't, but she'd damn well work on one.

3

SHIRLEY, NEW YORK

Laura had banished Rick to the family room with Marissa where they were catching the end of the first game of a Mets doubleheader. She'd retreated to her office and its computer.

They'd argued all the way home from Hari's office, but she'd finally prevailed: He wasn't going to Cape Town alone; she was coming along. She'd used all the basic arguments of two heads being better than one, how she'd act as his Gal Friday and his sounding board.

She didn't give him the real reason: that he'd need her along for protection. Not from any external threat—he was eminently qualified to handle that. No, he needed someone to protect him from himself.

Rick had become emotionally invested in finding his brother. That was fine when operating from afar, but it could cloud his judgement when he reached South Africa.

She'd volunteered to book the flights. He might book only one seat if she left it up to him.

She heard someone enter the office behind her.

"How's it going?" Rick said.

"The best time to Cape Town out of JFK is nineteen hours via South African Airways."

He gave a low whistle. "All nineteen in the air?"

"Mostly, except for a layover in Johannesburg. No nonstops. In all your travels, you've never been to South Africa?"

"Never set foot on the African continent."

"With 'Rick' as a name, you should have made a point of stopping in Casablanca at least once."

"Never had a chance."

"Well, then, it'll be the first time for both of us."

"Hey, about that . . ." He lowered himself into the chair beside the desk. "Can we rethink your coming along?"

"No."

"This could be dangerous. We know little or nothing about this Jeukens guy. I can't see how he's done all this alone. He's got to be working with other people. Hell, for all we know, he's been blackmailed into acting as a front. The situation's too unsettled. Too damn risky for me to feel comfortable taking you along."

"I'll stay in the background, out of danger."

"That's not gonna help Keith, so why come at all?"

Didn't he see? Didn't he get it?

"I'm not going along for Keith, I'm going for you."

"For me?"

"Yeah, you big dummy. What if you discover . . ." How to say this? "What if it's the worst news?"

He looked away. "You mean if Keith's dead."

"Yes. Exactly. I want to be there for you."

"Oh." His expression softened. Obviously no such thing had occurred to him. "Well, I appreciate that. I really do, but—" His cell phone gave off a faint vibrating hum. He pulled it out and checked the display. "Text from Stahlman."

"On a Sunday?"

"Answering mine. I need to arrange next week off. Want to do it face-to-face. Says to meet him in a warehouse in Long Island City." He pocketed the phone. "Can we finish this conversation later?"

"Of course. You go see Stahlman. We'll talk when you get back."

He stared at her a moment. "Why do I get the feeling that as soon as I walk out that door you're going to reserve two seats to Cape Town?"

"Why, whatever do you mean?"

"Wait, okay?" he said, pointing to her. "Just . . . wait."

"Uh-huh."

With an exasperated sigh he headed for the front door.

As soon as she heard it slam, she logged onto South African Airway's website where she snagged two first-class seats nonstop to Johannesburg—expensive, but worth every penny on a flight that long. From there they had only a short hop to Cape Town.

Next she called Steven. She needed someone to stay with Marissa and who better than her own father? Fortunately she and her ex were still on good terms. When Marissa had been recovering from her stem cell transplant, Steven would come and spend his designated weekends in the Shirley house, while Laura would move into his Manhattan apartment.

"Sure," he said. "Always glad to spend some extra time with my best girl. How long we talking?"

He was good that way—loved Marissa like crazy and would do anything for her. His public relations business allowed him to work anywhere. His laptop, his phone, and a wi-fi connection to social media were all he needed. He'd told her the only reason to have an office these days was as a place to meet clients.

"A few days should do it."

"Where is the world traveler off to this time?"

"South Africa." Using the KISS rule, she added, "A friend's brother has had some sort of breakdown and we're going to go bring him back. You might have heard of him. Keith Somers? The author who disappeared a while back?"

"Oh, right. I do recall something about that. He had a bestseller, right? Look, if he wants to make hay from his disappearance, send him to me. I'll have his face and the title of his book all over the place once he's back. That's my thing, you know."

Laura knew. And he was very good at his "thing." He could seduce public opinion into buying anything he told them to. If he'd limited his seductions to public opinion during their marriage, he and Laura might still be together.

"I'll be sure to ask. Meanwhile, I'll get her off to school in the morning and you be here when she comes home."

"No problem. Or better yet, I could come over tonight and—"

"Tomorrow will be fine."

He laughed. "Okay. Safe trip."

4

LONG ISLAND CITY, NEW YORK

The 35th Street address Stahlman had given Rick turned out to be a huge warehouse in the industrial zone between Queens Boulevard and the LIE. Looked like it had been around since just after World War II. Its two floors had to total a quarter mil square feet, easy. Rick had been involved in the security end for many of Stahlman's ventures, but he hadn't known about this.

The building might have had truck bays around back, but he saw only one entrance on this side—a steel door under a heavy-duty roll-up security shutter. Inside, a square-jawed side of Hispanic beef in a rumpled suit sat behind a battered desk. Rick recognized him—he'd vetted him for a security guard position last month—but couldn't recall his name.

"Hey, Mister Hayden," he said, rising and extending his hand. "Good to see ya. The boss said you'd be stopping by."

As they shook, Rick said, "I remember pretty much everything about you, Guerra, except your first name."

"Adão."

"Right." No wonder. "How's the job going?"

A shrug. "It's quiet. But that's okay. We get some shaky types nosin' around, but they move on."

"Quiet's good."

"I'm with you there," Adão said with a smile. "Gives me a chance to study."

"GED?"

"You got it."

"Keep it up. Where's the boss?"

Adão turned and punched a code into a keypad next to the door behind the desk. "Right through here."

The door buzzed open and Rick stepped through to find Clayton Stahlman staring at a monitor as he tapped on a keyboard. His desk was bigger than Adão's, but just as battered.

Rick didn't get to see Stahlman much—most of their communication was via phone, or email, or text—so he still experienced an instant of surprise at how healthy he looked. Before the *ikhar*, he'd been frail, feeble, and moon-faced from his meds. Got out of breath shifting in his wheelchair. Now vigorous and fit in his late sixties, gray haired in a turtleneck and jeans, he looked the picture of health, although his barrel chest remained a legacy from his pulmonary fibrosis.

"Mister Hayden." He'd never once called him Rick. "Good to see you! What brings you to the wilds of Queens?"

He gave a quick run-down of Keith's disappearance and the need to go after him.

"By all means, take as long as you need," Stahlman said. "You never take time off anyway. Do you need anything? Any way I can help?"

"I think I've got it covered." Rick gestured around. "But what is this place anyway? This why you need the extra security?"

"Still getting it set up, but yeah. I brought in some men like Adão from other spots for now. It's a little project I've wanted to start for a while. Thought I'd never get to it but, thanks to you and Doctor Fanning, it's now full speed ahead."

"Okay, but what is it?"

"We can talk about it when you get back."

Just then a door to Rick's right opened and a middle-aged woman stepped through.

"The latest scans," she said.

Stahlman raised his eyebrows. "Anything?"

"All normal."

Rick had a glimpse of a large space behind her. About twenty feet away a man in the lotus position floated two feet above the floor.

The woman retreated then, shutting the door behind her. Rick grabbed for the handle but it had locked shut before he could pull it back open.

"Wait . . . did I just see . . . ?"

Stahlman was smiling and nodding. "Probably."

"But . . ."

"All in good time. Right now the main thing for you is to focus on finding your brother. As I said: Call me when you get back. And if you need anything before that, you have my number."

Rick headed back to the street. Had he seen what he'd seen? He shook it off. He had more pressing concerns. The first was keeping Laura from going to South Africa. Marten Jeukens seemed like a harmless, middle-class businessman, but looks could be deceiving. He could be a dangerous psycho fronting a criminal enterprise. Rick didn't want Laura anywhere near him.

5

THE MOZAMBIQUE CHANNEL

The Afrikaner stepped into the pilot house. In some indefinable way he had changed since Amaury had last seen him on Friday. He did not have the field glasses that had been a fixture around his neck, yet he seemed just as tense.

"So, *monsieur,* how did you spend the past two days?"

"Mostly in a fruitless endeavor which involved unsavory types."

"Really. Do you care to elaborate?"

"Not particularly." He nodded ahead, at the foredeck. "Although the unsavory types I mentioned were not unlike the two in your current employ."

"Bakari and Razi? Yes, they look like they would eat your children for breakfast, but they are good workers."

The brothers lounged near the bow, by the ladders bungeed to the side rails. Both had dark, almost tar-black skin, broad shoulders, and round faces. But Bakari's face was pockmarked while Razi's was smooth, which proved handy because otherwise they'd be easy to confuse.

"Also they know how to keep their mouths shut," Amaury added.

"How do you know?"

Amaury shrugged. "There have been times when the exotics we've brought back have been on certain lists."

"Endangered species?"

"Those lists exaggerate the danger to the creatures. I take good care of them, find them good homes, but to do this I must operate—you know the expression 'under the table'?"

The Afrikaner's narrow lips twisted into a wry smile. "I know the expression well. I've had a few dealings down there myself."

"This weekend, perhaps?"

"Not worth talking about." Jeukens squinted ahead at the glaring water. "We seem to be moving faster than our previous trip out."

Amaury nodded, impressed. "You have a good sense of—*comment dit-on?*—of velocity. Yes, I have pushed us to ten knots. Last time we had no firm destination so I was conserving fuel. This time we know where we are going. No wasting our tank on a grid search as before. We shall be able to travel out to the island and back without stopping at Toliara."

Marten said, "I did a rough estimation from Maputo to the island and came up with a distance of just about five hundred miles, maybe a little less."

"I came up with the same. The weather maps show no fronts coming through, so we should have calm seas. We will drop anchor there Tuesday morning."

"Good," Jeukens said. "And you're sure we'll have enough fuel to return without stopping?"

Why was he so concerned?

"Yes. We burn more fuel going out because we are heading northeast and must push against the southward flow of the channel. On the way back we head southwest so we can ride the current and make better time."

"Excellent!"

Another question had been nagging at Amaury. "You said you were going to study the primates. Are you planning on staying behind when we head back?"

Jeukens sighed. "Not this trip. I first must get the lay of the land inside the caldera so I'll know what I'll need for a more extended stay. Like, are there food sources? A bunch of breadfruit and banana trees or coconut palms would make a nice supplement. What's the drinking water situation? No, I'll be heading back with you this trip. But next time . . . next time I'll know what I'm getting into and come prepared."

"Before we head home we will be sure to catch one of the proper sex for you."

Jeukens frowned. "Proper sex?"

"Yes. As a mate for your little friend."

"Mate?"

"But of course. You want a breeding pair, *oui*?"

"Not at all. She's dead."

"I am shocked. What happened?"

Jeukens pressed his fists together, thumb to thumb, and gave them a sudden, violent twist.

"I snapped her scrawny little neck."

6

SHIRLEY, NEW YORK

Rick kept his voice calm but Laura could tell he was furious that she'd made reservations for both of them.

"I thought we'd agreed to discuss this when I got back."

"And here I am, ready to discuss," she said in her sweetest, most reasonable voice.

"But you've already made the reservations."

Same voice: "I can cancel mine if you convince me otherwise."

"But—" His cell gave off a by now familiar vibrating hum. Checking the display, he said, "Hmmm, that was fast."

"What was fast?"

"I put in a call to one of the few people in the Company who remembers me. Asked him to check out Jeukens—any known criminal associates, things like that. He's got access to databases we can't get near."

"And?"

"Texted me with a link to a public website in Mozambique. I'll read it off so we can check it out on your big screen there."

As Rick dictated, Laura typed in the URL—a word she didn't understand followed by *.gov.mz*—then hit enter. Text flashed onto the screen, but all in Portuguese. She clicked the translate button.

"Looks like some sort of a police blotter," Rick said.

A subhead read "Maxixe, MZ" and was dated this morning.

"Where's Maxixe?" Laura said.

"You're the map savant."

"Somewhere in Mozambique is all I can say. Beyond that . . ."

The gist of the entry was that the body of a local helicopter pilot named Abilio Batalheiro had been found on a Maxixe street. Cause of death unknown at the time. The police weren't sure if it was an accident or foul play, but a South African named Marten Jeukens was the last person to engage Batalheiro's services and was being sought as a person of interest.

The bottom of the article listed Lieutenant Souza Mugabe of the Maputo police as the person to contact with any information.

Rick straightened. "I wonder if I should call this guy and ask if anything's changed since this went up."

"Well, unless he works the graveyard shift, chances aren't good he'll be available." When he gave her a questioning look, she tapped her watch. "It's seven hours later over there."

"And you know this because you're a map savant?"

She shrugged. "I noticed it's the same time zone as Israel, and I'll never forget Israel."

"Ah, yes. We'll always have Gan Yosaif."

Right. Fond memories of four bullet-riddled bodies.

She did a quick search for Maxixe and found it lay about three hundred miles up the coast from Maputo.

"A long way from Cape Town, and even Johannesburg. Are we sure it's the same Marten Jeukens?"

Rick shrugged. "Can't say. Doesn't seem like a common name, but for all I know, *Jeukens* is the *Jones* or *Smith* of South Africa. That report didn't happen to post his birthdate, did it?"

"I doubt it," she said, switching tabs, "but I'll check." No, no birthdate listed. She was about to click off when she noticed a *.jpg* link. "Hey, looks like they've got a photo."

She clicked it and a shot of a bald, bearded man in a safari jacket filled the screen. The caption said, *Marten Jeukens*. It appeared to have been taken in a hotel lobby. The photo was high-def with good lighting; so, even with a trace of motion blur, it gave a clear look at him.

She studied his face, saying, "You think he's the same guy? He looks different. I mean, he's still got the shaved head and the beard, but is that the same nose?"

Rick said nothing, so she added, "And didn't his eyes look different on his LinkedIn photo?"

Still no answer so she glanced over her shoulder. Rick's face had gone white and his mouth was hanging open.

"What's wrong?"

"Jesus H. Christ!" he said, pointing. "Keith! That's Keith!"

Laura looked at the screen again. She'd seen photos of Keith, watched his TV interviews, and this wasn't . . . Granted, he'd sported a full head of hair and had been clean shaven at the time, but this man was much thinner and . . .

"No. It can't be."

"The hell it can't! He's lost a lot of weight and shaved his head, but I know my brother, and that's Keith!"

TUESDAY

May 24

1

DAPI ISLAND

Amaury gazed up at the sheer lava wall of the mysterious little island and could only pray that the rest of this trip went as smoothly as these first two days. The waters of the channel had been placid, the current gentle, and the John Deere engine had purred like a kitten. Bakari and Razi, who often fought as only brothers can, behaved themselves. Even Jeukens had relaxed enough to exchange a few words with them—not that they cared to have much to do with an Afrikaner. The brothers spoke Portuguese, Ronga—they were Shangaans, a Bantu tribe—and could manage some very broken English. So English, by default, became the *Sorcière*'s lingua franca.

Its anchor had found firm footing about a hundred yards from the western shore and the ship bobbed gently in the current. Amaury and Bakari were rowing the inflatable fifteen-foot raft he'd brought along. The cargo: the ladders and the tents.

As they approached the shore, Jeukens and Razi waded out to their knees and pulled them the rest of the way in.

"The ladders," Jeukens said, scowling. "At last, the ladders. We should have brought them first."

So anxious to climb up and over that wall.

"And if we had, where would you be now? We would lose you to those monkeys when we need every available hand to haul our equipment to the other side."

"I am not part of your crew."

Amaury had anticipated this moment. Jeukens had been a client on the first trip out here. As the man who had chartered Amaury's boat, he'd had major say in the *Sorcière*'s course. But on this trip he was a passenger, with no say. With Bakari and Razi watching and listening, this had to be settled here and now, once and for all. The Shangaans' father had fought in the Mozambican civil war against South African–funded forces. He'd lost a leg to a land mine. They were naturally suspicious of foreigners. Neither Amaury nor Jeukens were natives, but Amaury's color was on his side, and he had to show the brothers that not only was he their boss, but the white man's boss as well.

"Ah, but in many ways you *are* crew. And I am your captain—onboard, and ashore while we are here. We need—what is the English expression?—a pecking order. Yes, a pecking order if things are to run smoothly. Bakari and Razi understand that. You said you did too."

Jeukens looked as if he were about to make an angry retort. His teeth were clenched, as were his fists. But he stood silent for a moment, then he spoke.

"You are right, of course. I . . . I apologize. 'Impatience does become a dog that's mad.'"

"Yet another quote, *monsieur*?"

"Shakespeare. *Antony and Cleopatra*."

Amaury had never read it, but at least he'd heard of Shakespeare.

"You agree that I am your captain?"

The Afrikaner nodded stiffly. "I agree."

"Then apology accepted," he said, surprised how easy it had been.

Of course, he knew Jeukens did not mean a word of it. But, at least on the surface, a proper chain of command had been established. He glanced at the brothers, who seemed satisfied.

"I have never been known for my patience," Jeukens added. "And you must understand that this island is completely unexplored. For all we know, we are the first humans ever to set foot on it. Who knows what wonders wait on the other side of that wall?"

Amaury winked at Bakari and Razi. "You are thinking maybe dinosaurs, *monsieur*?"

The brothers laughed and elbowed each other.

"Do not make light of this, Captain Laffite. Something of enormous importance awaits on the other side of that wall."

Yes, Amaury thought. A fortune in cutesy creatures.

"We shall know soon enough, *monsieur.*"

Bakari and Razi unloaded the two extension ladders, each expandable to twenty-four feet, and carried them to the base of the wall. As they stretched one of them to its full length, Amaury inspected the nearly vertical lava. After the Afrikaner's brief trip ashore on their first voyage, Jeukens had said the wall was not climbable. Amaury had taken him at his word and was glad of it. The lava was peppered with tiny pocks, worn almost smooth by eons of wind and weather. The vegetation that studded its surface clung precariously, offering no useful handholds.

Ladders were the only way up.

The brothers leaned an extended ladder against the wall with its top rung ending just shy of the rim. Jeukens stepped toward it but Razi was quicker, darting in front of him and clambering up the rungs like one of the primates Amaury intended to capture.

With Bakari steadying the ladder from below, Razi hoisted himself up to the rim and rose to his feet. For a few seconds he stood with hands on hips, staring into the caldera, then he turned, wide-eyed, and began babbling in Ronga. Amaury had picked up some Ronga during his years in Mozambique, but Razi was rattling too fast for him to understand.

"What did he say?" he asked Bakari in Portuguese.

"He says it's full of trees."

Excellent. Many trees meant many primates.

Jeukens reached again for the ladder up but Bakari blocked him.

"*Capitão* first."

Ah, yes. The pecking order. Normally Amaury would have allowed Jeukens to go, but because of the Afrikaner's earlier challenge, he grabbed the rungs and ascended.

Soon enough, though, all four of them were standing on the rim, staring in fascination at the canopy of green. Well, three of them, at least. Jeukens seemed more interested in an area about ninety degrees to their left along the circular rim.

"Do you see something we do not, *mon ami?*"

Jeukens stiffened, then relaxed. "Just looking for signs of the primates."

Why over there? he wondered. Why not directly below? Did the Afrikaner know something he was not sharing?

"And?"

"No sign of a single one yet."

"Let us hope that changes once we are inside . . . which should not be too difficult to reach."

The inner slope of the wall was much gentler than the outside, with larger vegetation, even a small tree here and there making itself at home on the incline. The climb down looked easy, but it appeared to be a lot farther than twenty feet.

They began the arduous task of hauling up all the supplies and equipment—food, water, tents, Coleman stove, all the traps, and one cage—on ropes. The task was made somewhat easier by using the second ladder as a skid, but with no shade on the rim, and no clouds to shield them from the blazing tropical sun, they'd all soon soaked through their shirts.

By early afternoon, everything was arranged on the rim. Razi broke out bottles of water and protein bars. As they rested and let the westerly breeze cool them, Amaury felt a nudge. He glanced up to see a grinning Bakari pointing toward the caldera.

Amaury almost dropped his water bottle.

The leafy canopy was alive with little blue-eyed primates, clinging to the swaying upper branches as they stared at the newcomers. Some were as close as twenty-five feet.

"These are the lemurs we trap?" Bakari said.

No, not lemurs, but Amaury didn't correct him—at least not yet. People all over the world were going to make that mistake. And that would be fine at first. The eyes would sell them. But Amaury would also whisper that his little pets were being intensely studied because they were suspected of being the missing link. If Jeukens ever published the connection, excellent! If not, so what? The mere possibility that someone might own the missing link would drive up the price.

Soon all four humans were staring back, though Jeukens seemed the least impressed.

"How many you see?" Razi said.

Bakari waggled his finger in the air in a show of counting. "Many hundred."

"And they don't seem the least bit afraid," Amaury said.

"Why should they be?" Jeukens said with a shrug. "We don't pose any obvious threat."

Razi grinned. "Not yet."

Jeukens waved his arm over the canopy. "Right now they're kings of their little castle. I'll bet they have no predators on this island."

"No big cats or snakes?" Amaury said.

"I wouldn't be surprised if they killed them off ages ago."

"Killed? They are little monkeys."

"They're also smart and adaptable."

A group of five primates—three males and a female with a baby clinging to her back—cautiously moved to within a dozen feet. Bakari broke off a piece of his protein bar and tossed it their way in a high, gentle arc. The one with the baby snagged it out of the air with a one-handed catch. She sniffed the fragment, took a tiny test bite, then screeched. It must have been a happy screech because the other three immediately began fighting for it.

"This is going to be easy, *mes amis*," Amaury said, raising his palm. "So easy!"

He and the brothers exchanged high-fives while Jeukens simply stared at the creatures.

"We're back in the lemur business!" Razi said in Portuguese.

"Lemurs?" Jeukens said. "Did he say 'lemurs'?"

"Yes. They are called the same in English and Portuguese."

"They are not lemurs," Jeukens said. "You know that."

"Then what?" Bakari said. "Big eyes . . ."

Amaury shrugged. "No one knows."

"What we call them?" Razi said.

"I propose we call them *dapis*," Jeukens said. "They resemble an extinct species called adapiform primates. We can shorten that to dapi. That is, if no one objects."

Dapi . . . Amaury liked it. Easy to say and easy to spell meant easy to sell. A cute little name for a cute little creature. Perfect.

"Dapi it is."

2

MAPUTO, MOZAMBIQUE

By the time she and Rick set down at Maputo International Airport, Laura was tired enough to cry. They'd left JFK late Monday morning and arrived in Mozambique shortly after noon—but the next day. Nineteen hours travel time, counting the layover in Johannesburg, and one whole day extracted from their calendars.

Bad enough that she hadn't slept on the planes—or at least not enough to matter—she'd barely slept the night before as well.

After recovering from the shock of seeing Keith in that photo, Rick had blown off Cape Town and was hell-bent for Mozambique. If Keith had been spotted in Maputo, that was where Rick was headed.

The arguments against Laura coming along had vanished. Rick was no longer going out to confront a potentially dangerous, even murderous criminal. He was going after his brother. He now seemed to welcome her company. To head off any second thoughts on his part, Laura volunteered to adjust the travel arrangements and sent Rick home to pack. She kept the JFK-to-Johannesburg flight but switched the short leg from Cape Town to Maputo.

On Monday morning, Laura and Rick had met at JFK's Terminal 4 to begin their African odyssey.

She found the Maputo airport surprisingly modern. As they exited the jetway they were funneled to the customs and immigration area. Everyone entering Mozambique—except citizens of a few neighboring countries—needed a visa. Rick and Laura were ahead of the game because they'd put their layover time in Johannesburg to use purchasing single-entry visas. While Laura had filled out the tedious forms, Rick purchased a supply of Mozambique meticais at the *cambio* booth. So they hit the Mozambican ground running.

Once they were through the bureaucratic mill, they headed for the baggage area. Rick had brought a simple carry-on but, not knowing how long she'd be traveling, Laura had packed for every contingency.

Rick had been flinty-eyed and withdrawn the entire trip. Despite her best efforts to draw him out, all he'd offered were monosyllables.

And now, out of the blue, he said, "Do we check in to the hotel first and then find this Lieutenant Mugabe, or go straight to the police department?"

"That might be the longest sentence you've spoken since Sunday."

"Really?" His mouth twisted. "I guess you're right. Sorry. It's kind of a lot to process."

"Your brother dropping out of sight for almost two months and then reappearing with another identity as a person of interest in a suspicious death? Yeah, it's a huge amount to process. I'll admit planes and airport waiting areas and immigration lines might not be the best places to discuss something like this, but it's just the two of us now. So give. How do you feel?"

He shrugged, looked uncomfortable. Feelings weren't his forte.

"Numb . . . I guess that's the best word. Numb with shock at first. The shock's pretty much worn off, but the numbness remains. Confused too. The things he's done . . . those aren't the actions of the nerdy guy I grew up with. If I believed in demonic possession, I'd say that's what happened: Keith's been possessed by a demon who's forcing him to do these things. But you and I both know there's no such thing. So what the fuck is going on? Excuse the 'fuck.'"

"No excuse necessary. Rarely has 'fuck' been more appropriate. I've never met him, but just from what I've seen on those interview DVDs, I totally understand the confusion. He comes across as a distracted intellectual and, well, ineffectual."

"An ineffectual intellectual . . . yeah, that's a good sum-up. But for now we should put his personality and all that aside. We need to back-burner wondering how a guy like Keith managed to pull this off, because *how* isn't the big question. For now we simply accept that he found the ability within himself and leave it at that. The big question is *why?* What drove him to all this?"

"It's got to be Mozi," Laura said. "As Professor Keith, he found his little pet primate in Mozambique. A few months later he returned to Mozambique as Marten Jeukens. If I had to guess, I'd say he came back to find another Mozi."

Rick slapped his free hand against his thigh. "But why come back as someone else?"

"We're back to *why*. When we can answer that, I'm betting all the other answers will fall into place."

Rick was shaking his head. "I'm not saying Mozi isn't part of the why, but it's got to be bigger than simply finding another like her. You don't sell nearly everything you own and assume a new identity just to hunt down a goddamn monkey. Those are the actions of someone who's planning on not coming back."

Laura shrugged. "Maybe he is coming back. He didn't sell his apartment."

"Maybe he didn't have time. He seemed in a big hurry."

"I'm not pretending to understand him. I'm just pointing out that he left a big door open if he decides to return."

Laura's bag was waiting when they arrived at the baggage claim area. Rick grabbed it and they headed outside to catch a cab.

"Warm day," he said as they stepped into the afternoon sunshine. "If this is their spring, wonder what their summer's like?"

"This is their fall."

He stared at her a moment, then, "Of course. Duh. We're south of the equator."

"We're also just south of the Tropic of Capricorn. Which makes this climate the equivalent of Thanksgiving in South Florida."

"The map savant strikes again," he said, his mouth twisting into a wry smile. "They speak Portuguese here, right?"

"Well, I'm glad you know *something*," she said with a huff, knowing he'd catch the sarcasm. "Do you happen to know any?"

"Not a word. You?"

She spoke English, Spanish, French, and the Mayan Yucatec dialect, but no Portuguese. However . . .

She held up her phone. "No, but I downloaded a Portuguese translator app before we left."

"You need an app? I'd have thought you'd have learned the language on the way over."

"Very funny."

"So I repeat my long sentence: "Do we check in to the hotel first and then find this Mugabe guy, or go straight to the police?""

If they stopped at the hotel she might never leave—she could see herself collapsing face-first on her bed and never waking up.

"Let's face the fuzz first."

"You got it."

Rick hailed one of the waiting cabs. An aging white diesel Mercedes without hubcaps pulled up and extruded its big-bellied driver. His round black face glistened with perspiration. As he put their bags in the trunk, she and Rick settled in the backseat. The car had seen better days. The windows were open. She sensed air-conditioning was not in the offing. No biggie.

She activated the translator app and spoke into her phone.

"Please take us to the police station." She tapped the translate icon and held the phone over the back of the front seat. *"Por favor, leve-nos à delegacia de polícia."*

The driver grinned. "Modern technology is amazing, is it not?"

Laura felt herself redden. "Sorry. Guess I should have asked if you spoke English."

"No sorry necessary. I am very happy that you tried. Many drivers speak a little English, but not all."

A compliment was in order. "You speak very well," she said.

"Thank you. We have five police stations in town. Which do you wish?"

"Five?" She shrugged and looked at Rick

"We need to talk to Lieutenant Souza Mugabe," he said. "Where would we find him?"

"Ah. He will be at the station on Avenida Guerra Popular, very near our beautiful train station and the Museu de Moeda."

"Museu de Moeda . . . that means . . . ?"

"The Money Museum. Money from all time and from all over the world. You should stop in and see it."

"Maybe some other time," Rick said. "Sounds like this Guerra Popular station is where we want to go. You know this Mugabe fellow?"

"I know only that Tenente Mugabe is a hard man if you break the law. I will drive you and your bags to Avenida Guerra Popular for eight hundred meticais. Agreeable?"

Laura didn't see a taxi meter on the dash. So the fare was negotiable?

"Eight hundred? That seems awfully—"

"It's about sixteen bucks," Rick told her, then leaned toward the driver. "How about we make it a thousand and you get us there as quickly and smoothly as possible."

The driver laughed. "You have heard about our famous potholes, yes?"

"Yes, indeed."

"They have been fixed! Well, most of them."

The cab lurched toward the exit and onto Avenida Acordos de Lusaka. The airport seemed integrated into the city because almost immediately they were on residential streets. Laura saw plenty of cars and rickety minibuses, but by far the most common modes of transport were bicycles, motorbikes, and plain old foot power. Roadside vendors sold from carts or small stalls or simply spread out a blanket on the ground to display their wares.

The houses they passed were mostly one-story, some outright shanties, others hidden behind walls, still others looking like they'd been constructed of brightly painted stuccoed cinder block. Every window and door was barred, however. That said a lot.

Rick must have noticed her concern. He leaned close and muttered, "Welcome to the Third World. Anything that can be carried off is fair game."

Apparently the driver overheard them. "He is right. When I bought this car it had four hubcaps. I did not have it two days before all four were stolen while I was sitting in traffic."

Laura's voice jumped an octave. "While you were in the car?"

He nodded. "Three of them and only one of me. What could I do?"

Ahead she saw a policeman standing at the side of the road.

"At least they've got police on the street."

The driver barked a laugh. "The biggest thieves of all!" The cop stepped out and waved the taxi over. "As you are about to learn for yourselves."

"What do you mean?"

"Get your passports out. Put five hundred meticais in each. If you don't have enough, ten U.S. will do."

"*What?*" Laura said as Rick began to remove his passport from a jacket pocket. "You can't be serious!"

"He waits here every day for cabs from the airport. If they carry tourists, he stops them and checks passports."

"Fine." She pulled hers from her shoulder bag and handed it to Rick. "Ours are in perfect order. We just came through customs."

"He can check them quickly or he can take a very long time. Which do you prefer?"

"I prefer not to be blackmailed."

She glanced at Rick, expecting to see that stony look in his eyes turning to steel. Instead she watched him tuck a ten-dollar bill inside each of the passports.

"Don't you dare give in! It's extortion!"

She knew she sounded self-righteous, but this infuriated her.

"Bribes grease the axles of the Third World," he said. "The wheels don't turn without them."

"Doesn't it irk you?"

He smiled at her. "Not in the least. You might as well be irked because all these foreign countries don't use English as their native tongue and have the audacity to develop their own language."

"No, it's not like that at all. It's—"

"It's the way they do things. You're not going to change it, so go with the flow."

The driver pulled up beside the cop. They exchanged some familiar greetings, then the cop stuck his hand through the open rear window.

"Passaportes."

Laura watched as he opened the passports, crumpled the bills in his hand, and handed them back.

"Proceder," he said, waving them on.

"See?" the driver said as the taxi picked up speed again. "No delay."

Laura growled; Rick laughed.

She wasn't naïve about graft. She saw plenty in Suffolk County and knew New York City was even worse. But having to pay off a cop just to ride down the street . . . ?

As they penetrated deeper into Maputo, the streets widened and the buildings grew taller and more modern, although some ornate remnants of the Portuguese colonial times remained.

Their current *avenida* suddenly morphed into a divided thoroughfare and changed its name to Guerra Popular.

"Hey!" Rick said a few blocks later. "Did we just pass Avenida Ho Chi Minh?"

"Yes," said the driver. "We also have Avenida Karl Marx and Avenida Mao Tse Tung as well. Many communist countries funded our revolution and the civil war that followed. This is how we show our appreciation."

"What? No Avenida Che Guevara?"

"No. But maybe someday."

Laura muttered, "I'm sure for the right price you can have an Avenida Rick Hayden."

Rick nodded. "Got a nice ring to it."

Their driver stopped before a nondescript brick municipal building and got out. As he was unloading their bags from the trunk, he pointed farther down the street.

"*Olha!* Our beautiful train station!"

Beautiful? Well, not exactly. But Laura had to admit the huge gingerbread building had a certain ornate charm.

"It was designed by Senhor Eiffel who built the tower in Paris."

"Fascinating," Rick said with ill-disguised disinterest as he handed over the fare.

"Around the corner is the Money Museum," the driver said with a wink. "Remember that when you are talking to the police."

"What did he mean by that?" Laura said as they trudged inside with their luggage. And then it hit her. "Oh, I get it." She shook her head. "Amazing."

They came to a chest-high counter with a uniformed man on a platform behind it.

"Tenente Souza Mugabe, *por favor,*" Laura said.

He rattled off some machine-gun Portuguese.

"*No comprendo,*" she said in Spanish, figuring it would be close enough to Portuguese for the guard to understand.

Eventually, through a combination of the translator app and the guard's rudimentary English, she came to understand that Lieutenant Mugabe was here but was busy.

"Tell him we've come all the way from the United States with important information on Marten Jeukens," she said into her phone and let the translator app do its thing.

The cop gave them a curious stare as he shook his head.

Rick handed his passport to the cop, who lowered it out of sight to examine. Laura heard the crinkle of paper money, then the passport was handed back as the cop picked up his phone. A long fusillade of Portuguese was followed by two shorter volleys, then he hung up and motioned for them to follow.

"Let's hope the lieutenant speaks English," Rick said as they wound their way to a rear office.

"Let's hope you don't run out of cash," Laura said.

Rick only smiled.

A tall, lean man, almost gaunt, met them at the door. He wore an open-collared white shirt with two buttoned-down breast pockets tucked into dark uniform pants. He reminded Laura of Lance Reddick. He stood before a cluttered, battered desk; sitting front and center on it was a six-inch great white shark carved out of ebony—which, Laura decided, made it a great black shark. A large map of Mozambique occupied the rear wall.

"I must confess I am intrigued," he said in lightly accented English.

Laura released a sigh of relief. "I'm so glad you speak English."

"It seems one cannot get far in this world without it." He did not sound too happy about that.

Rick introduced himself and Laura, and after handshakes and invitations to sit, Mugabe got right down to it.

"Right. So what can you tell me about Marten Jeukens that I don't already know?"

"Well, first off," Rick said, "he's not Marten Jeukens."

Laura expected some show of shock or surprise, but Mugabe gave only a slow nod.

"I know."

Rick straightened in his chair and saying, "You know? How did you find out?"

"We tracked down the real Marten Jeukens. It was not hard. The fake Jeukens was renting an apartment not far from here. We traced his credit card back to a Johannesburg bank, and from there back to Cape Town where we found the real Marten Jeukens, a very industrious Afrikaner who has been spending every day at his plastic bottle cap factory. Since he could not be in both places at once, we could draw only one conclusion."

"Identity theft," Rick said, his expression grim.

"Exactly."

Rick looked at Laura. "The plot sickens. But why a South African?"

"Skin color, obviously. And I suppose because of the open border with Mozambique. Jeukens was completely unaware that he'd been compromised. What I do not know, and what I am hoping you can tell me, is who is pretending to be Marten Jeukens?"

"A zoologist named Keith Somers. He disappeared from New York City April first. The first time anyone has seen him since then was that picture you put up—your 'person of interest.'"

Mugabe began writing in a notebook. "S-u-m-m-e-r-s?"

Rick gave him the correct spelling.

"And your interest in this is . . . ?"

"He's my brother."

"Ah. Then you know him well."

Oh, I wouldn't go so far as to say that, Laura thought.

"Do you know of any connection between your brother and Mister Jeukens?"

"None whatsoever and no idea why he would steal this particular man's identity. I do know my brother has traveled to East Africa many times, so maybe they met here. But that's just a wild guess. The question of why he'd assume *any* other identity has been plaguing us."

"Was he in some sort of trouble with the authorities at home?"

"He's a bestselling author in the States, a respected zoologist with a position at New York University. It makes no sense."

Mugabe looked up from his scribbling. "It certainly does not—in more ways than one. Usually identity theft involves monetary theft as well. Mister Jeukens—the real Marten Jeukens—is not missing a single centavo. Most unusual."

"No argument there," Rick said. "But what about this 'person of interest' business with the dead pilot? What that's all about?"

Laura detected a change in Mugabe then. He'd been engaging and pleasant when the information was flowing toward him. But now that someone wanted it to go the opposite way . . .

He gave his head an emphatic shake. "Sorry, no. I cannot comment on an ongoing investigation."

She had been content to sit quietly during the exchanges, watching, listening, fighting off yawns and longing for a bed. Now she saw a way she might make a difference. She reached into her purse and pulled out one of her cards.

"I'm with the medical examiner's office outside New York City," she said, sliding it across Mugabe's desktop. "Perhaps I could speak to your coroner about the pilot's cause of death. You know, doctor to doctor?"

"The coroner is awaiting toxicology reports and will not be able to tell you anything until they are back."

Toxicology . . . She filed that away.

"I work with the police all the time back home. I've—"

Mugabe shook his head again. "I am very sorry. It is simply not possible to discuss."

And then she saw Rick slipping a hundred-dollar bill into the maw of the carved shark. She wanted to snatch it from him but held back.

Go with the flow . . .

"Then again," Mugabe said, barely missing a beat, "since you are, in a sense, a fellow law enforcement officer, I can tell you that we have the pilot's log book. On the last page he scribbled the name 'Jeukens' and some coordinates."

Rick leaned forward. "Coordinates for where?"

"That is the problem." Mugabe started tapping on his keyboard. "Coordinates to nowhere." After a few seconds he turned the monitor to show a page from a small pocket notebook. "This what we have. As you can see, the numbers were hastily written and hard to read."

Laura memorized the sequence as Rick nodded toward the map on the wall behind Mugabe. "Can you point out the spot on that?"

"It is off the right margin of that map. Do not waste your time. There is nothing there but empty water."

Laura wanted to get back to the dead pilot. "You mentioned toxicology studies. Do they think the pilot was poisoned?"

Mugabe nodded. "The coroner says he appears to have died from a powerful neurotoxin." He drummed his fingers on his desk, his expression grim. "I have seen the body. Mister Batalheiro died horribly. The idea that someone here has a substance that can kill like that is very frightening."

Rick said, "So it's pretty clear this isn't some random mugging that went south. Sounds more like your pilot guy was targeted."

Mugabe was nodding. "Exactly. And if you are wondering why a police officer from Maputo is handling this investigation, Maxixe is in Inhambane Province and Inhambane does not have the resources for this sort of investigation."

"Is there any reason to believe my brother had anything to do with it?"

"No, but he is wanted for identity theft and is one of the last people to see the pilot alive, though I must say he has not acted like a criminal during his stay here. His movements have been quite transparent—even his trip to Madagascar."

"Whoa," Rick said. "Madagascar? What was he doing there?"

"He charged hundreds of gallons of marine gas at a dock in Toliara."

Rick's was incredulous. "He took a *boat* over to Madagascar? He could barely drive a car!"

"Not his own boat. The *Sorcière des Mers,* owned by Amaury Laffite."

"*Sea Witch,*" Laura said. "Who's this Laffite?"

"A dealer in exotic animals. A man of questionable ethics."

Laura exchanged a quick glance with Rick.

"Keith and an exotic-animal dealer at sea, burning hundreds of gallons of gas. Almost as if they were looking for something."

"An island?" Laura said.

"An island that is not there," Mugabe said.

Rick said, "Can we talk to this animal dealer?"

"Laffite? Yes, we would like to speak to him as well, but he and his ship have sailed again."

"When?"

"Sunday morning. The same morning we lost track of your brother."

Rick spread his hands. "Isn't it obvious? Keith is back on the *Sea Witch.*"

Mugabe nodded. "That is my guess as well. We will be waiting for him when he returns. He has questions to answer and charges to face."

"We'll be waiting right there with you," Rick said, rising and offering his hand. "Thank you for being so forthcoming with us. I can't tell you how much we appreciate it. May we stay in touch about my brother's return?"

"I will share what I can."

"Thank you *so* much."

"Wow," Laura said when they'd reached the sidewalk. "You were pretty unctuous at the end there. I was worried I'd slip and slide on my way out. I mean, why? You'd already bribed him."

Rick shrugged. "Best to let him think he holds the reins."

"Doesn't he? I mean, are you and I and our cabdriver the only honest people in this city?"

Rick only stared at her, his mouth twisting as if fighting a smile.

She sighed. "Did that sound as sanctimonious as I think it did?"

He nodded as the smile broke through. "Yep. Maybe even more so."

"I was afraid of that."

"Oh, and our cabbie? He flashed his lights to that cop as we approached. I'm guessing a signal that he had tourists on board."

"Aw, no."

"It's the way of life here, Laura. You're too much of a straight shooter to ever accept it, but that's what makes you you."

Sometimes it's a drag being me, she thought.

He pushed on. "Here's how I think it went down. Keith came here looking for another Mozi. He hooked up with an exotic-animal dealer who owns a boat and they went searching for Mozi Island. They found it at those coordinates—which I memorized, by the way."

"Me too."

"Took it for granted you would. Now the two of them are headed back to capture a bunch of Keith's favorite little primates."

"It fits," she said, "but what's the motivation? And you're leaving out the copter trip. Why make a day trip back to a place you just left?"

Rick smiled. "Well, we'll just have to ask him when we meet up with him."

"You mean when he comes back? But Mugabe—"

"Mugabe shmoogabe. We're gonna catch up to Keith on that island."

3

DAPI ISLAND

With gravity now on their side, lowering everything to the caldera floor was immeasurably easier than hauling it up. Marten was glad Laffite had brought extra-long ropes. On his earlier journey inside he'd been shocked to find the floor a good eighty feet down. But when he thought about it, he realized nothing said the floor of an oceanic volcano's caldera had to be at sea level. In fact it rarely was.

But what a floor . . . what a sight.

On Saturday, Marten's first view had stunned him with its beauty. Today's view was just as mesmerizing. The huge, thick, smooth trunks of the magnificent *Adansonia grandidieri* baobabs, spearing toward the sky like massive Romanesque columns, the greenery at their apices exploding eighty feet above the floor to form the main canopy. Their leaves let through enough light for a luxurious subcanopy of various species of twenty- to forty-foot trees, including traveler's palms and a few banana palms that had been stripped of their fruit. A thin, eight- to ten-foot understory of spindly trees, ferns, and clumps of bamboo overhung the grasses and underbrush carpeting the floor. Colorful parrots flitted from branch to branch. He noticed a large leaf nearby start to move, but a closer look revealed only a two-foot Malagasy chameleon, its green perfectly matching the leaves around it.

Marten closed his eyes and swallowed back a surge of bile at the thought of what he was here to do. That was a residue of Keith reacting. But he was Marten. He had no such compunctions.

He looked around. Had anyone seen his momentary queasiness?

No. The other three were busy setting up the camp. Even though the work was progressing quickly and relatively easily, Marten had to hide his frustration at the delay. He had to be circumspect. *Caution* was the byword here. Laffite had already caught him staring at the northern quarter of the caldera where he'd rolled the canisters off the rim.

Had one or both ruptured when they hit bottom? He prayed not. All his plans would be ruined. He'd have to be extremely careful when he finally did get a chance to go looking for them. VX was non-volatile with a high persistence factor, clinging to leaves and grasses, hanging around and contaminating everything. Since plants had no nervous systems, and no acetylcholinesterase to block, they remained unaffected. But anything that moved under its own power had better beware of brushing against that innocent-looking greenery.

Such carelessness on his part—caught looking away from the dapis. Stupidity, really. Laffite was no dummy, and a career criminal to boot. To stay ahead of the law, suspicion bordering on paranoia had to become second nature. Because everyone was a possible traitor. A trusted co-conspirator yesterday could be turned by the authorities today, or suddenly decide he no longer needed a partner.

Laffite probably wasn't worried about Bakari and Razi. Marten had made an effort to get to know them. The language barrier made communication difficult, not helped by their distrust of his skin color, but he had come away with the impression they were a pair of barely educated back-country Bantu Shangaans who had migrated to the capital with no ambition beyond simply getting by in the big city.

Laffite seemed to understand the brothers, but clearly did not understand Marten, which hardly surprised Marten because he was still trying to understand himself. He suspected the Frenchman would have been more comfortable if Marten had demanded an equal share in the profits from the dapis trade. *That* he'd understand—not as a threat, but as the start of a negotiation.

But research? Wanting to study the little profit centers and not pocket any cash? That he would not understand. And what he couldn't understand ignited suspicion.

Which was why Marten had dropped that idiotic "missing link" remark on the first trip. He had seen the dollar signs flash in Laffite's eyes, just as he knew they would. This strange Afrikaner became an asset then, rather than a liability, but an asset he did not understand and therefore could not fully trust.

So Marten had to be extra circumspect this first day on the island, had to play it close to the vest.

He ground his teeth in frustration. This whole boat trip would have been unnecessary if only he had been able to do what needed doing on Saturday. If only the caldera weren't so deep, if only that pilot's winch cable had been longer, if only the helicopter had had a big enough fuel tank to allow Marten the time he needed, if only the pilot hadn't seen the VX on the scraped canister . . .

If only, if only, if only . . .

He began unpacking his gear.

"I need a place to set up my tent," he called to Laffite. "Where do you suggest?"

"I am thinking right here," he said, waving an arm at the underbrush around him. "Grab a machete and start clearing."

A machete? Start clearing? Was he insane?

But no, he didn't want to challenge Laffite's authority again. That had been poor judgment. He wanted no confrontations. Laffite was welcome to his captaincy. It wouldn't last long. If things went according to plan, by tonight Marten would be the only living human on the island.

He grabbed one of the three machetes, pulled the crude black eighteen-inch steel blade from its sheath, and went to work on the underbrush. In minutes his palms were burning. His hands weren't used to this kind of work. He'd have blisters soon. He'd have brought work gloves had he known.

"*Olha!*" Razi said in Portuguese. "They watch."

Marten straightened and looked around. Sure enough, the subcanopy was teeming with dapis, clinging to branches or leaping from tree to tree, their tails stretched out behind them—leaps of ten to a dozen times their body length.

"They're always watching," Marten said.

Laffite gave him a quizzical look. "I thought you didn't speak Portuguese?"

Uh-oh.

Marten hadn't told anyone he knew Portuguese—*some* Portuguese. As Keith he had taken the Rosetta Stone course on his trips back and forth to Mozambique. But as Marten he'd decided it better to let people like Laffite think he didn't know the language. Laffite's English was far better than Marten's Portuguese anyway.

Besides, people tended to speak frankly about you when they thought you couldn't understand them.

"I don't," he replied in English. "But you can't spend time around here without picking up a few words. I certainly can't hold a conversation."

Laffite gave a slow nod along with a calculating stare.

More suspicion. Not good.

Bakari jabbed his machete into the dirt and strode toward the traps. "We catch one."

The live traps collapsed flat. Laffite had brought along a dozen, and two larger holding cages, which did not collapse.

"How do you plan to work this?" Marten asked, eager to get off the subject of languages.

The Frenchman's stare lasted a few more heartbeats, then he said, "I am figuring on heading back with two dozen males. That should allow me to test the market. If things go as I predict, the first group will create a buzz among exotics enthusiasts. Once they sell out and word gets around that there aren't any more, demand will soar."

"As will prices."

A big grin. "Exactly! So, when we have a dozen in this cage, we will take it back to the *Sorcière* and bring over the second. When that is full, we head back to Maputo."

Bakari was walking their way with a fully expanded live trap big enough to hold a raccoon. It would certainly hold a dapi. Even two.

Marten caught himself about to say, *We call those have-a-heart traps back in the States.* No, no, no! Marten was a South African.

Instead, he said, "I'm not familiar with this model."

A total lie, but Laffite didn't need to know that.

"They're quite ingenious," Laffite said. "Bakari, give our friend a demonstration."

Bakari set the trap down and knelt beside it. It ran about thirty inches long and maybe a foot high and wide. Five sides were quarter-inch steel mesh. A handle protruded from the center of the top, and a galvanized steel plate blocked the entrance.

"This is a one-door trap," Laffite said. "It is very strong. Once in there, a dapi will not be able to get out."

"But how does it get in?"

Bakari unlatched the slanted front panel and retracted it until it was positioned flat against the top of the trap. He latched it there.

"The door is spring-loaded," Laffite said, "with the trigger in that little plate on the floor of the trap. When the dapi takes the bait . . . watch."

Bakari stuck a slim twig through the top of the cage and poked the trigger plate. In an eye blink the steel panel snapped off the top and into the open end, blocking it.

"The door can't be opened from the inside, only the outside. The dapi is unharmed and safe from predators until we collect it." He smiled. "It even has a snack to munch on." He looked at Bakari. "Speaking of which, what will you use for bait?"

Bakari lifted a protein bar. "This. They like." He pulled a hunting knife from a sheath on his belt and cut off a piece.

"On Madagascar we bring sliced bamboo shoots for lemurs," Laffite told Marten. "They of course can forage for their own, but we've found that soft, moist, sliced shoots fresh from the tin are a delicacy for them. We brought a case of those."

Marten looked up and around and saw dozens of dapis watching them intently.

Just then the sunlight dimmed. Marten checked the sky, expecting a cloud, but no. The sun was starting to dip behind the rim—not setting yet, just slipping out of sight.

Suddenly the dapis started howling, heads raised, lips pursed, filling the air with discordant, high-pitched ululations. Bakari and Razi pressed their hands over their ears, but Laffite was smiling, his expression fascinated. Marten imagined his own expression mirrored the Frenchman's.

But the discordance gradually diminished as the disparate tones found each other and blended into a single note echoing through the canopies, filling the caldera. They held that note for a long, long time. And then, as abruptly as it had begun, it stopped.

"*Mon dieu!*" Laffite said, eyes wide. "I am . . . I have never . . . what was *that?*"

Marten was equally amazed. The indri lemurs of Madagascar sang, but their "songs" were more like prolonged hoots and howls. They did *not* sing in unison.

And now that the dapis had finished their song, they resumed watching the human interlopers.

"We must catch," Bakari said in Portuguese as he resumed resetting the trap. "We must!"

Marten glanced again at the audience of dapis, then turned to Laffite. "You might want to hide how the mechanism works when you unlatch the door."

"Why?"

Marten gestured about. "They're watching."

"So?"

"So they learn very quickly. They're highly intelligent."

"But they are also very little. You said yours weighed less than a kilo. These weigh no more, from the look of them."

"I'd say you're right."

"Well, then, that means their skinny little arms will be unable to overcome the power of the door spring. It is quite strong."

He was probably right, but Marten had felt obligated to say something, just to show the Frenchman that he was on his side and wanted to help him succeed.

But Marten had no intention of allowing Laffite to succeed.

He watched Bakari reset the trap, then carry it deeper into the caldera. Marten had just resumed hacking at the undergrowth with the machete when Bakari returned not five minutes later.

"That didn't take long," he said.

Bakari grinned. "This is test. We see if—"

He was interrupted by sudden screeching from back the way he had come, entirely different from the singing of a few moments ago. This had a terrified edge to it.

"Ha!" Bakari cried, pumping a fist in the air.

He ran back through the brush, Marten, Laffite, and his brother close behind. In a small clearing, maybe one hundred yards from the camp, they found a crowd of dapis, all clustered around something. They scattered at the humans' approach, revealing Bakari's trap. And inside, a very frantic, frustrated-looking male dapi, hurling itself against the sides, pulling at the door that wouldn't budge.

Same brown fur as Mozi, same white belly as Mozi . . .

Marten's throat tightened. Keith trying to surface again. Down, Keith. No thoughts of Mozi allowed. Mozi is dead and gone and good riddance!

As the four humans surrounded the trap, the dapi quieted, shrinking into a wary, cringing crouch.

Above and all around, his fellow dapis clung to the surrounding branches and trunks, chattering as they watched.

"Always they watch," Razi said.

Yes, always watching, Marten thought. Watching and learning.

Laffite knelt beside the trap and studied the captive.

"Do not be afraid, little fellow," he cooed in Portuguese. "We are not going to hurt you. We are going to feed you and keep you safe and find you a good home."

He signaled to Bakari who lifted the trap by its top handle. This elicited a frightened scream from its occupant that was immediately echoed by the surrounding dapis.

"I not like dapis," Razi said. "They not scared like should be."

Though he knew exactly what he'd said, Marten asked Razi to repeat it in English, then responded: "Don't forget, this is their island. They've ruled here for millions of years. We are newcomers. They don't know us yet."

Laffite nodded. "But they will learn to fear humans soon enough."

Don't count on it, Marten thought.

As Bakari moved off with the trap, the dapis followed, seeming to fly as they leaped from branch to branch. Marten stayed behind. He'd noticed dapis clambering up the smooth baobab trunks and clinging there to watch. With no branches, how did they manage that?

He moved to the base of one of the cylindrical trunks, a good six feet across, so thick it would take three or four grown men to stretch their arms around it. He inspected the reddish-gray bark.

"Looking for something?" Laffite said behind him.

Apparently the Frenchman wasn't going to let him out of his sight.

"I'm trying to figure how they climb these trunks." He ran his hand over the smooth surface. "With nothing to grab on to, how do they—?"

He felt an indentation under his palm and took a closer look. A small notch, an inch wide and perhaps half an inch deep, had been cut into the thick bark about five feet off the ground.

Laffite moved closer. "What is it?"

"Not sure . . . give me a second . . ."

He felt around some more, higher this time, and found another notch, identical to the first, maybe two feet above it.

"Handholds," Marten said as wonder filled him. "They've cut handholds and footholds in the bark."

"'They'? Who? The monkeys? The dapis?" Laffite's expression was a study in skepticism. "That is crazy."

"Is it?" Marten said. "Who else is around to do it?"

"But why? They have all these other trees that are easy to climb."

"Right. But these baobabs produce a tasty fruit, and if you don't want to wait for it to fall, then you have to go up and get it."

Marten backed up for a better look. Yes . . . a third notch had been cut above the second.

"How did they do it?" Laffite said, his tone still incredulous. "What did they use? Teeth? Bite the bark?"

"These trees are amazingly resilient," Marten said, moving closer again, "and their bark is thick and tough." He inspected the notch at the five-foot level more closely, poking the tip of his little finger into it. "I don't see any teeth marks here. This looks like it was *cut* into the bark."

"Cut? With what?" Laffite barked a laugh. "Don't try to tell me they have little axes!"

Marten glanced at him. "In a way, they might. A sharp-edged piece of lava stone might do the job very nicely. It's hardly in short supply on a volcanic island like this. In fact, from the looks of these notches, I'll bet that's exactly what they used."

"But that would mean . . ."

"Yes. They use tools."

Marten continued to stare at the notch. This was a whole other level of intelligence. Mozi had been able to open a three-number combination lock, but that had been imitative behavior—she'd watched the attendants dial in the combination and simply mimicked their actions. These cut notches were a number of steps ahead of that. This meant not only confronting a problem—how to scale a smooth, branchless baobab trunk—and formulating a solution, it meant devising the means to implement that solution.

"I am very impressed," Laffite said. "This will make them even more valuable. Imagine what my customers can teach their new pets."

"Yes . . . imagine."

Grinning, the Frenchman put his hands on his hips and did a slow turn. "Look at this place. Pure. Clean. Untouched. It is very possible we are the first humans here, ever. It is a paradise. We must keep this secret."

"We've already agreed on that."

"But I was thinking of money then . . . only money. This is more important than money. We must keep this place . . ." He snapped his fingers. "What is your word for 'without dirt'?"

"Pristine? Unsullied?"

"Yes! Unsullied."

"Does this mean you won't be bringing dapis back to the mainland to sell?"

Laffite laughed. "Now you are making the joke, yes? Of course I will. But I will work extra hard at keeping others of my kind away from this little piece of paradise. I feel as if we have discovered the Garden of Eden."

The remark jolted Marten. The Frenchman didn't know it, but he was very close to the truth.

Even if they'd forgotten the way back to the makeshift camp, all they had to do was follow the noise. The trees around the camp were alive with chattering dapis. The cacophony was terrific.

They found Bakari standing over the trap as he pulled on a pair of yellow-and-black heavy-duty firefighter gloves. Razi, also gloved, stood nearby gripping the open door to the holding cage. In a single swift, smooth, practiced motion, Bakari slipped back the spring-loaded door with one hand and, like a snake striking, jabbed the other into the trap. The dapi screeched as the glove closed around his chest and he was eased out, kicking and struggling all the way.

Marten wasn't sure what happened next. The dapi's screech was replaced by a howl from Bakari, followed by a curse as he hurled the little primate to the ground. It landed hard and screeched again, but this time obviously in pain.

Razi scooped it up and deposited it in the holding cage, closing the door after it. Bakari was shaking his right arm and muttering a few more curses in Ronga or Tsonga—Marten couldn't tell them apart. His forearm was bleeding where the dapi had bitten him.

"How did that happen?" Laffite said, looking furious. "You've done a thousand transfers without a bite."

Bakari said only, "First aid," and went looking for the kit.

Marten and the others turned their attention to the cage where the captured dapi was clinging to the three-quarter-inch mesh of the side wall, whimpering. It tried to lower itself to the floor but yelped when its right leg touched down. It couldn't bear any weight on it.

"Damn it, Bakari!" Laffite shouted. "You broke its leg!"

Marten looked up. The dapis filling the trees around them had gone silent. They clung to their trunks and branches, staring. He felt a chill. They were more intelligent than he had imagined, and they'd seen everything.

The only sound was Laffite continuing his tirade against Bakari.

"You've ruined it! I can't sell it with a broken leg!"

None of that mattered, of course. Marten had no intention of allowing a single dapi to leave this island.

4

MAPUTO, MOZAMBIQUE

After checking into the Hotel Cardoso, Laura had settled in her room and called home to touch base with Marissa before she left for school. Someone knocked on her door just as she finished.

Rick.

"Time to make a few decisions," he said, waving a map.

She had her suitcase opened on her bed so he unfolded the Madagascar map on the tile floor. He pointed to a thick dot made with a Sharpie.

"Here's my best approximation of the coordinates Mugabe gave us—a hundred miles or so off Madagascar's west coast. If there's an island, that's where it is."

Laura sat on the edge of the bed, looking over his shoulder.

"But how do we get there?"

"We do what Keith did. We take a chopper, only we take it from Madagascar instead of Mozambique." He pointed to an area labeled *Morondava*, east-southeast from the coordinates. "That's the closest town big enough to have its name on the map."

"Fine," she said. "But how do we get there? And do they even have an airport? And if they have an airport, does it have a helicopter we can rent?"

Rick sighed. "Good questions. We need a travel agent, someone who knows this stuff."

"How about the concierge?"

"Now there's a thought. You take a nap while I go down and check this out."

"No, no," she said, shaking her head. "I'm on my second wind." Or was it her third? Either way, she couldn't sleep right now. "We'll go together."

The concierge was young and beautiful, with mocha skin and short black hair, straightened and shiny and close to her scalp. The brass nameplate on her desk read simply *BIANCA*.

The first thing Rick did when they sat down was slip a hundred-dollar bill across her desk. How many of those had he brought?

Bianca slid it back. "That isn't necessary, sir. I'm here to help."

Rick reached around and slipped it under her keyboard. "I have a feeling you're going to earn it. If you still want to return it after we're done, I'll accept."

She gave him a concerned look, but left the bill where it was. "How can I help you?"

"Tell me about Morondava."

"On Madagascar?" Her face lit, making her even more beautiful. "I've been there. Very picturesque."

Good, Laura thought. "Does it have an airport?"

She nodded. "A small one."

Better.

Rick said, "Do you know if there's a helicopter there we can charter?"

"No, but I can find out. This may take a few moments. If you'd like to visit the bar . . ."

Laura could have used a glass of wine, but drinks would have to wait.

"We'll just explore the place."

They strolled toward the floor-to-ceiling windows at the far end of the lobby.

"Do you really think you had to bribe her too?" Laura said.

Rick shook his head. "I consider that a tip. In a very real sense I've asked her to act as our travel agent, which is probably outside the scope of her concierge duties. I'm banking on that nice piece of change to fix her focus on us and put anyone else on hold."

Laura glanced back. "I don't know if you noticed, but she's a stunner."

"Oh, I noticed. Reminds me of Josephine Baker."

She laughed. "You're right! You're full of surprises, aren't you. How do you know about her?"

"What's so surprising?"

"Well, neck deep in the clandestine services, as you've been all these years, I . . ." She shrugged. "I don't see how you'd run across her. She's not exactly in the news."

"There's a place in the city where I grab dinner now and then. Called Chez Josephine. Supposedly run by one of her offspring. Paintings and photos of her in various stages of undress all around the place. Great risotto."

They stopped at the glass wall and looked out over the city to the blue waters of the Mozambique Channel. She glanced back and noticed Bianca waving to them.

"Hey, she's got something."

When they reached her desk she said, "There is someone with a four-seater helicopter who takes sightseeing charters along the coast."

Rick handed her a credit card and said, "Can you book him for tomorrow?"

She nodded and began speaking French into the phone.

"French?" Rick said, glancing at Laura.

"After Malagasy, it's the second official language of Madagascar," Laura said. Before he could ask, she added, "I looked it up."

She'd been happy about that, since her French was fairly decent.

"Done," Bianca said, hanging up. "You are reserved. Most of his business is on weekends so he is glad to have a Wednesday charter. Is there anything else I can do?"

"Yes. Book us on the next flight to Morondava."

Her smile faded. "I have heard an American expression that applies to this: 'You cannot get there from here.' You have heard this?"

"Unfortunately, yes. But the town's right across the channel. There's gotta be a way."

"Yes, via Johannesburg and Antananarivo."

Rick beat Laura to it: "Antananarivo? Where's that?"

"It is the capital of Madagascar."

Laura shook her head, dismayed. "So we're talking four airports and three flights?"

"I am afraid so."

Rick looked at Laura. "You need sleep. Stay here and I'll go."

Like hell. She couldn't count how many times she'd watched those *Madagascar* movies with Marissa, who absolutely loved King Julien. If she ever learned that her mother didn't go there when she had the chance, she'd never forgive her.

"I'll sleep on the way."

Rick looked like he was about to say something, then thought better of it. He turned back to Bianca. "Okay. Can you get us there sometime tonight?"

She pursed her lips. "I doubt that very much, but I'll try my best."

It turned out she could get them to Johannesburg tonight, but they'd have to stay over before traveling to Madagascar. They decided to stay where they were and head out early tomorrow.

They thanked her and wandered away. Bianca did not offer to return the hundred-dollar bill. Laura doubted Rick would have accepted it anyway. As they stepped into the elevator, she noticed a lost expression. She'd never seen that look on him before. It didn't fit.

"What? Something wrong?"

He sighed. "So strange to care about my brother after all these years. Don't think I thought about him once since I left home. Thought he'd rejected me, but you've made me see he was probably doing the best he could."

Watching this tough, macho guy, this trained killer, struggling with unaccustomed emotions, Laura felt a sudden urge to hug him and tell him everything would be all right—that together they'd *make* it all right.

Oh, hell, why not?

She threw her arms around him and squeezed. "He'll be fine, Rick. Really. And so will you."

After a couple of heartbeats' hesitation, he returned the hug. "If you say so."

"Let's go to my room."

Did I just say that? she thought.

Yes. She did. And she meant it.

Rick looked flustered. "Um, Laura—"

"Hush."

She watched the glowing numbers climb, her excitement, her *need* heating with every floor. When the doors slid open she half dragged him down the hall. She fumbled with her key and got the door open and pulled him inside. As it closed behind him . . .

"Now, where were we?"

"Laura?"

She didn't want to lose this momentum, couldn't let this feeling peter out. She put her arms around him.

"I believe I was like this and you were—go ahead."

He put his arms around her as before. "I . . ."

"This is where you kiss me."

Please don't say no.

Rick hesitated a second. "Are you sure?"

"Absolutely."

He lowered his head and their lips met.

Yes!

She started unbuttoning his shirt. "It's time, it's time. It's way, way past time."

5

DAPI ISLAND

Marten squatted by the Coleman stove and stirred the pot of *matata*.

Amaury and the brothers had been frankly dubious when he volunteered to cook dinner for the group. Even more so when he produced cans of premade matata from his duffel—they actually made faces. But when he produced a pint of port wine and a bottle of extra-spicy peri-peri sauce, they changed their tune.

The caldera had grown downright chilly with the loss of the direct sunlight—lava rock didn't hold heat very well—and his fellow explorers seemed to relish the idea of a hot meal.

He'd emptied the cans of the traditional stew of diced clams and crushed peanuts with spinach, garlic, onions, and olive oil into an aluminum pot. The fresh port wine he'd brought would give it extra flavor, and the peri-peri would add a spicy kick.

He'd brought along some extra olive oil as well. The canned stew already had enough but the extra amount would mask the oiliness of the VX he was going to add at the end.

No worry about the heat of the stew degrading the neurotoxin: Its boiling point was up near 600 degrees Fahrenheit. He wasn't going to let the matata get too hot anyway. He wanted his hungry companions to spoon it in quickly, to make sure they each ingested a lethal dose before the effects started.

He had an unlabeled six-ounce plastic bottle full of VX in his duffel, just inches away. He'd bought the bottle in a Maxixe drugstore on Saturday before his helicopter flight and transferred the leftover VX from the sprayer before boarding the *Sorcière*. An earlier plan had been to fill the port wine bottle with it, but VX was too clear to pass for port.

When the time came, in a minute or so, he would add it to the stew—all six ounces. Why take chances? Even if one or two of his fellow travelers didn't die, they'd be too sick and weak to pose any threat. Marten would be able to set about his tasks without worry of interference.

Razi wandered over and sniffed the stew. Grinning and nodding, he said, *"Bom!"*

Without asking he grabbed the bottle of port and took a swig.

Oh, yes. A very, *very* good thing Marten hadn't substituted VX for the wine.

Giving a thumbs-up, Razi returned to the others where they sat near the tents, playing cards in the fading light. They'd thrown a blanket over the holding cage and the injured dapi within had gone quiet. The primate audience had either wandered off or gone into hiding.

Continuously stirring the pot as he kept his eyes on the trio of card players, Marten slipped his free hand into the duffel and felt around for the VX. He'd chosen an opaque plastic model the size of a small mouthwash bottle, but with a sturdy twist-off cap. Leakage—or worse, breakage—would spell disaster. He found it, wriggled it free, and set it beside the Coleman, out of sight of the card players.

Now the risky part. Now . . . gut-check time.

Risky hardly seemed the proper term when his own agonizing death was a very real and proximate possibility, especially since he was going to have to open the bottle barehanded. With a human LD_{50} of only ten milligrams, a drop or two on one of his hands would not kill him, but would make him very, very sick. He had a syringe of atropine in the duffel for just such an eventuality. It would save his life, but all his secrets would come out, all his plans would be ruined.

He glanced longingly at Bakari's fireman gloves lying atop the covered holding cage. If only . . .

Opening it would take two hands, so he stopped stirring and—

Just then Laffite shot to his feet and stepped toward Marten. He nodded as he passed and picked up one of the battery-powered lanterns they'd brought along.

"Getting so dark it is hard to see my cards," he said as he turned it on and held it up.

"What are you playing?" Marten asked, just to be friendly and seem more casual that he felt.

"Poker. Five-card draw. You wish to play?"

"I'm not much of a gambler."

"We raise one metical at a time."

"Maybe after dinner," Marten said, secure in the knowledge that he'd be the only one standing by then.

Laffite leaned closer and frowned. "You are well?"

The question startled Marten. "Why . . . yes. I'm fine. Why do you ask?"

"You look . . . not well."

"No, I'm fine. It's just that it's . . . it's been a long day and I'm not used to so much physical exertion. But I-I'm fine, really, and I'm sure I'll feel even better once I get some of this delicious matata into me."

Laffite grinned. "Well, hurry up then. We are all hungry."

He returned to the brothers, set the lamp atop the cage next to the gloves, and resumed his card game.

Well, the dim light would work to Marten's advantage. He grabbed the bottle and gave the cap a slow, careful twist. It didn't budge. Totally paranoid about a leak, he'd put extra effort into tightening it. Now he had to undo that effort. And be discreet about it.

It didn't help that his hands were sweating. He tightened his grip on the cap and strained, but his damp fingers slipped. He pulled out the tail of his shirt, wrapped it around the cap and tried again.

Finally it gave. That was all he wanted right now. Just loose enough to unscrew when the coast was clear.

He checked out the trio of card players . . . all concentrating on their hands.

Now or never.

Holding the bottle vertical and rock steady, he quickly unscrewed the cap. Cries of dismay from the card players—someone must have lost with a good hand. He risked another look—still clear—and upended the bottle over the stew while he resumed stirring. As the last of the VX disappeared into the mix, he heard Laffite's voice.

"What's that you're adding?" He was ambling toward Marten and the stove.

Marten's heart began hammering against his ribs.

Oh-hell-oh-god-oh-shit!

"Just a little more olive oil."

"Oh, well, one can never have enough—wait." He pointed to a bottle standing next to the stove. "Isn't that your olive oil?"

SHIT!

"Oh, yes, well, you caught me there. This is a secret ingredient I use whenever I—I mean, I use it to dress up canned matata."

Laffite's eyes narrowed. "Is that so? What exactly is it?"

Marten kept stirring the pot to keep his hand from shaking. He forced a smile. "Well, now, if I told you it wouldn't be a secret, would it."

"I am not finding this funny, Monsieur Jeukens. Why can you not tell me what you just poured in the stew you are about to serve us?"

Bakari and Razi had risen and were now flanking Laffite. They looked just as suspicious as their boss.

Marten dropped the empty bottle to the side.

"All right, all right." What to say? What was an innocent clear liquid he could add to matata? *What?* A liquor? Tipo Tinto rum sprang to mind, but it was the wrong color. But that gave him an idea. "Since you insist: It's my . . . my own homemade rum."

"Oh, is it now?" Laffite said. "Is it really? And why did you not bring any on our search for this island? I might have enjoyed some. Or did you cook it up just over the weekend?"

"I-I-I've been letting it age." Damn, he wished he could stop stammering. "Wait till you taste it in the matata." He kissed his fingertips like a clichéd French epicure. "Delicious!"

"I am thinking that we do not want to taste anything that you do not taste first." He glanced left and right. "Is that not right, *mes amis?*"

The brothers crossed their arms over their broad chests and nodded.

"Você primeiro," said Razi, pointing to the pot.

No! He didn't dare *touch* the stew, let alone eat it.

Marten shot to his feet. "This is insulting! You are implying that I am trying to harm you? *Poison* you? That's ridiculous!"

"Is it? Maybe you want all these dapis for yourself."

Marten waved his arms in genuine anger. Did they take him for a fool?

"Now you insult my intelligence as well! If I meant to steal your dapis, I'd wait until you three did all the work of capturing them, *then* I'd poison you!"

The obviousness of his blurted words seemed to give Laffite pause. Marten pushed the advantage.

"The simple truth, Amaury, as I've told you all along, is I don't want to sell the damn dapis, I want to *study* them! In fact, the book I am going to write about them will net me more than your profits from selling them, no matter how many you move."

Highly unlikely, but it sounded good and Laffite just might buy it. He *had* to buy it!

But Laffite held firm. "So you say. But I want to see you eat your matata. If all is fine, then I will apologize and we will have a good laugh."

"Oh, I doubt that."

"But . . ." The Frenchman's eyes narrowed. "You *will* eat it."

Marten returned the stare while his mind raced. What to do? What to *do?* If he ate, even half a spoonful might kill him, or at the very least make him ghastly ill. And if he refused, they might very well force some down his throat. Either way, they'd know he was trying to poison them, and they'd kill him. He saw no way out of this.

Except . . .

He steeled his knees and grabbed a small plastic bowl.

"Very well. But I want apologies from all three of you after I prove my innocence."

He began spooning the matata into the bowl, careful to avoid getting any on his fingers. When it was half full, he flung it at the three, then grabbed the handles of the pot and hurled it.

Without waiting to check his accuracy, Marten spun and darted for the brush. Even though the sky still held a faint red glow, light in the caldera had faded to the point where it was dark as night among the trees.

Which meant he had to be careful. Running headlong into a baobab trunk and knocking himself out would make an already catastrophic situation worse. So he slowed his pace, lowered himself into a crouch, and eased through the underbrush with both hands stretched out ahead of him.

From behind came angry shouts. Had he splashed them with enough of the doctored stew to stop them? Their clothes would protect them to some extent, and the ingredients would have absorbed a fair amount of the VX—which wouldn't have mattered a damn bit if they'd ingested it, but it reduced effectiveness as a topical agent.

His hands banged against something wide and hard. A baobab trunk. Keeping in contact, he slid around it and took the opportunity to check out the way he had come. Beams of light flickered through the foliage.

Flashlights. They were coming after him.

Which meant he hadn't hit them with the stew—or at least not enough of it to matter.

Fighting the almost overwhelming urge to break into a blind run, he took a breath and took stock. He'd left a trail through the undergrowth. Moving blindly through the dark, no way he could not. But could they follow it in the dark, even with flashlights? Laffite was an excellent seaman but that didn't make him a good tracker. The brothers had grown up in a village in the western wilds of Mozambique but had spent much of their adult lives as city dwellers. If they'd ever had tracking skills, how much was left?

Marten decided to take a chance: He reversed course, moving toward them for half a dozen paces, then he dropped to the ground and belly-crawled into a thick patch of undergrowth. At least it felt thick. He waited.

Soon he heard them crashing through the brush, moving at a good speed, not trying to hide their passage. Damn, the stew hadn't even slowed them down! How had he missed them so completely?

He heard a murmur of voices, then started making out words.

"There! Broken branch!" Razi's voice, speaking Portuguese. "We are right behind him!"

Marten thanked his stars—and himself—for expending the effort to take that Portuguese course.

He tensed as Laffite's flashlight beam reflected off something dark and gleaming in his other hand. A revolver. Did he mean to shoot on sight?

Marten had discarded his own handgun in Maxixe. He hadn't wanted to get caught with it if he was stopped while racing back to Maputo.

"What if he's headed for the boat?" Bakari said, also in Portuguese. His voice sounded strained. "He could maroon us here."

"The ladders are back the other way," Razi said.

"Yes, but he could double back along the rim and climb down."

"Relax," Laffite said. "I would not leave the *Sorcière* to be stolen. I removed the fuse to the fuel pump, and I have all the replacements. No one is taking the *Sorcière* anywhere without me."

Good to know. Marten had had plans for Laffite's boat all along. Now he just hoped he'd live long enough to use this information.

"Why would he want to poison us?" Razi said. His tone sounded hurt.

"He is crazy," Laffite said. "I have sensed it all along. But I did not realize just how cr—"

A retching sound interrupted him as one of the brothers vomited. It splatted on the ground not two feet from Marten's face, but he froze in position, squeezing his eyes shut and staying statue-still as he held his breath.

Razi blurted something in Ronga, so Bakari must have vomited.

"Don't tell me you tried that matata!" Laffite said.

"Never! I just feel sick all of a sudden."

The Frenchman's voice rose in volume. "Look! It got on your pants. Maybe it goes through the skin! Take them off! Now!"

Another retch but this time the vomit landed farther away. Marten saw Bakari's jeans hit the ground.

"Come," Laffite said. "Let's get you back where we can wash off that leg. We'll look for Jeukens in the morning. This island is small and he's not going anywhere."

Biting back a sob of relief, Marten crossed his forearms on the ground and rested his head on them.

Safe . . . for the moment.

6

MAPUTO, MOZAMBIQUE

Even after they'd caught their breaths and lay in a quiet tangle of interlocked limbs on Laura's bed, Rick still couldn't quite believe it had happened.

Something about her eyes when she'd said "Let's go to my room" had hinted at this, but even as she'd dragged him down the hall, he'd written it off to wishful thinking.

But then the kissing, the unbuttoning . . . and then falling onto her bed . . .

"I needed that," she whispered, her breath warm on his ear. "You have no idea how I needed that."

He pulled her closer. "I feel like all my bones have melted."

An exaggeration, but not a big one.

Laura's bare breasts pressed against the side of his chest as she let out a long sigh. "I know just how you feel. *God*, it's been a long time."

"For me too."

She kissed his cheek. "Oh, no. I've got you waaaay beat. You're the first since Steven and I split."

"But that's been . . . years."

"Tell me about it. Not that it mattered most of the time. At first my anger at Steven carried over to all men and I was happy—no, make that *delighted* to be alone. And then Marissa got sick and I had more important things to deal with."

"And now?"

"Now she's better—thanks in large part to you—and you and I have been dancing around this since that night in Orkney."

Oh, yeah . . . their kiss in her hotel room . . .

He said, "I'll be honest: The might-have-beens of that night—I mean if Clotilde hadn't interrupted with such terrible news—they've followed me around ever since."

She lifted her head. "You too? Why didn't you say something?"

"I don't know. The time never seemed right."

He didn't say that *he* never seemed right—for her. Still didn't.

"You know, for such an alpha male, you've been awfully beta around me."

"Fear of rejection. No one's immune from it. Especially since our relationship is so important to me—even if it never got past friendship."

"What made you think I'd reject you?"

"Well, I wasn't picking up anything that said you wouldn't."

"I was ready to try another level back in Orkney—surely you sensed that."

"I did, but we'd both narrowly escaped being killed that day, and we'd just finished sharing two bottles of wine—not to mention haggis, a well-known aphrodisiac—so it may have been just the special circumstances, never to be duplicated again."

She frowned. "Haggis is *not* an aphrodisiac, and I thought I was sending signals."

"If you were, well, not on a frequency I'm tuned in to."

She gave a soft laugh. "Okay, I admit I'm out of practice in the signal department. But I get a sense there's more to it."

Should he say it? Aw, hell . . .

"Well, yeah. You could do better."

She narrowed her eyes. "Does this have anything to do with Düsseldorf?"

She'd homed in on that like a guided missile.

"It has to do with a lot of things. I've killed . . ."

"Tell me about it. I saw you gun down four men—right in front of me."

"Three. The fourth was friendly fire."

"Which you made sure went into him. I saw that with my own eyes and I'm okay with it. I mean, we'd both be dead if you hadn't."

He'd done so much worse.

"It's not that—"

"It's got to be Düsseldorf. But you told me all about that."

No, not all . . .

"Rick, you have to let go of that guilt."

"Trying."

But he wasn't. Not really. Because sometimes he thought the guilt might be the finest part of him, the part that kept him sane—well, reasonably so—kept him anchored, gave him hope for himself.

Those blue eyes bored into him. "'There is no try, only do.'"

He had to laugh. "You're quoting Yoda to me?"

"Whatever works." She stretched. "Well, at least now we've gotten this over with."

"'Over with'?"

"Okay, that didn't come out right."

He feigned hurt. "Was it such a chore?"

She kissed his ear. "You know damn well it was anything but. But you've got to admit it's been an elephant in the room ever since we got back. So allow me to rephrase: At least we've broken the ice."

"Yeah, but now that we're in the water, do we sink or swim?"

"We swim. Synchronized swimming. But we keep it on the down-low."

"Yeah. I don't think Marissa's ready for that."

She rolled her eyes. "You've got that right, so no PDAs."

"PD—?"

"Public displays of affection."

"God, no." Some of her glossy black hair had fallen over her face. He brushed it back and tucked it behind her ear. "So where are we? Lovers? Friends with benefits? Coworkers with benefits?"

"I don't know. Do we have to call it anything? I don't take this lightly, Rick. And I don't invite just any man into my bed. Well, to tell the truth, I've *never* invited a man into my bed."

"I'm honored to be the first," he said, meaning it.

"I'm not the same woman I was even just a few years ago. Back then I thought I had a faithful husband, a healthy daughter, and a secure sense that the universe functioned according to a fixed set of rules. But then I learned that said husband was having a string of affairs, that mutated cells were trying to take over my daughter's bloodstream and kill her, and that a legendary cure-all that breaks all the rules of science isn't legendary at all. Everything solid has turned to air."

He held her tighter. "I know the feeling."

"I know you do. That's why I feel connected. We've been through a fire together. My whole worldview has been upside down since we returned. But yours has been flipped for a lot longer. How do you do it? How do you handle it?"

He sighed. How to say this?

"When science lets you down and reality proves unreliable, you're left with people—you've got to find people to believe in."

She cocked her head. "Am I one of them?"

"Most definitely. That's why I've been hanging around, making a pest of myself."

"You're anything but a pest. And just for the record, I believe in *you*. That's why you're here in my bed. But I can't be the only one you believe in. There has to be someone else."

"Not really. Stahlman, maybe."

"Stahlman?" She looked shocked, and maybe a little disappointed. "Of all people."

"I know you have issues with him, but Marissa's alive because of him."

"I know, I know. It's just me being emotional. But of all people to believe in . . . he's just about money."

"He's comfortable letting people think that, but there's lots more to him. Anyway, let's not talk about Stahlman. What about us in the here and now? What have we got here?"

"Well, it's too early for love, don't you think?"

Not too early for him. He'd played musical beds since Düsseldorf—he blamed it on PTSD, which might be a cop-out, but as good an explanation as any. He'd cared for each of those women, but loved not a one. He'd never felt about any woman like he felt about Laura.

But he said, "If you say so."

"We've got trust, lust, passion, compassion, a bond of shared experience that few couples ever have." She smiled as she rolled onto her back and pulled up the sheet, covering her breasts. "They'll do for now."

Rick tugged at the sheet. "Don't cover yourself."

"I'm not twenty anymore. Allow a mature woman some modesty."

"You've got a goddess body."

"A goddess with stretch marks, in case you didn't notice."

"I did. In fact, I kissed them on the way down, in case *you* didn't notice."

"I had my eyes closed. And speaking of down . . . where on Earth did you learn—?"

"Uh-uh. A guy's gotta have his secrets."

"No, a woman's got to have her secrets; a guy's supposed to lay them all out on the table."

"Well, okay. On one of my many trips to the Orient, I studied with a master of—"

"Don't say it!" she cried.

"You don't know what I'm going to say."

"I do. Tongue-fu, right?"

"You ruined it."

She laughed. "You must have been an A student. I think I broke my previous record for consecutive orgasms."

The truth was, he loved to pleasure a woman, and nothing he could remember had given him more pleasure than pleasuring this woman today.

He slid down the sheet and nuzzled a nipple, darker brown against the brown of her skin. "Want to try for a new record?"

She gave a little gasp and arched against him. "It won't be easy. Especially since we have an early flight tomorrow and I need my beauty rest."

"I'm always up for a challenge."

7

DAPI ISLAND

"How are you feeling?" Amaury said in Portuguese.

Bakari's voice was a barely audible croak. "Sick."

Bakari had got the worst of it. Amaury and Razi had a drop here and there on their pant legs, but Bakari had caught a big splash from just below his left knee down to his boot.

And now he lay on a blanket, curled into a fetal ball, shaking uncontrollably, his pocked face glistening with sweat. Amaury had seen people in a malaria crisis shake like this.

"Are you cold?"

Bakari only shook his head and continued shaking.

"Your friend tried to kill my brother!" Razi said, his hands opening and closing as if yearning to fasten around someone's throat.

"He's not my friend!" Amaury shouted. "He was never my friend!" He lowered his voice. "But I never thought he was my enemy. I never thought he'd . . . try to kill me."

Amaury found it unfathomable. What did Jeukens have to gain by killing him and the brothers? If he had wanted to keep the secret of the island to himself—to guarantee that only he knew it existed—the time for murder would have been on the way back during the first trip. He could have killed Amaury, brought the *Sorcière* close to some deserted stretch of Mozambique's coast—no shortage of those—then pointed the boat south and swum ashore. It would have wound up adrift in the uncharted stretches of the Indian Ocean and might never have been found.

He'd always thought the Afrikaner a strange one, but not a murderer.

Amaury realized he felt hurt. Betrayed. And a little sickened.

Why not simply bring a gun along and shoot them? So clean and easy. And manly. Poison was for women. A Borgia game. A slow, painful death.

Did Jeukens hate Amaury so much?

And what had he used for poison?

Taking Bakari's gloves from atop the cage, Amaury pulled them on and lit a second battery lantern. He approached the Coleman, careful to avoid the splattered matata. The burner was still lit. He turned it off. He remembered Jeukens pouring clear fluid from a plastic bottle into the stew. He'd put it down when Amaury confronted him and—

There! The bottle, on its side, close beside the stove. He held it up to the light. A few drops remained in the bottom. He took a quick, cautious sniff but smelled nothing.

He guessed it killed if you ingested it—why else would Jeukens add it to the matata?—but, considering Bakari's reaction, it seemed to work through the skin as well.

Movement next to the Coleman caught his eye. A six-inch, blood-red millipede was undulating across the ground toward the spilled matata.

"You might not want to go there," Amaury muttered.

He watched it wriggle to within an inch or so of a splatter and stop. It raised its head, swayed back and forth, then turned and retreated.

Amaury couldn't smell anything, but this thing apparently could.

Which gave him an idea.

Squatting, he upended the bottle over the millipede and let the last three drops within fall onto its undulating back. It crawled on, but only for a few seconds. Then it stopped, shuddered, and began a frantic writhing. Within fifteen seconds it was curled into a twitching ball. Very soon after that the twitching stopped.

Amaury dropped the bottle and backed away. So quick. So awful. It looked like every nerve in the millipede's body had gone wild.

Some sort of neurotoxin.

He clenched his teeth. That was what Jeukens had planned for them? No question about it: They had to find him and kill him on sight. Amaury had never killed a man but he could not allow Jeukens another chance at murder.

Then again . . .

If Jeukens was truly going to identify these dapis as the missing link, the payoff would be enormous. That made him worth keeping alive.

Why was nothing ever simple?

And why hadn't he done a background check on Jeukens? Not that he had the resources for a deep backgrounding, but he hadn't even Googled the man. No reason to. He paid in cash, and cash was king in Amaury's business. But now that he was thinking of it, how did he know this man had any scientific credentials at all? He could be a psychopath who simply *believed* he was a scientist.

A psychopath who had decided to murder his fellow travelers.

A nightmare! This simple trip—return to the island, bag some pets, and then go home—had turned into some sort of horror film.

Amaury returned to Bakari, who seemed to be shaking less.

"Feeling any better?"

He nodded weakly. "A little."

Maybe they'd be lucky. Maybe they'd dodged the Afrikaner's poison bullet.

As he set the second lantern down on top of the holding cage, he noticed the blanket had been disturbed. Had the dapis been at it? He lifted it and saw the injured dapi still inside. He didn't know whether to be relieved or not. He didn't know what to do with it.

"I'm sorry you are hurt," he said in a soothing voice. "It was an accident. We wish to harm no one." He thought of Jeukens. "Well, almost no one."

Then he noticed that the cage latch was partially undone. His fellow dapis must have come down and tried to open the cage while he and the brothers were off chasing Jeukens. He'd have to arrange a better lock.

He glanced up into the trees and gasped as he saw the eyes . . . just the eyes . . . countless big blue eyes reflecting the light from the lanterns.

A galaxy of eyes, watching . . .

8

Once he was sure Laffite and the brothers were well gone, Marten lifted his head and looked around in the darkness.

Shit! Could things get any worse? He seemed cursed. Not that he believed in curses or any of that crap, but someone who did could make a damn good case that the place had doomed him to failure. He was stranded in a rain forest at night with no flashlight and no supplies. If he hadn't been under such pressure, he might have thought to grab his duffel, but escape was all he could think of at that time. So he had his hat, shirt, pants, shoes, and nothing else.

What else could go wrong on this damn island? Surely the island would think of something before the night was through—if he survived the night. He had little doubt that if Laffite and company caught up with him, they'd drag him back and force some of that stew down his throat.

He shuddered at the thought of what would follow.

He still had a chance. He knew exactly where he'd left his backpack. The canisters were another story. If his luck continued on its present course, both would be ruptured and the VX that hadn't soaked into the ground would be splattered on all the surrounding leaves.

But . . . if they'd survived the roll down the hill intact, he could salvage this. It might mean sacrificing his own life in the process, but he was ready for that. This was too important.

Humanity was depending on him.

WEDNESDAY

May 25

1

DAPI ISLAND

No-no-no-no-no!

The backpack was gone.

Marten had remained in the bushes all night, napping now and again, but too much on edge to allow himself to fall into a deep sleep. What if he started snoring? He'd exerted himself all yesterday and had planned to have the island all to himself—well, except for the dapis—by the end of the evening.

And so he'd been wide awake when the sky began to lighten. Soon he could make out details of the forest around him. The sun had yet to peek over the rim, but he had more than sufficient light to see where he was going.

He marked the brightest part of the sky as east and began heading in a northerly direction, sticking close to the wall as he moved. He didn't know whether he'd reach the backpack or the canisters first. It didn't matter which, just as long as he found them both.

He'd left the backpack by an odd-shaped rock. He'd chosen it because it resembled a heart—the Valentine's Day kind of heart rather than the real thing—and how many of those could there be? And now he'd found it, but no backpack. He was sure he'd left it behind this particular rock. He remembered standing back and taking a mental photo of it.

Along with the two bricks of C-4 and the detonator caps, the backpack contained two bottles of water and at least one, maybe two granola bars. He needed those other things to complete his mission here but, oddly enough, he missed the food and water more right now. He'd eaten one measly protein bar since yesterday afternoon, and he was starving.

Okay. Keep it together. Forget the rumbling stomach and find the VX canisters.

If they'd ruptured and spilled their contents, the backpack no longer mattered. *Nothing* mattered then, because he was doomed. Amaury and the brothers would start tracking him soon and inevitably find him.

And, with the *Sorcière* disabled, he had no way to leave. Even if he did manage to elude them, eventually they'd leave him here. How would he survive? He had no survival skills. He—

Stop! Just . . . stop.

This defeatist thinking was counterproductive. Focus on the goal: Find the canisters and the backpack. They had to be nearby. They couldn't walk away by themselves, and no one was around to move them, so they had to be where they'd come to rest on Saturday.

Unless . . .

The dapis!

Even with coordinated effort, they weren't strong enough to move the canisters. But the backpack . . .

They'd sniff out the granola bars inside and go after them. With their intelligence, they could figure out the zippers through trial and error, and easily gnaw through the buckle straps. They'd eat the granola, maybe even chew holes in the water bottles—easy with how flimsy they made them these days.

But what about the C-4? They couldn't eat that. They might think it was edible at first, but if the smell didn't turn them off, one bite would.

And the detonator caps? What interest could they possibly have in those?

Okay, they'd raided the backpack and carried it off. Mystery explained. He could still find it, or what remained of it, but even more important, he had to find those canisters.

So he began a methodical hunt, moving quickly along the base of the wall until he came across some crushed vegetation. He followed the damage inward and found the first canister. He now realized it had been a blessing and a curse that Mahdi had painted it olive drab. The color hid it from the casual passerby—Amaury and his crew would never spot it by accident—but it had made the task of finding it more difficult for Marten.

He approached it cautiously, looking for cracks in its surface or fluid puddled around its base. The lack of odor made VX more useful as a weapon, but he wished now it had some kind of stink. He checked the ground around it for dead insects—it had been invented as a pesticide, after all—but found none.

Everything looked dry so he gave the canister a gentle push. It made a quarter roll and still showed no sign of damage. Another push . . . still good.

Marten let out a breath. One canister, fully intact. He was halfway there.

He went in search of the other. It shouldn't be far. And it wasn't. He found it thirty feet away. Also undamaged.

He gave a little fist pump. He was still in business. Well, almost. Now he had to—

High-pitched howling suddenly filled the air, the same discordant ululations he'd heard yesterday evening. And just like yesterday, the discordance gradually diminished as the disparate tones modulated and blended into a single thousand-throated note that filled the caldera. The dapis sustained that note until, as if receiving a signal, they all cut off at once.

Marten looked up. He saw no dapis, but he knew they were there, watching . . . always watching. What he did see was sunlight beaming across the top of the baobab canopy. The sun had crested the rim. Morning had officially arrived in the caldera.

Was that what that howling signified? Saying hello and good-bye to the sun? But that would be a . . . ceremony.

A ceremony? Marten felt a pinching at the back of his neck. These little primates used cutting tools and had developed a sun ceremony. All very primitive, but they should have neither. They were exhibiting a level of sentience that should be well beyond them. Could it be their screwed-up genome? They carried hsa-mir-3998, but even that shouldn't account for their unexpected behaviors. Or could it?

He shook himself. Moot. All moot. He had to concentrate on his next short-term goal: Find the C-4 and those detonators.

2

"That's the last of them," Bakari said in Portuguese as he sliced off a piece of protein bar and affixed it to the trap's trigger plate. "*Now* can we go find him?"

Amaury set the spring on the trap's door and reined in his temper—just barely. "Not yet, damn it!"

He and Razi had taken turns on watch through the night while Bakari slept the sleep of the dead. He'd brought his old beat-up Llama .38 revolver to the island on the chance that they might need defense against predators. Who would have guessed that the predator would be Jeukens? He doubted he'd return but hadn't wanted to take the chance. He'd gone through the Afrikaner's duffel and found the usual travel gear: extra clothing, toiletries, canned food, a flashlight, batteries, a satellite phone, but no mysterious little bottles that might contain poison.

Amaury had lent Razi the handgun for the first four-hour watch, and he had taken it back for the second. He wouldn't tell anyone, but he had drifted off during his watch. If the howling of the dapis hadn't awakened him and the brothers as well, they all might still be asleep.

Bakari seemed to have recovered but was moving slowly. He complained of hurting all over. The violent tremors of last night had left him with agonizingly sore muscles, but not sore enough to keep him from wanting to hunt down Jeukens.

Amaury had had plenty of time to think on that during his night watch, and he'd decided they should accomplish their mission here first.

"He tried to kill us," Bakari said. "He very nearly succeeded with me. You are not hurting. You do not care."

As bad as Bakari felt, he had insisted on helping to set the traps. While Razi, armed with the Llama, watched the equipment, Amaury and Bakari were out here setting up half the traps in scattered spots around the caldera. They were baiting all six with pieces of protein bars. Razi would go out later and bait his six with bamboo shoots. Lemurs loved the canned shoots but dapis might be different. They would find out. It didn't matter which bait worked better; neither was in short supply.

"Of course I care. But we came here to capture these little primates, these dapis, and that is what we are going to do. When we have a couple dozen of them all secured on the boat, then, and only then, will we start searching for Jeukens."

"But—"

"No buts, Bakari. He is not going anywhere. When I have what I came for, we can devote a few hours to search for him."

He frowned. "A few hours? I want to *find* him—I *need* to find him." He pounded a fist into his palm. "I have a score to settle."

"Of course you do. But we're not going to waste a lot of time on this. If we don't find him, we'll leave him here."

Bakari gave him a puzzled look. "We let him get away with it?"

Bakari was a good trapper, but not the brightest.

"He's not getting away with anything. When we leave we will be taking his duffel with his food, his phone, his clothes—everything. He will be marooned. He will have to find water, he will have to figure out what he can eat and what he cannot. When we return in a few weeks for our next batch of dapis, I don't think we will have to go looking for him. If he has managed to stay alive I will bet you he comes looking for *us*!"

Bakari's expression remained grim. "I do not wish to wait that long."

"But you might have to. Sometimes delaying a satisfaction makes it so much better when you achieve it." He saw no comprehension in Bakari's eyes. He felt as if he were talking to a child. Well, if that was the case, he might as well drag out one of his mother's old sayings: "And remember, all good things come to those who—"

From off to their left came the unmistakable sound of a trap door snapping shut.

"Do you hear that, *mon ami*? Already one takes the bait! That is the sound of money in the pocket! We may be looking for the Afrikaner sooner than you imagined!"

He led the way to the trap they had set just before this one. They found it as empty as they had left it. Emptier, in fact: The trap door was down and the bait was gone.

"What?" Amaury cried. He lifted it, examined it up and down. "How . . . ?"

The only thing inside was a two-inch length of twig. He dropped the trap and rushed back to the next in line where he found the same thing: a sprung trap but no dapi and no bait. And another short twig.

"Impossible!"

Wait . . . impossible for dapis, yes, but not for a human.

Amaury turned and leaned close to Bakari. "Jeukens," he whispered. "Don't look around!" he added as Bakari began to turn. He raised his voice: "Let's go check the other traps!"

They'd set six. The next was the third they'd set, and they found it just as empty of bait and prey as the previous two, though it too contained that short twig. Was Jeukens leaving it as a calling card of some kind?

They continued on to the first two traps they'd put out and found something different. No dapi trapped within, though the door on each had been sprung. But these still contained the bait. It made no sense.

Was the Afrikaner toying with them?

They had one trap left to check—the last one they'd just set. They rushed back to it and Amaury wasn't terribly surprised to find it sprung and empty except for another twig.

It had to be Jeukens. He had no food, so he was raiding the traps for the pieces of protein bar. But why had he left the bait in the first two?

He brushed that concern aside. Why didn't matter. They had to stop him from sabotaging their traps.

Keeping his voice low in case the Afrikaner was nearby, Amaury said, "Reset the trap with a larger piece of a bar. While you're doing that, I'll beat the bushes to see if he's nearby."

Amaury hurried through the undergrowth, ducking under the branches of saplings. He covered a fifty-foot radius and was pretty sure Jeukens was not about. Probably elsewhere looking for more traps to raid.

When he returned to Bakari, the trap was reset with a good-size chunk of protein bar on the trigger plate.

"You go that way," he whispered, pointing south. "Go as far as you can without losing sight of the trap, then hide. I'll do the same this way. He's hungry. He'll be back. And then you'll have your revenge."

Bakari's yellow grin was not pretty. He nodded and loped off.

Amaury headed north. He found a spot thirty feet or so away where he could crouch behind a stand of bamboo and watch the trap.

It didn't take long for company to arrive, but not the sort Amaury was expecting: Four dapis scurried down from the trees and headed toward the trap. They didn't scamper on all fours, but crossed the gap in bounding leaps like exaggerated skipping, very much like he'd seen lemurs do when out of the trees. They seemed at ease, not cautious in the least. One hopped on top of the trap while another paused before the open end. The two remaining stood back to back on their hind legs, their forepaws dangling in front of them, much like meerkats do. What were—?

And then he knew: sentinels. They'd set up a pair of lookouts.

All right. Dapis instead of Jeukens. He'd settle for a dapi. They were the reason Amaury had come here in the first place.

"Go ahead," he whispered. "Don't be afraid. Go in and grab that delicious bait."

Then he noticed that the dapi atop the cage, a female, was holding a slim twig, maybe six inches long. She worked it down through one of the slots in the trap door, then guided it through the mesh of the top and a couple of inches farther into the trap.

The small male darted inside, yanked the bait free of the trigger plate, and dashed out again, all without the door closing. The female on top snapped the twig at the level of the trapdoor. The released spring pulled the door down and slammed it shut as she followed the male and the two lookouts into the trees.

Amaury's mouth hung open as he rose and hurried toward the cage.

What just happened here?

He reached the cage a few seconds before Bakari.

"Did you see that?" the big man said, his expression slack with wonder.

Amaury dropped to his knees beside the cage and found just what he expected: the little two-inch length of twig on the floor of the trap. They'd figured out the mechanism. But how was that possible? They were dumb little animals.

Then he remembered the Afrikaner's words: . . . *they learn very quickly . . . they're highly intelligent . . .*

But this was almost human-level intelligence.

And he remembered something else: Yesterday Bakari had stuck a slim twig through the top of the cage to poke the trigger plate . . . a twig very similar to the one the female dapi had used.

Jeukens had warned Amaury about not letting the dapis see how the trapdoor mechanism worked. Hide it from the watching dapis . . . the always-watching dapis.

Watching and learning.

Clearly, Jeukens hadn't been stealing the bait. The dapis were behind it.

He saw it all now. The dapis had failed on the first two traps. They'd stuck the twig through as they'd seen Bakari do, triggering the trapdoor. But in the course of doing so the female had seen how the door worked. So she stuck the twig through one of the slots in the door and into the mesh beneath it, preventing the door from moving. That left the male free to go in and remove the bait. After he'd escaped the cage with his prize, she broke off the twig and let the door slam closed.

My God, if they could learn something that complex that quickly, surely they could be toilet trained. He grinned. An adorable missing link that could be toilet trained . . . The asking price for these little creatures kept going up and up . . .

The smile faded as the immediate consequences of what he had just seen slowly dawned.

"We are fucked," he said softly. Then he shot to his feet and kicked the trap across the little clearing as he shouted to the trees. *"Fucked!"*

"What is wrong?" Bakari said.

"The traps—they're useless. The dapis know how to get around them. We'll never catch a single one!"

Which meant this trip had just become a complete waste of time. He'd have to go home empty-handed. Or rather, go home with only a broken-legged male, which was as good as empty-handed.

Or was it?

His thoughts ranged in all different directions. There had to be a way to salvage this.

A breeding pair.

Yes! He had a male. If he could catch a female, just one, he could start breeding his own dapis. Breeding primates was always a challenge, and he had a feeling these dapis would find ways to make it even more difficult. But they'd be worth all manner of trouble if he succeeded.

The problem was . . . how to catch that one female?

On occasion he'd captured parrots and other exotic birds with fine-mesh nylon nets. He had a couple stowed on the *Sorcière*. Maybe he could entrap a female with one of those. He and the brothers would have to be on her immediately before she chewed her way out.

Amaury nodded. Yes. He could make it work. Maybe once, twice at most—they learned too fast. He'd never catch the two dozen he'd planned on. His dream of a quick score had been crushed, but he could make do with a slower, long-term plan.

The most important question was: Were the nets still on the *Sorcière* or had he moved them into storage at the dock? He prayed he'd procrastinated about them. Because—

A faint sound caught his attention. As it grew louder, he recognized it as engine noise.

No. This couldn't be happening.

He looked at Bakari. That *wup-wup-wup* sound could only be . . .

"A helicopter?"

3

"Finally!" Marten muttered as he fairly leaped upon the fourth and last detonator.

He'd been following a bread crumb trail—extremely odd bread crumbs—through the grasses and undergrowth for what seemed like half the morning. The first thing he'd found were the granola bar wrappers with no sign of the bars. Apparently they tasted pretty good to the dapis. Next came the empty water bottles.

Then . . . pay dirt: the two bars of C-4 within half a dozen feet of each other. Each showed signs of nibbling through the black wrappers and into the off-white plastique beneath—very little nibbling on the explosive itself. The polyisobutyline binder probably tasted awful. Same with the roll of duct tape he found nearby—nibbled, then tossed.

A short way farther on he'd found two of the detonators in a Gordian tangle, and nearby, his satellite phone, looking as if it had been dumped from the backpack as not worth a second look. Next came the ripped backpack itself, hanging from a branch. He checked inside and almost shouted with relief when he saw his two trigger phones and their batteries still attached to their plywood bases.

At that point he was pretty much back in business, but he'd wanted the last two detonators. Theoretically—and practically, as well—he needed only one per block to set off the C-4, but his mission was too important to leave anything to chance. He wanted two detonators per block. And now he had them.

Most of the damage to the backpack had been to the outside pockets, so he loaded everything back into the main compartment and lugged it all back to the VX.

After arranging the two canisters side by side, he realized the situation was far from ideal. But he'd make do.

First he used the duct tape to affix a block of C-4 to each canister, wrapping the tape all the way around. Then he poked holes in the wrappers and inserted the detonators deep into the claylike material.

Now for the phones.

Shortly after arriving in Mozambique to begin his search for Mozi's kin, he'd picked up three satellite phones. One he used for calls, the other two he'd modified to act as detonators. All three were tied to Mcel, the government-run provider, which supposedly allowed him access to five Intelsat satellites. His phone had worked well on the earlier trip to the island, but would it work *on* the island? Would the wall enclosing the caldera affect the signal? It shouldn't, but there might be something in the lava . . .

He held his breath as he turned on his phone, dreading the sight of a *No Service* message on the screen. But no, it found a signal. One of the Indian Ocean satellites was in range and in line. He had service.

Instead of the elation and anticipation he should have felt, dread filled him. He was about to commit an atrocity.

Between trips up and down the coast, he'd worked on the trigger phones, exposing their vibrators and soldering wires to opposite sides of the vibrating chamber. When the vibrator went off, it would close the circuit between them. Then he'd glued each phone, along with four interconnected AA batteries in a waterproof pack, to a small board. Three alligator clip wires—two red, one black—completed the process. Some of the clips had come loose in the mishandling of the backpack by the dapis. He reattached these and was ready to go.

He taped the phone boards next to the C-4 blocks on the canisters and turned on the trigger phones. He'd been keeping them charged in his apartment all along. Before he attached the detonator wires, he made sure each of the four AA Energizers in the battery packs was properly oriented as to positive and negative. Then he checked that each phone was working. He had the numbers on speed dial and, after attaching a circuit tester, called each. The tiny bulb lit on each call. If the detonators had been connected, they would have exploded.

Ready.

To be extra safe, he turned off his calling phone before attaching the alligator clips to the detonator wires. The worst-case nightmare scenario in a situation like this was some stranger calling his mom or his girlfriend and misdialing a digit so that the number just happened to match the trigger phone. Though in the realm of possibility, the odds were overwhelmingly stacked against that happening. And here on the island, the odds were astronomical, because a simple cell phone wouldn't reach; the unwitting dialer would have to be using a satellite phone.

With the detonators attached to their triggers, Marten rotated the canisters so that the C-4 block on each was facing and almost touching the other. This guaranteed success. All he had to do was trigger one block. The force of its explosion would set off its brother block, vaporizing the contents of both canisters.

Ideally, Marten would have liked one canister positioned on the north end of the caldera and one on the south, but that was impossible now. He couldn't risk getting caught in transit.

This would do the trick. When he made the first call, the combined blast would create a VX-laced shock wave, destroying nearby vegetation, but more importantly, sending a cloud of vapor throughout the caldera, filling every nook and cranny with deadly toxin, killing everything: reptiles, mammals, amphibians, birds, insects—anything that moved. And that included humans and dapis.

If his first call failed, he had the second number, the second phone, wired to the second block of C-4.

The trees and grasses and brush would remain, unharmed, thriving in their tropical paradise. The VX would eventually dissipate and other life would return. Birds and insects at first, and perhaps even a mammal or two would find their way here.

But no dapis. The dapis would be extinct.

The question was: when to make the call? And from where? He could detonate them from anywhere in the world.

If his original plan had worked out on Saturday, he would have wired up the canisters at each end of the island and detonated them from the helicopter on his way back to Mozambique. But that had gone belly up, forcing him to improvise.

Now everything was set to blow, but he had no way off the island. He was willing to die to see this end the way it must, but only if he could find no other way. And there was almost always another way. If—

He froze as he heard an unmistakable sound. A helicopter. But where was it coming from? The sound echoed off the lava walls, filling the caldera with noise that seemed to come from everywhere.

But-but-but . . . the only pilot who knew the island's location was dead. So who was up there now?

He headed toward where the sound seemed loudest.

4

"I am amazed," the pilot said in French through Laura's headphones. *"Who would have dreamed . . . ?"*

Laura gazed in wonder at the tiny, sheer-walled island below. Definitely volcanic. From up here it resembled a potted plant, a rough-hewn stone bowl filled with sprouts, although these sprouts were trees.

The pilot had been amused and downright condescending when they'd shown him the coordinates they wanted to explore. He'd echoed Lieutenant Mugabe almost to the word.

"There's nothing there but empty ocean."

Rick had convinced him to humor the two crazy Americans. The pilot had shrugged and said it was their money and no difference to him.

The day up until then had been hectic—no, beyond hectic into frantic. They'd awakened early, made love—not as languidly and as leisurely as she would have liked, but still a wonderful way to start the day.

She tingled at the memory of yesterday and this morning. She felt more at peace than she had in a long time. She supposed their lovemaking had something to do with that. She wished they could have spent the rest of the day in bed, but . . . not possible. Not today.

Quick showers and then off to Maputo Airport where they caught the first South African Airways shuttle to Johannesburg. For breakfast they gobbled lemony braided pastries called koeksisters during their brief layover before flying Air Madagascar to Antananarivo.

Their first argument of the day occurred in the Antananarivo airport. Rick wanted her to wait at a hotel—read, tour the capital, hang out at the pool, that sort of thing—while he tried to find his brother. If he found Keith, he'd either convince him to come back or not, but either way, Rick would be back in Antananarivo by nightfall.

He lost that argument.

From Antananarivo they had an hour flight in a propjet to Morondava and their helicopter. Bianca had given them the pilot's cell number, and Laura had called before boarding. The pilot had not been hard to find in the tiny airport. His name was Antso Rakotomalala and he'd looked hungover. He told them his *oiseau*, as he called it, could give them three hours in the air.

Then she and Rick had their second argument. Rick didn't know how skilled their pilot was or how well he maintained his chopper, they were headed out over open water where they wouldn't be able to make an emergency landing should the need arise, they had no idea what they'd find at the coordinates, if anything, blah-blah-blah.

He lost that argument too.

By the time they sighted the island, they'd used a third of their air time. But Laura was glad she'd come along. The flight itself had been no fun, what with the incessant noise and vibration, the uncomfortable seat, the monotony of empty open water in all directions, but the discovery that their trip had not been in vain made it all worth it. The island had appeared as a bit of cloud on the horizon and had grown into this tiny jewel in the middle of nowhere.

Rick made a circular motion with his hand. *"Tell him to look for a place to land."*

Laura relayed the message in French. Antso spoke very little English but he was already nodding and banking his *oiseau*.

They cruised around the south end of the island and, as its west side came into view, they all pointed out the anchored cabin cruiser at once. Rick signaled to descend and they buzzed by at twenty feet above the waves. *Sorcière des Mers* was clearly visible across the transom.

"*Sea Witch*," Laura said. "The animal dealer's boat. We've found the right place."

"*Now we just have to hope we're right about Keith being with him.*"

"He has to be," Laura told him. "Where else can he be? The police say he's disappeared from Mozambique. If Mozi's family is here, it's the only place he *wants* to be."

"*The boat looks deserted.*"

Laura had to agree. If anyone was aboard, they surely would have come on deck to check out the racket of a helicopter buzzing them. She looked past the *Sorcière* to the island where she spotted something gleaming behind a palm tree.

"Isn't that a ladder against the rocks there?" she said, pointing.

"*Sure is.*"

"Everyone must be on the other side."

Rick was twisting back and forth in his seat. "*We need to find a landing spot.*" He made the circular motion again.

Antso took them around the north shore back to the eastern side. Laura hadn't seen any expanse she considered wide enough to set down, but she was no pilot. He flew them across the top of the leafy canopy, unbroken except for the opening over a central lake.

"Can you land?" she said in French.

Antso's head shake was emphatic. "*Non.*"

"*You're kidding me,*" Rick said, looking disgusted. "*You've got to be kidding me!*" He looked around the cabin. "*He wouldn't happen to have an outside winch, would he?*"

Laura asked and received another *Non.*

Before they'd taken off, Rick had mentioned how he'd have preferred a chopper with pontoons in case a water landing was called for, but Antso's was the only helo for hire, so they'd had no choice.

The plan had been to land on the island—if they found it—locate Keith, and let Rick try to convince him to return to his old life. If that didn't work, at least find out *why*—get a clue as to what was going on in his head, what had triggered this crazy, uncharacteristic behavior.

But none of that would happen if they couldn't land. It looked like they were going to have to return to Maputo and wait for the *Sorcière* to return to its dock.

After a moment of brooding silence, Rick said, *"Tell him to circle the rim."*

Laura translated and the pilot complied.

After a full circuit, Rick said, *"Tell him to head back to the north edge."*

As the chopper banked around, Rick turned to her.

"All right, here's the plan. I'm gonna get out at the widest section of the rim." He glanced at his watch. *"By my estimate, he's got forty-five minutes of hover time before he has to head back. That's not enough for me to locate Keith and do any meaningful convincing."*

Laura immediately saw where he was headed but kept her comments to herself.

"So here's what I want you to do: After I'm down on the rim, you and Antso go back to Madagascar and wait till you hear from me." He held up his sat phone. *"I'll take this with me. When I'm ready to head back, I'll call you. You then call Antso and have him come back to pick me up—either with Keith or without him."*

As Antso reached the northern section of the rim and hovered there, Laura nodded, repressing a smile. Rick had it all figured, a perfect solution—for him, anyway. One that left her sitting on her hands back in civilization. She appreciated his wanting to protect her, but he should know by now that she was no novice where exploring a jungle was concerned. She'd spent her first two years after graduating medical school as a very well-paid bioprospector in Mesoamerica. Despite Rick's SEAL training, she could probably find her way around that island better, and locate Keith before he did.

But she made no protest. No point in arguing. It would simply waste time.

"How are you going to get down from the rim to the base?"

"Inner slope's gentler." He was snapping closed all the pockets on his bush jacket. "Looks like an easy climb down."

Laura had noticed that too.

"When do you want to do this?"

"ASAP. Explain it to him and see if he's cool with it."

She did.

Antso looked at Rick as if he had two heads, then said in French, *"You will have to pay for another charter, of course."*

"We realize that," Laura told him. "Same as this one."

He seemed to like the idea. With a Gallic shrug, he said, *"Bon."*

"Great," Rick said. *"Would you please tell him to set down here, just long enough for me to hop out?"*

Laura relayed the message, but Antso shook his head. His *oiseau* was already wobbling in the updraft from the channel side.

"Trop dangereux!"

Rick didn't need a translator for that.

"Okay, ask him to get as low as he dares."

Laura translated. Antso nodded and eased his *oiseau* down to about half a dozen feet off the uneven but generally flat surface of the rim.

Rick cupped his hand behind her neck and pulled her close for a kiss.

"Wish me luck."

He pulled off his headset, unbuckled his seat belt, and slid back the door. With a last backward look and a wink, he eased himself onto the runner, then leaped. He landed in a crouch, then bounded up to standing.

Antso started to rise and pull away, but Laura put a hand on his shoulder. "Wait."

With a quick wave, Rick stepped to the inner edge, eased himself over, and began to descend.

As he disappeared from sight, Laura tapped Antso on the shoulder, and made a thumb-down gesture as she unbuckled her own seat belt.

"Take me down."

Antso looked at her as if she had not two but three heads. *"C'est fou!"*

Not crazy in the least. That island down there was like a time capsule, an insect in amber locked away from the rest of the world for millions of years, with flora and fauna unlike anywhere else on the planet. A bioprospector's dream. Rick wanted her to return to Morondava to sit in the airport lounge and twiddle her thumbs until he called? Or maybe knit a sweater? No freakin' way.

"Head back to the airport and await our call," she said. "It may take us a few hours to settle our business here."

"*Business? Here? No one has business here. What kind of—?*"

"It's a family matter. Wait for our call."

Shaking his head, he lowered his copter again, getting the skids even closer to the lava this time. In deference to her femininity? Possibly. Whatever, she appreciated it.

She looped the strap of her shoulder bag over her head into a cross-chest position, then slipped out onto the skid just as an extra strong updraft wobbled the craft. She gritted her teeth and hung on till it passed, then leaped.

5

As Rick headed down the wall—it turned out to be even easier than it had looked from the air—he heard the sound of the chopper increase in volume.

That shouldn't be. It had started to fade, but now . . .

Was something wrong?

He scrambled back up and crested the edge of the ridge just in time to see Laura jump from the chopper's runner. She took a couple of stutter steps to keep her balance, then turned and waved at the pilot. Antso was shaking his head as he waved back and banked away.

No-no-no-no-no!

Rick pulled himself up over the edge and onto the rim, all the time waving to get Antso's attention. But the chopper's rotation took him out of Rick's line of sight and then he was beelining east toward Madagascar.

Damn!

"Laura!" he shouted. Damn, he was angry. "For Christ sake! What are you doing here?"

She turned with a startled look. "I thought you'd be halfway down to the bottom already."

It had turned out to be farther than he'd thought, but that wasn't the point.

"Heard the chopper come back and thought something had gone wrong. Never dreamed it'd be *this* wrong. Are you crazy?"

"Look, I'm as ready for this as you are. You've got sneakers, I've got sneakers. We're both in jeans, I've got a long-sleeve T, and you've got your bush jacket."

Saying she was worried about mosquitos and malaria, she'd insisted on the long sleeves for both of them this morning.

"But we don't know what we'll run into down there."

"Yes, we do. A jungle and your brother. I think I can handle those as well as you can."

"Did you forget he's traveling with poachers? Guys who might not like anyone interfering with their illegal—may I emphasize, *illegal*—activities?"

"'Poaching'? You can't call it 'poaching' when nobody even knows the place exists, when everybody tells you the place does *not* exist."

Okay, she had him there.

"Fine. But we're heading into the unknown and—"

"Exactly! Who knows what's waiting down there?" She waved her hands excitedly. "Flora that no one's ever laid eyes on—ever. Millions of years in isolation."

"Right. *The Land That Time Forgot*. That's what I'm afraid of."

She made a face. "You're not seriously worried about dinosaurs."

"Of course not, but—"

"Listen, the vinca alkaloids used in chemotherapy came from the Madagascar periwinkle. There could be a revolutionary cure for cancer waiting down there. And I could be the one who finds it!"

Was she serious? Sometimes he found it hard to tell. Was she playing the cure-for-cancer card just to get him on board with her tagging along, or did she mean it?

He decided she meant it. With Antso and his chopper a dwindling dot in the sky, she was already here and she was coming along.

As if, after last night, he could deny her anything.

And even if last night had never happened, like he could stop her anyway.

"All right. We're going. But I go down first. You stay right above me."

That way if anything dangerous was waiting down there, he'd meet it first.

She snapped to attention and saluted. "Sir, yes, sir!"

He sensed she was wired . . . dying to see what was down there. And he wanted her to see it. But he also wanted her safe.

The jungle wasn't the problem—she knew jungles better than he. Humans were his worry. Those below were interested in trapping animals; he and Laura had no intention of interfering but they might not see it that way. The remaining human was Keith, and he was no danger to anyone but himself.

Rick returned to the place where he'd begun his previous descent and started backing down the slope. Between narrow ridges and small out-croppings for footings, and ferns and saplings for handholds, the going was fairly easy. But about twenty feet down he had to call a halt.

"Can we stop a sec?" he said.

"Bushed already?" she said with a smile.

He turned and waved an arm at the massive trunks looming among all the greenery. "You've seen your share of jungles. Have you ever—*ever*—seen anything like this?"

"Never. I'm *sooo* glad I didn't let you talk me out of this. It's a once-in-a-lifetime experience."

He was glad for her. Her eyes fairly glowed with excitement. She was eating this up.

"It's deeper than you'd think. I guess that allowed those trees to grow so huge. Look at those trunks—like bridge supports."

"That's normal size for this species of baobab. Don't they look surreal with all their leaves at the top? When I first saw the canopy, I didn't real-ize it was composed entirely of baobab leaves. We're now between the canopy and the subcanopy, which starts about another twenty feet down. I can see various palms down there. Below that, where there's less light, the understory should be sparse and spindly. The floor will be thick with low-light, high-moisture grasses and undergrowth." She waved her hand in a get-moving gesture. "Come on. I'm dying to see the rest."

What he really wanted to do was grab her and pull her close and kiss her. He found her overwhelmingly attractive, now more than ever.

Despite all the warnings to himself to keep his distance—warnings for her sake, not his—they were now *involved*. What to call it? An affair? Okay, fine. He'd fallen headfirst into their affair and saw no easy way out. Truth was, he didn't *want* out. The only thing that eased his conscience was the conviction that he'd wear on her after a while and they'd drift apart, and then she'd be free to find a worthy mate and he'd never have to tell her the whole truth about Düsseldorf. When it was over he'd watch her from a distance and feel privileged to have spent any time at all with her.

Is this me? he thought. Really me?

Yeah, this was who he'd become.

They continued down, with Laura maybe five feet uphill from him, offering a nice view of her delightful butt every time he looked up.

"Are you staring at my butt?" she said as if reading his mind.

"I wouldn't say 'staring' exactly. I might be catching an occasional glimpse in passing."

Suddenly Laura was much closer.

"Hey, what're you—?"

"It's farther down than I thought," she said. "And you're going too slow. Beep-beep!"

Now she was beside him, grinning.

And now she was passing him.

"F'chrissake, be careful!"

She kept going. "Come on, slowpoke. Time's a-wastin'!"

He wasn't going to play this game. If they both fell and broke something—

Oh, hell, she was getting way ahead. If he let his feet slip on the mulch he could sort of shoe-ski down and—

No. Somebody had to be the grown-up. Usually it was Laura, being the mom and having the MD degree and all, but not today, apparently. She—

"Stop!" shouted a male voice. "Who are you?"

"I'm—" Laura started to reply but was cut off.

"You can't be here!" A very agitated voice, speaking some kind of accented English. "You've got to leave!"

Laura cried, "Hey, put that down!"

Rick broke through a tangle of ferns just in time to see someone in a floppy hat aim a dead tree branch at Laura's head. He was swinging for the fence but Laura was too quick. She ducked, then stumbled back. Rick wasn't about to allow a second chance. Rage flaring, his instincts prompted him to land a haymaker on the guy's bearded face, but training took over, reminding him how that was a good way to break some of his own bones. So he switched to a backhanded chop against the base of the neck where it joined the shoulder.

The hat flew off and hit the ground beside the dropped branch as the guy wailed and fell to his knees, clutching his shoulder.

Still raging, Rick was about to add a kick to the gut for good measure when the guy looked up at him. He froze.

"Keith!"

A surge of elation gave him a buzz. Keith was alive and well and Rick had found him. If he knew a victory dance, he'd do it right now.

His brother looked pained and puzzled. "That's not my name," he said through a groan.

His shaven head was sprouting a little bit of brown fuzz, his scuzzy beard hid much of his face, and he'd lost a lot of weight, but the eyes hadn't changed. This was the guy in the photo Mugabe had posted. This was his wandering brother, in the flesh.

The brother who'd just tried to crack Laura's skull.

"Keith, you dumbass!" He pointed to Laura, watching wide-eyed a dozen feet away. "You could have killed her! What the fuck were you thinking? And how did you just happen to be waiting here when we arrived?"

"I followed the sound of your copter, of course," he said, still gripping his shoulder as he jammed his hat back on his head and struggled to his feet. "And stop calling me Keith. My name is Marten—Marten Jeu—"

"Jeukens. Yeah, right. Cut the crap, okay? We tracked down the real Marten Jeukens and you ain't him."

Keith looked genuinely confused. "What . . . what are you talking about?"

Aw, no. Did Keith actually believe he was Marten Jeukens? If so, how was Rick ever going to convince him to come home? His brother would need a psychiatric hospital and all sorts of therapy to bring him around.

Rick looked at Laura. "What do you think?"

She shrugged. "I'm not a psychiatrist, but he could have had some sort of break. Or he's a very good method actor."

"Don't talk about me as if I'm not here. Or as if I'm insane. I'm perfectly sane!"

"Yeah. It's everybody else that's crazy."

"And I'm not acting." He looked at Laura. "Who is she, anyway?"

Rick motioned her forward. "This is Laura Fanning. She's a doctor."

Keith looked at her. "A medical doctor?"

"Yeah. The MD kind, not the Ph.D. kind." Rick decided to leave out the medical examiner part.

"No, I don't think you're acting," Laura said, staring at him. "You're so different from Keith. I've seen interviews with Keith and he rarely makes eye contact. But you have no problem with that, do you, Marten?"

Why was she calling him Marten? That only reinforced the delusion.

"Why should I have a problem?"

"And your English," she said. "You've developed an accent . . . almost like German, but not quite."

"More like Dutch," Rick said. He spoke fluent German and Keith's accent was different.

"I'm a South African," Keith said. "Afrikaans is a daughter of Dutch."

Laura looked at Rick. "It's like he's become a completely different person."

"Yeah, whatever. Look . . ." He wanted to add *Keith* but figured he'd play along like Lauren. "Whoever you are, you owe Doctor Fanning an apology for almost—"

"I will not apologize for trying to drive you off!" he blurted. "You can't stay here, either of you. It's too dangerous. You've got to leave, get off the island!"

"Fine. But if we do, you're going with us."

His gaze shifted back and forth between them. "You'll take me?"

"Sure. That's why we're here."

"Wonderful! Can we leave now?"

The response rocked Rick. No way had he seen that coming. But hey, he wasn't complaining. If Keith was going to come along willingly, they'd have no problem getting him back to New York. They simply had to avoid Mozambique, which would be easy enough. Once home, an army of shrinks could get his elevator going all the way to the top again.

"It'll be a few hours before we can leave." He turned to Laura. "How long you think?"

She glanced at her watch. "Antso should be landing within the hour. If he can refuel and head back immediately, we're talking two, three hours."

"Okay," Rick said, turning back to Keith. "You heard her. And while we're waiting, let me ask you something: Do you know who I am?"

"Of course. You're Keith's brother Garrick."

"Really? How do you know that . . . Marten?"

"I know everything about Keith. *Everything.*"

His brother had been Keith up to the day he'd disappeared. When had he changed? Maybe the exotic-pet guys he came with could shed some light on how long he'd been like this.

"The guys from the boat," Rick said. "Where are they?"

"Keep your voice down," he said, looking around. "They could be any-where."

"And that's bad?"

"They tried to kill me."

"They *what?*" This was taking a turn for the worse—way worse. Laura was here, damn it. Or was this just another delusion? "Why would they want to do that? Because of that hat?"

"It's hardly a joking matter. It's true."

Okay, it might be true. *Might.*

"Why?"

This wasn't the *why* Rick most wanted answered—*Why are you calling yourself Marten Jeukens?* topped the list—but it seemed of the most im-mediate concern.

"They want to capture dapis and—"

"Dapis?"

"They're little adapiform primates with big blue eyes."

"You mean like Mozi?"

His eyes widened. "You know about Mozi?"

"Yeah. All about her. Your research assistant Grady gave us the low-down."

"Keith's assistant, you mean."

Rick did a slow count to three. "Okay, Keith's assistant. Anyway, you say these guys want to catch these—what did you call them?"

"Dapis."

"Right . . . dapis. You must have known that when you boarded their boat."

"Of course I did. I came along to stop them. I can't allow a single dapi to leave this island."

"Why the hell not?

"The world isn't ready for them."

"Hey, you had one and the world didn't end."

"Keith had her. He couldn't do what needed to be done, so I did it for him."

"Did what?" Lauren said, her expression saying she wasn't sure she wanted to hear. "What did you do?"

"I killed her." He made a twisting motion with his hands. "Snapped her neck. And then Keith had her cremated."

"Kind of cold-blooded, don't you think?" Laura said, looking offended.

"You do what you have to do for the greater good."

"Why?" she said. "What was the reason? Her genome?"

He jumped like he'd been poked hard in the ribs. "What do you know about her genome? You know *nothing* about her genome!"

Laura had zeroed in on something here—touched a raw nerve.

"I know it spooked Keith."

"Keith was a pussy. He couldn't handle it. That was why he turned to me."

"What was it?" Laura said, pressing. "What couldn't he handle?"

Keith's gaze suddenly averted, roaming the ground, the underbrush. Was the real Keith coming back, or did Marten simply want to avoid giving an answer?

"You wouldn't understand."

"Try me. I'm a doctor."

He sneered. "Doctor! What are you—an internist? A gynecologist? A pediatrician? Unless you're an oncologist or a geneticist, you couldn't begin to understand. So forget about it. Just trust me, no way is the world ready for the secret hiding inside these little primates."

Rick remembered Laura saying something to the same effect—that genetics had advanced so far so fast since she'd graduated that it was like she'd never studied it at all.

But now, more than anything, Rick wanted to know the answer. He was sure someone could reduce the explanation to kindergarten level for him. But another question reared its ugly little head.

"Just how are you planning to keep the dapis secret?"

"Don't worry your head about that, Garrick Somers. Aaaaall taken care of."

Something about the certainty in his tone tightened the muscles in the back of Rick's neck.

"And what about these trappers you're with? What—?"

He stopped as he sensed movement in the thick surrounding greenery. Someone here . . .

He heard a twig snap behind him, and as he turned, a beefy black man charged in from his left. He roared as he bulled into Keith, knocking him clean off his feet. Then he leaped on him and began pummeling him. Rick didn't know if the guy was mad at Keith or at Marten, but either way, somebody was putting a beat-down on his brother, and where Rick came from, you didn't stand around and let that happen—even to a someone who was adamant about not being your brother.

Rick hauled the guy off Keith and slammed the heel of his palm into his nose. Blood shot from both nostrils as bone and cartilage broke. The guy staggered back. As Rick watched, waiting to see how much fight was still in him and if he'd have to hit him again—he hoped not—he felt a pair of strong arms wrap around his chest and lift him off his feet. Rick wriggled a few inches lower, then rammed his head back. Once again came the familiar crack of a nose flattening. The second guy cried out and relaxed his grip just as the first shook off his pain and began to charge.

The second stood with his hands over his nose, and behind him, Laura swung the same branch Keith had tried to use against her. It landed square atop the second's head, shattering in the process and doing minimal damage. Seemed it had been on the ground too long, with termites doing their thing.

Before the splinters could settle, Rick grabbed Number Two by an arm and swung him in an arc like a hammer-throw into Number One. They both went down in a tangle.

And damn, they looked alike. Brothers?

He guessed these were the trappers who'd brought Keith.

The worst thing Rick could do now was let them regain their feet and get organized. Time to start wrecking knees. Number One, the one with a pockmarked face, seemed the closest to standing again. Time to nip that in the bud. Rick had completed one step of a charge when a shot rang out behind him. He skidded to a halt and turned.

A skinny, dark-skinned guy with a ponytail held a bruised Keith by the collar with one hand and had a revolver—looked like a Smith & Wesson Model 10—pointed in the air with the other. Rick stepped closer to Laura and pulled her behind him.

"Everyone stop!" he shouted with a thick French accent.

The pockmarked guy didn't seem to hear. He charged straight at Keith again. But halted when the Frenchman lowered the gun and pointed it at his face.

"*Stop!*" He looked around with a dismayed expression. "What is happening here? What has happened to my beautiful island?" He shook Keith. "Bad enough you try to poison us! But now you bring strangers?"

Whoa. Keith tried to kill *them*? Someone was lying. Who? The Frenchman seemed genuinely distraught, while Keith looked guilty as hell.

Rick remembered what he'd said a few moments ago: *You do what you have to do for the greater good.*

Had poisoning these guys seemed like a greater good?

The Frenchman shifted the revolver toward Rick. "Who are you? Where did you come from?"

As much as he didn't like to have a gun pointed at him, Rick saw no reason not to tell him. He said, "We took a chopper out of Morondava."

"And you simply *found* this place?"

"No, we had the coordinates."

Frenchie's eyes bugged. "Where did you get them?" He shook Keith again. "Did *he* give them to you?"

"No. The police found them—"

He cut off as Laura squeezed his back. He'd used the squeeze technique on her during an interrogation in Israel when he'd wanted her to keep quiet. Was this the same?

Aw shit! They'd got the coords off the dead pilot's notebook—dead from suspected poisoning. And Frenchie here just said Keith had tried to poison them.

Sickened, Rick stared at his brother. Really, Keith? Really?

"What police?"

"Maputo. It's complicated."

"Ah, *oui*. It must be *très* complicated, *monsieur*. You find coordinates in Maputo and decide to hire a helicopter to go there and when you find an island where none is supposed to be, you decide to explore it?"

Laura stepped out from behind Rick and said, "Look, there's a logical explanation." She looked back at Rick. "Okay? I think it will simplify everything if we just lay the cards on the table."

She winked the eye that only he could see. He got it: *Trust me.*

Well, he trusted her like no one else in the world. And she was smarter than he'd ever be.

"Do it."

She turned to the Frenchman and pointed to Rick and Keith in turn. "This man and that man are brothers. I don't know what you're calling him, but that man's real name is Keith Somers—"

"Is not!" Keith said.

The Frenchman slammed his gun against Keith's shoulder.

"Silence!"

"He's a famous zoologist in New York who—"

"*Zoologiste?*" the Frenchman said with a smile. This seemed to make him happy. "Go on."

"He disappeared without a trace almost two months ago and his family has been searching for him ever since. It's been a long, strange trip but we tracked him here. His mother and sister are waiting for him in Morondava and our helicopter pilot will be coming back to pick us up in a couple of hours."

The last two were outright lies—she hadn't had a chance to call Antso about the return trip—but Rick understood the reasoning. She was putting them on notice that other people had the coordinates and knew they were here.

Yeah, she was the smart one.

The pockmarked one's fists were opening and closing with suppressed fury as he glared at Keith and mumbled something that sounded like Spanish but wasn't. Had to be Portuguese. He seemed to have a real case against Keith.

The Frenchman rattled back in the same language, saying "Bakari" in a soothing tone. He pointed to the other black and said the name Razi.

While they were yammering, Rick noticed movement in the trees. He glanced up to see dozens and dozens of the little primates Keith had called dapis. They hung on branches, clung to the fat trunks, and stared with those big blue eyes.

"Laura," he said softly, nodding above him. "Check it out. Mozi's relatives."

She looked up and gasped. "The island must be crawling with them."

When he was finished, the Frenchman turned back to Rick and Laura. "My two Shangaan associates are also brothers and they are going to search you."

"They can search me," Rick said, "but they keep their hands off her."

"You are in no position to make demands, *monsieur*—"

"Anyone lays a finger on her and I'll be on you like a fly on shit and if you think you can stop me before I reach you and ass-whack you and your two errand boys, think again."

He didn't know how well he could back that up, but he intended to try. Apparently he was convincing because Frenchie took a step backward.

"We are not here to harm anyone or cause offense. We are civilized people." He shook Keith again. "Which is more than I can say for your brother here. She may empty her pockets and hand the contents to Razi."

He rattled some Portuguese. Razi looked disappointed, but nodded.

Laura started emptying what little she carried in her pockets into her shoulder bag as the bloody-nosed Bakari patted Rick down. Rick kept watch on Bakari's right arm, knowing the man would not be able to resist a retaliatory shot. He'd let it happen. When he saw the fist close and the biceps start to bulge, he tightened his abs as hard as they'd go. When the punch landed, it hurt, but caused nowhere near the pain it could have.

Rick gave an exaggerated grunt as he doubled over and staggered back. Let the guy think he'd scored a shot. Might mollify him.

Bakari let loose an evil laugh while his brother grinned, revealing a Michael Strahan–class gap in his uppers.

It took Bakari a while to check all the pockets of Rick's bush jacket. That was why he wore the damn thing after all: lots of pockets. He confiscated his satellite phone, passport, compass, and wallet, and seemed inordinately pleased when he came across Rick's stash of zip ties.

"Laffite!" he cried, holding them up. "*Olha!*"

Laffite? Was that the Frenchman's name? Like the pirate?

He looked from the ties to Rick. "You were planning to detain someone, *monsieur*?"

"A thousand and one uses," Rick said.

"I can think of one already." He snapped his fingers at Bakari. *"Me dê."*

As Bakari handed him the ties, he tucked the revolver into his belt and zip-tied Keith's hands behind his back.

"No more poisoning for you. Sit!"

After Keith had lowered himself to a cross-legged position on the ground, Laffite strutted over to Razi and pulled Laura's wallet from her bag.

"Laura Fanning, MD. Medical examiner, it says." He nodded toward Bakari. "We almost had a dead body for you to examine."

Bakari glared at Keith again. Rick guessed he'd survived whatever poison Keith had used.

Laffite moved on to Bakari and took Rick's wallet from him.

"Did he really try to poison you guys?" Rick said.

"Absolument."

"That's not like my brother."

"Still, it is true. Wait. Perhaps he is not your brother. Did you not say his real surname was Somers?"

"Correct." He knew where this was going. "Mine is Hayden because we had different fathers."

He could have added that they had different mothers as well, but no point in getting into family dynamics.

Laffite raised Rick's wallet and passport. "I will keep these."

That had an ominous ring.

"We came for my brother. We'll just take him home and leave you to your business."

Laffite sighed. "I wish it were that simple, *monsieur.* But it is not. I will need to control communications for now."

"Why?"

"I am not sure it is a good idea to let you take your brother home."

"Why the hell not?"

"I need him to research the dapis and to publish his findings. He—"

A cry of pain interrupted him. Keith lay on his side on the ground, curled into a fetal position. Bakari stood over him wearing a satisfied smirk. Rick hadn't seen it, but he was pretty sure Bakari had kicked him in the gut.

"Fucking coward!" Rick yelled, following Laffite as he strode toward the pair.

"Rick!" Laura said, giving her head a quick shake. "Stay out of it."

Rick wanted to ignore her, but realized she was right. He watched Laffite give Bakari a tongue lashing in Portuguese, then direct him away from Keith. He returned to Rick without a backward glance.

Rick said, "Kicking a guy whose hands are tied—that's a low-rent shot."

"Bakari has a right to be angry. He almost died from your brother's poison."

Damn. What had gotten into Keith?

"Then why keep him around? He'll just be trouble. Let us take him off your hands."

Laffite was shaking his head. "These dapis will be valuable on their own, but they will be worth even more after your brother announces to the world that they are the missing link."

Stunned, Rick looked at Laura and was sure her shocked expression mirrored his own.

Whaaaaaaat?

6

The Frenchman, Laffite, led the way, with Keith directly behind him. Laura walked beside Rick, just behind Keith. The two native brothers brought up the rear.

Laffite hadn't threatened them or drawn his gun, he'd simply announced that they all were heading to their camp near the western wall. Keith had been pulled to his feet, she and Rick had been nudged by Razi, and they'd all started moving in the same direction.

She'd given Rick a quick nod that she hoped conveyed her wish that he cooperate. She knew how quick he was and how deadly he could be at close range. But the Frenchman seemed sane and reasonable. She felt sure they could all reach an accommodation that would allow everyone to go their separate ways.

At least Rick hadn't hit her with an I-told-you-so—*Did I or did I not say you should helo back to the airport?* And he probably never would. Not his style.

As they marched—with the indigenous blue-eyed fauna following through the subcanopy and understory above—she used the opportunity to check out the flora below. So many plants she didn't recognize. New species and subspecies for sure. And others she was sure were prehistoric, found only in fossil records. This island was like a time capsule. If only she could stop and examine them more closely.

Finally they arrived at what might pass for a camp—a small, hacked-out clearing with three tents, a Coleman stove, animal traps, and a larger cage holding one lonely dapi. Her heart went out to the little thing as it watched all the goings-on with its wide blue eyes.

"You three stay here," Laffite said.

He wasn't a bad-looking man. He needed a shave and a haircut, but he had a certain magnetism about him. Not as tall as Rick, not as solid, but he exuded a certain roguish charm. Maybe it was the French accent. Maybe because he bore a famous privateer's name.

"Can she have a blanket at least?" Rick said. "To sit on?"

"Yes-yes. I will get her one. But you stay together—close together. I do not want you moving about. Bakari is going back to the boat to gather some equipment, and Razi is going to check the traps. Do not think this is an opportunity for something foolish." He patted the revolver in his waistband. "I will be watching."

"How about my hands?" Keith said. "Can you untie them now?"

"No. I have not yet decided what to do with you."

As the Frenchman wandered away and busied himself around the camp, Rick turned to Keith and spoke in a low voice.

"What's this 'missing link' bullshit?"

"What makes you say it's bullshit?"

"Your assistant Grady told us there are lots of missing links along the evolutionary tree, not just one."

"Grady is *Keith's* assistant, not mine, but he's right. There *are* many. But Laffite doesn't know that. It makes me valuable to him."

"Right," Rick said, anger growing in his voice. "So valuable that he wants to keep you here—and us too. I want to get Laura off this island, so tell him the truth."

Keith shrugged. "It wouldn't do any good. It's something he wants to believe and he'll think I'm changing my story just so he'll let me go. Besides, I'm not ready to leave the island yet. There's something I need to do first."

"What?"

He smiled. "That's my business."

Rick shook his head. "I can see why they want to kick your ass. What's happened to you?"

"Necessity was the mother of my invention."

My invention . . . the way he said it gave Laura the impression he'd attached another meaning to the cliché. He was speaking as Marten Jeukens. Pieces were staring to fall into place. Was he saying . . . ?

"What necessity?" she said. "What did Keith find in Mozi's genome that led him to invent you?"

The question clearly shocked him. And, judging by Rick's expression, him as well.

Keith sputtered but managed to say nothing, so Laura pressed further. "Was one of the so-called God Genes involved?"

"A ridiculous term!" he said. "I hate it. If you must know, Mozi's genome showed that she was a member of a supposedly extinct primate species known as *adapiformes*. Do you even know what that means?"

She flipped through the mental notes she'd made. "She's a transitional species, with characteristics of both . . ." What were the terms Grady had used? ". . . Haplorhini and Strepsirhini, right?"

His eyes widened, then narrowed. "Oh. Your talk with Grady, right? He loves to talk."

"He found your diagram that showed how you were tracking the appearance of one of the God Genes that—"

"Do *not* use that term in my presence!"

"Very well. The diagram tracked your hunt for a gene connected with human creativity." She paused. She wanted to get this right—she had to get this right. Memory, don't fail me now. "Hsa-mir-3998."

"He told you about 3998? That's confidential information!"

Here was where Laura was going to go out on a limb. Mozi's genome had caused Keith to freak out. Using the data she had, she could come up with only one scenario that would shock the hell out of a researcher.

"I'm betting that you—I mean Keith—found something in Mozi's genome that didn't belong there. As an adapiform, she should have been extinct but wasn't. An exciting find."

"You might say," he said. "Sometime in the late Miocene they managed to

reach this natural vivarium. They're smart enough to have wiped out whatever predators and competitors were here before them. With a safe, stable
habitat they no longer had environmental pressure to adapt or evolve and
so their genome has remained pretty much the same for millions of years."

Laura nodded. "Right. So finding her alive would be exciting but not
shocking. Discovering that Mozi carried hsa-mir-3998, however, would
have been mind blowing."

"You're just guessing," he said, his voice hoarse.

"But it's an educated guess. And I'm right, aren't I."

She knew from his expression that she'd hit the bull's-eye.

"Only partially right. Yes, 3998 should not have been there. It's an
astounding anomaly but not, as you put it, 'mind blowing.'"

He was trying to wriggle off the hook, but Laura wasn't about to let
that happen.

"Sure it is. You couldn't find the gene in *any* primates or hominids until
you got near *Homo sapiens*, where it appeared seemingly out of nowhere,
just like miR-941 did a few million years ago."

"All true," he said with a sad smile. "I guess I underestimated you."

Not the first time she'd been underestimated along the way.

She wasn't about to let him know she was ninety percent faking it. She
had to keep pushing ahead before she revealed the true superficiality of
her knowledge of genetics. But raised voices stopped her.

Over by the cage, Laffite seemed to be throwing a hissy fit with Razi in
Portuguese. He'd told them he'd sent the brother to check the traps. Razi
didn't have any dapis with him, so she guessed he'd come up empty.

She turned back to Keith, trying to picture the chart Grady had shown
them. "Okay, you couldn't find this 3998 creativity gene in the Neander-
thals, and it wasn't in *heidelbergensis* or any primates before it. Yet you find
it in a transitional species that should have been extinct for millions of
years. Isn't that mind blowing?"

He shrugged. "Ever hear of HGT?"

"Horizontal gene transfer? Of course. It's how bacteria share antibiotic
resistance."

"We've learned that it happens in mammals too."

It did? That was a new one for Laura. But she didn't keep up with evolutionary genetics.

"We're talking eukaryotic cells?"

"Well, yes," he said, his tone turning testy. "That's the kind we mammals tend to have."

"No need to get snarky," Laura said.

"Whatever. HGT often has a viral vector. If a human retrovirus could have infected a dapi germ-line cell with 3998 from a human, the gene could be passed along to all that dapi's subsequent generations."

"That's kind of far-fetched, don't you think?"

"Far-fetched or not, what matters is we *know* HGT happens in mammals, which means Mozi carrying 3998 is not impossible. We have a mechanism to explain it."

Laura felt as if she'd suddenly been scooted back to square one.

"But-but-but—" She caught herself. She sounded like a damn motorboat. "But then why the big freak-out?"

"That's what I want to know," Rick said, getting in Keith's face. "I've been keeping my mouth shut here because I've understood maybe half of what you two've been talking about, but the takeaway seems to be that there's a scientific explanation for this human creativity gene being in your monkey pal. If that's the deal, let me echo Laura by asking, why the freak-out? Why kill Mozi and incinerate her body and erase every trace of her genome?" He waved his hands up and down at Keith. "And why all this bullshit? The shaved head, the beard, the accent, the stolen identity, the disappearance? *Why?* If there's such an easy explanation for 3998 in her genome, *why the fuck are we here?*"

Couldn't have said it better myself, Laura thought.

Keith took a deep breath. "Imagine you've lived all your life alone in a huge, dusty, dirty mansion with so many rooms you've yet to visit them all. It's powered by a generator in the cellar that has a lever in the on position. The lever can't be moved—when it was pushed into the on position it locked in place and keeps powering the house. And then one day you happen upon a well-lit, inordinately neat bedroom, with clean sheets and not a spot of dust anywhere. What conclusion would you draw from that?"

He's going to answer us with riddles? Laura thought. Like some Delphic Oracle?

She was about to challenge him but Rick beat her to it.

"We're not here to play games, Keith. We want—"

But before he could finish, Laffite appeared with Razi. The Bantu grabbed Keith's arm.

"We are exiling you," Laffite said as Razi began pulling him away.

Keith looked frightened, flustered. "What? Why?"

"We do not want to look at you, so we are hiding out of sight. Exiling you to your own little Elba, you might say."

"Exile?" Rick said, his voice grim. "What are you really going to do to him?

"No harm, I assure you," Laffite said, watching him stumble away. "Actually it is for your brother's own good. I do not trust Bakari near him. The poison made him very sick. No telling what he'll do if he has to look at him all the time."

Laura was ready to scream with frustration. Keith had looked ready to spill.

"Why the freak-out, Marten?" she called after him. "What did you find in Mozi's genome? You never answered the question!"

He looked back at them over his shoulder. "It's never been about what was in Mozi's genome. It's all about what *wasn't* there."

7

Razi led Marten about fifty feet from the camp to a large stand of bamboo. He felt his bladder clench as the Shangaan pulled a wicked-looking knife from a sheath attached to his belt.

"Wait! Wait, you're not—!" Razi grabbed a shoulder and roughly turned him around to face the bamboo. "Wait! Please!"

He felt the knife begin to saw through the zip tie. Was he freeing him?

He was spun back to face Razi who pulled one of Garrick's zip ties from his pocket and handed it to Marten. Through hand signals Marten gathered he was supposed to tie it around his right wrist. He did as indicated, making sure he didn't pull it too tight. Razi turned him around again and pushed his face against the green bamboo rods. From the corner of his eye, Marten watched as a second zip tie slipped through the first and was fastened to a particularly sturdy-looking rod—a good four inches in diameter—locking Marten in place.

Okay . . . one hand free. At least he could take a leak when he needed to. But more importantly, he could use his phone. They'd searched Garrick and his woman, but not Marten. After he'd fled, they'd no doubt searched his things and found the phone he'd brought along, but it would never occur to them that he'd had another waiting for him here. It rested now in a back pocket, under his loose shirt.

The big question: Should he use it?

As far as he was concerned, Amaury and his men were expendable. They were the worst sort of people, profiting from the sale of living creatures. The world would be a better place without them.

But Garrick and the woman . . . what was her name? Laura. Yes, Laura. They were innocent, and they were the best sort of people. Keith had thought Garrick had no regard for him, yet he'd traveled thousands upon thousands of miles to find him. Downright shocking, one might say. Shocking in many ways. They'd been raised in the same family but they shared no blood, and Garrick had been estranged from the family for years. His name was never mentioned—certainly not by his mother—and he'd made no attempt at contacting Keith or even Cheryl, with whom he'd had a decent relationship in their formative years.

And yet . . . here he was. All those miles, all that effort, and he'd found the island, of all things. Who'd have thought he cared so much?

Garrick apparently had unplumbed depths, and Marten did not want to be responsible for his death.

One way or another, however, the C-4 would be detonated and the VX dispersed throughout the caldera—ideally, with Marten and Garrick and Laura airborne or shipboard miles away. But if Marten had no choice, if his back were to the wall and he was faced with sacrificing innocent lives to do what he must, then he would not hesitate.

Razi made a final inspection of the zip ties. He must have thought the tie around Marten's wrist was too loose, because he gave it a firm tug. The loop became snug enough to keep Marten from wriggling free but loose enough to keep blood flowing to the hand and fingers.

Satisfied, he started to walk away, but stopped short. For a heartbeat or two he stared at the back of Marten's shirt, right at the spot where the phone hid.

No!

Marten rotated his body away but Razi was having none of it. He grabbed Marten and pushed him roughly against the bamboo again. He patted down his backside and grunted when his hand landed on the phone.

No! Please!

He pulled it free and waggled it before Marten's face, as if to say, *Naughty boy!*

Whistling tunelessly through the gap in his teeth, Razi strolled off without a backward glance.

Marten didn't know whether to laugh or scream. The numbers of the trigger phones were programmed into the speed dialer. If anyone decide to test them out . . .

8

After Razi had disappeared into the trees with Keith, Rick turned to Laffite.

"He needs psychiatric help. Keith trying to poison anyone is totally out of character. Whatever price bump you think you'll get from any scientific paper published by him will be cancelled out once people realize he's got a bunch of stripped gears in his head."

The Frenchman glanced at Laura. "You tell me he is a respected *zoologiste, oui?*"

"Yes, but—"

"That is enough. People get 'missing link' in their heads and it will stay there."

Laffite stared at Laura, giving her a long, hard look that made her uncomfortable.

"What?" she said finally.

"The card in your wallet says you are a medical examiner. A *coroner?*" He used the French pronunciation.

"Yes."

"This means you see only the dead?"

"Only the dead."

"But in your training, you must fix a broken bone at some time, yes?"

"I did some ER moonlighting where I splinted an occasional simple fracture until they could get to an orthopedist. I've helped apply a cast, but I've never done one by myself."

Where was this going?

"What's with the twenty questions?" Rick said, restless beside her. "Is someone hurt?"

He smiled. "Not 'someone.' Not a person. Come. I will show you."

He led them to the cage with its solitary occupant. The dapi backed away at their approach. Its crippled gait answered a lot of questions. And engendered more.

"How did he break its leg?" she said.

Laffite offered a totally Gallic shrug. "An accident. We do not wish to harm the dapis, only find them good homes."

"Out of the goodness of your heart, right?" Rick said.

Laffite pursed his lips. "Well, a man must eat, and these trips are expensive. But I want to know: Can you fix this poor creature's leg?"

"I don't know."

Laura squatted next to the cage and checked out the dapi. The little male stood with its back pressed against the opposite wall and stared at her with its huge sky-blue eyes.

She'd seen the photo of Mozi, but it conveyed only a fraction of the reality of these things. Like a lemur but much more appealing.

"The way he stares . . . it's mesmerizing."

"*Oui,*" Laffite said, squatting beside her. "One could drown in those eyes."

Laura didn't know why, but she replied in French. "*Tout à fait extraordinaire.*"

He gasped. "*Vous connaissez la langue?*"

She waggled her hand. "*Un peu.*"

"*Intelligente et belle et vous parlez français. Je pourrais tomber amoureux de toi!*"

"Don't get carried away, *monsieur.* And we'll stick to English for the sake of my friend here."

He glanced over his shoulder to where Rick stood with his arms crossed, watching them.

"He is a big one."

"Right. And don't forget it."

She refocused her attention on the dapi. He stood on his left leg, with his right knee flexed to keep weight off it. The lower leg was swollen. Fractured tibia? If it wasn't displaced—or better yet, incomplete . . .

"I might be able to make a splint for that leg."

"We have a first-aid kit."

She snaked her index finger through the mesh of the cage.

"Careful," Laffite said. "He bites. He bit Bakari."

"The splint will be easier if we can be friends."

And if I were an animal trapped by that brute, I'd bite him too.

The dapi held back. At least he wasn't attacking.

"What have you been feeding him?"

"They like the protein bars we brought for ourselves."

"Give me one."

Laffite pulled a bar from a breast pocket and began unwrapping it. The name *High5* flashed on the label. She'd never heard of that brand. Laffite handed her a piece.

"What flavor?"

"Banana vanilla."

"Maybe that's why they like it."

She dropped a piece through the mesh to bring the dapi closer, but he still hung back, his gaze repeatedly flicking to Laffite. Maybe he associated him with getting hurt.

"Why don't you and Rick back off a bit. Give me and my little friend some space."

As the two men moved a dozen or so feet away, Laura wiggled her finger and made cooing noises. She dropped another bit of bar through the mesh. Finally the dapi made a tentative move forward on three legs, keeping the rear right leg flexed and off the floor. He stretched and snagged the piece of bar closest to him. After gobbling it down, he reached for the second. All the while, Laura kept wiggling her finger and cooing.

When he'd swallowed the second piece, he stayed there, his gaze alternating between Laura's face and her finger.

This is where he either takes a piece of out me or . . .

He reached out and poked her fingertip with his own.

Laura stifled a laugh. "Not quite a high five," she said softly, smiling at him. "But a high *one* is a start."

"Check it out," Rick said from somewhere behind her. "You've got an audience."

She craned her neck. Sure enough, the branches above and all around were crammed with dapis, chattering and watching.

And then her dapi wrapped his little hand around her finger and rubbed his face against it, almost like a cat.

He's lonely, she thought. *Hurt and lonely.*

She worked three more of her fingers through the mesh and played with the little guy for about ten more minutes.

"Are we ready?" Laffite said.

"Ready as ever, I guess. Bring that first-aid kit over. Better yet, have Rick bring it over."

Rick tried to play with the dapi as she inventoried the kit. He could fit only his pinky through the mesh. The dapi backed off at first, but he seemed to have become desensitized to humans and soon was fondling Rick's finger.

Laura in the meantime had found some cotton, gauze, tape, and a packet of tongue depressors.

Yeah, this might work . . . if she could immobilize the dapi long enough.

Razi returned then. Speaking in Portuguese, he handed Laffite a satellite phone. Laffite held it up and called to Rick.

"Razi found this on your brother. Did you give it to him?"

"No. I assume that's his."

"But we have his phone. He left it here when he ran off after trying to kill us. This is different. Where did he get it?"

Rick shrugged. "No law against having two phones."

"No, I suppose not. I wonder who he was calling." He began tapping away at Keith's phone. "Hmmm . . . only two numbers here . . . both with Mozambique area codes . . . called early this morning. I wonder who they are."

"Well, if you hadn't sent him to 'Elba,' you could ask him."

"I told you: He has been exiled for his own good."

"So you say." Rick's tone told Laura his patience was fraying. "Hey, if you really want to know who he called, instead of standing there talking about it, why don't you dial them and see?"

"I believe I will do just that."

Laura could feel her own patience thinning. "Can we save the phone games for later? I'm going to need help here."

9

In an attempt to break the towering bamboo rod that held him fast, Marten hung all his weight on it.

He used to weigh more, but his wandering up and down the Mozambique coast in search of another Mozi, combined with the lack of fast-food places along the way—how he missed Starbucks—had melted a lot of his fat. Not that weight mattered much in this case. Being a grass, green bamboo tended to bend instead of break. And even if it did break, he doubted very much it would snap off like a dry twig. But he had to try.

He guesstimated the time at a couple of hours past noon. If he was going to get free, he needed to do it in daylight. Direct sunlight cut off early in the caldera, and after sunset the darkness down here became impenetrable.

The rod suddenly jerked lower as he heard a crack near its base. Could it be? Was it going to break? He swung a leg over and hauled himself up into a precarious straddle. He remembered seeing a Chinese movie once—something with a nonsensical name—that had a scene with a man and a woman leaping from rod to rod in a bamboo forest.

He started bouncing up and down on the rod, steadily gaining momentum while fighting to keep his balance. Suddenly a louder crack like a shot, and the rod dropped to the ground. Pain shot through him as the rod jammed against his perineum.

He rolled off in agony. He'd done it! He'd broken the bamboo but damn near castrated himself in the process.

When the spasms subsided, he dragged the zip tie around the rod as near as he could to the base. He groaned when he saw it. Yes, the rod had broken, but it was a green-stick break, with the majority of the fibers still intact. He'd need a sharp knife or axe or, better yet, a saw to cut through those.

He looked back along the twenty-five-foot length of the rod. Wait a minute. He didn't need to snap it off. It tapered toward the top.

Marten slid the second zip tie along the length of the rod, ripping off some of the larger leaves along the way. In minutes he was free.

But now what? He needed his phone and he didn't see any way to sneak into that tiny camp and retrieve it.

That left the almost unthinkable: He'd have to throw himself upon the mercies of his enemies. They wouldn't accept Marten, and would only exile him again, more securely this time.

But they might accept Keith. And he knew he could fake Keith.

10

"Done?" Rick said.

Laura leaned back and wiped perspiration and a few strands of hair from her forehead. "That's as good as it's gonna get. I hope it works."

She'd been great—gentle but firm about getting the job done while he'd kept a tight grip on the little creature. Watching her work, he'd been amazed by her concern, her constant stream of encouragement, even though the animal couldn't understand a word she was saying.

The dapi seemed to have calmed now. The splinting process had been one hell of an ordeal. He hadn't liked being immobilized—had struggled and screamed bloody murder through the whole procedure. Not from any real pain, as far as Rick could tell. More from fear and frustration.

Holding him steady hadn't been easy. The protective gloves Laffite had provided were clumsy and the dapi had had a field day snapping at them. But Laura had managed to wrap the leg and tape a tongue depressor along its inside and outside, starting above the knee and ending below the foot.

And all around and above, the other dapis watched her every move, their chatter subdued by the drama below.

"If I remember," she said, "you're supposed to immobilize the joint proximal and distal to the fracture." She took a breath. "Been so long. I hope I did this right. Okay. Put him down and let's see how he does."

"Don't let him run off!" Laffite said.

"I don't think he'll be running anywhere for a while," she said.

Rick eased the dapi gently to the ground where it stood uncertainly, bearing all its weight on its three good limbs. It swayed awkwardly because it couldn't bend the right leg—Laura had immobilized the knee. It looked at Laura, then back at Rick, then at Laura again. Slowly it lowered its broken leg until the tips of the tongue depressors below the ankles touched the ground.

Apparently it didn't hurt, or didn't hurt anywhere near as much as it had before, because it took a tentative step, and then another. It limped in a slow circle and then stopped to stare up at Laura with what Rick could only describe as wonder in its huge eyes.

Laffite laughed. *"Splendide!"*

Just then Bakari blundered in, carrying a large canvas sack over his shoulder, and in his other hand . . . were those spears?

The dapi screeched at the sight of him and leaped straight at Laura. To her infinite credit, she didn't duck but caught the little creature and clutched him to her chest. It clung and stared at Bakari whose broken nose was only slightly less swollen than before.

The native seemed upset about something but Rick couldn't tell what. Maybe more than one something.

Bakari and Laffite shared an animated conversation and gradually Bakari calmed. Rick wished to hell he understood Portuguese. Laffite turned to Laura.

"Our little friend seems to have bonded to you. I thank you very much for what you have done, but now he needs to be returned to the cage."

"Aw, let him stay out a little longer."

Laffite shook his head. "I am sorry, but we cannot risk his escaping."

Rick gestured to all the watching dapis. "Not as if there's any shortage of replacements."

"But that is just the problem, *monsieur*. These dapis are very clever. Too clever, perhaps. They have learned to . . . to *circonvenir*—what is the English?"

"Circumvent," Laura said.

"Ah, *oui*. They have learned to circumvent our traps. They take the bait and do not get caught."

Rick remembered the videos of Mozi when she'd been caged at Schelling, opening the combination lock. He wasn't surprised they'd found a way to hack a Havahart trap, or whatever they were called in these parts.

Rick shook his head. "That sort of makes your trip a waste of time then, doesn't it?"

And ain't that just too damn bad for you, froggy.

Rick couldn't ever imagine himself going the PETA route, but it galled him to see a bunch of poachers barge into a pristine ecosystem like this and mess up the balance. Laura had said he couldn't call them poachers because the island was unclaimed and no one had jurisdiction over it. Uh-uh. As far as Rick was concerned, these primates had jurisdiction. This was dapi turf. They'd been here millions of years without screwing it up, so in his book, they had squatters' rights. The island belonged to them.

"It might prove to be a waste of time and treasure, yes," Laffite said. "Then again, it might not."

Uh-oh. Rick didn't like the sound of that.

"Meaning?"

Laffite smiled. "I am not about to let these little primates, no matter how clever they might be, get the better of me."

Rick gestured to the pair of six-foot spears Bakari had brought along. "Gonna have your guys run them through?"

"Of course not. The brothers always bring their spears on our trips. Often they catch us dinner. We will be staying here longer than I anticipated. Maybe they can find a wild boar or the like. Have you ever eaten fresh wild boar, *monsieur*?"

"Tried just about everything once, so I'm pretty sure I have. Don't know how fresh it was, though. So if not spears, what? Tranquilizer darts?"

"An excellent idea, but I did not bring any because I never dreamed we would need them." He gestured to the bag Bakari had brought. "So I must improvise with netting."

He took the heavy gloves from Rick and slipped them on. The dapi screamed when he wrapped his hands around its body and pulled it from Laura's arms. Carefully, gently, he returned it to the cage and latched the door closed.

Remembering Mozi, Rick thought about suggesting a better lock, but

decided against it. Let Laffite learn the hard way. Not that this dapi would
be doing much tree climbing for a while.

"I'm back," said a voice. "In more ways than one."

Rick turned to see Keith strolling into camp from the opposite end.

"Jeukens!" Laffite cried.

"No, not Jeukens," Keith said, looking Rick's way but not making eye
contact. "I'm really back. It's me. Keith."

Laffite turned to Razi and shouted something in Portuguese. Razi
looked cowed but his brother reacted with fury. He charged Keith.

Rick reacted, stepping in front of Bakari and thrusting the heel of his
hand into his solar plexus. The man's forward momentum enhanced the
force of the blow, dropping him to his knees.

"No," Rick said, wagging a finger at him. "No touch."

It took Bakari a good half minute to catch his breath. He got to his feet
and glared past Rick at Keith. He pulled his knife from its sheath in his
belt; holding it in a forehand grip, he pointed the six-inch blade at Keith.

"He die."

Rick kept his eye on the blade as he shook his head. "No touch."

"Laffite!" Laura cried. "Stop this! Please!"

Rick noticed that Laffite had drawn his revolver but held it down
against his thigh.

"I tried to prevent this," the Frenchman said, "but his brother would
not cooperate and stay out of sight. So here we are. This has been brewing.
It is time it is settled."

Bakari switched to a reverse grip, not the usual choice of experienced
knife fighters, because it shortened the blade's reach. Maybe Bakari had
been in close-up knife fights where it worked for him. Maybe he'd found it
had an intimidating effect. If close enough and fast enough, a backhand
slash against an opponent's throat before he could react would end the fight
then and there. But Rick would be ready for that. And maybe he could use
the shorter reach to his advantage, making Bakari switch his grip.

"Amaury," Keith called from behind him, "if you don't want to stop
this for my sake, do it for yours."

"Mine?" Lafitte said through a laugh.

"The dapis are watching. Your man is giving them a course in the use of
a knife against humans."

Rick tuned him out and concentrated on Bakari's blade. His SEAL training had involved armed and unarmed confrontations with knife-wielding opponents. Ideally you wrapped something like a shirt around your non-dominant hand as a shield of sorts. Rick had nothing handy and couldn't risk removing his bush jacket just now.

So he'd do the unexpected instead.

Bakari crouched and shuffled forward, elbow flexed, the knife held close at mid-chest level. Rick put his hands on his hips and held his ground as he lifted his gaze and stared into Bakari's eyes. He saw confusion. The usual response from an opponent would be shuffling backward in an arc to Bakari's left, away from the knife hand.

When Bakari lunged with a throat slash, Rick danced back a step. As the blade passed harmlessly by, he knocked the arm down with his left hand and landed a right jab on Bakari's already broken nose.

That had to hurt.

Bakari roared and switched to a forehand grip.

Thank you.

When he lunged at Rick's chest, Rick slammed his right palm into the inside of Bakari's wrist and his left against the back of Bakari's hand.

The knife went flying.

But Rick didn't stop there. He used Bakari's continuing forward momentum to flip him off his feet, through the air, and flat onto his back. He landed hard and lay there groaning.

Out of the corner of his eye he saw Razi start forward but Laffite stopped him. The Frenchman raised his revolver to waist level.

Pretending not to notice, Rick picked up Bakari's knife and stood over the supine man. Here was a delicate moment. Things couldn't go on this way. Either he killed or crippled the man, or tried to arrange some sort of détente.

Even without Laffite's gun at his back, he would have opted for détente. He'd done enough killing. And Laura was here.

He stood over the supine Bakari as the Mozambican pushed himself up on his elbows and looked up at him, eying the knife. Rick switched it to his left hand and extended his right. Bakari looked like he was going to spit on it, but did nothing. Rick bent, bringing his hand closer.

He hoped he was doing the right thing. Where he came from, this was a gesture of respect for a fellow warrior. He hadn't turned his back on the fallen man in contempt; instead he was offering a hand up. But Bakari's culture might see it as something entirely different.

To his relief, Bakari gripped his hand and allowed Rick to pull him up. Now, the biggest risk: He held the knife by the blade and offered it to its owner. A ton of anger in this guy—certainly justified against Keith for trying to poison him, but he seemed to have lots more to spread around.

"Brother bad man," he said.

"No. Brother good man. Do bad thing. He is sorry."

"He no say."

"Keith!" Rick called, keeping his gaze fixed on Bakari. "Are you sorry for what you did?"

"Yes!" cried a voice behind him. "God, yes! That wasn't really me. I am terribly sorry, Bakari."

The Mozambican's pockmarked face remained impassive, but he took the knife and slipped it back into its sheath. With one last glare for Rick and Keith, he turned and strode back to where his brother stood.

"Thank you, Garrick," Keith said. "I think I owe you my life."

"You '*think*'?" Laura said, stepping closer to Keith. "I thought Laffite was exaggerating when he said you were safer in exile. I guess I was wrong."

Laffite slipped the revolver back into his waistband and ambled over. He appeared to have no idea how easily Rick could take that from him if he wanted. But the situation seemed to be morphing into a more agreeable balance. Better not to jeopardize that unless he had to.

"You handled that remarkably well, *monsieur*. For a moment there I thought you might attempt a more permanent solution."

Rick forced a smile. "Then I'd have to deal with his brother and you. I chose not to."

Laffite looked mildly surprised. "You speak of consequences. Killing him would not weigh on you?"

Rick didn't feel a need to answer that. The truth was, if Bakari had threatened Laura with that knife, it would be lodged in his throat right now. And Rick wouldn't give it another thought.

He tried the diplomatic route: "Well, he's the one who drew the knife. But I remember hearing somewhere that showing kindness to an enemy is like pouring burning ashes on his head. Or something like that. Forget who said it."

Staring at the ground, Keith said, "It's from 'Romans': 'If your enemy is hungry, feed him; if he is thirsty, give him something to drink. In doing this, you will heap burning coals on his head.'"

Rick realized his Afrikaner accent was gone.

Laffite turned on him. "You! You are the cause of all this dissension. I hid you away to bring peace, and you come back and almost cost your brother his life!"

"It's very complicated," Keith said.

The Frenchman turned to Laura. "Your *hélicoptère* should be back soon, yes?"

Crap, Rick thought as Laura fumbled for a reply. No way to lie their way out of this. Better to come clean.

"Actually," he said, "we're supposed to call him when we're ready to go back."

Laffite looked from Rick to Laura, frowning. "But I thought you said . . ." He shrugged. "No matter. He knows the way here without you along?"

Rick nodded. "I assume he still has the coordinates we gave him on the way out."

"*Bon.* You will call him now and have him come immediately."

Laura's expression was dubious. "You're letting us go?"

"It was never my intention to hold you prisoner."

"What about my brother?"

"Yes! Take him! Please! He is nothing but trouble. The sooner the three of you are off this island the better. Then my men and I can get on about our task." He turned away. "I will give you your phone."

"Oh, can I have mine?" Keith said.

Laffite gave him as suspicious look. "Which one? You have two."

"Uh, well, both."

"You may have them when you leave."

"But I—"

"Only the good doctor uses her phone, and only for one call."

As Laffite walked away, Keith turned and wandered to a corner of the little clearing, as far as possible from Bakari. He stood at the foot of one of the giant baobab trees and stared up at its pillar of a trunk.

"Do you have any idea what's going on with him?" Rick said in a low voice. "He's back to the Keith I remember. Well, sort of. And that weird accent is gone."

"Right," said Laura. "And did you notice how he's making only minimal eye contact? Marten looked you square in the eye."

"So what's he got? A multiple personality disorder?"

"They call it 'dissociative identity disorder' nowadays. Movie hound that you are, you've seen *The Three Faces of Eve*, I assume?"

"Sure. Creeped me out."

"Well, the concept of separate and distinct personalities operating independently of each other and unknown to each other is considered controversial at best, and BS by most. I think this is different. I think Keith created Marten to do something he hasn't the stomach for—to give him a skewed worldview and morality—and crawled into his skin. More like method acting than a psychotic break."

"You mean killing Mozi? Marten said Keith 'couldn't do what needed to be done,' so he did it. *He* killed Mozi."

Laura shook her head. "I think it goes beyond that. He said the world wasn't ready for the secret hiding inside Mozi. And 'you do what you have to do for the greater good.' That's kind of scary."

"Ya think? Marten's one scary guy. I've got this awful feeling he killed that helicopter pilot he hired."

"Right. He was poisoned. Possibly with the same stuff."

They both looked over to where Keith was standing alone, staring into the trees.

"I'm so sorry," Rick said.

"For what?"

"For getting you into this mess."

If anything happened to her . . .

"I don't recall giving you much choice. You had me started on my way back to Morondava when I jumped out."

"Still . . ."

Yeah. Still. Still he should have put the kibosh on her coming along back in Shirley. If he had, that's where she'd be right now: safe at home. But the idea of the two of them together on the road again had been irresistible. The time they'd shared last month hopping from country to country and continent to continent just might have been the best days of his life. The hunt for Keith had offered a second helping of that and he hadn't been able to say no.

"Look," she said. "It's been a little messy, yes—"

"A *little*? That guy over there, a guy I grew up with, someone I thought I knew, is a pretty safe bet to have murdered somebody, and then tried to kill three more. And then one of the guys he tried to kill just tried to knife me because I was standing in the way of his killing Keith. In my book, that's more than 'a little messy.'"

"Okay, but we're on our way home, or at least on our way back to Madagascar."

"Almost." He looked at his brother again. "Need to talk to him and find out what started all this madness. He was just about to tell us when Laffite had him dragged away."

"Don't you dare leave me out of that conversation," she said. "Remember the last thing he said: how none of this is about what he found in Mozi's genome, but all about what he *didn't* find."

"Yeah." It had been driving Rick crazy wondering about it. "You think he really meant it, or was he just screwing with our heads?"

"Oh, I think he meant it. I just don't know what he could have meant *by* it."

Rick was at a loss. "You know more about this stuff than I do. What gene in Mozi could have been conspicuous by its absence?"

She shook her head, looking baffled. "I haven't the faintest. He found a human gene that didn't belong, but that didn't seem to bother him. But he didn't find . . . what?"

"Well, it's a long trip back to New York. He'll have plenty of time to explain."

And Rick would throttle it out of him if he held back.

"The first leg of that trip is a step closer," she said. "Here comes our phone."

Laffite arrived and handed Laura her phone.

"One call only," he said. "I will wait."

Laura turned on her phone and waited. "We've got service," she said, then tapped a couple of buttons.

"You know this pilot's number so well?" Laffite said.

"It's in recently dialed."

After a short wait, she started babbling in French. Apparently what she heard was not to her liking because she raised her voice and began an angry tirade. Rick had no idea what she was saying, but Laffite understood and it seemed to amuse him. Finally she hung up and slapped the phone back into his palm.

"He is coming?" Laffite said.

Still seething, Laura said, "You better believe he's coming. Or else."

Still grinning, Laffite turned and walked away.

"Something wrong?" Rick said.

"Antso tried to hold us up for more money, or he wasn't going to pick us up."

"Really? Maroon us here?"

"Oh, he said he knew there was a boat here that could take us back to civilization, so he wouldn't be abandoning us."

"So how much extra are we paying?"

"Nothing. I told him yeah we had a boat and we'd sail it directly to Morondava. I told him I hope he remembered the man I was with because immediately upon our arrival in Morondava that man was going to kill him."

Rick wasn't sure he'd heard correctly or, if he had, if she was telling the truth.

"You really said that?"

"Damn betcha."

"And did you really just say 'damn betcha'?"

She grinned. "Damn betcha."

God, he loved this woman. He wanted to wrap her in a bear hug right now and never let go.

But this was not the place so he had to make do with: "You're pretty cool for a medical examiner, y'know."

"The cool coroner. That's me."

11

Laura headed back to the clearing after emptying her bladder in the bushes. She'd found a spot she thought was private but a horde of dapis had followed her through the branches above and watched with rapt attention while she'd relieved herself. She'd never had such an audience before.

Just as she stepped from the underbrush, she heard Laffite start to shout something in Portuguese. He sounded frantic and upset.

And then Laura saw why. A large female dapi was bounding across the clearing with a smaller male clinging to her back—a male with a splinted leg. She leaped for the trunk of a palm and scampered up out of reach of the three humans close on her tail.

Laffite roared incoherently and did a furious dance before the palm. The brothers stood by, gaping at the swarming dapis above, while Rick strolled toward her, grinning.

"Only a matter of time before that happened."

She nodded. She'd thought the same thing when she'd seen the simple latch on the cage. She was tempted to say "damn betcha" again but thought she'd gotten enough out of that.

She returned his smile. "Not a matter of *if*, just a matter of *when*."

"Exactly."

Laffite quickly cooled, then began giving orders in Portuguese. As the brothers got moving, pulling out the large canvas bag Bakari had brought back from the boat, Laffite came over to them.

"You two and the brother—Jeukens or whatever his real name—will come with us."

"Where?" Rick said.

"We go to catch dapis. We have wasted enough time."

Laura glanced at her watch. "But our helicopter will be here in an hour or so."

"You will not miss it. Its noise fills the air down here. But I do not wish to leave you three on your own while we are in the field."

"We're not thieves," she said.

He shrugged. "So you say. I do not trust any of you out of my sight. So you will come and be silent and watch. Get your brother and be over by the cage in ten minutes."

As Laffite strode away, Rick looked at her and shrugged. "No point in raising a fuss. We'll be on our way back to civilization soon and never see him again. And to tell you the truth, I'm curious to see how they plan to outsmart these little guys."

Laura had to admit to some curiosity in that regard herself. She was rooting for the dapis.

They pulled Keith away from his reverie by the baobab, regurgitating Laffite's dictum along the way. He accepted it without question. He seemed to be in a fog. Laura wondered if he was transitioning personalities again.

Bakari and Razi had gone ahead. Laffite met them by the cage. Keith seemed to notice for the first time that it was empty.

"What happened to the Prisoner of Zenda?"

Laura listened for the Afrikaans accent but it all she heard was northeastern United States.

"Escaped," Rick said. "Where were you?"

Keith looked confused. "I . . . I'm not sure."

"Come," Laffite said and led them toward the center of the island.

They'd walked maybe a hundred feet when Laura heard a clatter behind her. She turned to see a horde of dapis swarming the campsite. Laffite rushed back, waving his arms to chase them away. After they'd retreated into the trees, he started back toward them.

"Just out of curiosity," Keith called. "Are there any knives left?"

Laffite gave him a strange look, but did a quick search. He returned with a concerned expression.

"Not a one. How did you know?"

"Remember, I warned you?"

"The machetes are gone too."

Keith looked around. "Not good. Not good at all."

His ominous tone disturbed her. "What are you thinking?"

"I'm thinking they've seen how useful a sharp blade can be—they've watched us cut up things with them. I'm hoping they want to use them to cut more notches in the baobab trunks. But they've also seen Bakari try to slice Garrick."

He said no more as Laffite led them to a small opening in the trees—not a clearing, just an exceptionally shady spot where undergrowth was thin. One of their live traps sat in the middle. Bakari and Razi were busy suspending a large square of black nylon netting, easily twenty feet on a side, above it.

Rick said, "A little obvious, don't you think?"

Laffite shook his head. "Not if you've never seen a net."

Laura had to admit he had a point. The dapis would not associate that strange material with a danger to themselves.

"Even if it works," she said, "how many times do you think you can fool them?"

He shrugged. "Maybe twice. Maybe we catch five or six. I take them back to test the market for selling them. I take orders and deposits. We return with tranquilizer darts and bag as many as we please."

Great. Just what she didn't want to hear.

He pointed back along the path they'd just traveled. "The three of you stand back there where I can see you and you won't get in the way."

They retreated as directed. She could tell by the stiffness in Rick's shoulders and the flint in his eyes that taking orders from the shifty Frenchman rankled him. She put a hand on his arm.

"Hang in there, partner. We'll be out of here soon."

"'Partner,'" he said with a smile. "I like that. And 'patience' is my new mantra."

"Right there!" Laffite called.

Rick's eyes turned flinty again. "But if we weren't leaving within the hour . . ."

She patted his arm. "I know, I know. But we are."

She turned to Keith. Now was as good a time as any to get the answers she was dying for.

"Keith," she said, waving a hand in front of his eyes to make sure she had his attention. "Earth to Keith. Come in."

He blinked and looked at her mouth. Not full eye contact, but close. "Yes?"

"It's time for you to come clean: What wasn't in Mozi's genome that made you change your whole life?"

He looked away. "You must swear that you will never whisper a word of what I am about to tell you, not to anyone else in the world. Ever."

"Okay."

I guess.

"'Okay' isn't good enough. You must say, 'I swear.'"

"Very well. I swear."

"Garrick?"

"Yeah, sure. I swear. Now what didn't you find?"

"All right. Remember the mansion I mentioned?"

"Yeah-yeah," Rick said. "Dusty, dirty, with a generator in the cellar."

"Don't forget the generator's lever is in the on position. And especially don't forget the well-lit, inordinately neat bedroom, without a spot of dust anywhere. As I said before, what conclusion would you draw from that?"

Laura gave Rick a let's-play-along shrug. "Okay. I'll bite. I'd conclude that I wasn't alone in the house. Someone else has been there."

"Exactly. Being clean is very important. The room didn't clean itself—somebody put in a lot of effort to get rid of all the dust and dirt. Or . . . it might have been an add-on, new construction."

"Okay," Rick said. "It could be either. So what? What does this have to do—?"

"And what if," Keith said as if Rick hadn't spoken, "on the bed you found a mold for the lever that turned on the generator?"

Wait. This wasn't a riddle. Keith was constructing an allegory. So what was the lever and what was the generator?

She had it.

"Are you saying the lever is hsa-mir-3998 and the generator is human creativity?"

A big grin but still no eye contact. "Bingo!"

"The room is Mozi's genome."

A wider grin. "Double *Jeopardy!* winner!"

"So what?" Rick said. "We knew that!"

Keith's grin vanished. "It's staring you in the face! All the dust and dirt were missing from the room, either cleaned out or never there in the first place! Think! *Think!*"

The answer was doing a tantalizing Chippendale dance on the edge of Laura's consciousness but her reach was just a tad too short to grab hold of it.

Keith ran out of patience. "Mozi had no non-coding DNA!"

Laura looked at Rick, certain that the bafflement on his face mirrored her own. And then . . . and then . . .

"Oh, shit! Oh, crap! Oh, *fuck!*"

Keith looked away, pointing a waggling finger at her. "She's got it! She knows!"

"Knows what?" Rick said, his head swiveling back and forth between them like a radar dish. "You made Laura say 'fuck.' Laura never says 'fuck,' so I know it can't be good. In fact, it's gotta be awful. *What?*"

Right. She never said *fuck*. In her younger days, sure, every now and then, but with motherhood she'd purged the word from her vocabulary.

But this deserved many *fuck*s. Many, many, *many* fucks.

She grabbed Keith's arm. "No junk DNA?"

"'Non-coding' is the preferred term."

She wanted to punch him. "Who cares what it's called?"

"It's important in this case. Biological *activity* often gets confused with biological *function*. All DNA that had no useful function, biologically active or not, was absent from Mozi's genome. Better than ninety percent of the average primate's DNA is just taking up room on the chromosome— dust and dirt, if you will. Mozi's was half that."

"That . . . that's impossible."

"Tell me something I *don't* know. Why do you think I ran and reran her genome so many times?"

"But that means . . ."

"Yes," he said, nodding vigorously. "Somebody cleaned the room."

Rick had his hands folded as if in prayer. "Will one of you *please* . . . ?"

Poor Rick. He had no background in any of this.

She faced him. "Every creature on Earth carries what's known as junk DNA." She held up a hand to stop Keith from correcting her again. "It contains all the leftovers from our evolutionary past—mutations that didn't work out, bits and pieces of viruses, non-primate genes."

"Evolution I get. But what—?"

"As a species evolves, all that junk stays onboard and is passed up the line. The mutations that work are put to use, the ones that don't are consigned to the junk pile."

She was oversimplifying the process, but she felt the end point was valid.

Rick was frowning as the light began to dawn. "So I'm gathering from what you're saying is that somebody cleaned up Mozi's junk pile." He shook his head. "Is that possible?"

"No!" Keith said. "It's way, way beyond any existing technology. That's the whole point! As Laura said, primates—and humans and dapis are primates—share DNA with all sorts of lower life forms. We share a sixth of our DNA with daffodils and more than a third with the common fruit fly. But the dapi genome has been cleaned up—no extraneous DNA from prior species, also no non-functional DNA. It's like it was custom-designed, streamlined to produce a designated species. And it contains a human-specific gene—hsa-mir-3998."

Rick was nodding. "One of the so-called God Genes."

Keith threw his head back. "How I loathe that term! But that's what the creationists and the intelligent-design crowds will be shouting from the rooftops when they hear about it."

"So what?" Laura said. "Science is on the side of human evolution."

"Science *was* on the side of human evolution. Not anymore. Anyone with half a brain who looks at the dapis' genome will have to come to the conclusion that this species did not develop through natural selection and mutation, but was either altered or *manufactured de novo*."

"Where?" Rick said. "By whom?"

"The billions of believers around the globe will say in Heaven by God, of course."

"What do *you* say?"

Keith shrugged. "I don't know. I haven't a clue. But what I *can* say is that it's powerful evidence that we humans are the result of deliberate genetic manipulation. The dapis were *created*—I use that term advisedly because all the evidence points to deliberate genetic manipulation. Beyond that, I can offer only suppositions that will sound wild and off the wall and totally insane to anyone listening."

Rick began the stuttering bass line of "Ice Ice Baby."

Laura groaned.

Keith said, "Why are you making that noise?"

"Try me, bro. Just try me." Rick's grin was hard and humorless. "I can outdo you in the 'wild and off the wall and totally insane' department any day."

Laura hadn't seen it before, but this situation fit snugly with Rick's scenario of the human species being manipulated by outside forces. Perhaps a little too snugly for comfort.

"Right then," Keith said. "How's this? The dapis were placed in Africa millions of years ago to insert this specific gene, one related to creativity—hsa-mir-3998, to be specific—into the hominid line via a retrovirus or some other means of horizontal transfer."

"Do you think they knew what would happen?" Rick said.

"I don't even know who 'they' are, so how can I answer that?"

"Do you think your 3998 was the first gene they tried to insert?"

"Who's this 'they' you keep referring to?"

Rick had that look.

"You're going to get into that now?" Laura said.

"How can I not?" He turned to Keith. "Okay, try this on for size. Forces we cannot understand—intrusive cosmic entities, intellects vast, cool, and unsympathetic, call them what you like—placed a seed species with a manipulated genome among the African primates and sat back to see what happened."

"Ridiculous. You're talking a wait of millions of years to find out if it worked."

"Maybe millions of years isn't such a long stretch for them."

"You're adding a whole extra layer of supposition to the situation."

Rick smiled. "I'm allowed. Because Occam's razor doesn't work here. You already have evidence of outside manipulation of a primate's genome. It didn't happen by itself, right?"

Keith shook his head. "No, certainly not."

"Well, I'm offering a possible explanation. If you've got a better one, or even an alternate theory, I'm all ears. Shoot."

"I . . . I don't have one."

"Okay, then we'll go with mine for now. So, these intellects placed the dapis here to kick-start a brighter species of primate. And now that the resultant species is self-aware and self-sufficient and seated atop the food chain, maybe it's time to throw them a curve. Maybe it's time to let them know they're the cosmic equivalent of a genetically modified strain of lab rat, then sit back and watch the ripple effects of that revelation."

Keith snorted. "That's preposterous!"

"No more preposterous than all these gene carriers clustered here on an island that's somehow been missed by all the sailors and mapmakers and satellites. No more preposterous than a certain zoologist—one who has the knowledge and access to the technology to decode exactly what that primate is—just happening upon one of the species in a street bazaar. Don't you see? *We're all being played!*"

Keith waved his hands in the air. "Noise! Nothing but noise! I've introduced you to the equivalent of an evolutionary hydrogen bomb and you reduce it to the level of a freshman dormitory bullshit session with an inane cosmic conspiracy theory!"

"If you'd seen what I've seen . . ." He wagged his finger back and forth between himself and Laura. ". . . what *we've* seen, you wouldn't be calling it 'inane.'"

"It doesn't matter what you think or I think. It doesn't matter whether the changes in the dapi genome are the result of divine or unnatural intervention. None of it changes the inescapable fact that not one dapi can be allowed to leave the island. I knew the moment I sequenced Mozi's impossibly clean genome that I would have to track down her species and kill every last one of them."

Laura felt her jaw drop. "Wh-wh-what? Why on Earth . . . ?"

"To save human civilization."

"What the hell are you talking about?" Rick said.

"Science has led us to believe that we struggled up the evolutionary chain, mutation by mutation, pulling ourselves from the DNA muck to build a globe-spanning civilization that has driven a golf buggy on the moon and sent probes to the far reaches of the solar system and beyond. But the existence of the dapis is proof we were jump-started from outside. Whether it's attributed to a divine power fusing a bit of itself into us or the result of an experiment by extraterrestrial intelligence, either way, the implications of the dapi genome diminish us as a species. We go from movers and shakers and builders and explorers, from masters of our fate to . . . pets. Yeah, that's what this means: We're house pets."

Rick spread his arms. "Hallelujah, a convert! He's seen the light!"

"Don't joke about hallelujah. If the truth about the dapis gets out, it will be taken all over the world as proof of humanity's divine origin. And that will set science back centuries—creationism will be legitimized, intelligent design will be taught in science courses, human progress will stagnate. Politicians who don't toe that line will fall and theocracies will rise."

"You don't know that," Laura said.

"Oh, but I do, I do. The divine origin of mankind is taught by all the Abrahamic religions. The Jews, all the Christian sects, all the Muslim sects—we're talking billions of people here—will all buy into it, because that's what they've heard all their lives. The Hindus to some extent too. Even for people who've been on the fence in their belief, the God Gene is proof."

"The UFO crowd could make just as good a case for alien origin," Rick said. "They can say the artificial dapi genome means we *Homo saps* are the result of some sort of experiment."

Keith gave a derisive snort. "Pissing in the ocean. They're an infinitesimal minority of kooks who will be drowned out by the overwhelming majority of True Believers. The growing theocracies might even martyr them. Scientific inquiry will not only be discouraged under those theocracies, it could well be forbidden. No need to do research for answers when we already have the answer to everything: God." He slashed the air with his hand. "No! Nobody can know about this. And the only way to assure that is for every dapi to be hunted down and destroyed. The species should have died off millions of years ago. It's time to make their extinction a reality."

"Wiping out a species," Rick said with a slow shake of his head. "I never thought I'd hear you say that."

Laura tried to catch Rick's eyes but couldn't. "He can only say it. He can't do it. Can you, Keith?"

Keith kept his eyes fixed on a point somewhere past Laura's left shoulder and said nothing.

"Keith Somers could never do such a thing," Laura continued, "but Marten Jeukens can, isn't that right?"

Rick gave her a nod and jumped on board. "How convenient that the dapis are all in one place."

"How *in*convenient they exist at all! They should be extinct with all the rest of the adapiforms."

Laura said, "But you could have invented Marten Jeukens without selling everything you own."

"I didn't know where the dapis were or how long it would take me to find them. I thought it might take the rest of my life to track them all down. Now it's clear it won't, but . . . after Marten does what he has to do, I don't think I can go back to being Keith."

"Well, with the police after Marten now," Rick said, "you can't be him either."

Keith shrugged. "I'll work something out."

"'After Marten does what he has to do . . .'" Laura said. "Marten knows how to solve the dapi problem?"

Keith nodded. "The plan is in place. All it needs is to be set in motion."

"What's he gonna do?" Rick said. "Nuke the island?"

A sad smile. "If only he could." He looked toward where Laffite and company were toiling. "I'm tired of talking. I'm going to go watch what they're up to."

He wandered away, but not too far.

"He's really gone off the deep end," Rick said.

"You mean you don't believe him about the dapi genome?"

"Oh, I do. But of course I would. What about you?"

"I think he's telling the truth, and I think it unhinged him." She looked at Rick. "It's momentous, isn't it? I mean, it changes *everything*."

"Well, it doesn't change the world as it is, just how you look at it. If it gets out, it'll rub everyone's nose in the secret history."

"Secret history . . . what's that?"

"There's consensus history, which is what people agree on as to what happened and why. Then there's the secret history of what really happened and what was really behind those events."

"But do you think he's right? About the theocracies and new dark ages?"

"I can see the news changing the world to some degree. If I adopt a god-the-creator belief-set, whether that god's Yahweh or Allah or Brahma, I can see myself calling 3998 the God Gene and feeling, well, exalted that the creator had inserted a piece of himself—or herself or itself—into humanity. The world's already got somewhere between four and five billion believers in a divine creator. I can definitely see that number jumping. But I don't know about Keith's plague of theocracies."

"It could happen," she said. "With science seemingly legitimizing creationism, voters would maybe start leaning toward candidates who want to combine government with religious teachings."

"Bad news if you're gay or an atheist. Or just someone who sees it as proof that humanity is nothing but an experiment—"

"I know where you fall."

"Just a guy who asks the next question."

"Yeah, but your 'next question' isn't like most people's."

Rick was silent a moment, then, "Maybe Keith shouldn't have accepted the dapi genome at face value."

Laura frowned. "I'm not following."

"I'm going out on a limb here."

"You seem at home there. Shoot."

"Okay, what if the dapis are an elaborate hoax? What if the 3998 gene developed within us by the normal evolutionary route? What if ICE created the dapis with an unnaturally clean genome, and then popped 3998 into it?"

"For what purpose?"

"Same purpose as the panacea—to screw with our heads and see how we react."

"Now you're trying to screw with *my* head! That's too far out, even for you!"

"Is it? There's no fossil record of dapis."

"But lots of branches on the evolutionary tree are missing fossil records. And besides, the dapis have been isolated on this island for millions of years."

"Have they? How do we know how long this island's really been there?"

"Oh, come on!"

Was he serious?

"It's a 'next question.' Work with me here. It appears on no maps, no satellite photos, ships have been sailing the Mozambique Channel ever since men learned that wood can float and no one's ever reported it. But Keith comes along and there it is."

"What is it? *Brigadoon*?"

He shrugged. "I have no idea *what* to believe. I can envision different scenarios but can't say for sure which one is right."

"Don't you accept anything at face value?"

"Wish I could. Life would be so much easier."

Keith returned then, looking agitated. "We must leave this island. Where's that helicopter?"

As if in answer, a low thrum began to reverberate through the trees.

"Thank god," Laura said as relief flooded her. "We're finally going to get off this rock."

Laffite must have heard it too. He and the brothers were approaching.

"I need my phone," Keith said.

"You can buy a new one in Madagascar," Rick told him.

"No! I need *my* phone. I can't leave without it!"

"You are worried about phones?" Laffite said, stopping beside Laura. "I think maybe you should worry about *this!*"

Laura felt something metallic press against her temple. It took her a few seconds to realize Laffite was holding his revolver to her head.

"Hey, what the—?" Rick said, lunging toward him.

"Stay where you are, *monsieur*! I do not wish to hurt this pretty lady, but I will if you force me."

Rick backed up, hands raised. "What's going on?"

"Bakari is going to bind your wrists with the ties you so thoughtfully brought."

Laura's knees wobbled. For the first time since she'd left New York, she was truly frightened that she might not get home, might never see Marissa again. This didn't make sense, and that made it all the more frightening.

"Why?" Laura said, her voice shaking as Bakari moved behind Rick. "Our ride out of here is—"

"A ride you will not be taking."

Bakari pulled Rick's arms behind him. Laura was sure Rick would have been able to overcome him if Laffite didn't have a gun against her head. No dummy, Laffite. He'd neutralized Rick through her. Once Rick was removed as a threat, Laura and Keith would be easy to deal with.

Invisible above the various layers of green, the helo flew directly overhead, filling the caldera with a deafening roar.

When Rick was securely bound, Laffite lowered the gun.

"There. That was easy, wasn't it? Now Razi will bind you two and then stand guard while Bakari and I deal with your helicopter."

"Deal?" Laura thought as a queasy feeling roiled her stomach. "What does that mean?"

Razi pulled her hands behind her, looped a tie in a figure eight around her wrists, and zipped it tight.

"It means I will tell him you no longer require his services and send him away."

"He'll want his money."

Laffite smiled. "I will tell him to send you a bill."

Razi finished binding Keith and stepped back.

"I thought you wanted to be rid of us," Laura said.

"What I want right now," he said, waving his gun at them, "is for the three of you to sit." When none of them moved, he added, "If I shoot you in the knees you will sit. I do not wish to waste the bullets, but if I must, I will."

They sat or knelt in the scrubby brush.

"*Bon.* As for wanting to be rid of you, I have changed my mind. I do not want you out in the world, talking to the wrong people while I am here. You will stay until we are ready to leave, then you will sail back to Maputo with us."

He said something in Portuguese as he handed the gun to Razi, then gestured to Bakari. The two of them trotted off toward the tents.

Laura glanced at Rick, but his expression had turned to stone and his eyes had gone flat and unreadable. That couldn't be good. What was he thinking?

12

Amaury led the way to his tent where he grabbed the rifle case.

"Hurry," he said. "We don't want him leaving."

He thought it unlikely, but not beyond the realm of possibility. He had heard the doctor woman arguing with the pilot. He seemed a mercenary sort.

When they reached the ladder against the inner wall, he motioned for the faster Bakari to go first. He slung the Marlin's case over his shoulder and followed. The ladder allowed them to ascend the first twenty or so feet quickly before engaging the craggy lava of the wall itself where the going was slower.

What else can possibly go wrong? he wondered as he picked his way upward.

The traps were useless, Jeukens had turned into a crazy murderer—in fact, Jeukens had turned out to be someone other than Jeukens, someone with a brother who had somehow managed to track him down to this island,

Amaury's island.

That was how he'd come to think of it: *my island.*

But even worse, the brother and his lady friend had hired a helicopter to come here. Which meant the pilot knew the location of Amaury's island. And what would he do with that information? Exploit it, of course. He would soon be flying charters to a "secret mystery island" known only to him.

Which meant Amaury's island would remain secret no longer. Madagascar would waste little time claiming it. And once the world learned about the dapis, a virtual fence would rise around it,

Amaury would not be allowed to set foot on his own island.

But he'd seen a way to prevent that . . . or delay it, at least. A way that would have been unthinkable under different circumstances.

He had to stop this pilot from returning to Morondava.

He and Bakari were rising through the subcanopy now. Bakari maintained the lead. Amaury was less used to exertion; the extra weight of the Marlin and its case, though less than ten pounds, was taking its toll. He was breathing hard by the time they neared the top.

"Stop," he puffed before Bakari broke through the canopy to reach the rim. "Wait here for a second. Don't let him see you yet."

He unzipped the rifle case and pulled out the Marlin 336. He'd reaffixed the Nikon scope. Not a sniper scope by any stretch. Designed for shooting a deer or a bear within 150 yards. Five flat-nosed, 170-grain .30-30 Winchester rounds were lined up in the tubular magazine, waiting for their moment. Five shots at his disposal.

He tried to work the lever but his sweaty fingers slipped on the metal. He wiped his shaky hand on his pant leg and tried again.

Snikt–snikt.

The rifle was ready. He took a deep breath and shook his head.

I'm not cut out for this sort of thing.

But this island was the find of a lifetime and he could feel it slipping away. He had to save it, by whatever means necessary.

He listened for the helicopter. The noise was less thundering up here, and he could localize it. He remembered how he could double or triple the volume on his iPod simply by placing it in a bowl. The island acted as a bowl with the same effect on the helicopter.

The noise seemed to be originating on the far side but growing louder. It sounded like the pilot was patrolling the rim in search of his passengers.

Amaury tapped Bakari's arm. "He's coming this way. Get ready!"

Amaury and Bakari had discussed strategy while setting up the net for the dapis. The brothers knew they stood to make a pretty penny assisting Amaury with the dapi trade, so they were up for anything that would protect it. The plan was to coax the copter as close as possible to the rim. And while the caldera was reverberating with its throbbing roar, Amaury would shoot the pilot.

No one below would hear the sound of his rifle. He didn't want Jeukens and the other two to know what was happening up here. That was why he had made a show of giving his revolver to Razi. Only Jeukens knew about the Marlin, but he wouldn't know that Amaury had brought it ashore. Otherwise they would assume they were next to die, and that would make them difficult to manage—especially that Garrick fellow.

And they might be right. He might end up killing them too if he did not think they could keep the island a secret. But he wanted to avoid that if at all possible. He was not a killer.

Really? Then why am I up here with a rifle readying to shoot a man?

Because I must.

As the thrum of the copter grew louder, he gave Bakari a shove, sending him up to the rim. There, as planned, he began frantically jumping up and down and waving his arms over his head. Amaury eased into a spray of weeds on the inner edge of the rim and got as comfortable as he could.

He settled the Marlin against his shoulder and found a smooth spot in the lava rock to steady his elbow. He sighted through the scope, adjusted the magnification, and waited.

Not a long wait, as it turned out. The helicopter raced by, made a wide, looping turn over the water, then eased back to hover just off the rim. While Bakari made a show of shouting something and pointing down at the thin strip of beach below, Amaury found the pilot through his scope and centered the crosshair reticle on the his face.

Now . . . squeeze the trigger. Don't pull, just squeeeeeeeze . . .

Sweat dripped into his eyes. He quickly wiped it away and found the pilot's puzzled face again. No way could the man hear what Bakari was trying to say, but if this agitated fellow was suggesting that he land his copter, he was having none of it. As he shook his head and gave a dismissive wave, Amaury again tightened his finger on the trigger and—

He couldn't do it. The pilot was just another working man, trying to make his way in a primitive part of the world. A bit of a hustler, maybe, but he might have a wife and a child or two that he was feeding and clothing. Amaury had thought he could do anything to protect his island, but not this. Not cold-blooded murder.

Bakari was still waving and shouting. He glanced impatiently over his shoulder at Amaury, his expression saying, *Shoot! He's right where you want him! Shoot now!*

Amaury could only shake his head.

Bakari ran to him and snatched the Marlin from his slick hands. As he turned and aimed at the helicopter, the pilot spotted the rifle and immediately pulled his copter out of its hover and into a roaring turn.

Bakari fired, quickly worked the lever and fired again, and again, and again, the spinning brass cartridges gleaming in the sun as they spat from the side of the receiver. After five shots he ran dry and still the chopper kept racing away.

Amaury pressed a hand over his eyes as a sob built in his throat. He'd failed. Failed himself, failed the island, failed Bakari and Razi. Swallowing it back, he looked up to see Bakari stalking toward him, his expression furious. Amaury was suddenly glad the rifle was empty. Bakari still might use it as a club, though.

As Amaury cringed, he noticed the helicopter was sinking. Two or three hundred yards offshore it was racing toward the water, tilting as it banked to the left, its angle increasing until it was flying sideways.

"Look!" he cried, pointing.

Bakari turned in time to see it hit the water at terrific speed. The main rotor tore off and ripped through the fuselage. It must have hit the fuel tank because the copter was torn apart by a huge blast, scattering flaming debris over the surface.

In no time the heavier pieces sank, leaving only bits of lighter debris floating south in the current toward the trackless Indian Ocean.

Bakari's bullets had either hit the pilot or damaged one of the control mechanisms. Either way, the island's secret was safe. For now.

He should have felt happy, relieved, but he felt only wrenching guilt. He said a silent prayer for the fallen man. The only bright spot he could see was that the pilot's life was on Bakari's soul, not his.

With a contemptuous look, Bakari shoved the rifle at Amaury and stalked back toward the caldera. Amaury realized he'd lost face with the Shangaan. He might still be his captain on this voyage, but he no longer had his respect.

Amaury wondered if he'd ever earn it back.

13

As Rick sat cross-legged in the weeds and waited for the crack of gunshots from the rim, he watched Razi toy with the revolver, sighting on imaginary foes or prey, jerking it with imaginary recoil. He guessed the native had never owned a handgun, and wondered if he even knew where the safety was.

If only his hands were free . . . that .38 would be his right now and the dynamics of their situation would be dramatically different.

As the roaring, echoing thrum of the chopper eased back a bit, he nudged Keith with his knee.

"Laffite have any other guns around?" he shouted.

Keith nodded. "A rifle."

"Know what kind?"

"I think he said it was a Marlin. Can that be right? A Marlin is a fish. Why name a rifle after a fish?"

Rick didn't bother explaining that the "fish" in this case was a gunsmith named John Marlin. Nice hunting rifle, but not heavy on fire power. Probably chambered for .30-30s. Good for bringing down a deer, but a chopper? Maybe. Entice a small civilian helo like Antso's close enough and fire from cover . . . Yeah, it could work.

"Did he bring it over?"

Keith shook his head. "No."

"You're sure?"

"Of course I'm sure. I damn near broke my back lugging the equipment up to the rim and then down this side. The rifle's in a distinctive camouflage case. If it had been along, I'd have seen it."

He caught Laura giving him a questioning look. "What are you thinking?"

"Never hurts to know the enemy's assets."

"'Enemy' is kind of strong, don't you think?"

"Your hands are tied behind your back and that guy over there is holding a gun. In my book, that puts us in the hands of an enemy."

She shook her head. "I guess you're right. I know I'm going to sound naïve, but we're no threat to him."

"*We* know that. The big question is: Does *he* know that?"

The chopper thrum increased in volume again, making conversation difficult at best.

He didn't want to frighten her, but he was pretty sure Laffite and Bakari had headed up to the rim to shoot down Antso and his chopper. Maybe that idea was sitting in the back of Laura's head. Or maybe she'd accepted Laffite's story of simply sending Antso on his way.

Ten to one: Bakari had brought over the Marlin—three and a half feet long, tops—in the big netting bag, and poor Antso was going to be on the receiving end of a .30-30 slug.

Which brought him to Laura's we're-no-threat-to-him position.

Rick remembered how interested Laffite had seemed when asking if the chopper pilot had the coordinates. When Laura had confirmed that he did, the Frenchman had immediately handed her the phone to call him.

The only answer: Laffite wanted this island to himself.

Which left the most pertinent question: Would he risk killing a New York medical examiner to keep the secret? Rick had reinvented himself as a nobody, Keith had already vanished, but Laura was a state official who had left a well-marked travel trail.

If positions were reversed, Rick saw an easy way he could get away with the triple murder. He could only hope Laffite wouldn't see it.

The copter cacophony suddenly dropped in volume and faded away.

Laura's shoulders slumped. "There goes our ride."

Yeah, Rick thought. Straight into the drink.

He still hadn't heard any gunshots. But that didn't mean anything. The chopper noise could have masked them. So he waited. Maybe one of the pair—either Laffite or Bakari—would give it away.

"That leaves the boat as the only escape route," Rick said. "If we can get free, we can find our way to the beach and swim to it. Then it's bye-bye, Laffite, and hello, Mozambique."

"The boat won't start," Keith said.

"What do you mean? How do you know?"

"I overheard him say he'd pulled the fuel pump fuse and brought it and the spares to the island."

Crap. Not that it mattered with his hands secured behind his back.

Laffite and Bakari reappeared maybe ten minutes later. Bakari's pock-marked face was as impassive as ever; if anything, the perpetual chip on his shoulder seemed even bigger. But Laffite . . .

Rick couldn't help glaring at him, and it took all he had to keep from leaping up and head-butting him. The fucker had held a gun to Laura's head. And though he might not have had any serious intention of pulling the trigger, he'd frightened the hell out of her. Nobody got away with that.

Laffite retrieved his revolver from Razi and tucked it into his belt, then clapped his hands once.

"So! It is done! Your pilot is on his way back to Morondava. Razi, *mon ami*, free these good people."

He was not the same man who had walked off just a little while ago. The hail-fellow-well-met façade was as thin as a coat of paint and riddled with cracks. Something had happened, something had rattled him. And Rick could guess just what.

Laffite seemed to imagine himself something of a rogue, a freebooter of sorts like his namesake, bending the rules, breaking the laws, dodging the authorities. A smuggler. A modern-day Jean Lafitte. But Rick was pretty sure that until today he'd never been a party to murder.

He'd crossed a line that didn't permit crossing back. A part of him had died up there on that rim.

"So we're prisoners here until you decide to leave?" Laura said as Razi cut her zip tie.

A weak smile. "You are not *my* prisoners. You are prisoners of circumstance."

"Not much difference."

"No-no. You are free to jump in the channel and start swimming any time you wish."

Laura's tone turned bitter. "Right. Like any of us can swim a hundred miles."

"Actually longer, considering how the current will drag you steadily southward."

She rose, rubbing her wrists. "How long till you head back?"

Razi had cut Keith free second, and now approached Rick.

"That depends," Laffite said. "Hold on a second, Razi." He stepped closer to Rick and stood over him. "I have gathered the impression, Monsieur—Hayden, is it not?"

"Right. Like the planetarium."

"I have no idea what that means. Regardless, in the short time since we have met I have gathered the impression that you are a rather dangerous man and that it would not be in my best interests to free your very quick hands."

You got that right, froggy.

"I sense a proposal coming."

"You are perceptive. I have also gathered the impression that you are a man of breeding who will keep his word. So, if you will give me your word as a man that you will not attack me or Razi or Bakari, or sabotage any of our equipment, I will free you."

Your word as a man . . .

He'd heard the phrase in movies but never in real life. But yeah, he could live with that deal . . . within limits. Certainly not forever. Because threatening Laura's life came with a price tag. Someday, someway, a reckoning would come.

Another reason to make the promise popped into his head: He'd spotted a loophole.

"Okay. I will give you my word not to initiate force, but I *will* defend myself and these two from any sort of attack."

"That is only fair, I guess."

He continued to stare down at Rick.

"What?"

"I saw how you looked at me when I returned. I understand your anger for threatening your woman, but it was necessary to make you cooperate. You see that, don't you?"

Rick forced his jaw muscles to relax. "I see it."

"I am not sure I believe you. That is why I am having second thoughts."

Laura said, "Look, if he says he won't attack you, he won't. You can take it to the bank. He's a Boy Scout in that regard."

A Boy Scout . . . that was a first.

"Very well. But I will also need your word that you will not try to escape either."

"You mean swim away?"

"Do not play the fool. I mean try to steal the *Sorcière*."

Damn! That had been the loophole.

"Okay. No escape attempts either."

"*Bon*. Razi?" He pointed to Rick.

As Razi cut the tie, Rick saw a way to go for the knife but . . . he'd given his word.

As Rick stood and stretched his back and knees, Laura spoke.

"When I asked you how long till we head back, you said 'That depends.' Depends on what?"

"On the success of what we are about to attempt. If we succeed, we will spend the next day or two filling the cages with captured dapis. If we fail, we will pack up and head home tomorrow." A brief, sour smile twisted his lips. "Which means you will be hoping for failure, I know. But that is the way it is. Do you wish to watch?"

"Wouldn't miss it for the world," Rick said.

"Then watch from here. And be silent."

As Laffite walked off toward Razi and Bakari where they were fiddling with one of the live traps, a shadow began to stretch across the area. Rick looked around. He couldn't see the rim through all the greenery, but from the angle of the light he figured the sun was sinking behind it.

With the coming of the shadow, the constant chatter of the dapis grew silent, but only briefly. The air suddenly filled with a high-pitched howling, a variety of tones, growing in volume, clashing at first but gradually changing pitch and blending into a single note, loud as all hell.

He turned to Laura. "They're singing?"

She shrugged, her blue eyes filled with wonder.

The dapis held the note forever. At least it seemed like forever. And then, like someone cutting power to an amp, they stopped. After a few seconds of silence—probably to catch their breaths—their chatter resumed.

Rick found Laura giving him a wide-eyed stare as she spread her hands in bewilderment. "What the—?"

"It's a ceremony," Keith said. "They do it every evening when the sun drops out of view and again in the morning when it crests the rim."

"A 'ceremony'?" Laura said. "But they're animals."

"Not just 'animals.' They're primates, and very smart ones."

"But doesn't a sun ceremony imply awareness of something, I don't know, bigger than yourself?"

Keith nodded. "Yes, it does."

The thought gave Rick a chill—not across his skin, but through his brain.

"Don't you find that just a little bit . . . creepy?"

"More than a little," Keith said. "It means their 3998 gene is actively coding."

"And you want to wipe them out?" Laura's tone was scolding. "Seriously?"

He didn't seem to hear her. He waved an arm at the dapis watching from the trees.

"Have you noticed any predators on the island? I haven't. More than that, no competitors for the food supply either. If any of those ever existed here, the dapis wiped them out and claimed the top of the food chain. Now we arrive, probably the first intrusion on their environment in millions of years. We've awakened something in them. They're stimulated by our presence, they're responding to us, they're *learning* from us. We've changed them and they'll never be quite the same."

"Learning how?" Rick said.

"They watch everything, drinking it all in. That's why whatever Laffite is planning here at the moment will fail. He may capture one or two with his net, but that will be it. He'll have initial success because they've never encountered a net before. But as soon as they see how it works, they'll either circumvent it or avoid it."

"And you want to wipe them out?" Laura repeated. "That's almost . . ."

"Genocide?" Keith said. "I feel the same way. That's why Marten is necessary."

"But why? I still don't understand."

Keith's expression turned impatient. "We've already had this discussion."

Yes, they had, and Rick didn't want to suffer through that save-humanity-from-itself nonsense.

"So how did they catch the first one?" he said. "The one with the broken leg."

"In one of the traps. But that was the last one they caught that way."

"I'm not surprised," Rick said. "Not after seeing those tapes of Mozi out at Schelling."

Keith looked surprised. "You were at Schelling?"

"All part of tracking you down, bro."

"I could be impressed. I could even be touched."

"'Could be'?" Laura said.

Yeah, Rick thought. That's my bro.

Keith's smile seemed almost self-deprecating. "Well, easier said than done."

Wow. Was that a flash of self-awareness?

Keith pointed to Laffite and company. "I think they're about ready."

It looked like they'd baited the trap and set the spring door, and now they were fanning out from it.

They'd suspended the net from trees, tying its corners to branches so that it bellied down over the trap like a giant black veil of mourning. Rick guesstimated its area at about 400 square feet, more than enough to trap a few unwary dapis.

The three humans had donned heavy-duty fireman gloves. Bakari stationed himself at the far end, holding two of the tethering cords; on the near side, Laffite and Razi each held one. They didn't have to wait long before four dapis scampered down from the trees and skipped-bounded toward the trap.

"That's the weirdest form of locomotion I've ever seen," Laura whispered.

"They're largely arboreal," Keith said. "I've been watching them since I got here. They spend their days leaping from branch to branch, almost flying, so it makes sense they'd incorporate leaps when traveling over ground."

As soon as the four dapis reached the trap, Laffite waved an arm and all three men pulled their cords. They must have been tied with slip knots because the cords fell free, allowing the net to drop. Spotting the dark mesh wafting down, the dapis stared up at it with apparent fascination. Too late they realized that this might not be a good thing and started to flee. They managed one leap before the net engulfed them.

"Well," Laura said, her voice heavy with disappointment, "that's four for the cage."

"The last four," Keith said. "I guarantee no dapi will ever venture under that net again."

The trapped dapis began screeching and struggling against the mesh. Their fellows in the trees above took up the cry, scrambling about and making agitated jumps from branch to branch. Laffite and Razi high-fived each other and, walking on the net, headed for the cluster as Bakari approached from the far side.

Rick noticed that the dapis under the net weren't taking their capture lying down.

"They'd better hurry," he said. "They're starting to chew their way through."

Laffite and the brothers must have realized this too because they picked up their pace.

And then . . .

. . . it began to rain dapis.

Suddenly the air was full of them, leaping from the trees onto the trappers, landing on shoulders and arms and heads, clawing or taking a quick bite, and then leaping off to be replaced by another. Human cries and roars of shock and pain and rage mixed with the screeches of the attacking dapis.

Laffite, Bakari, and Razi were stumbling around in ragged circles as they batted and grabbed frantically at their attackers. But the dapis never stayed put long enough to take any damage. As he staggered about, Bakari's foot caught in the netting and he went down onto his hands and knees. One of the larger females landed on his back and jumped up and down, screeching and thrusting her long, skinny, hairy arms up in victory like Rocky at the top of the museum steps. She pulled his knife from its sheath and raced over to the trapped dapis where she began cutting at the net.

She wasn't alone. Other dapis had knives and were using them to the same end.

It ended as quickly as it had begun, leaving the three humans atop the net and no dapis beneath it—only four ragged holes where they'd been. The assault hadn't been a true attack, merely a delaying tactic to allow the rescuers time to cut their trapped fellows free. As soon as they were loose and headed for safety, the raid was called off.

But not the noise.

Rick didn't understand dapi noise. Did they have a language? Whatever, the sounds they were making now were different from anything he'd heard before.

"Is that cheering or jeering?" he said to no one in particular.

Bakari was still on his hands and knees. The female who'd jumped on his back dropped from the trees and stood a dozen feet in front of him where she repeated her Rocky victory dance, waving his knife above her head, then scampered back to a branch.

"Jeering," Keith said.

"Yeah, that's what it looks like." The female was now acting as cheerleader—make that *jeer*leader—for the rest of the dapis. "But why Bakari?"

"Because he's the one who broke the little male's leg."

Rick couldn't help grinning. "And she just so much as said, 'You're my bitch now.' Ooh, burned!"

Bakari jumped to his feet and stalked away from the net in the direction of the tents. At his departure, the jeering doubled in volume.

As he passed them, his face and arms were bleeding from numerous bites and scratches, his expression a mask of pure rage.

Well, Rick thought, looks like we're gonna find out if the Marlin is on the island or still on the boat.

But when Bakari returned he was carrying a spear instead of a rifle. He walked straight to the edge of the net. Laffite tried to stop him, grabbing his arm in an attempt to dissuade him, but Bakari roughly pushed him aside.

Above, the female dapi was waving the knife and still acting as jeer-leader when Bakari set his feet and raised the spear over his shoulder.

"Oh, no!" Laura gasped. "He's not really—"

Rick tried to turn her around. "Don't look." But she wouldn't turn.

Bakari let the shaft fly. The dapi had her back to him, facing her fellows, and didn't see it coming. The steel spearhead pierced her through, jutting from her breast bone as she was flung forward by the force of the impact.

She hit the ground on her side, kicked once or twice, then lay still.

And from the dapis in the trees . . . dead silence.

"Oh, this is not good," Keith said. "Not good at all. Because they watch . . . they watch and they learn."

14

Amaury and Razi finished folding the net, useless now because of the holes the dapis had cut through it. But holes could be repaired. Amaury wasn't so sure about the damage Bakari had caused.

"Because of what your brother has done," he told Razi in Portuguese, "the dapis will fear us now."

"Yes," Razi said. "They will fear us. And that means they will respect us. They had no respect." He held out his scratched and bitten arms, the oozing blood dried now. "Look what they did to us."

Amaury examined his own arms. They looked the same.

"They were only helping their fellows."

"Yes, but they jumped on us because they did not fear us or respect us. They will not jump again."

"Fear or respect or whatever you call it . . . as a result they will be harder to catch after this. Much harder."

Bad enough that Bakari had killed that female, he hadn't stopped there. He'd retrieved his knife from beside her body and cut off her head, then held her up by her feet to drain her blood onto the weeds. That done, he'd found a sapling, stripped off its leaves, and set her head onto the crotch of its slim branches.

But it got worse. He'd gathered up dead wood and started a fire. Next he gutted her, then sat down and began skinning her.

And through it all, the horde of dapis watched in silence.

As Amaury and Razi walked back, carrying the netting, they passed the sapling with the dapi's head. Her big, sightless blue eyes seemed to regard them reproachfully. Then they came to Bakari who had begun roasting her limbs over the fire. He did not look up as they passed.

Amaury found Jeukens and the other two by the tents.

"How could you let that happen?" the woman said.

"I wish very much that it had not happened, but I have no control over Bakari."

"It's barbaric."

He waited until he and Razi had stowed the netting next to the tents, then turned to her.

"You are an intelligent woman, I have no doubt, but you are ignorant of the native ways here. The brothers are Shangaans. They and other Bantu tribes do their share of farming and raising livestock, but they also eat the wildlife. Boars, monkeys, even the occasional gorilla. It's called 'bushmeat' and what he has done is no more barbaric than one of your fellow New Yorkers shooting and field dressing a deer for its venison."

"But-but these primates are special."

"Not to a Shangaan. They're just another source of bushmeat."

She seemed to give up on arguing. Good. He was too tired to argue, and hated being in the position of defending Bakari. The Shangaan had taken a deteriorating situation and made it immeasurably worse. If Razi weren't here, Amaury could see himself pulling out the Marlin and shooting Bakari—and this time he *would* pull the trigger. With the greatest enthusiasm.

"I think we should leave now," Jeukens said.

"You have no say in when we leave," Amaury told him. "I and only I shall decide, and I have already decided we shall leave tomorrow as soon as it is light."

"Well, that's a relief!" the woman said.

"Fine," Jeukens said. "But am I allowed to suggest that we sleep on the boat then?"

"Why would you want to do that?"

"You and your men, especially Bakari, have introduced a level of aggression to this island that I doubt these creatures have ever seen."

The big man, Rick, who had been standing aside in stony silence, looked at Laura. "Like a crab in a fish tank."

This meant nothing to Amaury but appeared to hold some significance for the woman. He ignored it and replied to Jeukens.

"You are being dramatic. I know animals. In any colony there is always aggression to determine who is alpha and who is not."

"That's normal and natural. This is different. They watched us use knives, then stole them and used them to free their brothers. Now they've watched one of their own speared, dismembered, and roasted."

"It is unfortunate, I agree, but what can I do?"

"You can get us off this island!" Jeukens said.

"We leave tomorrow. What are you afraid of?"

Jeukens pointed to the trees. "They *learn*, damn it! They learn by watching, and Bakari just put on one hell of a workshop."

Amaury had to admit he had a point, but he could not back down.

"So what are you telling me? That they will attack us during the night?"

"They might. We don't know enough about them. They might take the loss of the female in stride. She let her attention drift and paid the price. *C'est la guerre*. And even if they do mourn her loss, their brains might not be developed enough to grasp the concept of revenge. Let's hope not. Because we already know they can act in concert, as demonstrated by all those cuts on your face and arms. And that was just harassment to buy time for their captured fellows. I'd hate to be the target of a maim-or-kill assault."

Amaury shook off a wave of cold dread.

Rick said, "At least let Laura sleep on the boat."

She gave him a grateful look but shook her head. "Out there alone on the water? I don't think so. I'll take my chances here with you folks."

Rick looked ready to respond but something on the periphery of their camp caught his attention. "Oh, look. It's the monkey-meat man."

Bakari had arrived, gnawing on a dapi thigh as he approached. He clutched a variety of roasted limbs in his other hand. He stopped before Razi and handed him the other thigh. Razi asked something in Ronga that Amaury didn't understand. Bakari shrugged. Razi took a bite, chewed, swallowed, then returned a shrug.

Behind him he heard the woman say, "Ugh!"

Amaury guessed how the exchange went:

How is it?

Not bad.

Bite, chew, swallow.

Yeah, not bad.

Next stop: Amaury. Bakari shoved an arm at him. The scrawny limb had little meat on it, most of it crisped by the fire. It had been skinned down to the wrist but the hand had remained intact, the little fingers curled from the heat.

"I'm not hungry."

True enough. The sight of that little hand made his gorge rise.

"Eat," Bakari said, pushing it closer. "Eat and you are with us. Do not eat and you are with them."

Was that what this was? Some sort of initiation rite to separate *us* from *them*? The dark-skinned from the light-skinned? Prove that you are fit to lead us?

Some of the restaurants in Maputo served bushmeat now and then. He'd eaten monkey before, and even snake and aardvark. And boar, of course. So why not dapi?

He shrugged and accepted the arm.

He heard Rick say, "Oh, you've got to be kidding me."

Amaury ignored him and turned the arm back and forth, looking for something edible that wasn't charred. Finally he took a bite of the biceps.

Ugh. Stringy, tough, overcooked, and completely without seasoning. Tasteless. Like chewing rope. But he managed to swallow.

There. He'd done it.

Bakari grinned and clapped him on the shoulder.

Hourra for me. I've joined the club.

Bakari moved onto the others, offering the remaining arm.

The woman turned away, Jeukens shook his head, and Rick said, "Thanks, but I'm cutting back."

Bakari returned and took another bite of the thigh, indicating that Amaury should partake again.

Amaury pointed to the host of dapis watching in silence from above and quoted Jeukens. "They watch and they learn."

Bakari grinned. "That is right. And they have learned to fear me. Eat."

Amaury nibbled on the triceps and forced it down.

Glancing up, he felt the weight of the gazes from the crowded trees and wanted to vomit up the meat. But it stayed down.

He knew he wasn't going to sleep tonight.

THURSDAY

May 26

1

Marten opened his eyes.

He'd been feigning sleep, watching Laffite's pup tent through slitted lids. His mind longed for sleep. Pretending to be Keith was exhausting. While he'd watched, his mind ranged across the possible courses of action left open to him. He hadn't come up with many options.

One decision was irrevocable: He was going to die today.

Not out of any noble impulse, no misguided idea of being a martyr for humanity. As Camus said, "Martyrs have to choose between being forgotten, mocked or used. As for being understood—never."

Marten had no hope of ever being understood.

And besides, he *deserved* to die.

He had killed the pilot in Maxixe. The man's blood cried out for justice and retribution. And he would have it.

Marten's death would mean Keith's death too, of course. Keith didn't deserve to die. But Keith *needed* to die. Keith was the only one who knew the secret of the dapis, the only person, living or dead, who had seen the genome firsthand. With the theocracies waiting in the wings, Keith had to die.

Obviously Laffite and Razi and Bakari had to die as well—especially Bakari. He'd murdered and eaten a dapi. Unforgivable. But even if he hadn't, he knew of the island. Worse, the unholy trio were engaged in the exotics trade. They'd be shipping dapis back to the mainland and selling them to every Tom, Dick, and Harriet. Only a matter of time before some taxonomist got hold of one and ran its genome. And then . . . disaster.

He thought of Kahlil, the NYU geneticist rotting in an Iranian jail because his research went against the Quran. After the dapis were seen as instruments of God, church would merge with state and unsanctioned science would start being persecuted in Christian countries as well.

Thinking of dapis raised a question: What were they doing? He'd spent last night under the trees just like this and they'd seemed in constant motion through the branches above. Tonight they were silent. Frightened off by Bakari?

But dapis aside, the big question was what to do about Garrick and Laura. Besides the dapis, they were the only innocent parties on the island. He'd told them the secret of the dapi genome, but that was only hearsay on their part. And they'd both seemed skeptical, which was good.

But they knew the location of the island, and that was a capital offense. If only they *hadn't* found it. True, they'd come in good faith, looking for Garrick's missing brother, but that didn't change the fact that they could talk about it at any time. They knew the coordinates. They'd already brought a helicopter pilot here. They could bring researchers as well.

Marten sighed. No way around it: Everyone had to die with the dapis.

A glow began within Laffite's tent. At last!

Marten had given his own pup tent to Laura while he'd leaned his back against a tree perhaps a dozen feet away and pretended to doze. Garrick was also slumped against a tree, but his was right next to Laura's tent. Bakari and Razi had disappeared into the larger tent they shared.

Marten wondered if anyone had gotten any meaningful sleep tonight. Whether the threat of a dapi attack was real or not, the idea had to be on everyone's mind. But Marten had stayed awake for another reason.

He'd been waiting for Laffite's bladder to nudge him from his tent. Bakari and Razi had already been up. Even Garrick had left his post for a few minutes to do his business. Only Laura and Laffite had yet to heed the call. Marten knew it was an inevitable trip for Laffite. The Frenchman had downed one of the bottles of the wine he had brought along. To rinse the taste of roasted dapi from his palate, perhaps?

And there he was. The flaps of his tent parted and Laffite emerged with a penlight. He quick-flashed the beam around the site, confirming that everyone was where they should be, then made his way into the bushes. One of the prime rules of camping: Don't excrete where you might put your feet.

As soon as Laffite had turned his back, Marten was up and moving. He crawled into the tent and began feeling around. A penlight of his own would have been nice but the tent was so small—

Here—in the far right corner under a backpack: four phones in a pile. They could only be Garrick's, Laura's, Keith's, and Marten's. In the dark he couldn't tell which was which and couldn't spare the time to sort by touch, so he took them all.

As he returned the backpack to its former position, he realized the fuses for the *Sorcière*'s fuel pump might be stowed within. Did he dare? No. The temptation to use them for escape might prove too much. He had to die with the others.

As he exited the tent he had an instant of panic when he bumped into a dark figure right outside the flaps. But he was too tall to be Laffite.

"What the hell are you doing?" Garrick whispered.

"Trying to save us all," he said. "He'll be back any second. Get back where you were. Trust me."

Garrick hesitated, then nodded.

Marten stuffed the phones inside his shirt as he returned to his tree. Within seconds everything was as Laffite had left it. When he returned he flashed his light around again, then reentered his tent.

Trying to save us all . . . trust me . . .

How easily the fabrications tripped off his lips. Lying was an art which, like any other skill, improved with practice, practice, practice. And Marten had had so much practice lately.

He waited and watched, and soon was rewarded with the sound of snoring from Laffite's tent. That was his signal. He rose into a crouch and crept off through the underbrush. Garrick undoubtedly witnessed his departure but made no sound. Marten was not worried he'd follow. Garrick was not about to leave Laura unguarded.

Dealing with noble people was always a pleasure: They were reliable and, best of all, predictable.

He took his time, moving carefully. He saw no need to hurry to his own death. Then again, why put off the inevitable?

When he guessed he'd traveled about a hundred yards from the camp, he knelt in the weeds and pulled one of the phones from his shirt. He fumbled with it in the dark until he found the on button. He used the light from the screen to identify his own phone. He'd kept it turned off to preserve the battery. He turned it on.

Please work . . . . please-please-please.

The screen lit.

Yes!

What am I so relieved about? It means I can die now . . . as in *now*.

He pressed and held the 2 button and within seconds the number of one of the trigger phones appeared on the screen.

Now, all he had to do was press talk and a signal would flash up to a satellite over the Indian Ocean and then back down to Earth. The trigger phone would receive the incoming call, sending its vibration rotor into motion, which would complete the circuit to the detonator caps lodged in the block of C-4 taped to its VX canister. The explosion of that block would detonate the second block just inches away. The combined explosions would vaporize fifty gallons of the most potent neurotoxin known to man, sending a toxic cloud sweeping across the caldera. Contact or inhalation would doom any life-form with a nervous system. Those receiving a higher dose would die more quickly than those with a lower dose, but eventually all would die.

The *Sorcière des Mers* would be the only external evidence of human visitation. Sooner or later one of the many violent storms or typhoons that swept across the channel would tear loose her anchor and she would drift south into the Indian Ocean where she might be discovered as a mysterious ghost ship, or she'd sink to the bottom, lost forever.

With the heat and humidity of the island's tropical climate, all the bodies, human and dapi, would quickly rot into the soil, leaving no trace as they nourished the plant life in the timeless cycle of death and rebirth. The island would remain toxic for a long, long time, however, and woe be to the unfortunate explorer who stumbled upon her before the VX had been broken down by time and the elements. The central lake would stay toxic the longest.

Marten poised his thumb over the talk button. Did he really want to do this? Wasn't there another way?

No. Humanity could never deal with the truth about itself, and must never know. He was the custodian of that truth.

He realized he was delaying, subconsciously finding ways to put off the inevitable.

Reminding himself to take a deep inhalation of the vapor cloud as it rushed over him, he closed his eyes, gritted his teeth, and pressed the button. His bowels clenched as the call went out.

Sweating, shaking, he waited.

No explosion.

What was wrong? His phone was working. Was the satellite out? Unlikely.

He pressed the button again.

And again, nothing. He put the phone to his ear and heard ringing. The other phone was receiving the call.

Not good, but not the end of the world. Well, *his* world. At least not yet. Murphy's Law had prevailed: If something can go wrong, it will. But he'd prepared for this eventuality. He had another trigger set up just inches from the first. All hail redundancy.

He hit *3* on his phone and the second trigger's number appeared on the screen. No drama this time, no hesitation, no tense deep breath. He was too annoyed with his first trigger for any of that. He pressed talk.

And waited.

And nothing.

No. This couldn't be. Not *both* of them faulty. Impossible!

Sobbing, he began jamming his thumb against the button again and again. All he'd done to get to this point, all his sins, all his efforts to execute this perfect plan. It had to work, it *had* to!

But still no explosion.

He took a deep breath and calmed himself. Okay. Be logical. The problem wasn't the satellite. The problem was here on the island. That meant the solution was here as well. He'd tested all the circuits between both phones and their attached detonator caps, but something might have gone wrong. No, something obviously had gone wrong, something as simple as an alligator clamp falling off.

But on *both* of them? That wasn't right. None of the humans of the island had discovered the canisters or they'd have raised a stink. Then what? Something as simple as a falling branch? Or—

Oh, hell. A dapi. A curious dapi investigating something it had never seen before. That had to be it.

When he had enough light he'd find out what had happened and make it right. And then . . .

An idea occurred to him. If he detonated the C-4 while he was standing there, he wouldn't have to suffer the agonies of death by a neurotoxin. His end would be instantaneous. Like turning off a light switch.

He smiled. Every cloud did indeed have a silver lining.

2

Rick knew he'd be the first Laffite would question when he realized Keith was gone. And sure enough . . .

Faint predawn light was filtering through the canopy when the Frenchman crawled out of his tent. He stretched his back, looked around, and stiffened when he noticed someone was missing. He strode straight to where Rick sat with his back against one of the fat tree trunks.

"Where is your brother?" he said, standing over him.

"Am I my brother's keeper?"

"I want an answer."

Rick rose to face him. "I don't have one. I saw him walk off into the bushes an hour or two ago. I thought he was going for a leak. He hasn't come back yet."

All true. Of course, he'd left out the small detail of the phones Keith had stolen from Laffite's tent.

"An hour or two?"

Rick shrugged. "I didn't check my watch, but it seems about that long."

Laffite turned in a slow circle. "He should be back by now."

Yeah, he should be, Rick thought.

He'd been wondering what Keith was doing in the bushes with those phones. Calling for help? Not a bad idea. If Laffite knew help was on the way, he'd have to keep the three of them alive.

He'd also wondered if he'd found the fuse Laffite had taken from the boat. If he had, and had slipped back into Marten mode, he might very well have sailed away, leaving them all marooned.

"Maybe the dapis got him."

"Do not even joke about that."

"Hey, it's possible."

"If you truly believed that, you would be out looking for him."

Rick shrugged again. "It's not like he can go far."

"True, true, but—" Laffite's eyes widened. Rick had known a certain unpleasant possibility would eventually occur to him. *"Merde!"*

He whirled and raced back to his tent. Seconds later he emerged with a backpack in one hand and his revolver in another. He stalked toward Rick.

"Where *is* he?"

"No idea." He held his ground. "And that's the truth."

He gathered that Keith hadn't taken the fuse, else Laffite would be scrambling up to the rim to make sure his boat was still here.

"Well, then, you will go find him."

Rick smiled and shook his head, trying to provoke the Frenchman.

"I don't think so. I'm sure he's just fine where he is."

Laffite raised the revolver and shoved the muzzle toward Rick, placing it within easy reach.

Thank you.

"You will go find him now or someone you care about will suffer!"

That did it.

He lashed out with his right hand, grabbing the barrel and giving it a vicious twist as he pushed the gun down and away. It discharged with a loud crack as Laffite's finger caught inside the trigger guard, firing one round into the ground. Rick wrenched the revolver free and the Frenchman screamed as his finger broke.

"That's the last time you threaten her," Rick said.

Bakari and Razi scrambled from their tent and he heard Laura cry out behind him.

"What happened?"

"Nothing important," Rick said. "Everything's cool."

Laffite was bent over, cradling his broken finger.

Rick examined the revolver. Not a Smith after all. A near-antique Llama clone of the Model 10. He found the release and swung the cylinder out. He dumped the rounds, fired and unfired, into his palm, then hurled them into the brush. If he'd had a screwdriver handy he would have removed the cylinder and done the same with it. Instead he left the cylinder out and hammered it against a baobab trunk until it wouldn't fit back into the frame. Then he tossed the whole thing out of sight.

There. That leveled the playing field. Well, a little. The brothers still had their spears and he presumed Laffite still had the Marlin in his tent. But nobody would be strutting around with firepower tucked in his belt.

"You broke my finger!" Laffite said.

"And you threatened Laura again. I don't call us even, but it'll do for now."

More light was filtering through the trees. Laura was out of the tent and looking around.

"You sleep okay?" he said.

She gave him a dumb-question look. "Yeah. I mean, I knew you were out here, so . . . yeah."

He loved her for that simple acknowledgment. It made the whole long night worthwhile.

"Where are the dapis?" she said.

"We do not care about the dapis!" Laffite groaned, clutching his injured hand. "We need to find Jeukens!"

"We need to get off this island, is what we need," Laura said.

"He has all your phones."

Rick tried to look surprised. "Really? How'd he manage that?"

"He must have sneaked into my tent."

"You say that like it's a bad thing."

Laffite only glared at him.

"Come on," Laura said, grabbing the Frenchman's arm. "Let's find the first-aid kit and see what we can do for that finger."

As she led him away, Rick said, "Hey, he just threatened your life again."

She gave Rick an eye roll. The doctor part of her had taken over and she didn't take the threats seriously. But she didn't know about Antso and his helicopter.

On the way to the first-aid kit, Laffite shouted something to the brothers in Portuguese. They took off, in search of Keith, no doubt. Rick was tempted to start his own search, but he wasn't letting Laura out of his sight.

He looked up at the empty trees.

And yeah, where were the dapis?

3

Marten was lost. His own damn fault for trying to find the canisters before sunrise oriented him. But what little he could see of the sky showed a lid of clouds. With no firm idea of east, he'd have to guess about north. Because north was where he'd left the canisters.

He hadn't seen a dapi since dark had fallen. No reflective eyes watching from the trees, no chatter. Almost as if they'd deserted the island. The overcast would prevent the sun from cresting the rim. Would that mean no ceremony this morning?

At last he located the canisters hidden in the underbrush as he'd left them. And immediately he saw the reason the detonation had failed.

Shit! Shit! Shit!

Four of the alligator connectors—two from each board—were missing. The black wires were still there, but the reds were gone.

Just as he'd suspected: dapis . . . had to be the dapis. But why? Were they attracted to red? What the hell was he going to do now?

Movement behind him made him turn. A dapi male hung from a low branch, staring at him. And around his neck . . . four red wires. He'd learned how to work the alligator clips and made a necklace for himself.

Slowly, avoiding any sudden moves, Keith checked his pockets on the off chance he had a protein bar somewhere on his person. But no. Nothing. He needed something to entice the dapi closer . . . close enough to grab those connectors. All he had were phones.

During his train and bus trips up and down the Mozambique coast he'd downloaded an app or two to help pass the time. He had the old standby, Tetris. He'd heard about Angry Birds and tried it but found it ridiculous. Same with Candy Crush—mindless. He couldn't believe people actually spent hours with—

Wait . . . didn't Angry Birds feature a red bird?

Maybe . . . just maybe . . .

He began searching through his apps, praying he hadn't dragged it to the trash can.

4

Without an X-ray, Laura couldn't tell if Laffite's right index finger was broken or merely badly sprained. Either way, it needed immobilization. She could try a tongue depressor as a splint, but decided instead on simple buddy taping: She used strips of adhesive bandage to strap the injured index to the healthy middle finger.

"*Tu es une belle femme*," he said as she worked. "*Un homme peut se noyer dans vos yeux.*"

She shook her head. He had to be kidding. Coming on to her in French so a certain someone wouldn't understand?

"*Il est une brute*," he continued. "*Repartir avec moi.*"

"Tell him you'll go only if he promises to take you to the Casbah," Rick said from a dozen feet away.

Laura laughed. "Since when do you speak French?"

"I don't, but when someone like him goes all Pepé Le Pew, I can suss out the gist of what he's laying down. The Casbah or nothing."

Laffite looked puzzled as he replied in English. "The Casbah? In Algiers?"

Lauren played along. "Of course. Is there another?"

"I would not take such a beautiful woman to such a terrible place." Then he shrugged. "But of course, if you wish—"

A man started screaming somewhere out in the woods. She glanced at Rick who looked like a panther ready to spring.

"Keith?" she said.

He shook his head. "One of the brothers."

Laffite agreed. "It sounds like Razi."

His cries were agonized.

"He's hurt," Laura said. "How—?"

Laffite rose to his feet. "We should go see."

"Be my guest," Rick said.

"You are afraid?"

"Terrified," he said casually. "Laura and I will stay put. But you feel free to go."

Laura doubted Laffite was going anywhere.

And then the cries choked off.

All around . . . silence.

Laura had to ask: "Has anyone seen a dapi this morning?"

Rick shook his head. "Not a one. Although I wonder . . . I mean, I hope it's not true, but I'm wondering if Razi just found them."

They all waited in silence. Her patch-up job done, Laura left Laffite and gravitated to Rick's side.

"Do you really think it was the dapis?"

He shrugged. "Dunno. I saw my first living dapi less than twenty-four hours ago, so I have no idea what they're capable of. But from the sound of it, something bad happened to Razi out there, and I'm pretty sure it had nothing to do with Keith."

Something was plunging toward them through the brush.

She grabbed his arm. "Hear that?"

Something heavy, too heavy for a dapi.

And then Bakari, his face a mask of grief and fright, burst into their little clearing carrying Razi across his back in a sort of fireman's carry. He knelt and eased his brother to the ground.

A yelp of shock escaped Laura when she saw the prone figure.

"Putain!" Laffite cried.

Rick said, "What the fuck?"

Miniature spears, each about a foot long, jutted from each eye socket and each ear canal, two had been jammed into Razi's blood-filled mouth, and another poked skyward from his larynx.

Bakari, distressed to the point of panic, raised his bloody fists and howled at the trees in helpless rage.

Laura felt as if her feet had grown roots. She stood frozen, unable to move as the implications washed over her, then she broke free and knelt beside the fallen brother.

She felt Razi's throat for a pulse, but his carotid was still. She pulled open his bloody shirt and pressed her ear to his chest to check for a heartbeat. Nothing. She straightened up and looked at his blood-filled mouth, the spear in his larynx. It looked like he'd choked to death on his own blood. Still, there might be a chance . . .

She eased the stick from his throat. No spearhead atop the shaft—little more than a sharpened stick. She tossed it aside. No air gushed from the hole, but no blood either. The spear had performed a crude tracheotomy. With an airway established, if she could kick-start the heart into beating again, he might survive.

Laura started hand-on-hand compressions of Razi's chest, timing them to the recommended tempo of the Bee Gees' "Stayin' Alive." But after fewer than a half dozen, she saw blood clots blocking the hole. And then Bakari pushed her away with a growl.

"Hey, asshole!" Rick said. "She's only trying to help!"

"He doesn't understand," Laffite said. "And it doesn't look like there's anything to save here." He made a face. "Look what they did to his eyes."

Rick had picked up the mini-spear and was examining it. "Looks like it's been chewed to a point." He looked around. "This must be what they spent the whole night doing."

"'They watch and they learn,'" Laura said, quoting Keith as she stared down at Razi's pierced eyes and throat. "And this is the result of their latest lesson."

Rick threw the little spear at Bakari. "This is *your* doing, fucktard! They'd never seen a spear until you demonstrated how useful they are!" He pointed to Razi. "Happy? Happy?"

Bakari jumped to his feet, looking confused and angry, but ready to fight.

"Easy, Rick," Laura said. "You're talking too fast for him. He doesn't understand you."

"He understands just fine." He took a breath and turned away. "Sorry, Laura. It's just that the profound stupidity of all this makes me . . . makes me crazy."

Laura understood. Bakari's actions had turned a gentle community of tree hoppers into a murderous army of warriors. And now the humans were the enemy. She wanted to scream at him herself.

She lowered her voice. "But why Razi? I'd've thought—"

"Was wondering the same myself. Maybe they thought it was Bakari. They're brothers, after all." Rick turned to Laffite. "Hey, ask your pal here what happened out there."

Laffite spoke to Bakari in Portuguese and received an elaborate reply accompanied by a series of hand and arm gestures.

When he was done, Laffite said, "They were searching for your brother, walking maybe one hundred feet apart, when a dozen dapis jumped on

Razi and began stabbing him with their sticks. By the time Bakari arrived to help, they were done and gone."

Laura studied the fallen Razi. The dapis had struck at his most vulnerable parts, and ones most crucial for defense. Humans were so much bigger and stronger, but the dapis didn't have to be seasoned warriors to realize that their target, no matter what the physical advantages, didn't stand a chance once deprived of sight and sound. They were smaller, so they'd swarmed, much like Paleolithic humans did to bring down mastodons.

"So what next?" Rick added, wandering aimlessly about. "They decapitate us and dismember us and cook us up for dinner? I mean, that's what they saw this cretin do! He set the example."

Laura couldn't see the dapis taking matters to that extreme, but . . .

"They've become dangerous," she said.

"They may have been dangerous all along but never had a reason to show it until we provoked them."

Laura could see only one course of action. "Which means now, more than ever, we need to get off this island."

"I agree," Laffite said. "We will leave all the equipment—it will be fine until I return. We will head for the boat immediately."

"What about Keith?"

"He is welcome to come along, but we cannot risk searching for him. Look what happened to Razi."

"I traveled all this distance to find him," Rick said. "I'm not leaving without him."

Uh-oh.

"I think he's made his choice," Laura said.

"When I hear that from him, fine. Then it's full speed ahead away from here. But until then . . ."

"Okay. Where do we start looking for him?"

He shook his head. "Not 'we.' You're getting on the boat."

"And leave you here on your own?" Her turn to shake her head. "Not happening."

"Look, be reasonable. I'll be able to move faster without you."

She stamped her foot. She was trying to break herself of that habit but not having a lot of success.

"First off, not true. I can move just as fast as you—maybe not in an open field, but in all this jungle, we're even. Second, two pairs of eyes are better than one. And last, we're a *team*, damn it! We came here together, we'll leave together."

"You two are welcome to continue arguing," Laffite said, "but Bakari and I are heading for the safety of the boat. I will wait an hour. If you are not on the shore by then . . ." He smiled and waved. *"Bon voyage."*

A cold lump grew in the pit of Laura's stomach. She had a feeling he wouldn't wait a single minute.

"You can't maroon us here," Rick said.

Laffite shrugged. "Face it, *monsieur*. Your brother has either decided to stay with his beloved dapis, or he has already suffered Razi's fate. Either way, you are wasting your time—and mine."

He said something in Portuguese and gestured toward Razi. But as Bakari bent to lift his brother's body, he cried out, reaching around for a short, slender spear lodged in the back of his right shoulder.

The trees above and around erupted in a cacophony of screeches—war cries? Victory cries? Laura couldn't tell.

As Bakari clawed at his back to remove the spear, more wooden missiles darted from the trees. Most of them missed or landed sideways and bounced off without causing harm. But one did manage to pierce the skin of Laffite's forearm.

"Run!" he cried.

He spun and made a dash toward the area where the ladder leaned against the inner wall, but ran into a hail of little spears. Crossing his arms before his face, he reversed and charged past Laura and Rick.

"We can't stay here," Rick said.

He grabbed Laura's arm and pulled her into a crouching run.

She looked back to see Bakari bringing up the rear. Behind him, a horde of dapis swarmed to the ground where they retrieved their fallen spears and leaped back into the trees.

"Lucky for us they haven't had enough time to figure out how to throw those things," Rick said as they followed Laffite, dodging past slender saplings and monolithic baobabs.

"We appear to be on their learning curve," she said. "As targets."

"Once they figure out you hold a spear at its balance point, we're in trouble."

"And you know about spear balance points because—oh, never mind." She could guess his answer and she wanted to save her wind.

As the last in their running procession, Bakari was taking the brunt of the attack—which, as far as Laura was concerned, he fully deserved. The dapis had a justified beef with him. But did he deserve the same fate as Razi? Did anyone?

Gradually the attack eased off until the four of them were simply running. Laura was about to call a halt so they could reorient themselves, when the spears started flying at Laffite from straight ahead. He didn't hesitate: He made a sharp turn and disappeared off to the right. The dapis in the trees followed.

When Laura and Rick and Bakari reached his turning point, the dapis were moving away, leaping and flying through the trees as they chased Laffite.

Laura stopped. "Listen," she said, panting. "If they're going that way, let's go back the way we came."

"Great idea," Rick said. "Which way is that?"

Bakari, his shirt bloodied by a few superficial spear wounds, paused for only a few seconds, then started running again, continuing in the same direction they'd been headed.

"Let him go," Rick said. "Back is better."

She led the way, keeping a wary watch on the trees for spear-wielding dapis.

"You sure this is the way?" Rick said after a while. "Because none of this stuff looks trampled."

True enough. She'd thought it would be simple to retrace their steps, but had no idea where they were.

"I think we're lost," she said.

And when she spotted the central lake through the vegetation ahead, she knew it for sure.

5

Marten held the cell phone out to the dapi. He wished for one of those large-screen phablet models, but he'd have to work with what he had.

"See the birds?" he said, easing it forward as he repeatedly pressed the touchscreen to keep things moving. He hoped the red one was in motion.

The dapi seemed interested, cocking his head this way and that as he stared at the screen, but always glancing warily at Marten to see what he was up to.

Just a little closer . . . a little closer. Even if he couldn't grab the dapi itself, simply getting a finger hooked inside the red-wire necklace would be enough.

Just a little bit closer . . .

Now!

He dropped the phone as he lunged with both hands, but the dapi was too skittish and too fast. At the first sign of motion he screeched and leaped and was gone. Well, not quite gone. He stopped on a branch, looked back at Marten, and gave what sounded for all the world like a Bronx cheer.

Marten picked up the fallen phone and ended goddamn stupid Angry Birds. He wanted to hurl it into the trees but he still might need it. He stalked back to the canisters and stared at his trigger boards. How could he jury-rig the setup to—?

And then he saw it, staring him straight in the face. The dapi had taken the four red wires but left him the two blacks. But he didn't need any wires except the pair that sprouted from each detonator cap.

If this had been a chemical formula or an amino-acid sequence, he'd have solved any problem immediately. But something as simple as this . . . the solution had been so obvious he'd looked right past it.

He simply had to touch one of the detonator wires to the positive snap-connector terminal on the battery box and the other to the negative. *Boom.* Mission accomplished. And he'd never know what hit him.

He was reaching for the wires when he heard someone approaching from the jungle. Coming fast.

6

Laura's first thought upon seeing the lake was how thoroughly lost they were. The second, inanely, was how badly she needed a good scrubbing.

"This is not the way I thought we were going," Rick said. "Where the hell are we?"

"Well, the lake's in the center so—"

"Right, but are we on the north shore, the west shore, what? Damn, my sense of direction's usually pretty good. What is it about this place?"

Laura knew what he meant. "Yeah. Sound is strange here, so's the light. It's hard to keep your bearings."

They both craned their necks, looking up for a hint of the sun's position.

"Great," Rick said. "We reach the only place inside the caldera with an unobstructed view of the sky—albeit a narrow aperture—and we've got thick overcast."

"Did you just say 'albeit'?"

He cocked his head. "I believe I did. I never say 'albeit.' What's happening to me? Anyway, we seem to have eluded the dapis for the moment."

"Oh, I doubt that. They're busy chasing Laffite and Bakari, but I'm sure they've got scouts up there keeping tabs on us."

She checked the vanilla sky again. With the clouds allowing no clue as to the sun's location, points of the compass were a guess.

"If Pepé Le Pew hadn't taken my compass, clouds wouldn't matter. We need to figure out which way is west."

She knew the camp was near the western wall.

"You want to go back to camp?"

"Yeah. Get my compass from Laffite's tent and we'll never be lost again. Or at least not *this* lost."

"Well, we know we started off heading north."

Rick grimaced. "But we were being chased and not watching and following Laffite who was taking the path of least resistance. By the end we could have been heading in any direction."

"So the only thing we know is that we wound up at the center of the island." She heard herself and added: "Sorry for stating the obvious."

"No, it's okay." He was looking up again. "This is the only place down here that gets direct sunlight. Which means . . ." He looked around. "Which means that the old woodsman's lore about moss on trunks might work."

"Moss? In case you haven't noticed, there's no shortage of moss around here."

"That's due to a definite shortage of direct sunlight. But when there *is* direct sunlight, even for a few hours a day, moss tends to avoid the southern side of a tree trunk and accumulate on the north. So if we wade along the shore here—"

"You mean get in the water?" She didn't know about that.

"Just up to our ankles."

"But we don't know what's swimming in there. I mean, I've already seen prehistoric ferns and horsetails . . ."

"Don't tell me you're worried about an ichthyosaurus."

"No, but we can't afford to assume anything about this place."

"Suppose you're right. But if we can find trunks with moss on just one side, we'll know which way is north."

"No, it's a great idea, I'm just—"

She cried out as something landed on her back and started pulling on her hair. Another something landed on her shoulder. More joined the first two.

Dapis.

Nearby she heard Rick yelling in surprise and anger until the screeching of the dapis clinging to her downed out every other sound. Before her sight was blocked she had a glimpse of him spinning and swatting at the dozen little primates engulfing the top half of his body.

The good news was they weren't carrying spears. But the ones on her head and her right shoulder were yanking on her hair. The burning pain sent her stumbling blindly to the right. She bounced off saplings and smaller trees, but kept moving, determined to stay on her feet. If she fell, God knew what would happen to her.

Try as she might, she couldn't dislodge them. She called out to Rick, but if he replied she couldn't hear him over the dapis. If only she could see! Because if she could find the lake she just might dive in to get these creatures off her, and the hell with whatever might be lurking beneath the surface. But they continued to block her vision.

She didn't know how long she stumbled around, but after a while she got the impression the dapis wanted her to travel in a certain direction. She fought them but the painful tugging on her hair and the lopsided distribution of their weight on her upper body made it impossible.

And then, as suddenly they'd jumped on her, they left, fleeing for the trees and disappearing among the branches.

Finally able to see, she looked around for Rick, but she was alone. No lake in sight, leaving her more thoroughly lost than before.

She called out Rick's name, hearing her own voice echo around her. Almost immediately she heard a faint response, but it seemed to come from everywhere.

She kept calling and he kept responding, but she couldn't find a direction.

She gave it a rest for a moment, catching her breath. And suddenly a man started screaming in pain and terror. Much closer. Off to her left, she gauged. And then, just as suddenly as he'd started, he stopped.

He'd sounded an awful lot like Razi had this morning, which meant this was probably Bakari. If the dapis had attacked him in any way like they'd attacked his brother, he had no hope.

She listened for more, and through the quiet she heard voices . . . male . . . close . . . arguing.

Definitely from her left. She hurried that way.

7

Rick wasn't sure if he'd tossed the dapis off or they'd found something better to do. He had a definite feeling that they'd been trying to steer him somewhere but he'd fought like hell not to go there. And he thought he'd won. So maybe they'd simply given up.

But where the hell was he? He checked the ground and saw crushed vegetation. Not just from him. Looked like quite a few feet doing the trammeling. He followed it and, after maybe fifty yards, stepped into Laffite's makeshift camp.

He made an immediate beeline for the Frenchman's tent. He didn't bother crawling in, simply ripped its pegs and supports out of the ground and dumped all the contents.

There—the Marlin in a camo case beside the bedroll. He grabbed that, along with his compass, wallet, and passport. Now, where was the backpack? Right. Laffite had dropped it when his finger broke. He spotted it on the ground twenty feet away. Checked inside and found a box of Winchester .30-30s for the Marlin, and a clear plastic box holding a variety of replacement fuses.

Okay. We can get home.

Although who would be part of that "we" was still up for grabs. Laura for sure, Keith he hoped. Laffite and Bakari? Maybe. Before they stepped aboard they'd have to agree that the *Sorcière* had a new captain—at least until they reached the mainland. After that Laffite could have his boat back.

He pulled the Marlin from its case and checked the breech. Empty. As he began loading he heard Laura's voice, faint, calling his name. He returned the call, then heard her again. He couldn't get a fix on her location, so he checked his compass to choose a direction. The needle pointed north, so, what the hell, he'd go north. If her voice didn't become louder after a hundred yards or so, he'd turn around and head the other way.

Calling her name again, he started walking.

8

The dapis seemed to give up chasing him. Amaury staggered to a halt and was bending over to catch his breath—maybe even vomit—when he spotted Jeukens staring at him from behind a stand of chest-high bushes.

"What are you doing here?" the Afrikaner said.

"Running for my life." He looked around. "The dapis haven't attacked you?"

Jeukens showed a puzzled frown. "Of course not. They're not vio—" His eyes widened. "Have they made spears?"

"Yes! You have seen them then?"

"No, but Bakari gave them a beautiful demonstration of aggression and the use of a spear."

He looked nervous, edgy. Was he hiding something?

"What did you do with all the phones?"

"Nothing."

Definitely hiding something. Amaury stepped toward him.

"Let me see what you are doing back there."

"No-no. Stay where you are!"

Amaury pushed through the bushes and saw—what? What was he looking at? Two green cylinders . . .

"Those . . . those look like chemical containers."

Yes! A biohazard symbol peeked through the green paint.

Merde . . . this couldn't be good.

Jeukens moved to block him. "No, it's experimental—"

Amaury shoved him aside and moved closer. Something taped to the sides. Images flashed like sparks—phones . . . wires . . . putty blocks . . . battery packs . . . detonator caps . . .

"*Putain!*" Bombs attached to poison! He saw *VX* on the side of one canister. "VX? What is VX?"

"Nothing to worry about. It's just—"

And then screaming. Nearby. Someone thrashing through the undergrowth. It sounded like Bakari—had to be Bakari.

Then the man himself appeared, running blindly—blindly because of the screeching dapis clinging to his head, stabbing at his eyes, his throat. They leaped off as one, leaving him with miniature spears jutting from his bloody eye sockets and his own knife jammed into the side of his throat. Their departure unbalanced him. He tripped, fell. He landed face-first, right at their feet, driving the spears deep into his brain. All four limbs went into rigid spasms, his body convulsed twice, then he lay still.

Amaury heard a strangled sound—Jeukens was bent over, retching, but nothing came up.

He straightened and stared at him. "What have you done to this place—to them?"

What indeed? His Paradise, his Eden . . . ruined . . . lost.

He shook it off. None of that was important now. These two canisters— *they* mattered.

"VX? Is that what you tried to poison us with? And now you want to finish the job? Have you gone crazy?"

He started toward Jeukens, hands reaching for his throat, but stopped short when the Afrikaner held up a phone.

"All I have to do is press the talk button and all this goes up."

"I don't believe—but you'll kill yourself as well."

A sad smile. "That's become the plan."

He was serious. He intended to die here. Amaury's knees went rubbery. He wasn't ready for death.

He glanced at the canisters, saw the phones, the blocks of plastique—

Wait. On each . . . only one wire from the battery pack attached to the detonators. The madman hadn't finished wiring the devices.

Amaury leaped at Jeukens, got both hands around his throat, and squeezed with everything he had. They staggered in a circle, tripped over each other's feet, and tumbled to the ground next to Bakari. As they rolled back and forth, Jeukens's face began to purple.

Amaury hadn't been able to shoot the innocent pilot, but he could kill this murderous bastard—he *would* kill him. Strangle the life out of him, and enjoy every second of—

A blaze of pain—a searing agony enveloped his gut. He released his grip and struggled to his knees. Jeukens held a bloody knife—Bakari's knife. How . . . ? A glance showed it was no longer in the Shangaan's throat.

The pain toppled him back to the ground. He looked at where his hands clutched the wound . . . dark, dark blood leaking between the fingers. The world blurred. He was spinning . . .

9

Marten rose and watched Laffite writhe on the ground, clutching his belly, then go still. He looked at the bloody knife in his hand and felt his gorge rise. He dropped it and backed away.

Turning, he saw the woman, Laura, standing on the far side of the canisters, her hands over her mouth, her eyes wide and horrified.

"You saw it!" he cried. "It was self-defense! You're a witness!"

He had no idea why he was babbling like this. Did he want acquittal? Absolution? What did it matter? She was going to be as dead as Laffite in about ten seconds.

She lowered her hands. "I already know what VX is."

"Do you now?" He edged closer to the canisters. "And how does a county medical examiner know that?"

"Part of my training," she said, "was recognizing the signatures of various poisons."

Noise in the bushes and suddenly Rick appeared behind her, carrying a rifle.

No!

She smiled but didn't bother turning to look. "What took you so long?"

"Followed the voices."

Frozen in shock, Marten watched Garrick access the setup with the canisters in a heartbeat, then point the rifle at the center of his chest.

"Really, Keith?"

Marten wasn't sure whether Garrick would shoot him or not. Who knew what the CIA had turned him into? Better to play it safe and act the older brother.

"I told you why, dear brother. I can't think of anything to add."

"How about the possibility that you're wrong?"

Wrong? No, the end of human progress was at hand.

"I'm not."

Garrick sighed. "Y'know, when we were kids I used to think you were infallible. I thought you knew everything. I really looked up to you."

The words shocked him. He gave Garrick a closer look. He didn't seem to be lying.

"You could have fooled me. You treated me with utter contempt."

Keep him talking until the detonator wires were within reach. Don't look at the canisters . . . you're not interested in them. Just edge closer, half an inch at a time, and then touch one wire to the positive node, one to the negative . . . and no one here would ever talk again.

"That was later, when I thought you'd rejected me. Thanks to Laura here, I've come to realize you'd probably given all you could."

"Ah, yes, Laura." He made a point of looking at her and not the canisters while moving another inch closer. "The ME who knows what VX is."

"VX?" Garrick said in a hushed tone. "Aw, shit, Keith. You were gonna use VX to wipe out the dapis?"

The past tense was not lost on Marten. Garrick thought he had stopped him.

"Yes. An extinction event, you might say."

"And us as well?"

Collateral damage was, after all, *damage*.

"I couldn't let anyone leave this island. You see that, don't you?"

Closer . . . closer . . .

"No. You had options. We did swear to keep the dapis secret, remember?"

Time to raise his arms, as if gesturing toward them.

"Okay, then—"

Now! He reached toward the nearest board and—

No detonators—just holes where he'd inserted them into the C-4. Same with the other block.

"Where—?"

"Those silvery cigarette thingies with the wires?" Laura jerked a thumb at the jungle behind her. "I threw them back there while you were stabbing Laffite."

"You know about detonators?" Garrick said.

"I watch movies. I know what plastic explosive looks like too—same way."

Garrick's lips twisted as he gave her a nod.

"No!" Marten cried. "You couldn't have!"

"But I did."

Liar! She wouldn't throw them where he could find them again. They were still on her person, in one of her pockets. But with Garrick pointing that rifle at him . . .

Movement to his right, Laffite on his knees, face pale, teeth bared as he swung his arm. He had the knife!

The blade sliced into Marten's upper thigh, practically in his groin. He staggered back, pain flaring in all directions, bad, but not incapacitating.

And then he saw the red spray, the blood coursing from his thigh in pulsating gushes. He pressed his palm over it, trying to stanch the flow but it kept coming . . . kept coming . . .

10

Laura darted around the canisters to where Keith lay dying. And *dying* was the only word for it. Laffite had cut his femoral artery high up—too high for a tourniquet, but Laura felt she had to try.

The Frenchman had dropped the knife and pushed himself back against a tree where he sat clutching his bloody abdomen.

"You son of a bitch!" Rick said and kicked the knife into the brush.

Keith lay supine, face white as a tissue, lacking the strength to keep pressure on the weakly pulsing wound. Not at all a good sign. Five liters of blood in the body. Lose just two and shock started to set in.

"Your belt!" Laura said, pointing to Rick's waist.

He tossed the rifle aside and yanked off his belt. Stepping into the pool of blood, he squatted beside Keith and wrapped it around his thigh. He couldn't get it much above the bleeding so he cinched it directly over the wound.

"Keith?" he said, muscles bulging as he pulled the belt tight. Blood continued to run out under the strap. "Keith, hang on!" He looked up at Laura. "Has he got a chance?"

The answer was a definite no, but she hesitated to put it into words.

Keith saved her the trouble. His voice was a faint, hoarse, rasp. "I'm gone."

"Hang on."

"Did you . . . did you really think I was infallible?"

"Yeah, Keith. I did."

"You were right. I was."

The belt seemed to be working. The blood loss stopped. Or maybe no more left to lose?

She looked at Keith. His chest wasn't moving. She squatted and pressed on his other femoral artery, looking for a pulse. None.

She put a hand over Rick's where he gripped the bloody belt.

He blinked at her. "He's gone?"

She nodded, unable to say anything.

"We can try CPR and—"

She shook her head. "No use." The purpose of CPR was to pump blood to the brain and lungs. "You need blood for that, and Keith's . . ." She gestured to the red pool.

He released the belt and rose. She slipped her arms around him. "I'm sorry."

He looked down at his brother. "Keith, Keith, Keith . . . what the fuck?" He heaved a deep sigh. "At least he went fast." Then he shook his head. "Why do I care? He was going to kill us both."

"He was still your brother. Family doesn't need to make sense. Most times it doesn't."

Rick looked over her shoulder and said, "You!"

She turned and found Laffite staring up at them. His ponytail had come undone during his struggle with Keith. With his unshaven face and unkempt hair matted with sweat, he looked like a homeless man.

"I saved your lives," he croaked, pointing to the canisters with a shaking hand. "He was going to blow up the island!"

She shook her head. She doubted very much he'd been thinking about her. Then she noticed Rick had the rifle again and was pointing it at Laffite.

"Rick, no!" she cried.

The cringing Frenchman raised a hand as if to block the bullet and moved his other to expose his wound. "He stabbed me first."

Laura noticed the color of the blood—very dark. From the location she guessed a liver wound. He could survive that but only if he got treatment soon.

The tableau held for a few heartbeats, during which she heard dapis scurrying around in the branches above. No chatter. Silent, restless, watching.

Suddenly Rick growled and hurled the rifle into the bushes. She watched him take a few deep breaths, then turn to her.

"Nothing's simple here, is it?"

She shook her head. "I wish it were."

He stepped back to the canisters. "VX . . . I can't believe it."

"Where does anyone get stuff like that?" she said.

"Syria had a store of it. Supposedly destroyed, if you believe in fairy tales. The question is, what do *we* do with it?"

Laura was at a loss. "We can't dump it at sea. The salt water will corrode the aluminum. And do you really want to bring it back to civilization?"

He shook his head. "Best to leave it here, I guess. Unstressed, under these conditions, this sort of heavy-duty aluminum could take a long, long time to rot. By then the VX might be harmless."

"Then there's nothing to keep us here."

Laffite groaned. "You cannot start the boat without me, *monsieur.*"

Rick reached into a pocket and produced a box of fuses. "Think again."

"You cannot leave me!"

She looked at Rick. "No, we can't."

"Think he'll survive the trip back to Maputo?"

"No. But we can call Antso and have him come back. If we can carry him up to the rim . . ." Something about Rick's expression . . . "What?"

"You want to tell her, Pepé?"

But Laffite only looked away.

"Tell me what?"

He spoke to Laffite. "You didn't send Antso back to Morondava. You shot him out of the sky, didn't you."

"*What?*"

"That was Bakari!"

"Yeah. Blame the dead guy. But even if that's true, it was your idea and your rifle."

Laffite said nothing but his expression spoke volumes.

Poor Antso.

"And I'm sure he had similar plans for us," Rick added.

"Not true!"

"Shuddup. He wants this island all to himself." He shook his head. "You deserve to be marooned here, Laffite, but I'll make you a deal: If you can get yourself to the beach, we'll take you back. Don't expect any help from me. I've got my brother to carry—thanks to you."

Laura didn't know if she could leave him here, but didn't know how to help him either. He'd never survive the voyage.

"While I get Keith situated," Rick said, "why don't you toss those batteries into the brush, just for safety sake. The C-4 will deteriorate quickly, but those batteries might last a while."

She thought it was overkill, but didn't argue. So as Rick began lifting

Keith and positioning him across his shoulders, she started pulling the AAs from the nearest battery pack.

Behind her, Laffite started screaming. She turned to see him swarmed upon with spear-wielding dapis. They screeched as they stabbed him repeatedly in the eyes and mouth and throat, and then fled back up the tree trunk to perch in the branches.

Laffite made gagging sounds as his hands fluttered like wounded birds over his pierced eyes and mouth and throat. With a final violent choke he fell over sideways and lay still.

Rick stood with a stricken, fearful, helpless look, both hands occupied with steadying his brother across his shoulders.

"We're next, I'm afraid. You run ahead. I'll stay close behind."

Laura stared up at the dapis who had resumed chattering as they stared back.

"I don't know, Rick. I'm thinking back to when we were running from them. Did you get stuck by any of their spears?"

"A couple hit me when they bounced off Laffite but, come to think of it, no."

"And when they jumped all over us, did any of them bite you?"

"No. And I had a definite feeling they were steering me somewhere."

"I think we're there. I've got a feeling the dapis knew something wasn't kosher here—they were trying to guide us."

"But I resisted."

She smiled. "Imagine that. So did I, but I'm smaller than you, and they left me within fifty feet of this spot."

"Well, I'd like to *leave* this spot, if you don't mind." He shifted Keith on his shoulders. "I can trace my steps back."

"Can I help with him?"

His mouth twisted. "Don't make me say it."

She didn't know what he meant at first, then . . .

"No-no. I won't. In fact, *please* don't say it."

He nodded. "Follow me."

11

They found the camp occupied—by dapis.

The little primates were everywhere—one even sitting atop the cage . . . a dapi with a splint on its leg.

She guessed the splint on that little fellow was one of the reasons they'd been left alone, along with the fact that they hadn't partaken of Bakari's barbecue.

The dapis kept their distance but didn't flee to the trees as Rick, dripping with sweat, eased Keith's body to the ground. He'd been strangely silent during the trek back. Laura had wondered what was on his mind but gave him space to work it out.

"It's going to be a nightmare getting him back to the States," he said.

So that's what he'd been mulling.

"I can imagine."

"First off, the police are looking for him in Mozambique. Second, he entered the country under an assumed ID. And he sure as hell didn't die of natural causes."

Not to mention how he'd decompose on the trip back.

"You could bury him here."

He shook his head. "Paulette's gonna need closure."

He was thinking about his mother—good for him.

"Okay." She spotted Laffite's nylon tent crumpled on the ground. "We can use that as a shroud and keep him as cool as possible belowdecks. We'll do whatever's necessary with the authorities to clear him through."

"*I'll* deal with it. You've got a daughter waiting."

True, true. But they had that team thing going.

"How do we explain the absence of the boat's captain?"

He puffed his lips as he blew out a breath. "Been working on that too. We may have to sneak Keith's body ashore and send the *Sorcière* chugging back into the channel. A lot of details to cover, but we've got a couple of days at sea to work them out."

"A couple of *days?*"

"Probably more. I don't think that thing'll run more than ten knots. But I noticed it's got a radar pod so we can run all night if we take turns."

A couple of days . . .

"Let's get moving. And keep your fingers crossed that it starts."

"Oh, no! Don't say that! You have the fuses—"

"Let's just hope he didn't play any other tricks."

Feeling sick, Laura led the way to the wall.

12

"Here we go," Rick said as he pushed the gear lever forward. Relief flooded him as the *Sorcière des Mers* eased into motion. "Homeward bound."

They'd wrapped Keith in the tent and hauled him over the rim and down to the beach. Rick had rowed the three of them in the inflatable out to the *Sorcière* where he immediately replaced the fuel pump fuse and tried the engine. To his unbounded relief, it started right up.

As the engine warmed up, they'd placed Keith belowdecks and raised the anchor.

And now they stood side-by-side on the bridge.

Laura looked about to cry. "We survived. Somehow we survived."

Yeah, he thought, thinking of Keith's trussed-up body. *But Keith didn't.*

Which meant he'd failed in what he'd set out to do. But at least Laura hadn't been hurt.

He hugged her close. "We're going home, Laura."

"I can't believe what we went through in the last forty-eight hours," she said, her face against his chest. "The madness, the violence, the deaths, the . . . the revelations."

Rick glanced back at the island. A cool front was moving through, creating a mist.

"Look!" she said, pointing up to the rim.

A host of dapis lined the edge, watching them.

She waved.

Rick smiled. "What are you doing?"

"Just saying good-bye . . . and maybe good riddance."

One or two of them raised a tentative hand, so she waved again. A few more waved back. She waved a third time and a lot more copied her. The gesture seemed to catch on. Eventually all the dapis were waving good-bye.

"My God, they learn fast," she said.

Rick nodded. "As we know all too well."

The mist thickened as they pulled away. Soon the dapis and eventually their island were lost from sight.

"Do you think Keith was right?" she said. "I mean, the effect the truth about them would have on the world?"

Rick shrugged. "Who can say? I have a hard time buying it, but he was so *sure*. So it doesn't matter if he was right or wrong, he was convinced the secret of the dapis would usher in a new Dark Ages and he was saving human civilization. No way we were gonna talk him out of it."

"*Idée fixe*," she said.

"Hmmm?"

"A medical term for a mind-set or opinion that's set in stone, impervious to reason."

"Well, with no Dark Age coming, I guess we've helped achieve Keith's purpose. Which means, if the Intrusive Cosmic Entities who created the *ikhar* to screw with our heads also created the dapis for the same purpose, then we've been a part of wrecking both schemes. The world doesn't know the panacea is real, and no one but us knows the dapis exist."

He tilted his head back and thumbed his nose at the sky. This is for you out there . . . just for you.

"I just had an odd thought," she said. "What if there's disagreement among the intellects? One side tries to get a dapi into the hands of someone who can expose the secret, and the other side makes sure it's a man who understands the consequences and won't let the secret out?"

"You mean, it's like a cosmic game?"

"Yes, and you and I are caught in the middle." She pressed her face into his back. "Listen to me! I sound like you!"

He couldn't help grinning. Was it contagious? Had she caught it?

"I like it, I like it!"

"That's what worries me!"

He laughed. It felt good to laugh. Back there on the island he'd thought he might never laugh again.

The red, sinking sun peeked through a break in the clouds dead ahead.

She hugged him tighter. "I love this."

"Did you just say the 'L' word?"

They'd agreed it couldn't be love yet. Was she feeling otherwise?

"Wasn't that a TV show about lesbians?"

"Not that I know of. No . . ."

She said, "I mean just you and me on a boat in the middle of the ocean. Isn't it great?"

A sigh slipped out. "It's super."

She hugged him tighter. "Hey-hey-hey. You could show a little more enthusiasm."

"No, it's a wonderful thing. Wonderful for me, but . . ."

"But what?"

"Well, you can do better."

"Stop that!"

"Really. A guy without a ton of blood on his hands."

"Well, from what you told me, the world's a better place because of that blood."

"Some of it was innocent."

"That's not the point," she said.

"What *is* the point?"

"That *I'll* decide who's good for me." She snaked her arms around him again. "Rick, Rick, Rick. Is there any hope for us?"

He cupped a hand over hers. "There's always hope. I need you to keep me a little sane and you need me to keep you a little crazy. And I need . . ."

"Need what? Anything."

He was going to have to come clean with her. Now or never. She deserved to know everything.

"It's about Düsseldorf."

"Not that again. That's over and done."

"I need to tell you the rest of the story."

"There's more?"

He nodded as his stomach knotted. He took a deep breath. "I knew the barn with the kids was rigged to explode. I knew that if I set off the sickos' explosives that the kids would go too."

Her arms around his chest loosened. "You knew the kids would die?"

"I wasn't right in the head, Laura. I'd seen the kids . . . no eyes . . . no tongues . . . deaf . . . paralyzed. They weren't coming back from what the sickos had done to them. They had these looks of unrelenting horror on their faces as they tried to scream and scream but they had no voices and I . . . I decided they were better off dead."

Her grip slackened further. "You decided . . ."

"Yeah." He wanted to turn and face her but couldn't. "I know I had no right. But all they had ahead of them was endless, unremitting horror."

She released him and now he turned to face her. She was staring at him, arms at her side, expression unreadable.

"And no one knows?"

"You're the first, the only. I expected to take it to my grave. Then you came along."

"And you've lived with that all these years?"

"I keep telling myself I didn't do it *to* them, I did it *for* them."

"Does it work?"

He shook his head. "No."

"How many children?"

"Fifteen."

She gasped. "Then . . . at least one or two of them had to have been Marissa's age."

He said nothing. He couldn't.

"Why did you tell me this?" Her voice sounded on the verge of tears.

"I felt you should know . . . if we're headed toward something . . . toward being together, you have a right to know."

"You and your damn duty!" she said, voice rising, tears filling her eyes. She pounded both fists against his chest. Not terribly hard. Strength seemed to have deserted her. "Did you ever think I might not *want* to know something like that?" She began pounding him with every word. "Did—you—ever—*think?*"

He pulled her against him. She didn't struggle, but she didn't embrace him either. Simply leaned against him.

"Believe me, Laura, I didn't want to tell you at all, but I couldn't live with . . . not."

They stood statue-still for a while, then she pushed back.

"I have to think," she said turning away.

"Laura . . ."

"I have to think."

She left the bridge. He watched her make her way down to the aft deck where she sat on the transom and stared out at the water.

Now you've done it, he thought.

His chest felt heavy—*everything* felt heavy. Chances were excellent he'd just ruined the best thing that had ever happened to him. Should have kept his goddamn mouth shut. But that would be living a lie. He'd proved an expert at that during his years with the Company, but he refused to with the woman he loved. Sooner or later it would have come out, and the longer he waited, the worse it would be.

I have to think . . .

Would she ever forgive him? *Could* she? He'd yet to forgive himself, so how could she?

13

The sun had set and darkness stalked the *Sorcière* from the east. Laura watched Rick's silhouette on the bridge. Every once in a while he'd turn to look at her.

She'd recovered from the shock. She'd said she had to think, and that was what she'd been doing . . . thinking about Rick deliberately causing the deaths of fifteen children. Unthinkable, unspeakable on the surface, but . . .

She'd known he could kill. She'd seen him kill. But she'd never thought he could do something like *that*.

Neither had he, most likely.

And yet . . .

He was a good man. She knew that. His revulsion had been all too clear as he'd described what those sick people had done to the kids. And the kids were not coming back from those mutilations. Even the *ikhar* would be useless against that level of injury. It couldn't grow new eyes, a new tongue . . .

I keep telling myself I didn't do it to them, I did it for them.

And she was sure that was true. He'd done it *for* them. He'd known no one else would have the will, the plain guts to take the situation in hand

and save those children from the endless horror their lives had become and would continue to be.

So it had been left to him.

The easy way would have been to call the German authorities. Let them arrest the adults and stick them in mental institutions until they were either "cured" or escaped to start the same thing all over again.

And the children . . . house them where they'd live out their lives tumbling through a silent, formless black void, never again to hear a kind word or feel a gentle touch. And if science ever did reach a point where they could be helped, each would be irretrievably insane by then. If they weren't already.

Rick had spared them that.

And rid the world of the scum who had hurt them.

But still . . .

The contradictions buffeted her.

She couldn't help feeling betrayed. Not by Rick—he'd leveled with her. Betrayed by fate or life or whatever. She'd been closed off for years. Now, after finally opening up to someone, she learns . . .

But then again, back by the explosives and the VX, when she'd sensed Keith trying to distract her with all his chatter, she'd been doing the same to him, but hers had been a delaying tactic. For as sure as she knew the sun would rise and set, she'd known Rick was on his way. She knew he had her back. Wherever she might be, he'd have her back. And that was precious beyond compare.

So could she put his past behind her and look toward a future together?

Rationally, she said *yes*. She didn't fear him. Not in the least. Here was a man who would lay down his life for her or Marissa without a second thought.

Emotionally, though, she still didn't know.

But she wasn't going to find out sitting down here, was she?

Laura rose and headed up to the bridge. She didn't expect an easy fix, but they had hundreds of miles of water ahead to work out . . . something.

THE SECRET HISTORY OF THE WORLD

The preponderance of my work deals with a history of the world that remains undiscovered, unexplored, and unknown to most of humanity. Some of this secret history has been revealed in the Adversary Cycle, some in the Repairman Jack novels, and bits and pieces in other, seemingly unconnected works. Taken together, even these millions of words barely scratch the surface of what has been going on behind the scenes, hidden from the workaday world. I've listed them below in chronological order. (NB: "Year Zero" is the end of civilization as we know it; "Year Zero Minus One" is the year preceding it, etc.)

The God Gene is part of the Secret History.

THE PAST

"Demonsong" (prehistory)
"The Compendium of Srem" (1498)
"Aryans and Absinthe"** (1923–1924)
Black Wind (1926–1945)
The Keep (1941)
Reborn (February–March 1968)
"Dat Tay Vao"*** (March 1968)
Jack: Secret Histories (1983)
Jack: Secret Circles (1983)
Jack: Secret Vengeance (1983)
"Faces"* (1988)
Cold City (1990)

Dark City (1991)
Fear City (1993)

YEAR ZERO MINUS THREE

Sibs (February)
The Tomb (summer)
"The Barrens"* (ends in September)
"A Day in the Life"* (October)
"The Long Way Home"+
Legacies (December)

YEAR ZERO MINUS TWO

"Interlude at Duane's"** (April)
Conspiracies (April) (includes "Home Repairs"+)
All the Rage (May) (includes "The Last Rakosh"+)
Hosts (June)
The Haunted Air (August)
Gateways (September)
Crisscross (November)
Infernal (December)

YEAR ZERO MINUS ONE

Harbingers (January)
"Infernal Night"++ (with Heather Graham)
Bloodline (April)
The Fifth Harmonic (April)
Panacea (April)
The God Gene (May)
By the Sword (May)
Ground Zero (July)
The Touch (ends in August)

The Peabody-Ozymandias Traveling Circus & Oddity Emporium (ends in
September)
"Tenants"*

YEAR ZERO

"Pelts"*
Reprisal (ends in February)
Fatal Error (February) (includes "The Wringer"+)
The Dark at the End (March)
Nightworld (May)

* available in *The Barrens and Others*
** available in *Aftershock and Others*
*** available in the 2009 reissue of *The Touch*
+ available in *Quick Fixes—Tales of Repairman Jack*
++ available in *Face Off*